Praise for *A Dual Inheritance*

"This brilliant family saga captured me from its opening lines and kept me pinned to the couch—by turns laughing and sobbing—until I'd reached its stunning, satisfying conclusion. It calls to mind *The Corrections* and *The Emperor's Children,* as well as Cheever and Michener and Potok, but this is also a novel squarely in the tradition of Victorian social realism, of Eliot and Galsworthy and Dickens. *A Dual Inheritance* is a cracking story— populated with complicated, fascinating characters and fueled by surprising turns of plot—but it's also a deft analysis of class and race in America. With it, Hershon establishes herself as one of the most important storytellers of the new millennium."

—JOANNA SMITH RAKOFF, author of *A Fortunate Age*

"This insightful, worldly, and engaging novel, at once intimate and broad in scope, traverses continents and decades while hewing closely to the psychological shadings of its characters. A rueful comedy of entitlements and chagrins, it says volumes about the way we live now."

—PHILLIP LOPATE, author of *Getting Personal*

"Joanna Hershon's splendid new novel explores the choices of a generation through the lives of two friends—inextricably bound, in love with the same woman, and at war with themselves. Hershon creates a sprawling, spellbinding narrative that is as intimate with the lives of relief workers in Africa as it is with the inner workings of the boardrooms of Wall Street. *A Dual Inheritance* is stunningly wrought, compulsively readable, and Hershon's strongest work yet by far."

—HELEN SCHULMAN, author of *This Beautiful Life*

"A grand, engrossing, ambitious, and memorably populated novel. Hurray for Joanna Hershon!"

—ELISA ALBERT, author of *The Book of Dahlia*

"The intensely detailed love triangle is reminiscent of an East Coast elite answer to the Midwestern trio of *Freedom,* but with mere keen observation in place of that other novel's sweeping moral pronouncements. Hershon explores the ways we can, and can't, escape our backgrounds."

—*Publishers Weekly* (starred review)

BY JOANNA HERSHON

A Dual Inheritance
The German Bride
Swimming
The Outside of August

A DUAL INHERITANCE

A Dual Inheritance

A Novel

JOANNA HERSHON

BALLANTINE BOOKS

NEW YORK

Published in the United States by Ballantine Books, an imprint of The Random House Publishing Group, a division of Random House, Inc., New York.

BALLANTINE and colophon are registered trademarks of Random House, Inc.

Back On The Chain Gang, Words and Music by Chrissie Hynde © 1982 EMI MUSIC PUBLISHING LTD. trading as CLIVE BANKS SONGS. All Rights Controlled and Administered by EMI APRIL MUSIC INC. All Rights Reserved. International Copyright Secured. Used by Permission. *Reprinted by Permission of Hal Leonard Corporation.*

LIBRARY OF CONGRESS CATALOGING-IN-PUBLICATION DATA
Hershon, Joanna.
A dual inheritance : a novel / Joanna Hershon.
pages cm
ISBN 978-0-345-46847-5 (hardcover)
ISBN 978-0-345-53880-2 (eBook)
I. Title.
PS3558.E788D83 2013
813'.54—dc23   2012046548

Printed in the United States of America on acid-free paper

www.ballantinebooks.com

2 4 6 8 9 7 5 3

Book design by Dana Leigh Blanchette
Title page images: © *iStockphoto*

For Derek, Wyatt, and Noah

I found a picture of you,
Oh what hijacked my world that night
To a place in the past we've been cast out of,
Oh now we're back in the fight.

—CHRISSIE HYNDE

Contents

Part Three 1988

Part Four 1989–2010

Dual inheritance theory (DIT), also known as gene-culture coevolution, was developed in the late 1970s and early 1980s to explain how human behavior is a product of two different and interacting evolutionary processes: genetic evolution and cultural evolution.

Part One

1962–1963

Chapter One

Fall

Had he described Hugh Shipley at all over the past three years, *approach-able* would not have been a word he'd ever have used. But one warm autumn night during his senior year, Ed Cantowitz found himself grabbing Hugh Shipley's arm in front of Lamont Library the way he might otherwise grab a Budweiser at Cronin's. They were not friends; they'd spoken only in passing this year, and mostly after the Shakespeare seminar in which they were both enrolled, but Ed Cantowitz was not thinking of how Hugh Shipley might find him off-putting or offensive, because, as usual, Ed Cantowitz was thinking about himself.

"Keep walking," muttered Ed, and that's what Hugh Shipley did. He walked as if he hadn't even noticed the interruption, didn't so much as slow the trajectory of his cigarette from hand to mouth. Ed watched the cigarette and the dry fallen leaves on the ground—anything not to turn around and stare at the girl. "Do me a favor and keep walking and don't turn around. Do *yourself* a favor and just look straight ahead."

Shipley nodded. "Might want to take your hand off my arm," and Ed released his grip before offering a crazed smile as an afterthought, if not an apology. He knew he had a menacing voice, not to mention truly dark stubble (he'd forgone his much-needed second shave of the day), and his husky voice and bulldog build lent him not only an unsavory but even vaguely criminal air. Ed usually alternated between being pleased by these qualities and ashamed, but at the moment he was so focused he didn't care what Shipley thought. The two young men walked down steps and past a stand of pine trees, kicking crabapples out of their path, and Ed talked. "This girl," he said, and Shipley nodded again. Ed didn't sound embarrassed, because he wasn't embarrassed. This, he believed, is what men did for one another, all kinds of men, he didn't care who; in the face of beautiful women, men were allied soldiers, at least until proven otherwise. "I can't stop staring at this girl, but I'm under no illusions that I don't need strategy. You? You don't know a thing about strategy, am I right? Because you don't need it. I need strategy—and make no mistake about it, strategy does work—but when I held open the door for that girl just then, I knew if I let myself do something about her, it would have been the wrong thing. I needed to save myself from myself, as they say. Listen, can you tell me if she's still there behind us? Petite girl, big eyes—she's actually kind of cross-eyed—really really really nice knockers?"

Hugh Shipley looked slyly right behind them. He reported that he no longer saw the girl. "Hadn't noticed she was cross-eyed."

"Slightly," said Ed, stopping suddenly, short of breath. "Only if you look closely."

"Well," said Hugh, "glad to help." He sounded sincere, but Ed knew he might have missed the sarcastic edge. It wouldn't have been the first time. Ed was not a nerd—no, sir—but at this point in his college career, he had to acknowledge that he was—to put it kindly—an outsider. Being at ease around groups of other people—especially lighthearted other people—was not his strong suit.

He'd barely spoken to Shipley in the three years they'd been classmates; they'd had no reason to speak. Ed was on scholarship and was a rigorous and nakedly ambitious student with a government concentration and a gift for statistics. He was preparing to write his senior thesis on how China would dominate the twenty-first century. Hugh, on the other hand, skipped classes, often smelled like whiskey, and was rumored to be working with a lapsed graduate student on some kind of anthropology film project. He towered over Ed at roughly six foot four, and he was, of course, a Shipley, which lent everything he did a kind of simultaneous legitimacy and scandal. He'd grown up in the famous Brookline home of Clarissa Cadence Shipley—a ubiquitous stop on any Historical Homes of Boston tour. Ed had no idea how he knew this; the family was exactly that famous—one simply knew these things. One also often saw Hugh carrying a camera tripod and wearing dungarees as if he were headed off to the African savanna instead of crossing the street between classes, but—and this was the salient point—there was nothing comical about him. He looked as if he might, in fact, be more comfortable amidst a pride of lions.

"So it's Friday," Ed declared. "Friday night." He tried—unsuccessfully—not to laugh, which he often did when he had excess energy, which he certainly did just then. Sometimes his laughter came from shortness of breath, sometimes it even came from anger, but Ed was—as the expression went—quick to laugh. He was quick, in fact, with everything except a joke. Jokes he hated; they were never funny.

"I'm sorry I'm laughing," said Ed. He understood that he seemed strange, even vaguely crazy, and promised himself he would not be surprised if Hugh walked away right then.

But Hugh only nodded, as if he was waiting for Ed to stop. Then he stubbed out the cigarette on his shoe and began to strip it down. The wind carried the filter away and Ed stopped laughing.

Hugh grinned and shook his head. "Some strategy."

"How do you mean?"

"Well, after all that bluster, you're without a date on a Friday night." Hugh opened and closed his hands as if they'd been aching. "Maybe you should have figured out a strategy while you actually had the chance."

"Hey," said Ed, nodding toward Hugh's hands, "you got circulation problems or something?"

Hugh looked at his fingers as if he'd noticed them for the first time. "I guess."

"It's the smoking. Something about the tobacco. I read it somewhere."

Hugh's fingers were long and lean, aristocratic yet manly, and they impressed Ed more than the expensive clothes, carelessly worn, that signaled a prep-school past or the athletic gait and suntanned face. It was Hugh's hands that evoked in Ed Cantowitz a rare feeling of intimidation, but just as he was prepared to give over to the feeling, to acknowledge and make room for its uncomfortable presence, the intimidation was gone and what was left in its place surprised him: interest, plain and simple. He was rarely truly interested in other people, and, when he was, it was as if he had an intellectual obligation to follow through on it.

And something was nagging at him. He kept thinking of the Shakespeare seminar that Hugh and he were both taking, and how—maybe because Ed was alternately too willing to acknowledge that he understood little of what Shakespeare was talking about more than half the time or was overexcited about how much he *did* understand, and maybe because, okay, he tended to speak up more than most of his fellow students—Ed was laughed at, and often. He was used to being laughed at in class and didn't act offended—never looking away, preferring instead to look around at all the laughing faces—but of course he was offended. And when he looked around the room, there was one face that was never laughing, and that was Hugh Shipley's. Hugh always sat in the same aisle seat, his legs outstretched and inadvertently tripping the professor, who was fond of pacing as he taught. Hugh Shipley never laughed at Ed. And this fact was nagging at him and making it somehow essential that Hugh not walk away. He also wondered, as he always did when standing beside another man, whether—though Shipley had a good eight inches on him—he could take him in a fight.

"Ever boxed?" he asked.

Shipley shook his head. "I probably should," he said, in a way that suggested to Ed that this answer was more of a personal aside, alluding to a different, more complicated question. He offered Ed a cigarette, which Ed declined. Hugh shrugged again and lit up, squinting as the lamplights came on. Young men were illuminated up close and in the distance; young men were in a rush toward rooms and drinks. In groups and alone, they were saddled with bags—all canvas and army green—full of books, and books and books weighing them down but not holding them back. The whole scene struck Ed Cantowitz, as it often did, as somewhere between funny—a bunch of pack mules!—and poignant, even heroic. Harvard. He'd gone to Harvard. All of these mules and Ed was one of them.

He wondered if being out on the streets on a Friday night would always bring on this unmistakable charge, as if he were about to get caught for every dishonorable act he'd ever committed, every lie he'd ever told. He also wondered if he'd ever stop picturing his home, with his mother still in it, with the Shabbos table set and the smell of burned chicken and the ironed white cloth with the ghost stains of Shabbos past, stains that—like the people who'd spilled the wine and gravy, the too-salty chicken soup—were never completely gone. All those people no longer crowded into his parents' dining room, bearing poppy seed cakes and starting in with ritual complaints about their health and the changing neighborhood, the abandonment by their rabbi, the disintegration of their shul. They no longer clamored to compare statistics of how many Jews were left in their community or the steep increases in crime. There was no more lamenting how the *schwartzes* were moving in and taking over, dragging the neighborhood down. *"It's inevitable,"* yelled Uncle Herb, though he tended toward yelling as a rule, making little distinction between his civic frustrations and *"This chicken is very tender."*

They no longer sat around the table hollering and commiserating, drowning out his mother, who said little more than "Murray—enough," while busying herself with serving food, and Aunt Lillian with her watery eyes, who cried, "But what about the Jewish commitment to integration?" before blowing her nose and excusing herself. Those people no longer sat there at his father's table, but only his mother was dead; the others had merely stopped coming. They'd moved out to Mattapan and Sharon and, in one case, Newton. But even if they hadn't moved, or even if his father had moved along with them, Murray Cantowitz had stopped observing not only Shabbos but all of the holidays, even the High Holy Days, and there was no longer any God-given reason to gather together.

Murray Cantowitz had adored his wife. Ed, even as a child, had known his father was the kind of man who had enough love for only one person in this lifetime, and his mother was that one person. When he lost his wife, Ed's father had also lost whatever decency she had inspired. At first people said his incessant bitterness made sense; it was the grief, poor man. But after about six months they said nothing, because they stopped coming around, and Ed, age sixteen and then seventeen (what a birthday *that* was), was left alone with him. No Shabbos, no God, no mother. Only studying. Because he was—thankfully, although he'd never thought to be thankful about it—seriously smart and could leave this house and this town and never come back, propelled by the sheer force of his studying. He pictured his marks and his scores like the fiercest Kraut-bombing warplane—the North American P-51 Mustang—lifting him up to where he could see their building far below, until he was too far away to even tell the difference between the tenement where he had spent his youth and all the other tenements in Dorchester.

His mother had looked like an Italian film actress, with thick black hair shot through the front with a dramatic white streak. She moved slowly in the morning, regardless of how big a rush his father insisted he was in, no matter how early Ed needed to be at school. It was because of his mother that he'd attended Boston Latin, after one of his determined Irish teachers marched over to the Cantowitz home one spring afternoon and suggested—after impatiently refusing a cup of tea—that if Mr. and Mrs. Cantowitz did not pursue Boston Latin for their son, then Edward was sure to become bored and superior and make a mess of his life. His father had only scoffed, wondering aloud what Ed had done to both impress and annoy his teacher, but Mrs. Dora Cantowitz had taken Mrs. Patty Delany's words to heart and made sure her son took the necessary steps to follow his teacher's advice. No one would have mistaken his mother for an intellectual, but she had also been an elementary school teacher for a few years before marrying Ed's father, and she had a fierce, if sentimental, regard for education. She had been a beloved teacher, one whose students, years later, wrote her appreciative—nearly amorous— letters. After reading a letter aloud to Ed and his father, she would place it in a blue folder, kept on the top shelf of her modest but mysterious closet. Ed was jealous of these children; how could they have known her back then? Back when she was Dora Markov being courted by Murray "the Curl" Cantowitz, welterweight?

She'd seen him buying an orange at the fruit stand and said, "Good luck with your next fight!" the way kids did at the time. "It's gonna be a tough one" is what he supposedly replied. "Sure would be nice to see you in the crowd." "Oh," Dora had demurred, "my mother would never allow it." "I'll tell you what," said Murray. "See this orange? I bet you I can peel this orange in a perfect circle without even nicking the skin. If I can do that, you come to my fight. Leave your mother to me." They leaned against a liquor-store window as Murray unpeeled the orange and asked Dora for her arm. He squeezed a bit of the juice onto Dora's outstretched wrist. "Better than any perfume," he declared, and—as his mother used to say, quite cryptically—she was finished.

She was from truly poor Russian Jews; Cossacks had murdered her father while he was working in the fields outside Kiev, and her newly pregnant mother had somehow cobbled together enough money to get a passage to America with her sister's family. They had all raised this American-born daughter for something better than a welterweight, no matter how promising Murray Cantowitz's career looked at the time, and Dora had retained that idea that she was meant for better things, even after she had made her choice. She was a snob about manners and grammar and was prone to expressions like *I would never stoop so low* and *I never cared for her*. And she was superstitious. With all of her manners, she was not above throwing salt over her shoulder even while eating in a restaurant (which she generally treated with great seriousness) or spitting three times in the middle of the street if she saw a black cat or stepping on the foot of a person who'd mistakenly stepped on hers, nor would she utter the word *cancer*—even after it ravaged her body, even as she prayed for death itself—for fear of taunting the disease.

By age seventeen, there was no Shabbos, no God, no mother, but there were, finally, girls. After all of that time spent wondering over

what they wanted, what they liked, it was finally clear: Girls liked grief.
They liked when, after admitting that, yes, it was still difficult to talk
about his mother, Ed became so sad, so overwrought, that his desire
approached desperation. They liked how he gripped their hair and
faces and breasts as if he were suddenly terrified that they, too, might
drop dead. And if they weren't going to die in that moment, Ed *made
them feel* that they would one day, and that Ed would, too, that they all
would die, every last citizen of Dorchester, Roxbury, and Mattapan,
and that they—a girl and Ed Cantowitz—they were breathing (*Can
you hear my breath? I can hear your heart. Feel that. Come closer; no,
closer*), they were alive. It was as if Ed, with his recent status of mourner,
had been given permission to act out each year of pent-up sexual frustration and, with this permission, his very own seduction style had
emerged. If he'd been more of a cynic, he might have called it the
Death Threat, as if it were a new dance; he might have boasted of his
technique to the guys at Sam's, who placed bets on the number of spares
in a bowling game and played pool on one of the eight backroom tables
on any given night. He might have bragged to the boys who won their
cigarettes during poker games, boys with no one waiting at home for
them, making sure they weren't ruining their precious young lives. But
Ed wasn't that kind of cynic. Though sometimes he played pinochle
until he couldn't see straight and none of his hard-earned money from
working for his father remained, he wasn't that kind of boy. It was true
that at some point he'd become conscious of what he was doing with
these girls and began performing just a bit, but by then he was too
grateful for his success to return to behaving with any measure of
self-control. His mother would have called these aspiring young gam-
blers and such boasting *low class,* and he'd loved his mother without
reservation. They had joked around together in their pajamas up until
the very end—Ed lying at her side under rosebud-patterned sheets,
under ugly blankets crocheted by the Sisterhood, while his father
cursed doctors on the phone by day and friends in the kitchen by night.
"Why didn't you have more children, Ma?" Ed had asked her once
(only with hindsight did such a question seem cruel), as he dared to

imagine a world with only his father for family. "Oh; Eddie," she'd said. "Who was going to come after you?"

Ed's thrill with girls was not about conquest, but it was a thrill and as real as his very real fear of dying. Which was, of course, exacerbated when he was that close to a girl, because he felt like he really really really didn't want to die. Not when such happiness was possible.

There was Marla with the red sweater, who offered him a turn on her new bicycle, to take a spin through Franklin Field. They coasted down a hill and into a patch of sunlight. He told her he hadn't kissed anyone since his mother died. It was so easy; it was true. To feel her small lips parting, her squat hand in his hair, to tumble down behind the oak trees. When she left that summer to be a counselor at a girls' camp, he spent the better part of a Sunday wandering through the zoo, because taking a good look at the monkeys could usually cheer him up, but nothing did the trick until Peggy asked him the time in front of the antelopes and the camels. Peggy had been quick about it; the word *efficient* came to mind. Then one day Carol sold him an orange Popsicle. Carol had watched him lick the Popsicle and told him when she got off work, slipping him another Popsicle free of charge. Sarah Jane was covered with mosquito bites and was going mad with itching when she came into Twinies, where he was buying his father cigarettes. These were neighborhood girls; he had seen them all before, but he wasn't sure where. It could have been anywhere—the Wall on the High Holy Days amidst a sea of teenagers angling to show off their best-dressed selves, or maybe the Chez Vous roller rink, where he would've no doubt been too busy looking at their legs as they laced up their skates to remember their faces; he could have seen them while waiting on line to buy candy or comics. But never had he imagined how these girls—the very same ones who bought their parents Geritol at Twinies and challah and half-moons at the bakery and chatted with the cobbler about which shoes were theirs even when their ticket was nowhere to be found—would follow him to secluded spots or in some cases (Peggy!) lead the way. When he'd told his story of grief and loneliness, each one had offered him such succor. Sarah Jane had heard of him—heard that,

though he was smart, some people worried he'd get into trouble now
that his mother was gone. Marla had told him to lay his head on her
thighs. She had stroked his head and said *there, there* as if he wasn't full
of anger and hunger but instead was only a girl from her camp, someone longing for home.

Unfathomably (Ed couldn't help but think), Hugh didn't seem to be
making any move toward wherever it was that Hugh Shipley went on a
Friday evening. They both still looked on as students rushed about in
the twilight. Hugh lit up another cigarette.

"So what's on your agenda this evening?" Ed finally asked.

Hugh shrugged. "You?"

"When?"

"Now," said Hugh. "Where are you headed?"

"I'm not sure," Ed admitted. "Maybe go get a drink? You want to get
a drink?"

"Oh," he said, stretching his fingers again, "I was actually going to
see my father."

"Do you want to go see him?"

"Not especially."

"Then I'd consider it carefully. Maybe you need a drink."

Hugh laughed. "You think I need to have a drink before seeing my
father?"

"Maybe. Maybe you do. How the hell should I know?" He sounded
coarser than he'd meant to, coarser than he was, and as he cursed himself for how this so often happened, how he ruined whatever chance he
had to be affable and winning, Ed suddenly saw something on the
ground in the distance, a flash of light in the patchy grass, right where
the girl had walked. As he crouched down to collect it, he prayed for a
monogrammed brooch, a silver hairpin he'd need to return to the
slightly cross-eyed, perfectly buxom girl, but it was only a smashed bottle cap, the label worn away.

When he looked up and saw Hugh Shipley's back to him, and when he heard him beg off while walking away before the night had even started, he vowed to pursue Hugh and keep him interested, at least for the next five minutes.

"Hey, where are you going?" he called after him.

After three years as a Harvard student and four years of no religion, Ed had—just a month ago—decided to say kaddish for his mother. He had made this decision solely because his mother had come to him in a dream. She'd sat on his bed in the room he shared with Stan Landau, his roommate since freshman year (that Jews were assigned only Jewish roommates should not have come as a surprise, but it just so happened that Stan was the perfect roommate). In the middle of the night, with the lights from the river shining through the curtains, with the heft of her former zaftig self weighing down the end of the bed, his mother had stared him down and said, "Just say it for me." When he'd asked what she was talking about, she looked at him exactly the way she seldom had: brimming with disappointment. And so, though he'd had no intention of doing so perhaps ever again, or at least—more realistically—not so soon after the seventh and hopefully final infernal summer spent working for his father, laying steel pipes in the ground, Ed had gone home. He'd gone home for Yom Kippur. Of course the holiday had fallen on a day of lectures only days before his midterm examinations, and of course he'd had to give the professors a sufficient explanation, but he didn't apologize. He approached his European history professor and explained the Day of Atonement as if not only this thin-lipped man but also the entire faculty at Harvard had been clamoring to understand. Ed told him, in the loftiest voice he could muster (a voice that he'd learned not from three years at Harvard but from his own dead mother), that the very word *atone* meant to be *at one* with God. Then he walked to Central Square in his too-short dark suit, picked up an egg-salad sandwich to eat before sundown, and took the Red Line. He tried not to feel afraid that something would prevent his return.

His father was into a bottle of rye and barely acknowledged his presence. Forget about the fact that his father was drinking hard liquor after
sunset on Erev Yom Kippur—that he drank *at all* was still a shock. Ed
had been raised on the story of how, during Prohibition, his father's
uncle—a Brooklyn *rebbe*!—had been fond of making bathtub gin and
how one fatal night he'd mixed the wrong proportions and *the rabbi died
from drinking bad gin*. Ed had rarely seen his parents drink, aside from
some Manischewitz on Friday nights and holidays, aside from a glass of
sherry for his mother now and then, though he was starting to think that
maybe his father had always drunk and had—before his mother's
death—simply done so in secret. The night after Ed's mother was buried, after all of the mourners had gone home and the house was unbear-
ably quiet, his father pulled a bottle of rye from below the sink and a
glass from the cabinet above it. He sat down at the kitchen table, opened
the bottle, and filled the glass exactly halfway. He betrayed no awareness
that Ed was standing in the doorway, and his father drank from that
glass as if the whole action—the retrieval of the glass, the exacting
pour—was somehow inevitable.

Now Murray Cantowitz hid nothing. There was piss coating the rim
of the toilet seat and coarse hairs in the sink. *Well,* Ed thought, *at least
he's shaving.* The amber-colored couch coughed up clouds of dust when
he sat down on it, and when Ed rose to get a start on quietly cleaning, his
father yelled, "What're you doing?" as if he were tearing the place
apart. "Leave it!" And so Ed headed out the door to a different shul from
where he'd been bar mitzvahed, to the shul where most of the old embit-
tered congregants had relocated, having refrained from asking his father
one last time if he wanted to come along.

The night was chilly and clear, and as he became just another Jew
walking toward the shul, he was stunned by how calm he felt, as if he
were suddenly inside a recurring dream, where urgency was replaced by
prescription. All he had to do was get from the street to the shul. All he
had to do was say the kaddish. There was no reason to think any further
than that; the dream didn't allow for it. The sanctuary smelled like heavy
breath, aftershave, and dense floral perfume. He opened a prayer book

and felt its crumbling binding, sticking shut for a few final moments by old dried glue. Such humble materials for such supposedly holy words, and as much as he tried to hold the book together, out came the paper bits from the binding, out onto his trousers and reminding him of hay, which was a strange association, but once the thought was there he couldn't stop it and all the men in their jackets and *tallis* looked not like men but like horses, stooped and obedient. Enveloped in a not altogether bad smell of age and thoughtful hygiene and this blameless equine image, he let himself rock back and forth, and the keening familiar melody took hold of him and the Hebrew came without thought. Everything over the last four years had been about thought. He stayed inside the shul until the very last prayer. When he'd made his way through crowds of familiar faces—the bearded and the shaved, the powdered and the rouged—and their questions, so many questions, not only about Harvard but about his unfortunate father, after he'd been kissed and slapped on the back and when he was out the door and taking off his yarmulke, grateful to feel the air again, he saw Marla of the red sweater standing on the curb, evidently waiting for a ride. Without her red sweater she looked much more ordinary than he remembered and also, somehow, more appealing. He thought of saying hello, of asking what she was doing these days, if she still had that bicycle, but it was as if he'd turned into one of the horses he'd imagined while inside the shul. He watched in silence until saying hello became inconceivable, until a car pulled up and she looked both ways before getting in and taking off.

For years he'd dreamed of the much-heralded mystery and majesty of *shiksas*. But now that he was surrounded by Radcliffe girls on a daily basis—adorable ginger freckles, startled blue eyes—now that he was no more comfortable talking to them but *almost* accustomed to their extensive knowledge of not only tennis and Europe and oystering on private islands off the coast of Maine but also Aristotle and Freud and Keynesian economics, goddamn it all to hell, here he was in front of a synagogue, nostalgic about Marla and all of the others, the girls he hadn't called.

———

In Harvard Yard, Ed not only caught up with Hugh but within minutes he was buying drinks at Cronin's. "To make up for my accosting you," Ed had insisted.

"You did kind of accost me."

"Yes," said Ed, "and I'd like to make up for it."

"In that case I'll have a whiskey as well."

Ed suggested they share a ham sandwich. "I'm not the religious kind," Ed announced, and, though Hugh nodded, it was clear he had no idea to what Ed was referring.

"I don't really have any Jewish friends," Hugh explained, lighting up another cigarette. He didn't look uncomfortable, only direct.

"I don't really have any Shipley friends."

With his arm outstretched atop the booth, as if to claim a phantom girl, Hugh said, "You haven't been missing much." He was both plain-spoken and distracted. He was always looking around. Ed watched how his gaze followed the waitresses, the cooks in the kitchen, the salt and pepper on the table, and finally a pair of twin girls and their tense-looking dates who passed through the bustling doorway.

Ed finished his beer. "Would you look at them? They're *identical*."

"They're not."

"Of course they are. Imagine being one of those poor schmucks. Never knowing which one was yours."

"You'd know."

"You can't tell me you're able to see a difference."

"Of course."

"How?"

"Anyone can see they are different," said Hugh. "One has a scar on her forehead, and the other one's chin is more pronounced."

"They look exactly the same."

"You aren't looking in the right way." Though by all rights this was a condescending thing to say, Ed didn't feel particularly condescended to. Hugh just seemed as though he really cared what Ed did or didn't see.

"I'm an observant bastard, okay? Make no mistake about that. Listen, who noticed that the girl from the library—my girl—is cross-eyed. Who saw that?"

"Oh, she's *your* girl now?"

"Well, she's not yours, that's for sure."

"What's her name?"

"Oh, I have no idea," Ed said, able now to laugh at himself, at how his ardor seemed suddenly comical.

When the ham sandwich arrived, Ed grabbed his half quickly. He was, as usual, hungrier than he'd realized. As he savored the salty ham, the slightly stale bread, he looked at the twins and their dates waiting for a table. What was Shipley talking about? He saw no pronounced chin, no scar. The only difference occurred when one lit a cigarette, when the fact that her sister had not lit a cigarette made them both that much more exciting because they had made different choices. Her smoking style bordered on theatrical, and Ed wondered if he might have seen her in a Harvard Drama Club production. He had become an avid theatergoer. At first it had been to impress Radcliffe girls, but sometimes he went alone if there was no one with whom he really wanted to watch and (inevitably, afterward) discuss. This semester he'd seen a steamy *Cat on a Hot Tin Roof*, *The Little Foxes*, a terrific *Pajama Game*; he wanted to go to England and meet Harold Pinter and personally thank him for *The Caretaker*, which he'd recently seen at the Loeb. Though last week's offering was melancholy nonsense. He'd taken a troublingly tall date to see a play by García Lorca. Everyone had been dressed up like leafless trees, and a screechy cello droned on for hours.

"I always wanted to be a twin," said Hugh, who had moved on to a third whiskey. "Ever since I can remember."

"Oh God, no, nothing worse—another Hugh Shipley?"

"It wouldn't be another of me," Hugh quietly insisted. He apparently had no interest in lightening up. Did he speak this way with everyone? "It would be the other part, the missing part. Don't you ever feel like you're, I don't know, missing someone?" He looked up from the bright table lamp and squinted into comparative darkness.

"Yeah," Ed said. "I miss my mother." It was an absurdly weak thing to say. He wasn't sure why he'd said something so personal that it approached transgression, but he imagined it was because Hugh Shipley seemed to have forgotten Harvard's unwritten rule about maintaining a modicum of sarcastic affectation, or at least until one was properly drunk. And he also sensed that Hugh had chosen to confide in him and he wanted to offer something in return.

Hugh nodded. "When did she die?"

"Four years now."

"I'm sorry."

Ed poured another sugar into his coffee, though he had no intention of drinking another sip. He nodded. "Yeah," he said. "Yeah, thanks."

The twins and their dates were seated at the next table. It was difficult not to stare. They had the same auburn hair parted to the side, the same pearl earrings and cherry lipstick. If there was one girl, she would have been noticed solely for her solid good looks, but their twin-ness was even more striking than their prettiness. The smoker laughed and the other did not. Ed wondered if a joke had been made at the un-laughing un-smoking one's expense, though neither of their dates was smiling.

"In Mali," Hugh said, "twins are the only ones who are considered complete. The rest of us, we're walking around as halves. We're half people, all of us. No wonder we're all about to be destroyed by nuclear bombs."

"Goddamn right. I keep thinking I should follow every urge, every stupid idea in my head. Because who knows, right?"

"What is it that you want to do?"

"Oh hell, I don't know. I'm just talking. It's a goddamn unsettling thought that there are nuclear missiles off the coast of Florida. Can you argue with that? No news flash there. None at all. Where in Africa is Mali?"

"West."

"Uh-huh."

"That's where I'm headed."

"No kidding?"

Hugh nodded. "I'm going to take pictures."

"Well, I'm going to Wall Street," Ed said, and he couldn't stop his voice from sounding proud. "Different jungle."

"I'd say so. Save yourself. Come to my jungle instead."

"To Africa?"

"Sure. Why not? At least no one is sending nuclear bombs there."

Ed laughed and drank the rest of his tepid sweet coffee. "What are you after? You want to be eaten by savages, like Rockefeller? You want to—what?"

"He wasn't eaten by savages."

"So they say. Let's put it this way: Such a trip is not in my future."

"No? What is?"

"I want to make some real dough."

"*Real dough?*"

"Yes, indeed. Not a fashionable thing to say around here, I know. But I want to work hard and make money. Money like your oldest, richest Mr. Shipley made."

He tried not to sound fanatical, he truly did, but when he imagined a day that he wouldn't have to worry over how many times he could clean his dirty shirts before they fell apart, he tended to sound—he realized this—like an advertisement for the wonders of capitalism. He wanted the freedom to buy a new shirt if he was too goddamn lazy to take his to the cleaner's. Cardboard strip around the starched front—a new shirt, nothing like it. All that cardboard. He loved tearing it apart like wrapping paper.

Ed asked, "Why shouldn't I have certain pleasures in life if I'm willing to work harder than everyone else?"

"Why, indeed?" Hugh replied, but this time it was condescending. "But, just so you know, my family doesn't have any real money anymore."

"Believe me, your family has money."

"No, I mean it. It's all but dried up in our branch of the family. There was some kind of issue with the trusts. I don't know."

"What do you mean, you don't know?"

"I mean I don't care."

"You might start to care when you get malaria in West Africa and need to be evacuated and flown back to this fine country, threat of nuclear missiles or not. You might care if you need to get a job." He felt his neck tensing up, and he forced a smile.

Hugh nodded. "I understand."

"No, you don't. Not really."

"Okay, I don't. I don't. You got me."

"That's right."

"So will you give me a job then?" Hugh asked. "When I'm hard up and desperate?"

"You think it's a joke?"

"I don't think it's a joke, but I know too many people who have plenty of money, and they're wretched. They're also incompetent. Talk to me when you know more people with money."

"I will."

"Just so you know," said Hugh, sitting up straighter, "I hope you do."

"What about Romulus and Remus?" Ed blurted. "They were twins. No love lost there."

Hugh took his last bite of sandwich. He was the slowest eater that Ed had ever seen, with the exception of his aunt Lillian. He chewed every bit of that bite and finally, finally swallowed. "They were raised by wolves."

"Many great men were."

"Were you?"

"My mother—she was a peach. But my father has some wolflike tendencies, you bet."

"Like what?"

"Oh, I don't know—he never wanted to have children, so that probably has something to do with it." Ed laughed, but he could tell he sounded strained. "He wanted my mother and he wanted to make her happy, but he's made it clear, especially now that she's gone, that being a father wasn't what he was after. And where I'm from, children are everything. It's all about *the children*. It's just what they think about and talk about and live for, and I think all that fuss—it really got him riled up. I only figured out that children were such a focus—who notices such a thing when you *are* one of those children?—since he would point it out so frequently, deriding this one and that one because they talked, they thought, they *bragged*, about their kids too much. God forbid someone bragged. It was like his cause, how people gave kids too much attention, and what was implied was that it sure as hell wasn't going to be like that in our house."

"Too bad he couldn't have just come on over to our neighborhood. Don't laugh. He and my father—despite appearances to the contrary, I'm sure—would have plenty in common."

"Is that right? Well, I don't know about your father, but mine didn't like everyone lavishing attention on the children, because he always wanted to be at the center. See, he'd had a taste of it, a real taste of attention. Worst thing that could have happened to a guy like my father. He was a boxer, okay, and I guess a pretty promising one—"

"Your father was a boxer?"

"That's what I'm telling you." Ed tried not to sound frustrated, but he knew that if he didn't keep talking, he'd lose steam. This was the first time he'd told anyone at Harvard anything about his father. He'd guarded these stories, kept them close. It was as if telling them too frequently would dull their power. To Ed, the very existence of these tales proved that his father wasn't solely a bitter, drunk steamfitter. That there was some spark to his past. Some interest.

Hugh said, "I've never met a boxer."

"Yeah, well, unfortunately, he got knocked out early in his career. He lost his hearing in one ear and broke a few of his vertebrae, and I guess the recovery really took it out of him and his boxing days were over quickly. He went from being some kind of local hotshot to having not much of an education and a lot of aches and pains."

Ed thought about stopping, but he couldn't stop now, not when Hugh looked so genuinely interested. It was as if Hugh was counting on him, relying on Ed to deliver a good, engaging story. What else could he do?

"My mother always told me that was when he changed, although who knows. She met him right before he got knocked out. I guess by the time he was injured, she was sufficiently impressed. He was greeted with respect when he took her out and she was just a kid, she was from an extremely strict family, and when he showed her a night out in Boston—y'know, cocktails and dancing, the whole bit—she was charmed. He was handsome then, even after the injuries, a genuinely handsome man. I don't look like him—in case you were wondering—though I did get his shoulders." Ed sat up taller, grinned. "Not too bad, am I right?"

Hugh laughed, as if he couldn't believe anyone would say something so vain. "Hmm. Especially for your height."

"Ouch," he said. "*Ouch.* At any rate, my mother saw him through his recovery and he never forgot it. He loved to talk about how patient she was and also how tough. And how, after having me, my mother never gave him that kind of attention again."

"So he's a real tough guy."

Ed nodded, grinned. He told Hugh how—after eight straight amateur victories—during his father's first professional fight in downtown Worcester, he was felled by a roundhouse curse of a punch. How the press clippings stated that he'd been knocked out cold, but this was not the case. How he'd stood up by the count of eight. How those who'd been there that miserable night still sometimes stopped him on the streets of Dorchester to insist that he'd been robbed.

After an appropriately solemn shaking of the head, Hugh piped up, "Did he teach you to fight?"

Ed paused before nodding. "In the basement."

"That must have been . . . something."

"Oh, it was great. It was the best time we ever had."

He wasn't sure why he'd said that or how the lie had come so easily. He imagined the basement, where no lessons had occurred. The furnace was in the basement, and it had been Ed's job to put the hand-painted sign (COAL!) in the window so that the delivery truck would stop. The coal man rigged a series of steel chutes from the truck to the furnace, and the coal had crashed through the chutes and shot its way into the coal bin. He had grown up accompanying his father down to the basement, watching him shovel fresh coal into the steel door, fit the crank into the middle of the furnace, and slam that crank left to right as if his life were hanging in the balance and depended on the force of the slam. His father had brought him down to the basement to ostensibly train him to one day take over the task of the furnace, but Ed always felt that his father relished doing it himself and the real reason he wanted Ed to watch was to demonstrate just how strong he still was, despite his life-defining injuries. His father slammed that crank until the ashes of the burned coal came through the grate, onto the furnace floor, and, as soon as Ed could sweep, it became Ed's job to sweep the ashes into the ash can. Several weeks after Ed's bar mitzvah, his father had sent him down to the basement to get ash for the icy sidewalk. When he'd come up with a bucketful and stood at the top of the dark moldy stairs, the door had been locked and no one would answer. At first Ed thought his father had locked it out of habit, by mistake, but he soon realized his father was playing a joke on him, the kind of behavior that would come up with more and more frequency until his departure from home, and Ed would always be left to wonder just what was it that he had done wrong. But his father wouldn't admit it was a punishment. "It was a joke," he'd said. "You gotta learn to lighten up."

His father had not taught him to box—not in that basement, not anywhere. Ed had asked his father to do the honors, and at first he'd said of course he would, but after asking repeatedly and having his father say he was tired or in no mood or watching the game, it became clear that, for whatever reason, his father didn't want to. Ed had learned boxing from other teachers; they were never hard to find: his gym teacher Mr. Coleman; "Big Sully," who cleaned the monkey house; his gambling friend Schwartzy, who had good form as a boxer but lacked the nerves to compete. Ed was a good student in general; he knew this now. He was certain his ability to learn quickly was going to help him later in life, and more than boxing ever had. When his father was in his prime, he'd saved three Jewish boys from a bunch of Irish thugs. People had said how brave he was, how he looked out for his own, how he'd always be known as a hero. But this was no longer.

"My father's a decent man," Ed said, as if it was pity and not anger that consumed him.

The waitress cleared their plates away and Hugh said he'd pay.

"No," Ed insisted. "I offered. Besides, I thought you didn't have any money." With whom, Ed couldn't help but wonder again, did Hugh usually spend his time?

"I said *real* money. There's still a bit. The dregs. I'll buy you beer, coffee, and half a sandwich with the dregs."

"No," said Ed. And that was that.

They went to Adams House and drank gin with limes, and Ed met the head of the drama club and a *Crimson* writer whose work he admired. Ed watched as girls approached Hugh and Hugh ignored their not-so-subtle invitations. Ed marveled at how, like preening birds, they offered their pale necks, their bosoms, arranged their jewelry to catch the light as if lighting were the issue. He knocked back more gin; he drank until he forgot to add the lime. Ed and the girls listened as Hugh spoke softly about the Dani tribe of West New Guinea, how their culture was based on a never-ending war between neighboring clans, an ongoing quest to avenge the fallen, to pacify ancestral ghosts. Hugh talked about how human cruelty was paralyzing but compelling and that maybe these specific warriors could be seen as a microcosm for all warriors and that maybe, if people really paid attention to them, some positive change for our own culture—no matter how small—might just result from it. When Hugh was done speaking, the girls didn't stop listening. They listened to Hugh's silence and eventual progression into playing impenetrable jazz piano, which only invited them to settle in. One of the girls started listing all of the jazz greats who'd been taken from this life too early, who must have been too pure for this world.

"The fact that they were drunks might have also had something to do with it," Ed pointed out, and there was a collective sigh of indignation, though one of the girls did laugh before running out of the room to be sick.

"Let's go," Hugh said. "I need some air."

And on the banks of the Charles, Ed asked Hugh if he meant what he'd said about bringing change to America through studying savages in New Guinea. "There aren't any Negroes in Fenway Park. Hitler almost succeeded in wiping Jews off the planet. Do you actually think people are open-minded enough to see themselves reflected in completely primitive people? Do you think *you* are?"

"I'm not sure," said Hugh after a moment. "But, yes, I do think so."

"Okay," Ed said, skeptical. "We'll see."

"I know you think it's ridiculous," Hugh said, but not as if it really mattered.

"Look, I have another question. Why did you ignore those girls? Why did you seem so hell-bent on ending up alone or—worse!—still talking to *me* when you could be off seducing any one of them?"

Hugh picked up a stick and hurled it toward the tar-colored water. He tried to light a cigarette, but his lighter was jammed. "My heart's bashed in," he said.

"Your heart? Your heart is fine."

"What do you know?"

"Your heart is *fine*."

"You don't know."

"Hearts are very resilient."

"I'm sure yours is."

"That's true," Ed said. He was thinking not of Marla or any number of missed possibilities but of a girl he'd met in New Haven while tailgating two weeks ago; they drank bourbon from her brother's flask. "It is."

Hugh finally lit his cigarette and seemed marginally less pathetic. "Every now and then I'll take a girl out, even go to bed with her, but it doesn't make a damn bit of difference, no matter who it is. I'm all broken up. Have been for years."

"I see that. So who did this to you? Who bashed Hugh Shipley's weak and feeble heart? I'll change her mind."

Hugh started laughing, a great unruly laugh, the kind that can change a mood entirely and stop a night's potential downslide. "I bet you could," he said.

Ed jumped up on a bench and jumped off it, up and down until he was out of breath. "Tell me something funny."

"Funny," Hugh said, as if he was about to recite a dismal poem. But when he spoke up again, he was animated, maybe more than he'd been all night. "All right. I was sent to an Episcopal boarding school when I was eleven."

"*Eleven?* Jesus, I said funny—not Dickensian."

"I'm getting there. At this school—where, by the way, I refused to take communion—I was . . . *exploring* the storage room in one of the main buildings and of course I was smoking and I opened up a can of potassium sulfate or nitrate—I still can't remember which one it was—"

"I'm guessing nitrate."

"Right. And it exploded. Not supposed to be combustible, but I'm telling you I nearly burned the school down. This was unintentional and unconscious, until I read all of Freud during the summer of my senior year and had some fairly major revelations about unconscious desire."

"I'm still waiting for the funny part."

"So there I was, running up the stairs with this impromptu bomb, and I threw the bomb in the toilet. Clouds of smoke billowing, I was coughing—terrified—but what happened when I had the opportunity to let it all burn? That school that I hated? That venerable institution where my father broke all the records for athletics, including my grandfather's? Did I let it burn? Of course not. I saved it!" Hugh was laughing now, and Ed tried to but couldn't stick with it.

"I saved the school. *I* did. That's the way I saw it, at least. After the smoke cleared—so to speak—the headmaster took one look at me and said, 'Now I *know* I'm going to be able to kick you out of this school.' He was thrilled to finally have a good enough reason. But in the end—here's the funny part—he couldn't because my father was, and still is, an important trustee. Ridiculous," he said, laughing again. "So completely ridiculous. I nearly burned their school to the ground and still they kept me around."

"What did your father say?"

"Well, I'm fairly certain he was just relieved that I wasn't coming home. One of my father's favorite routines was to talk about how boring children were and to construct the kind of conversations he wished he could simply have had with the help, with regard to looking after me when I was a child. *See that pile of money over there,* he would say, *go on, over there, that pile in the corner—take it. Yes, the PILE. Take the PILE, just take care of the boy and for God's sake don't tell me about each sneeze!*"

"I've never met him, but you're a pretty good mimic," Ed admitted.

"The man can still make me laugh even though I basically hate him."

"I don't hate my father," said Ed, not because it was true but because he could never imagine saying so, certainly not to Hugh Shipley, not to someone whose father didn't understand what it meant to do any kind of work, not to mention the kind of backbreaking work that his father still did as a steamfitter, laying pipes in the ground, getting coated with dirt and unspecified grime, often narrowly escaping electrical fires because of what he called *Depression cheapo wiring.*

"That's good," said Hugh. "I'm happy for you." He tossed his cigarette and sat down on the bench.

"Is your mother funny, too?"

"My mother's dead."

"Oh," said Ed. "Oh."

"A long time ago," said Hugh, as if Ed had asked. "I barely remember her."

The river and the sky were far off in the distance, and all that felt real was the bench where Hugh was seated and the stubble of grass underfoot. Ed sat down on the bench, too. He wanted to say something, if for no other reason than he was uncomfortable with silence. He hated to sit in silence with anyone. He hated hearing other people's uncomfortable sounds—their toe-tapping, their throat-clearing, their quiet cracking-of-knuckles. He hated how driven he felt to make the silence stop, how a roar of discomfort filled his own head like a giant wave crashing to shore. Every few summers, his mother had prevailed and borrowed from the credit union so that they could go to Nantasket Beach, and that cold Atlantic once gave him the tossing of his life; he'd never forgotten the roar of it as the wave drew him up and over. The more he didn't say to Hugh, the more he withheld words of kindness or humor or whatever the hell he was supposed to say, the more absurd it felt to be there, hearing that ocean's roar. Why couldn't he simply say *I'm sorry,* the way that Hugh had done earlier this evening? *I'm sorry.* Hugh had said it strong and clear, and here Ed was, unable to say a word. They were strangers, he thought. They'd remain so.

But then whatever profound awkwardness he'd been feeling, whatever definitive *wrongness,* mysteriously tapered off and, like the halting of a violent storm, what was left felt akin to good fortune. As Saturday's rising sun became a sudden and tremendous possibility, what remained was nothing more extraordinary than two grown motherless sons.

What also remained was this: They were—despite sharing not a single interest or goal—going to be friends.

I grabbed Hugh's arm. I said, "Just keep walking." I must have been out of my mind, okay? But that's exactly what Hugh did.

I felt this . . . grip . . . on my arm, and what do you know, it was Ed. I thought, My God, this fellow is in some kind of state.

When they told this story many years later, both men said they could never remember how they'd gone from Ed's tight grip to sitting in Cronin's sharing a ham sandwich, but that wasn't true, because Ed had always remembered. He'd followed Hugh; he'd dropped a squashed bottle cap, brushed grass off his trousers, and run after him. He never forgot.

Chapter Two

Fall

As a freshman, Hugh Shipley had embarked on an English literature concentration, but after two years of earning decent marks despite rarely giving his best efforts, after forgoing much of Shakespeare and Virgil to play chess with a few quasi-bums in Davis Square, one of those quasi-bums, who hailed from Tennessee, gave him a seminal article about kinship theory during the autumn of his junior year, and although he'd read the article mainly out of an urge to be polite to someone who was masterful at chess and apparently—given his disheveled appearance and his refusal to discuss anything but chess—not much else, he'd reread the article just as soon as he was finished and immediately talked his way into an anthropology course, even though the deadline for enrollment had long passed.

Hugh Shipley then took a whole lot of NoDoz and wrote a paper about the incest taboo, which earned him the attention of the department head, resulting in a swift switch of concentrations. He upped his NoDoz intake, gave up whiskey for beer (more nutrients), and wrote both "*Cherchez la Vache*," about the single-minded obsession that the African Nuer tribe have with their cows, and "Fatness Comes Second," a detailed analysis of human size variation. He'd found himself staying up reading more than what was assigned, thinking about classes long after the professor had stopped speaking. He had finally—at age twenty-one—felt ready to begin his education, but it was only when he'd thanked the Southern quasi-bum for the excellent reading recommendation that he knew he'd found his true teacher.

For the quasi-bum was not a bum at all but a graduate student named Charlie Case, who—besides the two hours a day that were wholly dedicated to chess—spent his waking hours in a basement office at the Peabody Museum, editing reels of footage and writing proposals, who had—incredibly!—made an epic journey to New Guinea in order to shoot, vérité style, one tribe and their endless war. He'd been the *leader* of this expedition, the one who introduced Michael Rockefeller to New Guinea, where Rockefeller had returned that fall and disappeared mysteriously after capsizing a canoe. Hugh—bearing a famous last name and being a budding photographer—could not help but identify with Michael Rockefeller, which, of course, he had never admitted to anyone.

Over the winter and spring of his junior year, Hugh turned up regularly at the graduate student's messy office with sandwiches and Cokes, with offers to help in any way he could.

"Why do you want to help?" asked Charlie, whose beard always seemed accidental.

The one time Hugh had asked Charlie Case point blank what he really thought happened to the young Rockefeller, if he thought he'd drowned or been killed by natives or, as some purported, become absorbed into a local tribe, Case only said something about Rockefeller's eyes, how he couldn't get them out of his head, these eyes that were so inquisitive, always asking something of whatever or whoever happened to be in front of him. Charlie Case said that he wished everyone had a bit more of that quality and, goddamn it, didn't Hugh wish that, too?

Remind me, said Charlie Case. *Why do you want to help?*

He had started out wanting to ingratiate himself so that he might hear about Charlie's travels. He supposed, at first, he'd been after little more than some good old-fashioned exotic storytelling, as it always seemed improbable that these anthropology professors—the same ones who had chalk dust on their blazers, who walked their dogs and presumably (at least the better-off ones) lived in any one of the fine houses on Brattle or Larchwood or Oxford—made their way to such primitive societies, usually for at least one year. He'd heard tales of certain professors drinking hallucinogenic tea, disrobing, and speaking in tongues. In short, he'd been curious. What, he also wondered, *was* visual anthropology besides a relatively new field that—he had to admit, and forget about explaining it to his father—sounded awfully vague? But the footage (not a naked hallucinating professor to be seen) consumed him more than any book ever could, and by last spring he'd finally found what his father had long condemned him for lacking: a sense of purpose.

Never mind the fact that his father mocked his budding interests (hanging what appeared to be an effigy made of burlap, straw, and velvet from Hugh's bedroom ceiling as a welcome-home gag was one particularly unfunny moment in which his father's estimation of valuing other cultures was on ridiculous display, though Hugh had been impressed by his ingenuity—whom had he paid to sew such a thing?). Because of this footage, which depicted (among countless other images lodged in Hugh's brain) a naked man so focused on weaving that Hugh could feel the fabric with his own uncalloused fingers, because of his acquaintance with a similarly focused Charlie Case, he was able to study in a new way. The masses of reading assignments, which he'd previously had trouble completing no matter what the course, were no longer so forbidding. It was as if seeing all of Case's footage had unlocked some part of his mind and he began to be able to picture everything that he read, and when he could picture something—be it a tribal costume or a philosophical argument—it turned out he was able to engage. And engage he finally did. With this newfound love of analyzing centralized government and marriage and the way that women linked society together all across the world regardless of whether they wore rings through their dark noses or around their snow-white fingers, with his developing urge to analyze life's basic structures—structures to which he'd never previously given a thought—there emerged a curious freedom. He wasn't entirely sure what he felt while watching dark naked children rub clay around their eyes so that they might resemble birds or while watching people play out their lives under a belief system in which ghosts exist without a trace of kitsch but instead are more real—hyperreal—than anything, but he couldn't deny he was energized. He was also no longer consumed primarily with the blank expanse of the day—the hours and hours after waking and how he had to fill them. He no longer devoted the majority of those hours to thinking about Helen and wondering what had happened to her.

That springtime of his junior year he had been on some sort of full-fledged upswing, where the very weather seemed to support his plans and his mood, and this stirring feeling lasted throughout the summer, when he had worked (vowing it would be the very last time) at the yacht club on Fishers Island, where his ancestors had been founding members and where his two older half brothers still raced their boat. He vowed not to work at the club ever again—not because he didn't love sailing or even many of his cousins and crewmates (if not exactly his own brothers), but he knew it was a disgrace to belong to a club with discriminatory policies against Negroes. Jews, too, of course. Likely Catholics—who knew what the actual bylaws said? If he wasn't going to board a bus and march down South anytime soon, he could at least—for Christ's sake—forgo his favorite goddamn sport. Even if it was the only sport that he was not only good at but also actually loved. Even if he would miss how being a good sailor was about instincts and decision-making more than about any physical advantages that he also just so happened to possess. He would sail again, he told himself. He would sail not as sport but to get to where he needed to go.

He had gone so far as to arrange a meeting with the club president (an elderly distant cousin) to explain his feelings on the matter of discrimination, and, after a hand-folding pause, the president/cousin replied in a disturbingly kind voice, "I'm glad you have told me your feelings on this matter, Hugh."

"You are?"

"Of course. My door is always open. You know your family plays an important part in the history here."

"To be honest, sir, I don't care about my family's important history as much as I care about what is going on right here and right now."

"Yes," said the president, "I see."

"You see?"

"I do. Are you sure I can't get you something to drink?"

"I'm sure," said Hugh, desperately craving a beer. "Thank you."

"You know," he said, as he stood up and fixed himself a finger of gin on ice, "man is tribal."

"Yes, sir. That I know. Anthropology happens to be my concentration."

"You don't say."

"Yes, sir."

"And you're a Harvard man, too, just like your father. So you are the last person I need to explain this to, I'm sure." He looked Hugh in the eye and smiled. "We are tribal by nature." He wouldn't quit smiling. "And this, Hugh, is our tribe." He took a slow sip of his gin. If this man were a different kind of person, he would have shrugged his shoulders sheepishly. But he was not that kind of person, and, for this, Hugh was glad.

"It's hardly that simple," Hugh tried.

"Young man, this is our home. We have a right to choose who enters our home."

"But it isn't a home," said Hugh.

"Look," he said, with only the slightest hint of impatience, gesturing out the open window toward the blue sky and sea and rolling green hills and the freshwater ponds and hydrangea bushes and that slight breeze, which would soon carry the official whiff of gin at precisely five o'clock. "If you think that changing some policy is going to alter the essentially tribal nature of society, forgive me, but you need to reexamine your expectations."

This club president—who was in fact Hugh's grandmother's second cousin, a man named Tribby Eaton, a man Hugh had loved and admired as a child, who had once given him a bowl of peanuts and a Coke after he'd lost a sunfish race—was not stooped nor was he bent; he had a full head of white hair and the shoulders and hands of a man who knew how to sail under inclement weather and return a killer serve. "This is where you come from," he said, and again his voice was kind.

In Hugh's mind he was raising his own voice, telling the old man to go stuff it, to stuff the traditions and the island and all of his justifications, that all of those justifications came not from pride but from fear. But as Tribby Eaton showed him the door, Hugh couldn't help noting that the older man looked sad. And when Hugh told him that he wished to revoke his membership, there was none of the victorious feeling he'd anticipated. None of the moral clarity he enjoyed when he played out the scenario either before or after this moment (as he would go on to recount it more than a few times over the years). But the point had been made and it was he who had made it, and that meant more than anything else. Didn't it?

So he was feeling really good about his decision to never return to the yacht club, feeling good and highly principled, when he'd returned to the Peabody the first week in September of his senior year with a glazed donut and a bottle of Coke, only to find Case's office vacant. As he held on to his intended gifts, he also tried holding on to his burgeoning sense of hope and purpose, and he'd run through the halls in search of Case, or at least some voice of authority who might explain Case's whereabouts. And as he jogged by the offices on the fourth floor, where he had never been, as he began to sweat through his shirt and started to panic about panicking—he saw Helen.

She was *sitting behind a desk and talking on the telephone.*

He would not have been more shocked if he'd wandered into a burlesque show in the middle of the day and she'd been the main attraction. There was Helen for the first time in almost four years, and instead of walking straight in to the office and demanding an explanation for her past actions or throwing her over his shoulder and carrying her away or asking what she was doing in the Peabody Museum, apparently *employed,* he'd continued to run, and as he ran, he felt it all disintegrate. All of those notions about the world conspiring to support him and the weather matching his mood and all that crap—they were gone. But they weren't just gone—it was as if someone had ripped a rosy poufy opera scrim from his intractably gray brain. It was as if, when he sat down on a bench in the Yard and (as if trying to conceal some kind of evidence) wolfed the jelly donut and the Coke he'd brought for Case, everything went dark. There was Helen and he couldn't even bring himself to speak to her.

She'd acted so focused on her task, as if she were terrified to look past the ink ribbon on her typewriter. She had seen him; he felt sure of it. They had seen each other.

And he continued to peer into that office on the fourth floor during the subsequent trips he had made to the Peabody. Though he concealed himself behind a column, he was certain that she saw him, sure that she was participating in the same elaborate charade. He told himself he was going back to the Peabody to learn more about Charlie Case, although he'd learned very quickly that Case was hardly missing—he had simply gone to Hollywood to speak to producers about perhaps taking a more commercial direction with the film (and hadn't thought to let Hugh know).

But of course he'd really gone to see Helen. He was convinced she knew exactly when he was coming and that she even dressed up in her best clothes, wore her hair loose for him. There she was and there she continued to be: tall and blond, those delicate lips still delicate, and that long nose still bisecting her face in always-surprising asymmetry. There she was behind her desk—long neck, long limbs—still Helen. After all this time and after all he knew or thought he knew, his physical response to her was pitifully unchanged.

Over the next month, every Thursday afternoon, he was certain they spoke without speaking. He'd stand outside her office door and she'd pretend she didn't see him. In his mind it was a tentative silent conversation—*you look the same, so do you; you seem well, so do you.* But as she pretended to type, he began to silently speak about how he'd only found out about her pregnancy through a family friend after they had graduated from their respective boarding schools (*boarding school* being a WASP euphemism for *prison*, they'd both agreed, laughing, out in the woods behind her school's gymnasium, Fats Domino on the loudspeaker muffled in the distance, their breath and cigarette smoke mixing in the near-frigid air).

In the quiet of the Peabody, Hugh silently spoke of that cold spring night when they'd finally talked, after circling each other for years. How their gloved hands had fumbled with cigarettes, how she'd taken him to the inside of a fat hollow tree, how they had urgently come to that tree again and again and nobody had caught them. How they had always kept their relationship a secret, without asking each other why. Right there in the Peabody, on what he remembered as his fifth visit, Hugh silently said (and, he was sure, Helen silently agreed) that they had kept it secret to ensure it remained untainted by the exclusive society from which they were both inadvertently descended. They'd kept their alliance secret to protect it from all the loathsome rules and expectations that had so plagued the two of them before they'd found each other. They were two tall kids who'd always liked hiding anyhow, but now they had each other. They had their tree.

In silence, as Helen sat behind a typewriter, Hugh spoke of how the Shipley family friend had been gossiping at the very dining room table where Hugh had grown up learning about soup spoons and what it meant to be a traitor to one's class and how to properly debone a fish. Hugh had not—surprise—been paying attention to the luncheon conversation, when suddenly, incredibly, he heard the name *Helen Ordway*: Helen Ordway whom he loved and who had not returned a letter or telephone call since the last night they'd spent together, the night of the Last Hurrah, which they had each taken special precaution to ensure they could not attend. While their classmates donned tulle and tuxedos, they'd reiterated their elaborate excuses to the only ones left in their respective dorms that night. Hugh had not gone on the bus with the rest of the boys from his school but had instead waited until they'd all gone, and he'd hired a taxi to take him to the very same campus, only when he arrived he'd bypassed the festive decorations and golden light and made his way through the graveyard and toward their hollow tree.

The gossiping family friend asked Hugh's father if he'd heard about a recent *situation* with Helen Ordway—as in the daughter of Guy and Virginia Ordway—as in can-you-imagine-if-the-papers-got-a-hold-of-*that*-story Ordways—and though Harvard-bound Hugh had nearly retched as this family friend carried on about no one knowing who the father was, or who had *done this* to poor Helen (who'd always seemed a touch *off* somehow, no?), and how Helen Ordway had refused to say—even after she was shipped away to heaven only knew where for the summer—Hugh had not retched, but he had left the table, and though he'd lacked the energy to punch a hole in the wall (what he imagined to be the proper response to such information), he began what became (at least to his father) a comical extended crying jag, which would last on and off well into the fall.

Hugh told Helen in his mind and in that silence how he had cried in a house where men did not cry, where centuries passed and deaths abounded but men still shed no tears. Hugh told her how he'd written her letters not only that summer but also well into the fall of his freshman year, how he had telephoned her family and written so many letters, never receiving a single response. He asked her, within this silence—their silence—how she could be so cruel and if he was right to have finally begun to doubt the one thing—the one person—he'd known to be true.

He recalled their final night and how she'd still dressed up as if she was going to the Last Hurrah, even though it was just the two of them, outside by the tree as usual. When he'd seen her coming toward him across the damp grass—teal silk, pale skin, dark sky—he remembered feeling badly that he hadn't worn a tuxedo after all, that he should have done it for her. But as she came closer, removing her silver heels that had been sticking more deeply into the ground with each progressive step, it was clear she didn't give a fig what he was wearing. She kissed him and grabbed a cigarette from the pocket of his scratchy flannel shirt. "You look like Grace Kelly," he said.

"I do not. Have you been waiting long?"

"You look like a taller and slightly more peculiar Grace Kelly. It's like you're Grace Kelly's more distinctive sister—you know, the one that Grace doesn't want hanging around, because she makes Grace seem ordinary. That's you. You make Grace Kelly seem ordinary."

She did a twirl, showing off her dress, her legs. She didn't care for formal occasions or any of the debutante balls (including her own) to which they'd each been invited that year, but outside those contexts she enjoyed dressing up, and this, too, he loved about her. But in the months and years that followed, he'd wondered—and he wondered it in silence at the Peabody—if that night she'd already decided that it would be their last time and if she might not have been simply showing off.

Without being able to converse with Case and view his footage and without any *actual* conversation with Helen, Hugh became increasingly aware that he had to break the silence. Charlie Case was off to a film festival in Italy—Hugh had seen it in the *Crimson*. He'd tried and failed to not take it personally that Case had shared exactly none of his good news with him, and his recent ability to not only function but also excel had fallen away once again. He'd tried to get back on track several times—once being the weekend after he'd met Ed Cantowitz, when he'd spent his days not only studying but also leaving his room for appropriate amounts of fresh air, if only because Ed kept coming by and, with that more than slightly foolish but also *contagious* restless energy, succeeded in dragging him out of doors—but once again he was flailing.

Thanksgiving had been a recent disaster, one in which his brothers and their wives and children had opted to go to Bimini and both he and his father had drunk like they were in competition to reach oblivion, which resulted in insults lobbed back and forth between them, and by the time Aunt May and Uncle Peter had shown them the door, it was clear that neither father nor son had behaved acceptably. It all amounted to this: The longer he waited to speak to Helen, the worse off he became. He never wondered why she hadn't broken the silence; he assumed it was up to him. With hindsight he would wonder about this and would see it as the embodiment of his callow youth, but now there was no hindsight.

Now it was almost Christmas. He held a C- paper in his hands after retrieving it from his favorite professor. Now it was an unseasonably warm December day, when every student in his path seemed frantic with good cheer, and below the C- in watery black ink was: *You can do better than this*. Perhaps because his own father's style of censure was more along the lines of sarcastic rage, nothing had the power to undo Hugh more effectively than gracious condemnation. His favorite professor was a gentleman, brilliant and evenhanded, and Hugh couldn't feel more like an ass for handing in such a substandard (drunk) paper. He carried the C- as he paced the halls of the Peabody, only to find her right where he'd left her last week, when it had been raining and her hair was lank and the air humid and he'd watched her remove a lavender sweater and straighten out a white blouse with a rounded collar, which had reminded him of all of those evenings by the fat hollow tree and how—afterward—she had always pulled her skirts and blouses into place with quick, near-violent tugs.

And now there she was at a desk, the last place he'd ever thought to picture her. There were her long and bony fingers, blessedly naked of rings, the telephone chatter he strained to hear, the evidently poor typing skills and two small apples on her desk, half eaten.

And maybe it was because Cantowitz would not let up about his distractedness (*Wake up!* Ed would say, *Come back!*, clapping his hands in front of Hugh's face, midway through conversations), or perhaps it was because the previous Friday, after taking a very beautiful girl out on what had seemed like a perfectly fine evening, she'd told him that one day he'd regret his rude behavior, but this time when he saw Helen, he approached her.

"Care to take a break?" he said.

He didn't know what he'd expected. He hadn't thought that far ahead. But when she called out, "Oh dear God," he knew it hadn't been that.

"Sorry," he said reflexively. He thought his heart might actually give out right then, before he was able to say a goddamn thing.

She looked at him as if she not only couldn't believe her eyes but didn't particularly like what she saw.

"What?" he said. "What is it?"

She leaned back in her chair and didn't blink.

"It's nice to see you" came out of his mouth as if he were a parrot, albeit one who'd been raised in well-bred captivity. To make things worse, he added, "How's your family?"

"My family?" she asked.

There were three other women working in the room, all obviously watching, though none of them had given up the pretense of working, so the room looked like an even worse version of one of those Broadway musicals his late mother had apparently enjoyed so much and his childless, dear aunt May had insisted on taking him to when he was an ungrateful boy prone to saying things like, "Why don't they just say what they want to say instead of singing a whole song about it first?" She'd taken him to the 21 Club for a hamburger and "shown him off" to the maître d', who seemed like a nice man stuck with a shitty job and who always asked him if he liked baseball or football and, when Hugh replied, "Neither," had laughed too loud.

"Yes," he said, "your family. How are they?"

She abruptly threw the half-eaten apples into the wastepaper basket. "I could use a cigarette," she said, and with an expressionless and perhaps slightly queenly nod to the others, she hurried Hugh out the door. "What are you doing here?" she asked, whispering, as they shuffled down the corridor like a couple of spies.

"What do you think?" he said. "I'm a student here, Helen."

"Oh," she said. "Oh, of course."

"What did you think this whole time? Did you think I'd found you or something? That I've been coming on the train weekly from New Haven or—I don't know—New Jersey?"

"What *whole time?*"

"The whole time we've been . . . communicating."

They burst out the door into a suddenly windy day. She pulled the cuffs of her sleeves down as low as they'd go. Her arms were always too long for any of her sweaters. He remembered that.

"Um," she said, and bit her lip.

He handed her a cigarette. A bell rang far off in the distance, and he briefly wondered what time it was; he looked at the tiny white scar on her upper lip, the hollow at the base of her neck where a small ruby had once been suspended on a thin gold chain. That spot was now empty; it looked like the most naked flesh he'd ever seen, and the sight of it made him so dizzy with wanting that he thought he was going to grab her and he was afraid no matter how he tried otherwise that he would do it—whenever he did it, because he knew he would do it; he couldn't *not* do it—too hard. He cupped her outstretched hand, protected her cigarette as if it were the last cigarette, as if nothing could be more precious to him than this particular cigarette as he struck at his lighter with his thumb. People passed; people talked. His mouth went dry. As the flame struggled and ultimately singed the tobacco and paper, he kept his hand in place. It could not have felt more intimate if he had made his way under her gray skirt, if he had waged war with her merry widow, pulled her panties aside, and slid his finger right up inside of her.

After she exhaled, after she removed a stray bit of tobacco from her lower lip, she said, "How do you mean we've been communicating?"

"I've come here every week is what I mean. You've been staring right back at me."

"I have *not.*"

"Helen—"

"I have not been staring at you. This is the first time I've seen you in a very very very very long time. *Hugh.*"

He realized he hadn't lit a cigarette for himself yet, and the relief a new cigarette afforded him was considerable. "Ha," he said, lighting up. "Ha."

She looked up at him and she said, "I haven't seen you."

He nodded, and then he nodded harder until she said, "Okay?"

What could he do? He nodded again. He went over it in his mind a few times, how she had been so suspiciously focused on her work, how, when she removed her lavender sweater, it had seemed practiced, as if she'd been doing it just for him. He supposed it was possible he'd been standing far enough to the side of the door.

That he might have, in fact, done an excellent job of hiding.

He looked up at a faraway airplane flying in and out of clouds and wondered where it was going. "Do you ever feel relieved when the sun isn't out?"

"All the time," she said, and she smiled. When Helen smiled it was always a surprise, because she looked so profoundly untroubled, no matter what was going on. Her smiling face was such a stark contrast to her unsmiling face, because (he'd finally figured out) her teeth were *slightly* too big for her mouth, and this often gave the impression that she was either deep in thought or about to cry.

They walked aimlessly until a bench appeared as if they had special-ordered it. He sat down first.

"What's your concentration?" she asked.

"Anthropology," he said, too quietly. She asked again and he repeated it. It sounded so stupid and somehow distinctly offensive that he could have a concentration, that he was a senior in college, a senior at Harvard like his father had been and his grandfather before him, a student just like everybody else. "Everything since being with you has felt like such a lie."

"What do you mean?" she asked, and there was her smile again—misleading, he knew, he *knew*—but still she looked so completely fine: young and beautiful and fine. For a moment he wondered if the rumors had been nothing but that, and maybe she'd simply grown tired of him and moved right along to many others, never given him another thought.

"Sit down," he said. "Please."

"I'm cold," she said. "I'm suddenly really cold. And I should be getting back to work."

"What do you do here?"

She wrapped her long arms around herself, kept them there and shrugged. He wondered what was so familiar about her stance, why it made him want to say: *You remind me of someone.* Maybe it was that she reminded him of herself, her old self, which at this point felt like part of him, so often had he thought of her every gesture. "Secretary. My father got me the job," she said. "Shocking, I know."

"What part?"

"You know—of course he got me the job. Of course I'm a secretary—even though I can't type—positioned in a place to meet so many of our brightest, most eligible young men. Everyone is really hoping the best for me, everyone's just—you know—*hoping*! I think my father would settle for an old geezer professor at this point, he's so nervous." She was still smiling, but she no longer looked untroubled. "Hugh." She shook her head. "What is it you want me to say?"

She let her arms drop. And, as soon as she did, he realized who she'd reminded him of: a child in Case's footage. He couldn't have been more than six. When his playmate was killed with arrows shot by the neighboring clan, he wrapped his arms around himself in the very same way that Helen had.

Hugh stood up and put out his cigarette. He took her by the shoulders. "I want you to tell me what happened."

"Why?"

He didn't take his hands from her shoulders and she didn't shrug him off. Not until he started to yell, "Because I fucking need to know."

She shook her head. "Don't speak to me that way."

"I'm sorry," he said. "I'm so sorry."

"That's for me to do," she said darkly. She looked around as if she suddenly realized that they were in public and that she was not comfortable with being looked at, not comfortable with being talked about, although she was very much accustomed to both. "You knew," she said.

"What do you mean I *knew*?"

"I mean you knew. You knew I was pregnant; you knew it was yours."

"Well, I sure as hell didn't know because you had the decency to tell me. Do you want to know how I found out? I found out because Edith Billis was at my father's table and she was drunk. Does that constitute knowing? Should I have believed her? And how was I—" He was yelling again and he stopped himself, lowering his voice. "How was I supposed to help you if you never answered my letters or my telephone calls? And don't tell me you didn't receive any letters or messages."

"No," she said, "I did."

"Then . . . how?"

"I don't know," she said. "It was stupid. I'm stupid. I have to get back now."

"Helen," he said, and he knew he had to ask right then or somehow he never would. "Did you have it?"

She bit her lip. "No."

He opened and closed his hands. "Okay." He felt less relieved than he thought he would.

"In France they call them *angel makers*. My friend got one done there. Isn't that poetic?"

"No," he said. A stray hair fell into her eyes and he was grateful for it, grateful to have a concrete lead on touching any part of her, to feel her fine straw-colored hair as he smoothed it away from her face, to smell her perfume, which she once told him was made from tobacco flowers.

"I wanted you to be worse off."

"I feel terrible," he whispered, moving closer.

"Good," she whispered back.

Chapter Three

Winter

Ed knocked on Hugh's door. He knocked until the knocking turned into banging, which turned into sloppy bashing until Hugh finally opened up. "Fucking Cantowitz."

"Righto," Ed said. "Get up and get dressed."

"Because?"

"Because it's already afternoon! Get moving!" He sat in the walnut chair with the wine-colored cushion where he always sat before morning classes, with a view of the miserable swollen sky. It hadn't snowed all winter, and it was like the atmosphere was bloated and in need of relieving itself. As Hugh buttoned his shirt and struggled with the same moth-devoured navy cashmere sweater he wore at the start of every goddamn day, he mumbled to Ed about how he'd read all night long, how he hadn't slept until the sun came up. "Do you know that the Nuer people in Africa, as studied by Evans-Pritchard in the beginning of the 1940s, barely spoke of their lineage?" he asked.

"No, Hugh," Ed said flatly. "I did not know that."

"Bet you can't imagine a world where lineage was irrelevant." He looked under his bed and came up with two socks—not matching, not clean. "For the Nuer," he continued, while pulling on the socks and lac-

ing up a pair of tennis sneakers, "any divisions between men had nothing to do with lineage."

Ed fought the urge to sigh. "Maybe he only meant that the divisions
are so fucking obvious. Maybe it is like asking—okay—a *fish* to describe water. The distinction is so blatant it might not even seem worth
mentioning."

"This obsession of yours, this focus on our differences—it's not in-
herent."

"I would hardly call stating the obvious an obsession. And, incidentally, I'm not the one staying up all night reading articles about lineage.
I'm not the one bringing it up."

"Point taken."

Ed picked up a tennis ball from the floor and began to toss it up and
down. He wanted to bounce it off the opposite wall, but he knew that
Henley, who lived on the other side of that wall, would make him pay.
He knew everyone in Adams House now, and he knew that he con-
founded these people by wearing such consistently crisp clothing (he
hadn't come to Harvard to dress like a bum) and asking forthright questions about anything that popped into his head. He didn't need to be
bouncing balls off walls in addition to acting—so consistently—like
himself. He'd once asked a dark-skinned fellow lounging in the common room if he was an Arab or a Greek or what, and when Shipley
nearly gasped, with an expression that struck Ed as distinctly matronly,
Ed didn't understand what the great big deal was. He asked people
whether they'd been baptized, whether they'd ever met a Jew. He didn't
see the point in pretending that everyone had sprung from these Ivy
halls and that everyone came from Shipley-type homes; he'd read up on
the statistics of admission and knew this wasn't the case anymore.

And yet more often than not he'd felt as if he were on the set of a
Hollywood picture, in which everyone was doing his part to evoke a
certain collegiate fantasy, and part of that fantasy was erasing all pasts
except the popular ones—the houses and lawns and clubs from which
Harvard men had originally come and would indeed continue to come
for centuries. The way he saw it, *he* was the one interested in human

behavior. As it turned out, the dark-skinned fellow was not an Arab nor a Greek but an Indian from Bombay, and they'd spoken at great lengths about the aftermath of the Raj, the disastrous creation of Pakistan, and how he had no interest in returning home, where he was supposed to take over his family's textile empire.

"I know that when you talk about our different backgrounds you think you're simply stating the obvious," said Hugh now, "but do you ever think about the possibility that what is obvious to you may not be—I don't know—exactly true? You know it's very Marxist of you to focus on what tears a culture apart."

"I haven't had a goddamn cup of coffee yet today. Please," said Ed, "go easy with the rhetoric. And I am, as you well know, no Marxist."

"You shouldn't come here without having had a full meal. Otherwise you remind me of—and I'm sorry to say it—a certain French military leader. A short one—also highly ambitious—"

"I'm sorry," said Ed, "but I don't see the de Gaulle comparison at all."

"I'm talking about Napoleon, you imbecile."

Ed half-threw, half-pelted, the tennis ball at Hugh, who caught it just in time.

"Eat first," he said, tossing the ball back to Ed, while pulling on an overcoat. "At least drink some coffee. Seriously."

"Interesting that Evans—what was his name?"

"Evans-Pritchard."

"Right," said Ed, rubbing his hands together as they finally made it outside, which was cold but not numbingly so. "*Evans-Pritchard*. Some name. Interesting that he was making these observations while over in Western Europe some pretty important decisions were being made based on the contrary."

"I knew you were going to say that."

"That's because it is obvious. Anyone would say that."

"Not really."

"Forgive me, but it seems more than a little irrelevant, given the historical context of our time, that some Brit *in the 1940s* took down notes

on an African tribe about how *they don't care about lineage*. Well, bully
for them, right? And don't you think they're busy worrying over
more-pressing concerns, such as where to kill or gather their next meal?
Maybe this lineage obsession emerges when there are moments to think
about something other than the most basic survival. When I'm
hungry—like now—I don't give a shit about lineage, either. Hey—
notice something different?" Ed stopped suddenly, standing up straight.

"What are you doing?"

"What do you mean?"

"With your head. What are you doing with your head?"

"Gesturing. I am gesturing with my head. Toward my new car.
Christ, can't you just notice? With your profound powers of observation? Here—get in." Ed opened the passenger door proudly and made
his way around to the driver's seat.

"We're going to be late," said Hugh, skimming his hands along the
radio dial, the glove compartment; he flipped open the ashtray.

"Late to where?"

"Ah," said Hugh. "To class?"

"You're such an ass. It's Sunday," Ed said. He turned the key in the
ignition. "Boy, do I love that sound."

The car was a 1958 dark-green Ford Thunderbird convertible, the jewel
for which he'd saved during those deadly hours working for his father.
He'd studied the Kelley Blue Book all throughout his time at Harvard,
as if it were the one constant in an ever-evolving stream of canonical
classics, and though GM seemed to be a better value, it was the
dark-green Ford Thunderbird that he loved. The previous owner of the
Thunderbird had been stylishly shady—a travel agent with a vague
Irish brogue, in a great big rush to sell. The car was a good-looking vision, and Ed—neither for the first nor the last time—had been snowed
by good looks. As it turned out, the green Thunderbird had defective
gears that allowed for forward motion only.

"Now, as much as I appreciate your new car and as much as you've surprised and impressed me by sinking your savings into a thing of completely impractical beauty, *you are going to get us killed*," shouted Hugh, in order to be heard over the considerable wind.

The sun began a valiant fight with New England and her doleful skies. Light shot through the clouds, and Ed called out, "Jesus, it's cold! Don't you want to know where we're going?"

Hugh lit his cigarette, annoyed by all the wind. He finally exhaled a good cough of smoke. "Thanks to you—evidently—I know tomorrow is Monday. That's about enough knowledge for me."

"No kidding?"

Hugh nodded. "What."

"I can't imagine being woken up—especially on a weekend—and merrily going along with what somebody told me to do."

Ahead of them, a little girl waved madly through a station wagon rear window, and they both waved back immediately and without fanfare.

"But you're not *somebody*," he said. "You've gotten me out of bed for weeks. You've personally ensured my not flunking out."

"I haven't," Ed clarified. "I've only made sure you were already up, while on my way to class. It's not a big deal."

"Fine. But I appreciate it, is what I'm saying. I do appreciate it."

Ed kept his eye on the road. "It's not a big deal."

"Why can't I just say thanks? I have to pretend you haven't done me a few favors?"

"I'm just saying forget it. Let's talk about something much better. Who's the girl?"

"What girl?"

"I saw you talking with a girl maybe two weeks ago. You haven't mentioned it, so I'm curious. I was rushing to a class and I saw you across the Yard. You were sitting on a bench. Tall girl? Good-looking? At least from what I could see."

Hugh threw his cigarette into the wind. "I don't know," he said. "I'm trying to think. Could it have been Flossie King?"

"Not Flossie."

"I don't know," Hugh said, as if he were thinking it through. "I can't think of who that would be."

As Ed drove the highway, as the buildings grew squatter and uglier, he thought about how—when he had seen Hugh with this girl—he hadn't, in fact, been in any kind of rush. It had been a strangely empty twenty minutes or so, when he was trying to decide if he was hungry enough to buy a roast beef sandwich before shutting himself in the library for the night. He was putting off studying, putting off eating, and all the while he had a twitchy feeling, but he couldn't decide—even when he asked himself—what it was that he really wanted to do. In short, he was momentarily stuck, and when he saw Shipley he'd felt briefly relieved, for he now knew what he would be doing for the next gradient of time, and he knew it would shift his mood. He could say hello to Shipley and get swept up in some pointless argument, which would—especially if a few drinks were involved—break into incredulity at least once on both of their parts, which only heightened the stakes of the argument.

But before he could say hello, he'd noticed that Hugh was speaking with a girl, a stunning girl—he'd also downplayed that part of his observation—and that it was clearly no light conversation. First it had seemed that she was angry, but after watching for a minute it looked as though she was struggling to breathe.

Then Hugh had stood up and taken her by the shoulders, and—how could Ed explain this?—he'd looked scared. Ed watched them for another second, but it quickly started to feel as if he was not supposed to be watching, that no one should be watching, and that—though they were doing nothing but standing together—they should have been given complete and utter privacy.

"I wonder who you mean," said Hugh.

"I'm sure it'll come to you. Probably when you least expect it."

Ed had woken up this morning with a keen urge to drive his new car and figured that—especially with some company—he didn't need a destination. A Sunday drive. Wasn't that considered a normal—even a civilized—thing to do? Though he didn't feel particularly civilized. He wanted to know why Hugh was avoiding talk about this girl and why he was getting the distinct sensation of being placated. It made him want to drive faster.

"Do you really not remember your mother?" asked Ed, in a tone that sounded aggressive, even to his own ears.

"Very little," Hugh said. "I wish I did. What made you think of *that*?"

"I don't know," said Ed. "I don't want to say you were lucky that she died so young, but—"

"Then don't," Hugh said.

Ed looked at Hugh, and there wasn't a trace of a smile.

"Forget I said that," Ed said.

He suddenly remembered a place he'd heard about—a pond closer than Walden, a place that reliably froze each winter, no matter how mild the weather. Ed imagined sliding out on his shoes, looking down at the expanse of frozen water, out at the kids who'd inevitably be testing new skates.

In his mind's eye he could see himself speeding instead of slipping, feeling the air there just like he felt the air here on the highway, nearly raw on his face. They drove in wind-whipping silence and the road stretched out in front of them and, though the idea had never held all that much appeal—he was no great fan of the Beats—Ed briefly wished that they were setting out to drive across the whole country. He would drive and shut the hell up for once. But when they reached the turnoff into the woods—the one he'd heard about from a girl he'd taken out a few times—he made a sharp right, and they bumped along over rocks and branches until the trees thinned out and there was the silvery pond—*the Big Deep*, the girl had called it. She'd skated there when she was a kid.

It was a relief to get out of the car, to stop hearing the wind. Though he'd done nothing but drive, the air had made him feel as if he'd played hard in some outdoor sport. He'd make sure to put the top up on the way back. There were only two other parked cars, and one looked as if it hadn't been started in months. Ed scanned the pond for signs of happy shrieking kids, but there weren't any kids, only a stooped figure standing far enough away that Ed couldn't tell if it was a man or a woman, and this felt like a bad sign somehow.

Hugh jumped up and grabbed a thick branch, hung there momentarily before launching into chin-ups; he was short of breath by the time he let go. And of course Ed had to give it a try. As Ed pulled up on his fourth chin-up (Hugh had done five), Hugh said, "My father's mentioned that my mother would let me out and run me—you know, like a dog." He said it as if no time had passed between Ed's original question and now, and this was one of Hugh's best qualities as Ed saw it—the ability to pick up on lost queries, to not care if the moment was over, and to thereby create a sense of extended, even luxurious, time.

As Ed pulled up on that branch with every ounce of his strength, he watched how Hugh hoisted himself up onto the hood of Ed's new car, which should not have mattered, but Ed wanted him off the green paint.

"Whatever the weather," said Hugh, "if it was snowing or raining, she'd open the door and out I'd bolt."

"Huh," said Ed, after letting go of the branch. He'd done five chin-ups. His arms were shaking.

"He'd probably instructed her to train me," Hugh said. "Probably wanted me disciplined for athletics early. What a false start that was."

Ed recalled the previous month when they had gone to The Game. Hugh wouldn't pry the goddamn movie camera from his face, and Ed knew that Hugh wasn't capturing it for any sentimental reasons. Hugh cared less about football—and whether Harvard beat Yale—than about capturing the *naïve hysteria* of this game that Ed knew Hugh had grown up watching with his father and brothers each fall and that Ed, incidentally, wholeheartedly enjoyed. With his giant camera (which held by anyone else would have been awkward), Hugh was making some kind of avant-garde short film—at least that was what Ed deduced from Hugh's grudging description. All Ed understood was that the game in its entirety—when put forth by Hugh—would be rendered in fast motion and thus (Ed supposed) would seem suitably ridiculous.

"Hey, listen," said Ed, attempting his best impersonation of nonchalance. "Would you mind getting off my new car?"

Hugh did so without hesitating, and they walked toward the pond. "So that's all you remember?" Ed asked. "Running?" He was suddenly nervous about sliding out on the ice. There was likely a reason for the absence of the kids. And how could he know that the girl who'd told him about this place wasn't trying to exact some kind of revenge? He wasn't always terribly polite, especially when it was clear that a date wasn't going well. His social unease quickly became physical, and he often started to twitch. He couldn't remember if she'd told him about the pond before or after he'd suggested they call it quits.

"I think I remember this one window," Hugh ventured. "I have an image in my head of this small window—a picture window. Seeing it from outside. Seeing my mother's face and then the face disappearing. It used to seem like a memory I'd invented, but now I think it might be a real one, because I would have been outside in the cold and she would have been inside and the window would have fogged from her breath against the glass. And she would have been smoking, too. She's smoking in almost all of the pictures. So—there you have it—a memory."

"It wasn't for me to ask," Ed said.

Hugh gave a noncommittal nod.

"Even I know that," Ed admitted.

"Please, tell me something else so I don't have to be stuck with my one image of the window all day long."

"What do you want to hear?"

"I don't know," muttered Hugh. "Something."

Ed thought about how, as a little kid, he'd been terrified—petrified—of the dark. His mother had taken him into the windowless bathroom next to the kitchen, in order to get him over his fear. She shut off the lights and stood with him. At first he'd cry and then he'd settle down and then they'd just stand there, talking in the dark. He remembered her laughter and how she loved to talk and that she was truly good at it. When any conversation went off the rails, she could always, seamlessly, steer it back.

Ed had always thought of this as a happy story, and he considered relaying it to Hugh, but he realized it wasn't a happy story; it wasn't even a story. It was a mother and son talking in a dark bathroom, and that seemed kind of weird.

"Well?" said Hugh. "Give me *something*. What kind of kid were you?"

"Nosy."

"Big surprise."

"I asked my fourth-grade teacher—Mrs. O'Connor, a widow—if she'd ever had sex with her husband before he died. I'd just gotten a handle on the birds and the bees, and since she didn't have children I was confused. I was sure I was going to get a beating, but she nodded. And of course I couldn't leave it alone," Ed said, surprised at how embarrassed he actually felt with this memory fresh in his mind. "I asked her what it was like. *What was it like?* Jesus, what a mouth I had. Again I expected to get a beating, a bad one, but instead she looked very calm and still and—I'll always remember this—she said: *Lovely.*"

"I can't believe she didn't kick you out of class."

"*I* would have kicked me out of class."

"No, you wouldn't have."

"That's true. Who knows what I would have done. Probably would've given me a smack. God help my future kids."

They were standing on the banks of the pond. The water, to Ed's relief, wasn't frozen after all. It looked black in patches, and the sun had gone behind the clouds. Hugh just shook his head.

"You hungry?" Ed asked.

"I could eat."

There was a place on the road. Inside was nothing special. When Ed ordered raw sirloin, Hugh looked at him askance.

"Trust me. I know meat. My uncle's the supplier here."

When the raw sirloin arrived, Ed split it in two, seasoned it with salt and pepper, cut it up in small pieces, and—voilà!—steak tartare. He'd had steak tartare for the first time on a date last year with a Radcliffe girl who proclaimed it her favorite dish, and he'd figured why not make it himself for a fraction of the cost? He was so proud when Hugh tasted it and declared it as fine as any he'd ever had. They drank scotch and ordered more raw sirloin and ate more steak tartare.

Ed could not stop talking about money. "For instance," he said, making an effort to keep his voice lowered, as he knew that the subject—not to mention the drinking—would raise his voice automatically, "this check. If you pay it, I feel bad; if I pay it, you feel bad."

"I don't feel bad if you pay it," said Hugh, laughing.

"I just hate splitting tabs. I feel like a communist."

Hugh kept laughing, drained his last drink. "You're generous," he said. "I get it."

And it was Hugh's dismissive sarcasm in that moment (the same laconic sarcasm that Ed otherwise greatly appreciated) that clarified for Ed the true destination of the day.

He wanted—in fact he needed—Hugh to see his father's house.

If Hugh could only see where Ed was from—or so Ed reasoned—he would admit that he felt superior to Ed. Ed always *sensed* superiority, but each time he confronted Hugh about it, Hugh insisted he was being paranoid. There was an incident at the Museum of Fine Arts that still elevated his heart rate; Ed had mistaken a Monet for a Manet, gone on to elaborate for a good minute on the latter's life story before Hugh bothered to point out his mistake. And only after Hugh had let him go on and on.

The thing was, Ed didn't really mind if Hugh felt superior in terms of where they came from. In fact, maybe what he was realizing was: He preferred it. They were from two different places, and on venturing into the world Hugh had definite and specific advantages. Ed only wanted to hear Hugh acknowledge he'd had it easy in comparison, which Hugh never would come out and say. He preferred offering philosophical arguments, which were rarely enlightening, which were, in fact, irritating and only backed up Hugh's stubborn denial that any of it mattered.

Ed would get over this discrepancy in their backgrounds; he would. Because he was going to personally level the playing field, and he was looking forward to it. He didn't want to be an underdog forever.

Yes, they wanted entirely different lives, and, yes, Hugh cared little for Ed's version of success, just as Ed cared little about the Third World, unless it was in the context of untapped resources that might affect the marketplace. And perhaps it was senseless to frame anything between them as a competition, because there was no relevant contest. But could Hugh be *totally* uninterested in money? Could anyone be?

Ed only wanted the acknowledgment before they left the starting gate that he *was* the underdog. Objectively. And that maybe it wasn't fair, maybe it wasn't even important. But it was so.

As they drove along in his new Thunderbird (top up), Ed watched the circus that was Blue Hill Avenue through a faint whiskey haze: the fruit and fish stores. The sock and underwear stores. The bakeries and hosieries and crowds of people in transit. He watched the old men in skullcaps and long black coats, the Negro women in bright clothing, and the men in those wide-brimmed hats that Ed knew came from Roxbury's Hat Man; he watched the *balabuste* matrons haggling and lugging their goods. And Ed, of course, watched Hugh, who was also taking in the scene.

The Italian banana man called out, "Banana, banana, banana."

When Ed switched his focus entirely to Hugh, he saw two things: that Hugh's expression was unreadable and that the avenue—when he attempted to view it with an outsider's gaze—was, if nothing else, lively.

"Roosevelt rode his limo right here," Ed said, as if he had complete confidence that Hugh was even vaguely interested. "Thousands of Jews throwing rose petals—can you imagine? And JFK—he ate French fries in *kishke* grease right there." He pointed at the G & G Deli, with its enormous vertical sign. "Ever had *kishke* grease?" Ed asked.

Hugh shook his head, but whether this was an answer to Ed's question or whether he was simply overwhelmed was unclear. "I've never seen so many pharmacies," he said.

Hugh was quiet, and maybe Ed was imagining it but he seemed either overly respectful or profoundly uncomfortable as they parked in front of the triple-decker three-family home.

"He knows we're coming," Hugh asked, "right?"

"Not exactly," Ed said, getting out of the car. "It doesn't matter," he assured Hugh, but he sounded unconvincing—even nervous.

As he led Hugh up the steps and knocked on the door, Ed wondered if maybe this was a terrible idea. He was suddenly overcome with the fierce desire to have never revealed a single personal detail, not only to Hugh but to anyone he had ever known. Power emerged from mystery. And what the hell else was he doing besides killing any vestige of mystery he possessed? This was—he was sure now—a terrible idea, but when he heard his father coughing his way to the door, he also knew he didn't have it in him to run away, leaving his father (not to mention Hugh) to wonder why someone would do such a thing—such a little-punk thing to do to a broken man.

And then the door opened.

His father stood still, without greeting them. All that was missing in this initial exchange could be found in his yellowing undershirt, in the little hair left on his olive-skinned head springing up in peppery tufts, and in the plentiful hair that was everywhere else—erupting from under his shirt collar on his still-broad chest, springing from big knuckles and meaty forearms.

When his father leaned forward, peering through the screen door to make sure it was Ed, there was the unmistakable smell of alcohol seeping out of not-young skin, and Ed nearly said, *Sorry, Pop, sorry, but we gotta run. Just wanted to make sure you're still alive.*

But instead he pretended that he was happy to see his father; instead, he grabbed him in a hug—clearly aggressive in the strength of the grip but a hug nonetheless. Ed thought if he acted affectionate, then perhaps he might feel affectionate, and maybe all this affection wouldn't allow for Hugh to perceive his home to be as repellent as it really was. But hadn't he *wanted* Hugh to see it all, to see and understand?

Hugh Shipley shook Murray Cantowitz's hand, and Ed couldn't help but admire Hugh's confident handshake and imagine his father rating it the way he knew his father habitually did, though he hadn't shared these ratings with Ed since he was fifteen, when he'd rated Ed's handshake a five ("at best") and Ed had shouted at his father, who in turn had not spoken to his son for nearly three weeks.

Ed knew Hugh had scored high on the handshake test because, instead of proceeding right back to his spot in the living room and letting Ed and his friend fend for themselves, Murray Cantowitz shuffled in to the orange kitchen, and Ed and Hugh followed close behind. The refrigerator was nearly empty, but after a few moments of painfully awkward silence, wherein Ed avoided looking at Hugh by examining the refrigerator's contents, his father asked Hugh if he liked chopped liver.

"I can't say I've ever had it, sir," said Hugh. "I'm curious."

"It's like pâté," Ed explained, and his father gave a snort before emptying a half-empty box of crackers onto a plate, surrounding the plastic container of chopped liver—a plastic container that never would have made the journey from kitchen to living room, had his mother been alive. Hugh would never have been allowed into the kitchen at all. She would have carefully scraped the chopped liver into a glass bowl; she would have offered Hugh more and more until Hugh would have had to laugh and say thank you too many times, until it became a joke between them.

They followed Murray Cantowitz into the living room.

"What's with the shuffling, Pop?" Ed muttered, despite knowing nothing good could come of such a question, which his father, in any case, either didn't hear or chose to ignore.

Hugh sat down on the filthy amber couch, his legs splayed to the sides like a basketball player's, as his hands gripped the couch in between. Ed saw that Hugh was trying his best to sit up straight, but the couch sank so low that he was unable to do so.

Ed claimed the green armchair and dipped a stale cracker in chopped liver, which tasted kind of spectacular.

Murray Cantowitz didn't sit. He produced a bottle of rye and two glasses. "I know Eddie won't drink."

"Really?" asked Hugh, as Murray Cantowitz gave him a generous pour. Hugh reached immediately for his full glass, clearly pleased to have something in the way of common ground. "Nice to meet you," Hugh said in the way of a toast, before taking an eager sip. "I've heard a great deal."

"Shit, I hope not," said Ed's father, who still didn't crack a true smile. Murray Cantowitz hadn't looked terribly surprised that Ed was there, or that he'd brought a friend. He only set his drink on the mantel after all that shuffling back and forth. Maybe his father had quickly sized up Hugh and was attempting to appear more tragic than ever. Maybe his father wasn't immune to the fantasy of the wealthy stranger. The one who appears on an ordinary doorstep and turns shit into gold.

Hugh must have inspired that fantasy every time he left the house; he must have appealed to all the poor suckers who crossed his path, because Hugh just looked rich. No matter how earnestly he strived toward egalitarianism, no matter how threadbare his sweaters or how hard his living might ever get over the years to come, he exuded privilege. Ed could feel his father softening, sucking up to Hugh before he even realized he was doing it.

"What's doing, Pop?" Ed asked. His knee was bouncing up and down, with no end in sight. He knew that his twitch was forthcoming and that his father could not stand the twitch. "You getting outside?"

"Getting outside? You already forget how hard I work?"

"Of course not. Did you get an injury on the job?"

"What are you talking about?"

"Nothing."

"Nothing?" his father said mockingly.

"I thought you were limping or something."

Murray Cantowitz took a slug of rye and shifted his weight. "I hope you don't forget what hard work is." He shook his head. "I know you think I should pick up and leave with the rest of them. I just hope you don't forget how many years I been working here—right here—and coming home right there to where you're sitting." He gestured at Hugh.

"I can move," Hugh said, and Ed had to laugh.

"Stay where you are," said his father.

"Stay right there," said Ed.

"You planning on sitting down with us, Pop?"

Murray Cantowitz shook his head. "I like standing."

"Okay, then," said Ed. "Well."

A shard of light pierced the closed curtains, and Ed was overcome with the urge to go lie down on his old bed, to sink into a fast, hard sleep. He even closed his eyes for a moment, only to open them and understand exactly where he was and how infrequently he'd sat here since the twelfth grade. During summers, he'd worked so hard during the day that, by the time he made it home, he went straight to sleep, and in the morning he went from bed to door, drinking coffee with the guys on the job.

But here he was, surrounded by the same fake-wood paneling, the same fake-crystal bowls filled with decades-old lemon sours gathering dust on the shelf; here was the same fake-ivory sailboat surrounded by real faded seashells that his mother had collected during summers at Nantasket.

"Is that you?" Hugh asked, pointing to the portrait—oil on canvas— done by a neighbor when Ed was nine years old.

"That's Eddie," said his father—as if all American citizens were, by law, forced to hang portraits of their children on their living room walls and, were it not for such a senseless law, he would have never been trapped into hanging such sentimental nonsense.

"It's a good likeness," said Hugh.

"You think so?" asked Ed's father, in a manner that was unsettlingly natural.

"Yes," said Hugh. "Who painted it?"

Murray Cantowitz shrugged. "A neighbor kid."

"Huh," said Hugh, and, as Ed's father topped off Hugh's glass, "thanks."

"I wonder what ever happened to that kid," said his father.

"You never know," said Hugh. "That painting might be worth a mint someday."

Here were Hugh and his father conversing with ease. Here was his father with a not-particularly-bitter smile, and Hugh eating chopped liver with evident gusto, and it occurred to Ed that he was, in fact, the only problem here.

He was the one unable to see anything besides the closed windows and drawn curtains that had, for most of Ed's life, been opened each morning by his mother, who had once broken up the marital spat of a couple of strangers by offering her unsolicited opinion through the open window. He was the one seeing the dust coating the television, which surprisingly was turned off and facing Hugh, offering a dark mirror.

Ed imagined that he had switched places with his friend and that he was the one faced with his own reflection at that moment. That he had the legitimate right to be the one thinking: *What the hell am I doing here?*

His father coughed wetly. Finally he said, "You people almost finished with school?"

"That's right," Hugh said. "Ed sure is going places, isn't he?"

Among the spectrum of possible replies, Ed knew, there would not be anything close to a *yes* or an *oh yeah* or even a noncommittal nod.

"That depends on whether he does or doesn't," said Murray Cantowitz. "I'm not holding my breath—it's only winter. Lot can happen before the ink is dry on that diploma."

"That's true," said Hugh, indulgently, Ed thought. "We can't take anything for granted. At least I can't."

"A fellow like you!" his father exclaimed, as if he was a person who made pleasant comments from time to time. "Oh, I'd say you've got it in the bag."

Hugh shook his head with infuriating modesty. Ed's father was nodding.

What the hell was happening here?

Joanna Hershon

"Take it from me," said Hugh, "no one has a better shot than Ed."

Why did Ed want to punch Hugh right then? Why? When he was saying nothing but what Ed had always wished someone might say to his father on his behalf?

Murray Cantowitz still hadn't sat down. He'd been leaning on a side table and was now shuffling to the breakfront cabinet.

"Pop," said Ed, "you don't see how you're walking?" Even as he said it, he knew it was not concern that motivated him. And as his father chose to ignore his line of questioning yet again, as he opened the cabinet and took out a new bottle of rye, a voice rose up outside the window:

"All right now. AW-RIGHT! I am BACK. And see here: Ain't no one goin' home till this nigga gets some goddamn heat. You hear me, old man? You hear me?"

"Pop?" Ed asked, as his restless leg finally stopped bouncing. "Who the hell is that?"

His father only gestured, as if he was swatting at fruit flies.

"I am HERE!" the man shouted. *"On MY goddamn Sabbath!"*

"Pop? You gonna answer the man?"

"That *schwartze* isn't talking to me," said his father, with an expression that could only be described as revulsion, and Ed had the feeling that it wasn't the man outside the window who was the subject of his father's deepest scorn.

"Sure sounds like it," Ed replied. He could hear the panic in his own voice.

"He isn't talking to me," repeated his father. "You think I don't know?"

Ed felt the surge of heat, the particular heat that results only from the shameful words and actions of one's own family. Then he parted the curtain and looked for himself.

A Negro in a pair of brown trousers and a button-down shirt was raising his fist and hollering, *"You hear me, old man, I know you hear me. Make some fuckin' improvements on your goddamn building."*

"Goldblatt," said his father, pointing toward the top floor, where their landlord had lived for all of Ed's life. "He hasn't left yet, either. This *schwartze* keeps after him, I'll give him that."

"Quit using that word," Ed spat out, still looking through the window.

The man shook his head over and over.

"*Schwartze?*" asked his father. "You want me to stop with the Yiddish? In front of Johnny Harvard here, I'm embarrassing you with the Yiddish?"

"It's not the Yiddish," Ed said. "Just stop."

His father picked up one of his mother's seashells, a scallop. He fingered the ridges and held it in his hand. "You want to go to shul again? Have a heart-to-heart with the *rebbe*? You can mull it all over. You can talk about your beloved *schwartzes*—"

"Christ—"

"Sure, him, too—why not? You and Rabbi Steuyer and Jesus Christ can talk over how you and the *schwartzes* should create a new holiday. Why don't you go and do that? You can serve sweet potatoes with matzoh for the Seder. You're so fuckin' smart—we know all about that—so why not write up a Haggadah full of our slavery stories, because we really have so much in common. That's what Rabbi Steuyer wants to do, did you know that?"

"When's the last time you stepped foot in a shul?"

"Don't you worry. My information is good. Goldblatt upstairs gives me updates. You and Rabbi Steuyer—you could have long *satisfying* discussions. And then, when you're finished with your big discussions, when you're done with your bullshit about *tikkun olam,* when you're done with your important and noble plans, you can step outside and get your wallet stolen and your ribs kicked in for good measure."

It was all Ed could do not to take the yellowed undershirt in his fist and slam his father up against the bookcase and watch it all come down on top of him, every last disintegrating lemon sour.

"What's *tikkun olam?*" asked Hugh, predictably.

"It's an obligation to heal the world," said Ed.

Hugh nodded before standing up slowly. "Mr. Cantowitz," he said.

"My son should not have brought you," Ed's father nearly whispered to Hugh, so suddenly soft and low was his voice.

"No," said Hugh. "No, I'm glad he did."

"Everyone's gone," Murray Cantowitz said. "Everyone. You don't understand," he said, ostensibly to Hugh. "Nobody's even callin' me up to guess how little these houses will be worth in one year's time. Whole neighborhood's gone or leaving."

"What about the slumlord upstairs?" asked Ed.

"Yeah, he's here. Him and me. We're just alike, right? That's what you think?"

"Why don't you leave, too, then?" Hugh asked, in a fake-helpful tone that Ed heard as masked disgust. And Ed, though he knew he had no right to be, was irritated. He was annoyed with Hugh for speaking up, for acting as if he understood anything about this neighborhood.

"Fuck 'em," his father said. "Can't drive me out."

"Fine," said Ed, "fine." But still he didn't turn the knob on the front door. "Listen, let me ask you something: Why do you suddenly care about the *rebbe*? I'll tell you the last time you stepped foot in a shul, because I know. And you haven't even said kaddish. Nothing. Not even for her."

"You watch," said his father, clearly not listening to any of it. "You watch how Rabbi Steuyer leaves his devoted congregation of slumlords and working-class racists. Sure," he said, "he'll go somewhere morally superior, but watch how he will also conveniently leave the *schwartzes*. He'll go someplace far away, where he can cry about civil rights with the rest of the rich and deluded *mishpocha* out there in the suburbs, who are sending all of their money to Christian charities in Alabama while their own people—" He faltered for a second, and Ed and Hugh watched him do it. Neither interrupted, and when he noticed this, he just stood there, seemingly uninterested in finishing.

"You couldn't even sit down for a goddamn minute, let alone not embarrass me." Ed opened the door and then closed it again. "Let me ask you something else, Pop. Why can't you sit down when I come here with my friend? Why can't you show *me* that respect? You're shuffling around like some kind of martyr—"

He didn't know what to expect when he said that, but his father's face registered fury to its full—and in fact rare—extent, and though his father had hardly ever punched him, Ed had to stop his own hands from flying up, ready to protect his face.

Murray Cantowitz did not punch his son. He only ran his hand over his face a few times before he looked at Ed once more.

"You know why I can't sit down?" his father asked. "You want to know about it? I can't sit down because a *schwartze* youngster slashed my back pants pocket with a razor so that my wallet would fall to the ground. Happened to Sol Cohen and he only lost the wallet. Me? I can't sit down on my goddamn ass because the hoodlum wasn't so skilled—or maybe he was!—and I got cut."

Ed felt ill, physically ill, the same terrible feeling in the pit of his stomach and the very top of his skull as when he'd looked over at his father the one time during the burial, after he'd shoveled dirt onto his mother's coffin.

"You try lying facedown on a gurney while some medical intern sutures your ass," his father said. "You just try it."

"You should have called me," Ed said.

His father shook his head, and finally, carefully, sat down on the amber couch. "Any day now," his father said, wincing. "Watch that *rebbe* put his house on the market."

They drove back to Cambridge in silence. Ed was relieved that evening had come, that at least the light was cooperating in ending this awful day. There were boats on the river, cars on the highway, so many people busy with getting the most from their Sunday, before the week took hold. He felt the opposite and always had, even when he was a kid. The routine of school—its clarity and urgency—was what he enjoyed most, and he imagined that even if he had all the time and money in the world, he would always want to work. The weekends felt amorphous, and the absence of structure unnerved him. When he woke up each morning, he had to fill up the day somehow, fill it up until it stopped feeling so shapeless, so free.

"Sometimes I think it's good my mother didn't live to see him like this," Ed said at last.

Hugh only nodded.

"She would've been so ashamed."

"What do you think she would have thought?"

"About my father?"

"No," Hugh said, "the neighborhood. The—what was the word your father used?"

"I don't know," Ed said, agitated. "Why? How the hell should I know? Was my mother a political person? No, she was not."

Hugh didn't respond right away. He lit a cigarette and smoked. Only when he finally needed it did he flip open the glossy wood ashtray. "Why didn't you call your father?"

"What?"

"Why didn't you call him to let him know we were coming?"

Ed stepped on the gas and changed lanes twice. "What are you saying?"

"I'm not saying anything. I'm asking why you didn't tell him—warn him—that not only were you coming but that you were bringing me along?"

"Is that what you would have done?"

"Yes."

"Because you're so courteous?"

Hugh shook his head. Hugh said nothing, but Ed heard: *Because I'm not cruel.*

"You leave that house and you see who my father is, what an aggressive, bigoted person, and the first thing you say is that I should have given him fair warning? You think it would have made a difference?"

"Keep your eyes on the road," Hugh said.

"They are."

Hugh started to say something but stopped himself again.

"What."

"He was unwashed. He was embarrassed. If you know you're going to object to him to begin with, and if you know I am, too, why not at least give him the opportunity to present himself the way he wants to?"

"Are you saying he deserves that?"

Hugh shrugged. "I think I would at least do that for you—if not for him—if we were going to see my father."

"Your father is different."

"That's true. My father is very well dressed." Hugh forced a smile that went nowhere. "Okay, he went to Harvard and, yes, he's rich. But he is also a racist and a drunk *and* an anti-Semite on top of it, and so, if I was going to subject you to him, if I—for some mysterious reason—felt the need to do that, I would at least try my best to warn him to behave in front of you. That's what I would do."

Ed just nodded and kept his eyes on the road. He couldn't imagine he'd be able to look at Hugh after the car was long parked, after they were back in their world, which, it seemed to him now, was as fake as the ivory sailboat in his father's house. "You're right," he said.

"I know." Hugh rolled down the window and the air came rushing in.

"But you would never invite me to meet your father."

"Why do you say that?"

Ed willed himself to slow down and shut up, to stop plunging this day into an even greater decline. But though he managed to ease off the gas, this fake temperate voice did not stand a chance. "Because," he answered, "you won't even tell me the name of a girl you are obviously sleeping with." He saw the lights on the river, the familiar blur that was Cambridge, and felt a crushing nostalgia for the day he'd set out to have.

Hugh emitted a hollow laugh. "Are you saying I was lying to you earlier, when you asked about her?"

"I'm saying you're not interested in honesty."

He thought of how Hugh seemed somehow too eager to step into his father's house and to engage in a conflict that belonged to Ed and his father, a conflict—so *many* conflicts!—that was ugly and embarrassing and *theirs,* and how Ed could not imagine Hugh ever allowing any conflicts of his own to go anywhere beyond the realm of storytelling.

"I'm saying," continued Ed, "that with or without that Leica around your neck, you're a voyeur."

Ed parked, and—to his amazement—Hugh made no move to get out of the car. He didn't speak or look at Ed but sat finishing his cigarette. Finally—when they were back on the sidewalk, when they started walking the short distance toward their houses, before they would need to decide whether or not to split ways—finally Ed came out with it.

"I'm going to be blunt," Ed said. "What's the big secret?"

"What are you talking about?"

"I can't handle secrets. I'm too suspicious by nature and I'm too tense."

"No, *really?*"

"Listen—"

"No," Hugh said calmly, "no. You listen." He looked up for a moment at the evening sky. "You put me through some kind of test today, and I didn't appreciate it. You're impatient and aggressive—and that's not the same as being Jewish."

"I didn't put you through a test," Ed argued.

"Why did you want me to meet your father like that?"

"I wanted you to see where I come from."

Hugh shook his head. "Not really. You were just using me."

"Using you? You think I'm *using you?*"

"Sure. Isn't that what friends do?"

"No, not in my book. I don't want that kind of friend. I told you, I don't have any time for it."

"I see," said Hugh.

Some jerk honked his horn in one steady blare in the distance, and Ed saw Hugh wince.

"Come on," said Ed, giving Hugh a gracious punch on the shoulder. "The rest of them are the secret-keepers." He looked out on the Yard, where people were climbing steps and walking in clusters toward dinner on Mass Ave. "Not you. You're different."

"Is that right?"

"You know you are. Listen to you. You're taking me to task! You are so disappointed in me right now. You are disappointed in everything and everyone, and it kills you. That's why you're different. Because you can't stand it. And also, although you have shown nothing near your potential and you are in some ways—let's face it—kind of lazy, you want to save the world."

Hugh looked down at the sidewalk and, despite himself—Ed could tell—he smiled. "And you're going to help me do that?"

"No," Ed said, "of course not."

They started to walk again, and when Ed suggested they eat dinner, when he said he was starving and Hugh expressed little surprise, because Ed was always hungry—always *starving*—Ed finally said, "I apologize." But it lacked a certain sharpness.

"That's okay," Hugh replied. But it wasn't, not exactly.

Chapter Four

Spring

Guy Ordway had succeeded in life despite his education. His business credentials and background were the subjects of much speculation, but because he had married Helen's mother, whose family was one of the best on the East Coast, the speculation could go only so far. He'd married into a good family; he was protected, and because he'd never forgotten his shaky origins, he was adamant in wanting his daughter to marry someone if not of Wall Street *and* the Ivy League then certainly of the Ivy League. He made no secret of wanting to protect his legacy, to bolster it with the appropriate names.

He'd forbidden Helen to live in Manhattan, where (he reasoned) there was far too much trouble for someone like her, but he'd approved of Helen living on the bottom floor of a Brattle Street townhouse with her cousin Lolly (whom he remembered as always having been a well-behaved and frankly bland little girl) and her cousin's husband, Raoul Merva.

Raoul was Hungarian, twenty years older than Lolly, and chair of the Harvard mathematics department. After meeting Raoul at Lolly's father's funeral on Fishers Island, Mr. Ordway had gotten it into his head (and Hugh had a difficult time imagining how) that Raoul Merva—though problematically Catholic by birth if not practice—possessed a traditionalist sensibility that had boded well for keeping Helen out of trouble. That, and he was industrious; he'd come to the United States— to Harvard—to escape the clutches of Communism and had—as Hugh could best understand it—done something revolutionary with triangulation in applied mathematics as well as investing some of Lolly's money, which had made them a modest fortune. Part of Helen convincing her father to let her live with her cousin Lolly had involved Raoul phoning Guy and offering reassurance that he would keep a strict eye on Guy's daughter. Which was, of course, patently untrue. Raoul thought Helen should live however she liked. His only suggestion was that she go and get analyzed, after being brought up by a father like that.

Lolly was an excellent cook. There was always a glass pitcher of home-brewed iced tea in the refrigerator, along with roasted chicken and potato salad she'd learned to make when she and Raoul had lived in France, with mustard and oil and fresh dill that she grew in their back garden, along with grapes that, come August, would be fecund and fallen to the ground. Lolly acknowledged that her plants were overgrown and attracted bugs, but she was terrible at pruning.

"I'm afraid that nothing will grow back," she explained one evening, as they all sat outside under the burgeoning grapevine, drinking a bitter Hungarian liqueur.

Raoul took her hand. "My mouse. She is afraid of death."

"Everyone is," said Helen sweetly—thought Hugh—and reassuringly.

"Raoul isn't," said Lolly. "When he told me he didn't want children— you know, soon after we'd met—he said he had a similar certainty about not needing to continually publish."

Raoul solemnly nodded, not letting go of her hand.

"A similar certainty?" asked Helen.

"No fear of death," Lolly gently explained.

Each Thursday evening, Helen went to typing class (she really was a hopeless typist; in class she would eschew the instructive exercises, instead typing up lengthy descriptions of the people around her, which were rife with errors but amusing to read), Lolly went to her analyst, and Raoul invited a remarkably diverse group of professors to the house. His only requirement of the evening was that everyone had to drink the disagreeable liquor of his homeland and actively try not to be boring. His theory was that, by the end of two months, 50 percent would become Unicum drinkers for life. In addition to Raoul's mathematics colleagues, Hugh had met a Dante scholar, a few psychiatrists, physicists, poets, and several esteemed anthropologists, who'd all shown their slides of Amazonian jungles, the sand-swept Sahara, the mesas of New Mexico. In a matter of weeks, Hugh had met experts in smallpox, Freud, the Tzotzil Maya, and the Nuer. He kept waiting for Charlie Case to walk through the door, but the most anyone could offer were rumors about his completed film; one professor had heard that it was a shoo-in to win a big French prize, another mentioned (with evident distaste) that Charlie Case had become quite comfortable in Hollywood.

Ice clinked and highballs were refilled; the lilac bush brushed against the open window. Hugh watched the men: all sitting, all listening, as an unassuming fellow with thin pale skin (Hugh couldn't stop picturing it scorching in the African sun) who'd done extensive work in Upper Volta described a tribe called the Mossi as *the Japanese of West Africa,* due to their numerous rituals and greetings. The man started out speaking softly and grew more and more animated, until Hugh sensed him progressing toward an out-and-out performance. This little pallid man became a skilled—if vaguely campy—mime, bowing and scraping, even lying on the floor.

Hugh ran downstairs, retrieved his camera, quickly returned, and started shooting.

He hadn't asked Raoul if he might take photographs, he hadn't thought it through, but he knew that if Raoul admired anything about him it was what (toward the end of Hugh's first dinner at the townhouse) Raoul had heralded as his *independence.* Which may or may not have been a euphemism for *trust fund,* but Hugh had decided to be hopeful. After the first few kisslike clicks of his Leica, he attempted to catch Raoul Merva's eye, and when he did, Hugh felt nothing short of soaring relief as Raoul smiled and even mugged for the camera.

"Bravo," said Raoul. "Hugh will document these evenings. What shall we call ourselves?" mused their host. "A good salon needs a name," he said, with just enough absurdity in his voice for Hugh to realize that he was joking.

Paparazzo, thought Hugh mordantly, *that's me.* Though he'd be hard-pressed to discover more substantive and less attractive subjects, as he trained his lens on Raoul Merva and co. he imagined he was Marcello Mastroianni in *La Dolce Vita,* whose palpable self-hatred was somehow completely appealing. He thought of sitting in the Brattle Theatre last spring, staring into the eyes of that final moment's Umbrian angel and vowing to learn Italian. Which of course he never had. He thought of how he was a Shipley and it didn't matter what he did, because the peak of the Shipleys had already happened and the point of his existence was nothing more than to ride out the wave of the Shipley name until it dumped out onto the shore.

Although he maintained to Ed that inheritance meant nothing and that the individual self was everything, he often thought that this was bullshit, and if he remembered one thing from his spotty education it would be how the anthropologist Radcliffe-Brown, while doing field-work in Australia, went walking with an Aboriginal in the outback and how they met another Aboriginal to whom the first Aboriginal spoke for hours. How after this conversation (of which Radcliffe-Brown understood nothing) the first Aboriginal said to the anthropologist: *We're going to be killed.*

Why? asked Radcliffe-Brown.

Because, explained the first Aboriginal, *after two hours of conversation we still cannot find a blood link between us. This is why.*

Maybe this was all life amounted to. Maybe he was allowed to sit in this room and amuse himself by taking photographs because he was a Shipley and nothing else he might do in this life could ever come close to that.

But as he continued to shoot, he forgot about his pointless fate or even that he was ostensibly supposed to be capturing—for posterity—this evening's guests. He saw patterns emerging and he didn't shy away from capturing them, whether or not Raoul would appreciate it. He shot short men in the foreground to look enormous, while the taller men faded into the background like unfocused ghosts. Three men stood side by side with their hands pressed so tightly into the pockets of their sport jackets they looked almost frozen, and he shot them from below to exaggerate their immobility. As he retreated further behind the lens, Hugh began to identify these impressive men less by their contributions to scholarship than by their defining gestures—how they sat and stood became as compelling as what they were saying.

The proper way to greet your superior, the Upper Voltaist explained, was to drop to the ground and throw dirt on your head (which he promptly pantomimed), and Hugh immediately imagined himself under a mound of dirt, as he'd never understood so completely that he knew nothing. He also realized that he really had never gone anywhere and that he had to go everywhere, that he'd seen nothing and he'd have to try to see everything. He had just enough money that he didn't have to work, so long as he lived modestly. He was nothing if not the perfect candidate to be a perpetual student. Normally such a realization would have rendered him useless for days, weeks even, but at the moment he felt not only inferior to this room full of experts but also suddenly, shockingly motivated.

"May I have a volunteer?" the Upper Volta expert asked, back on his feet once again, and of course Hugh shot up from his seat near the door, towering above the professor and grinning like a dedicated fool.

"If you're greeting your equal," the expert explained, reaching out his small hand for Hugh to shake, "you simultaneously drop to the ground as you are shaking hands."

Hugh shook the professor's hand and they kept shaking and lowering, shaking and lowering, until it felt like dancing the twist with no Twist. He realized he was drunk when he lost his balance and fell to the floor, but no one appeared to care. In fact, his falling seemed to make everyone happier, as if he had proved some point for them. When Hugh cursed himself aloud and worried over the damage done to his camera,

Raoul Merva helped him up and ruffled his hair. His hand lingered there, and Hugh had the distinct sensation that his head was a basketball for Raoul to palm idly while waiting for a game to begin.

All of these gentlemen had traversed the globe, and Hugh, for that one moment, didn't mind that his connections were the only reason he was invited. He was too grateful to sit and listen and shoot rolls of film that he'd possibly never develop. And—miracle—he got to sleep with Helen afterward.

They lay in Helen's bed, staring at the ceiling, regaining their breath.

Months had passed since their meeting at the Peabody, when they'd taken right back up again, even keeping each other secret out of habit until Ed forced Hugh to admit he was hiding something. And when Ed finally forced the truth, Hugh had been left to wonder not only why he'd kept Helen a secret but why Helen had kept him a secret as well. This was something he always wanted to ask her about, along with the details of the abortion. But somehow he never did.

He didn't miss their tree. He *liked* taking her to dinner and meeting her on campus and introducing her as his girl. He liked watching people watch her. Sometimes, if they were meeting in the Yard or on a street corner, he would glimpse her waiting for him and stop for a moment or two, admiring not only Helen but also how other people responded to the sight of her. She seemed to inspire goodwill and good posture. He would feel the initial tinges of jealousy, only to remind himself that she was actually waiting for him.

Helen was funnier than he'd ever properly understood and a skilled conversationalist with nearly everyone. At first, this realization was disappointing. He'd always imagined that Helen suffered being misunderstood as distant and even (he was embarrassed to admit this) not very bright, due to her decidedly blond beauty and a sometime forgetfulness, and that he—Hugh Shipley—was the person who was uniquely suited to appreciate not only her outer self (absurd to imagine a personal claim to something so obviously appealing) but also her unique and complicated inner self. He now understood that she came across as distinctly nuanced and that any idiot would be able to see that.

But if, as she was fond of saying, he was her favorite person, well, then, he ought to feel a good deal better about himself than he was used to feeling.

He was starting to. Especially when he slept here at the townhouse. Especially when Helen crossed her ankle over his as if it were her own.

"Why do you think she does that?" Hugh asked, looking up at the ceiling. On the floor above them, Lolly's footsteps created a diversion; she liked to clean in the middle of the night.

Helen said she thought the act of cleaning during the daytime felt— for Lolly—too damningly bourgeois and depressing, but she somehow still couldn't bring herself to hire help around the house. "I'm sure she talks about this with her analyst."

Hugh laughed without averting his gaze from the ceiling. "I see you've given this some thought," he said.

"Tell me, Lolly," she intoned in her best Viennese accent, *"you like ʒe broom?"* Her narrow shoulders and small breasts moved up and down, and he had to kiss her again.

"I think we should go on a double date with Ed," said Helen. "I'll set him up."

"You mean it?"

She nodded, running fingers through his damp hair.

The only two times Ed and Helen had spent an evening together, Helen answered Ed's questions perfunctorily—with little to no warmth—until Ed had stopped asking, and it had fallen to Hugh to break the awkward silence, which was not exactly his forte. He was too surprised at their not getting along to have any idea what to do. When Hugh had asked Ed what he'd thought of Helen, Ed had countered, "Do you really want to know?" And of course Hugh didn't. Not really. Not if it meant Ed saying that Helen was cold and snobbish and all of the things that Hugh knew she wasn't. Though Hugh had to admit she had maintained a surprising remove when they'd all drunk bad coffee together at Hayes-Bickford.

"There's a girl from my typing class I think Ed would like," Helen said.

Hugh wondered how Helen could possibly have any idea of whom Ed would like—Hugh certainly didn't—or exactly what kind of girl she not only imagined might be interested in Ed but also of whom she'd approve. He was curious. "You were not exactly . . . nice to him."

"I was chilly," she acknowledged, "I know."

"Was it all his questions?"

"I found him off-putting," she admitted. "But, for whatever reason, he's your friend. I'll find something to like. I usually do."

"You do?" Hugh rolled onto his side and Helen nodded, turning her back to him. He folded himself around her, and when he was once again nesting in her softest place, he was all excited.

"Yes," she said.

"Is that right?" He put his hand on her hip.

"Or I pretend."

"Ah," he said, starting to rock back and forth.

"I pretend until it's true."

They stood outside the Casablanca on the kind of spring evening that makes anyone want to get along. The girl's name was Connie Graff, and she was petite and dark, and though she was dressed in a kilt and a cashmere twin set, the effect was somehow hard-edged, as if she was proving a point. She also spoke with a strange but compelling authority, and moments after the introductions, Hugh, Ed, and Helen became immediately and mysteriously cowed by her opinions. She assured them that it wouldn't be long before the Casablanca would be too crowded to enjoy a decent drink, because everyone—everyone—was out tonight.

"Connie just came back from New York," Helen said. "From job interviews on Madison Avenue. Isn't that right, Connie?"

Helen was, by anyone's account, a sophisticated girl who'd gone to all the right schools and had appropriated most of the accompanying cynicisms; however—and Hugh always forgot until moments like this one, and each time he was newly puzzled and charmed—she'd been kept somehow sheltered from New York City. So paranoid was her father about its corrupting influences, one had to wonder what he did over the course of each workweek. Mr. Ordway liked for the family to stay in Connecticut or preferably on Fishers, and Helen had been kept busy at boarding schools and clubs, and then there was *the situation* (as Hugh still could not help thinking of it, so haunted was he by that gossip's voice), when she was sent to live with the aunt in Stonington, so with the exception of certain approved balls, annual visits to her father's office, and maybe the ballet or the symphony, New York had remained a mystery. In any case, while Helen was not particularly mystified by someone as eccentric as Raoul Merva (so comfortable had she become living on the fringes of academia, where eccentricity held sway), she seemed genuinely awed by what Hugh's father somewhat derisively referred to as *normal life,* so long as the setting was the island of Manhattan.

"How were your interviews at Grey and BBDO?" Helen asked. "I haven't even had a chance to find out."

"Oh, fine," said Connie. "It was just fine," she said, as if there was clearly more to the story and that it wouldn't disappoint. But before anyone could ask anything, she continued. "Have you been to New York on a Friday afternoon? When all those cars pull out of town? Where are they all *going?*" she asked, as if she really wanted to know. "I mean, don't you want to see the inside of every single country house? Not that they're all so magnificent, of course, but *some* . . . Oh—" she said, peering into the dim light of the bar. "Goody. I think I see that big crowd heading out."

"After you," said Hugh. When Connie smiled, he was grateful to think: *nice smile.* He knew that later he'd be able to point out this feature to Ed, without having to think about it. When Hugh had proposed the evening, Ed had instantly agreed to come. He had been undeterred by the lack of information, had relied solely on Helen's recommendation.

But now that they were all here together, it was embarrassingly transparent why Helen thought Ed might like Connie: She was Jewish.

But after they sat down and ordered their drinks, Ed started laughing.

"What's so amusing?" asked Helen.

"Nothing," said Ed. "Forget it."

"Oh, that's awful," said Helen, clearly meaning it. "That is the most awful thing you can do to a conversation."

"Helen," said Ed, "you really need to stop with the compliments. You are too nice."

"She's right, though," said Hugh, lighting the two girls' cigarettes before his own. "Fewer habits—even of yours—are more unfortunate."

"It's only that, just because we're under the Brattle Theatre," asked Ed, "does everyone have to think they're Orson Welles or Ingrid Bergman? Look around. Everyone is mentally on their way to Europe, in the fog, with a tragic past."

"But not you," said Helen, rather pointedly.

"No," he said, "not me. Not you, either, Connie Graff. Am I right?"

"Ingrid Bergman is the *end*," said Connie.

"The end?"

"The *most* gorgeous," Connie continued, "the most chic. Do you disagree?"

Ed shrugged.

"Are you kidding? When David Selznick signed her for her first Hollywood picture and told her to pluck her eyebrows, cap her teeth, and change her name, she told him she wouldn't consider it. She speaks five languages. Her return after the scandal was triumphant. Truly. Who wouldn't want to be Ingrid Bergman?"

"Me," said Hugh, unsmiling. "I would not want to be Ingrid Bergman. I think such a sudden change would be very confusing for everyone."

None of the three (two of whom certainly knew he was trying to elicit a laugh) seemed entertained.

"It's chic to be sad, isn't it?" Ed said.

"I suppose it is," said Connie, leaning forward with a hint of con-spiracy. "Why is that, do you think?"

"I don't know," said Ed, "but it's irritating. When I look around, I'm irritated."

"We see that," said Helen. "Maybe you need to get some air."

"No," said Ed. "I'll stop."

"Well," said Helen firmly, "that would be nice." Then she gave Ed a surprisingly generous smile, a look that was almost . . . complicit, which Hugh noticed was all it took to make Ed relax. Hugh, too, was tempo-rarily silenced by Helen's assertion, and he would always use that night as an example of how—contrary to popular belief—one can never pre-dict the direction of an evening within the first five minutes.

Because not only was the "Ingrid Bergman night" (as they all even-tually referred to it) fun—and *so* much more fun than the beginning had promised—but after Ed got over the fact that Helen had obviously set him up with Connie solely because they were both Jewish, it became clear that Ed did like Connie and Connie liked Ed, and Hugh liked ev-eryone and Helen approved, and for a month or so they all hung around together. Friday evenings, they dressed up and had drinks in the Brattle Street townhouse (the Mervas had once again set off for the Dordogne), which led to dinner and—for Ed, Hugh, and Helen at least—eventually breakfast. Connie always returned to her dormitory and was never late. She was a proud virgin, and Ed's varied attempts at persuading her oth-erwise (at turns comic, pleading, and downright lewd) often punctuated these evenings. Connie didn't seem to mind and even relished the atten-tion, as they drank bottles of wine from Raoul's fine collection and Hugh looked through his camera lens, as if they really were—Ed and the two girls—subjects as worthy as members of the Nuer tribe, the Dani, or—at the very least—a few melancholy film stars.

By the time Connie Graff's high school sweetheart showed up in the middle of the Thursday typing class with *a ring that proved he wasn't playing around,* the Friday night routine was so firmly established that the absence of Connie Graff (who wasted no time in moving back to

New Rochelle) mattered less than any of them would have guessed. Ed continued dressing for Fridays and driving Helen and Hugh around in his convertible on Sundays. They returned to the Big Deep and ate egg-salad sandwiches and drank many bottles of beer. Helen filled the empty bottles with pond water and wildflowers, lining them up, week by week, along the water's edge. They drove to Somerville to see a big house that was completely round. While Hugh was aiming his lens at Helen in front of it, and while she was trying to pretend she didn't notice him doing so, an old man shuffled by, walking an equally old Labrador. "I always figured my life would be better if I lived in that round house," he said. "Go on," he told them, "go on and I'll take your picture."

Hugh handed over his Leica somewhat reluctantly, but the old man backed up and was nothing if not nimble as he fiddled with the lens. Hugh stood next to Helen, taking her hand.

"No need for any funny business," said the old man, though they were doing nothing but standing still. "That house is as regal a backdrop as you can ask for."

Ed made no move to join them—out of, Hugh imagined, respect—but the man nearly growled at Ed, "Time's a wastin'."

Ed—squeezed in the middle—made up for his reticence by throwing his arms around the two of them, the force of which caused Hugh and Helen (who were, Hugh knew, king and queen of the miserably stiff photo smile) to offer up something genuine. They each hated having their picture taken, but when the old man was gone, Hugh sheepishly asked Ed to take one of just Helen and him, if only to prove to himself that they could appear relaxed and happy without Ed's arms around them.

As for Ed: Each week he joked less and less about being a third wheel. In fact, it became evident that he enjoyed it and that Hugh and Helen enjoyed—after such secretive beginnings—maybe not a fawning audience but certainly a witness, and one who was not shy about making his presence known.

———

At Ami Henri, sunlight poured into the small pleasant rooms, and for a brief moment Hugh felt so contented that he thought there was something wrong with his head and that maybe he was confusing a positive sensation with a negative one, like when hot water is so hot it actually feels cold. He was jolted out of his blatant neurosis by the French proprietress, Mrs. O'Hagen—so named because of the American G.I. she'd married and promptly divorced after their arrival in Boston. Her name was at odds with her Gallic charms, and when Ed insisted on telling her so (this being his first time here), she leaned over the table, emitting the scent of onions and butter and something distinctly more earthy, and said, *"Merci,"* pointedly—Hugh couldn't help but notice—not to Ed but to him.

"My," said Helen, fanning herself with the worn yellow menu, "someone never warmed to American habits of bathing."

"She's phenomenal," said Ed. "I'm going to sleep with her."

"Is that right," Helen said, reading over the menu before placing it on the table.

"What's your fancy?" Hugh asked her.

"Snails, I think," said Helen, while looking at Ed.

"What?" asked Ed. "What's that look for?"

Helen started to laugh.

"Helen Ordway, are you saying I don't have a chance with Miss Bardot over there?"

"She's hardly Brigitte Bardot. Besides," Helen took her voice down, "she must be at least forty years old."

"Well, golly gee," said Ed. "Ever hear of a May–December romance?"

"You have to admit, your confidence is staggering," Hugh said.

"And?" countered Ed.

Mrs. O'Hagen approached the table again, and Hugh ordered a bottle of wine.

"I'm suddenly so hungry," said Ed, all the while looking at Mrs. O'Hagen as if she were a filet mignon. When Helen laughed, Mrs. O'Hagen shot her a withering look before sauntering off once again.

"You have to admit," said Helen, offering her cigarette to be lit, which Hugh did without missing a beat, "you are constantly on the make. I'm just not sure it's altogether healthy."

"And why not?" Ed asked, as Mrs. O'Hagen approached once more with an open bottle—an undeniably lovely sight. "Why not aim high?" he said, drawing out his words, watching *madame* pour and then leave. "Hugh, don't you think I should aim high?"

Hugh nodded, shifting in his seat as he watched an older couple order briskly after kissing Mrs. O'Hagen on both cheeks. He had a passing thought that the man looked like his father. But this man was shorter, balder, and his father was in the middle of the country, attending a Union Pacific shareholders' meeting; he was spending a week on a luxury train car, a high point of his year.

"I admit," Hugh said, "I don't understand how you can be so blindly confident despite—I'll go on and say it—a few rejections. You don't exactly take it in."

Ed knocked back some wine. "Take what in?" he asked.

Hugh glanced at Helen before settling into his chair. He tried to return to the pleasant sensation he'd had upon sitting down with Helen and Ed, but all he noticed now was the narrow space between two doorways where an African mask had always hung. The mask was gone, and it was terribly unnerving to see the empty space, which was no doubt contributing to his mood. When he'd asked about the mask several years ago, over an unusually pleasant dinner with his father, Mrs. O'Hagen had told him that she purchased it from an old woman in Dakar. She'd seemed pleased that Hugh was interested and had mentioned her decorative knives from the Congo; perhaps he might one day want to see them?

Hugh knew that Mrs. O'Hagen might remember him, but he was too reserved to ever act as if they'd met. There were reports that she conferred the honor of viewing her naked flesh upon a select few Harvard upperclassmen each year, but Hugh did not want to even consider that he could be among those few, as he would never—now that he finally had Helen—accept such a distinction.

"What?" Ed repeated. "What exactly don't I take in? Look." He put his elbows on the table and leaned in toward both of them. "When girls—not only girls—when *anyone* is skittish about my . . . personal candor, I know not to trust them."

"Is that so?" countered Helen.

"I know not to trust them, because they clearly haven't resolved their own personal problems. That," Ed said, "is why they're uncomfortable."

"Maybe," said Helen, taking a last long drag of her cigarette. "Or maybe they just find you overbearing."

Ed waved her off. "What would I want with people like that?"

Mrs. O'Hagen sauntered toward their table with a bowl of cornichons. She described *les especials*—especially a leg of lamb with some nice spring peas—quite tenderly.

"You are ready?" Mrs. O'Hagen asked meaningfully. "Do you know what you would like?"

When the cake arrived, it sported one lit candle, and Hugh and Helen sang a shy but boozy happy birthday. Ed's face lit up as if no one had ever done anything nice for him before that moment, and Hugh felt a strange flip in his throat that signaled his own special breed of crying (quick start, no end in sight) and he slugged down the rest of the Bordeaux. When Ed loosened his tie and raised his glass, it was easy for Hugh to picture how his friend would age, how he might lose his hair and get rounder at the middle but he'd always command a room without doing more than this: lifting a glass and—for one brief moment— looking deadly serious.

Ed twitched—a vigorous blink—just like he did when he'd been studying all night and insisted on recounting what he knew, even as Hugh had fallen asleep on the common-room couch, leaving Ed to rattle off dates and concepts until he was completely satisfied there was nothing he had missed. "You not only have to get it all in there," he'd explained, when Hugh asked why he had to say everything out loud, "but you have to make sure none of it leaks out." He talked about acquiring knowledge as if it was no different than fixing up a car, filling it with a full tank of gas.

"Hugh," he said now, "Helen." Again the big blink. "I want you to know that you are my friends. I would kill for you both, I really think I would."

Hugh and Helen started to laugh. Ed did not.

"Don't laugh."

"Sorry," said Hugh.

"Sorry," said Helen.

"Thank you for taking me to this restaurant on my birthday."

"You're welcome," said Hugh.

Mrs. O'Hagen came back to the table. She picked up the cake. "Happy birthday," she said to Ed. "I will cut this into pieces. And maybe some crème?" She turned, and Ed watched her go.

"I have to sleep with that woman," he said, his outpouring over their friendship clearly finished.

"What about getting back to how you'd kill for us?" said Hugh.

"She has slept with others," Ed maintained, as if to soothe himself. "It is not out of the question."

"I'd let that particular ambition fall away if I were you," said Hugh, and Helen nodded, offering another cigarette to be lit. "What do you really know about her willingness? I think it might be nothing but wishful rumors."

"John Winn has."

"I'm sorry," said Helen, "but that's John Winn."

"John Winn," said Ed, "is a drunk who was kicked out of Harvard for holding up a movie-theater cashier with a water pistol."

Helen shrugged giddily. "I'm only saying . . ."

"He held up a cashier—a movie cashier—"

"As if the type of cashier matters!"

"He held up a cashier with a water pistol. Are you saying he's more sexually appealing than I am?" Ed was grinning madly now. "Connie Graff liked me!"

"Connie Graff married a dermatology resident and moved to West-chester. This is Mrs. O'Hagen," stressed Helen, looking at Hugh for encouragement.

"It is," offered Hugh.

Suddenly Ed backed his chair away from the table and dropped his napkin. The kitchen was at the end of a long narrow hallway and they could make out half of Mrs. O'Hagen, whose back was to them. They watched Ed approach her, stopping just shy of grabbing her behind. They watched as Mrs. O'Hagen turned around, holding a dessert plate. Ed took the plate from her hand and set it back down on the counter. Hugh and Helen said nothing, the older couple ate in silence, and the few other tables in the restaurant were empty, but, even so, no one could hear what Ed said to Mrs. O'Hagen that produced such a laugh, a laugh clearly ripening to become either a giddy reproach or—remarkably—an invitation. No one could hear what he'd said. In fact, it was as if the room was filling up with a thick and difficult silence. Hugh and Helen sat back in the banquette and, as if in response to what could only be de-scribed as the very real heat that Ed had somehow managed to generate in that small kitchen, Hugh put his hand up Helen's skirt and Helen tilted toward him. But both of them still watched the kitchen; someone was bound to come back at any moment, after all.

Chapter Five

Solstice

"I've never been on a ferry before," Ed said. "How is that possible?" He stretched out his legs and rapped his knuckles on the wooden bench. The deck was neither crowded nor empty and it was unseasonably warm for June. The sun shone, gulls swooped, and as he breathed in deeply, a salt scent came not only from the sea but also from the potato chips four pregnant women were noshing.

"You realize," said Hugh, "we're headed toward a special kind of nature preserve."

Hugh had been talking cryptically and continuously since they'd boarded the boat half an hour before, and now Ed was barely listening. He preferred to look at all the mothers-to-be, at their tan calves and straw hats, and to imagine each one during their individual moments of conception. It certainly altered the view.

"Nature preserve?" Helen mumbled, from her prone state. She loved the sun; her eyes were closed.

Hugh lit a cigarette, looked out toward Fishers Island. "Sure," he said, nodding at the four pregnant women. "We're coming up on one of the last places left in the Northern Hemisphere where WASPs can successfully procreate without threat from outside forces."

Helen sat up, fanned herself with the ferry schedule. "Okay," she said. "That was funny. Now, are you almost done?"

"Sadly," said Hugh, "no." He stretched his arm around her.

"Hugh," she said.

"Ed should really prepare himself."

"I think I got the picture," said Ed. "The man is not a fan of the Jews."

"What did you tell him?" asked Helen, alarmed.

"Just the basic truth." Hugh shrugged. "But your father knows Ed's our friend. I imagine he'll behave himself."

"Yes," said Helen, her voice tight, "I imagine he will." She took a cigarette from her purse and Hugh lit it for her. "You know," she said, "my father happens to have a deep respect for hard workers. And, say what we will about Ed"—she smiled brightly—"he's a hard worker."

"True," said Hugh. Though he wasn't finished with it, he crushed his cigarette, stripped it to bits, and threw it out to sea. "Fishers Island is kind of like a zoo. A beautiful, impeccably maintained zoo. And there's a deep fear of having to live outside the zoo. Did you know that?"

"Really?" Helen asked. "And did you go and do all the necessary fieldwork with the monkeys and the lions? Did they reveal their deepest fears? Hugh, seriously. My father would be mortified."

"I would have assumed it anyway," Ed assured her.

"Well, that's hardly fair."

"But he *isn't*—as you so nicely put it, Ed—a fan," asked Hugh. "Is he?"

"Well, no," said Helen. "If you mean as a group? No, he is not."

"Maybe it's more of a hothouse than a zoo," Hugh persisted. "Everyone in their summer states of mind. The island mentality. Forgive me—and I *will* get this out of my system—but it's crippling being sequestered. People form dependencies. They stop paying attention." He shook his head, as if he was unable to shrug off his mood.

Two of the pregnant ladies looked up from their magazines. Ed caught one's eye and smiled. He imagined how her husband was likely finishing his week on Wall Street in an old-money firm, where—if you were from the right family—you could be a perfect idiot and somehow still, upon graduating, have a coveted position waiting.

"Please," Helen said quietly. "You said you wanted to come."

"Of course I want to come," Hugh said, also lowering his voice. "I'm sorry. It's your family. Of course I want to be with you if this is where you want to be. Plus, we're going to show Ed a good time before he starts making his *real dough* and we never see him again."

"It's gorgeous," Ed said, looking out at the horizon, heady from the saltwater, from other people's problems. He pictured Fishers Island the way it looked on a map—a few dabs of land between Long Island and Connecticut; nothing to get worked up about. "I don't care about any of this," Ed insisted. "I just want to go swimming."

"Sure you do," said Hugh. "You do care."

"Maybe," said Helen, "he doesn't care *right now*. Maybe we don't have to care about the deeper aspects of our society twenty-four hours a day. Even Bobby Kennedy goes sailing with some regularity, you know."

"Bobby Kennedy," scoffed Hugh. "Bobby Kennedy's a lightweight."

"Again?" asked Ed. "We're going to get into this again?"

"He was practically McCarthy's right-hand man."

"You know," said Ed, deciding *not* to spend the rest of the boat ride arguing about degrees of liberalism, "I actually have plenty of sympathy for how people marry their own kind here and—"

"Sure," said Hugh. "While playing golf and getting smashed and wearing their native attire, they're simply carrying out their traditions. The Dani ritually kill other tribes, and our people just keep everyone at bay and *pretend* they don't exist."

"Don't you think you're sounding a tiny bit silly?" Helen asked.

Hugh grinned in his half-grinning way, blue eyes squinting into the sun even though he had a perfectly good pair of sunglasses on top of his head. "Of course," he said finally. "Of course I am."

As if she'd been reading Ed's thoughts, Helen placed Hugh's sunglasses gently on his face.

"I'm a product of this place," Hugh said, by way of explanation.

"As am I," Helen said. "And guess what? Last time I checked"—she held up her finger, where the late Mrs. Shipley's engagement diamond sparkled so brightly Ed imagined it could start a fire—"you and I are getting married. We are marrying our own kind."

Hugh shrugged. "Sarcasm is my only weapon."

"You hardly need a weapon," Helen said. Ed had thought she was angry, but he was evidently wrong. She was smiling, even laughing, now that Hugh was done with being funny.

Ed Cantowitz peered around the ferry deck. Everyone seemed friendly enough. He looked forward to sleeping on good cotton sheets and drinking gin from crystal. He'd graduated from Harvard summa cum laude. His father had wept. This was going to be a great summer.

As the ferry docked, Ed noticed the redhead in the yellow Mercedes convertible immediately, but he was surprised when she started waving wildly in their direction, for, although Kitty was a beauty, too, she looked nothing like Helen. Besides the lavish red hair, she had great big breasts and (he noticed upon closer inspection, as he shook her soft hand) explosions of freckles across her fleshy chest. She was smiley and chatty and without a trace of self-consciousness about talking nonstop from the moment she said hello. "Come on now," she said. "I promised Mother we wouldn't run late. We need to dress for dinner, et cetera. You sit in the front, Hugh." She tied a scarf around her head and started the car. "Have you noticed she always thinks we're going to be late and we never are?"

"Where are J.K. and Susannah?"

"Left them with Mother," she said, backing out of the small lot. "Ooh, give me a cigarette, will you? Last time I left them with her it wasn't pretty—Mother was crying when I returned, muttering something about J.K. taking after Johnny, and then she said that there was a reason people came east for an education. I'd only gone out to buy my kind of coffee, because Mrs. Mulroney won't buy any of the 'fancy kind,' on principle. Even if I give her twice as much as she needs when she goes to the store! By the way, be sure to offer your condolences; as you might imagine, she's *distraught* about the pope's passing. Anyway," Kitty said, lighting up the cigarette, "let's get going."

Over a bumpy road, through a tunnel of trees, Helen's sister never paused for breath.

"Look at all the bunny rabbits!" she cried. "Do you see them? Ah, gee whiz," she muttered, as she swerved to miss hitting one. "And look up. See the osprey? Where did they build their nests before telephone poles? Helen, look, oh, look—do you remember how we got sick on blackberries right over there? Or was it oysters? I do remember getting awfully sick in that cove. Oh, and there's the Winston house. Hugh, you must remember Mrs. Winston from spending time here? You must. I adore her. She's still alive but you know her children don't summer here anymore. Just quick visits. Like me! Terrible! *I'm* one of those children now. I have to convince Johnny to let me bring the children for the whole summer next year. Don't you think? They'll be old enough to start sailing? Helen, do you know he wants to teach them to sail *on a lake?*"

She asked this as if it did not merit a response, which apparently it did not.

"As if there is any comparison!" Kitty continued, swerving again so as not to hit another bunny.

As the car swerved, Helen nearly fell into Ed's lap, and he felt a twinge of sadness when she composed herself, taking away not only her body but also her distinct scent, which was something he could never quite place.

"I'm just not a lake person," Kitty explained, ostensibly to Ed and Hugh. "I tried. Didn't I try, Helen? The lake is too still. I'm sorry, Ed—that's your name, right? I'm miserable with names; ask Helen. I was about to call you David. Anyway, you must think I'm terribly rude, I haven't explained what I'm talking about, and, knowing my sister, she didn't say anything—so, ready? I went and married a Californian."

"Really," said Ed.

"Seven years ago," said Helen. "It's not exactly breaking news."

The road was narrow, and Kitty had to pull over in order to let an oncoming Cadillac pass by. She waved to the old lady behind the wheel. "That was Mrs. Winston!" she explained triumphantly, as she continued on the road. "I swear! Her ears must have been burning. I just love how small this island is. I *miss* it. Although, as you might imagine, Ed, these narrow roads can make for some particularly awkward encounters. I swear, Helen, I *swear* to you I can't *tell* you how many times I've come face-to-face with Mouse since I've arrived."

"Mouse?" asked Ed. He had to.

"My ex-fiancé," said Kitty. "I met Johnny," she offered, as if Johnny was the end of more than simply her engagement.

"His name is *Mouse?*" Ed asked.

"Mouse is six foot six," said Kitty, explaining the evidently ironic nickname, as she made a sharp right turn.

"Easy on the wheel," said Hugh. "Please, Kitty," he added.

"You'd better get used to some windy roads, isn't that right? God knows what kind of roads they have where you're going. Remind me where you're going? Nairobi?"

"I wish," said Helen.

"Ethiopia," Hugh explained, "a village called Ciengach." As if he knew he'd be repeating this many times throughout the weekend and it was his sincere wish to remain patient. "I'll be assisting my mentor, Charlie Case, and another filmmaker from Paris."

"Well," said Kitty, *"c'est magnifique."*

"C'est magnifique?" Helen asked, rather bitingly.

"Oui," Kitty replied, as if to say: *Go climb a tree.* "Though I'm sure you'll miss my sister, Hugh. It's too bad you aren't getting married before you leave." There was an unprecedented moment of silence as they watched what looked like a turkey take its time crossing the road.

"You know what they say," said Helen. "Better pheasants than peasants." And they coasted down a hill.

"They don't say that," said Ed.

"Oh, but they do."

"I'll miss her very much," said Hugh.

"And how long will you be gone?" Kitty asked.

"Yet to be determined, actually." Hugh looked out at the passing trees. "One of the main things written about the tribe we're filming is that they're particularly visually striking, so . . . It sounds very promising."

"Mmn," said Kitty. "I'll say."

"Hugh is going to meet me in Paris when he's finished," said Helen. "Did I tell you? Raoul Merva set something up for me at the Sorbonne? Typing, yes, but typing in Paris."

"How nice for you," said Kitty. "I hadn't realized your French was that good."

"Oh, it isn't," said Helen. "But my accent is apparently excellent. And, besides, I'm sure I can find work in one of the fashion houses. They're always looking for tall girls."

"It's funny," Kitty said. "When you're driving around here you don't really realize how easy it is to make wrong turns," she continued. "You just think to yourself, *Oh, I'm going a bit over here,* but in reality—"

Ed noticed how Kitty tried to catch Helen's eye in the rearview and how Helen didn't look back.

"In reality," repeated Kitty, "you're going wildly out of your way."

The house was natural gray shingled with marine-blue shutters, as if whoever chose the color had sought to match the seemingly endless stretch of white-capped sea that lay beyond its windows. It was also in need of a paint job. At the bottom of a vast green lawn, the beach was rocky and the dock needed tending, but the sea was a perfect expanse, and it was hard not to believe that anyone who was lucky enough to live in such a house might be a little more perfect because of such a view.

"Hello?" cried Kitty, when no one greeted them at the door. "They're here! Mother?"

A worried-looking woman appeared from what Ed imagined as a warren of endless rooms. "Helen dear," she said, briefly taking Helen's hand and nodding toward Hugh and Ed.

"Mrs. Mulroney," said Kitty, "where are the children?"

"Your mother's thrown up her hands," said Mrs. Mulroney.

"Mother?" Kitty cried out. "For the love of God, I was gone not twenty minutes!"

There was the sound of pans crashing to the floor, and Mrs. Mulroney excused herself.

"J.K. and Susannah, if you don't come and give your aunt Helen a proper hello right now—" But Kitty was already advancing through the rooms, and the three of them followed.

In the library, the children were giggling under what might have been every blanket in the house. The couches had been robbed of their pillows and were strewn about the room. Kitty sat down behind the large mahogany desk.

"How can you do that?" asked Helen. "Just sit there like that? I still can't sit there," said Helen.

"Oh, he's a pussycat," said Kitty.

"Father is a *pussycat?*"

"Funny, that was not my impression, either," said Hugh.

From what Ed could gather, it was a point of great contention that Hugh had not asked for Mr. Ordway's permission before proposing to Helen. That, in addition to the various reasons Mr. Ordway found Hugh objectionable, beginning with his lack of serious employment and ending with the fact that he was "running off" to Africa without even having the decency to marry Helen first. When Ed had asked why he was, in fact, running off to Africa without marrying Helen first, Hugh had declared something vague about not succumbing to outside pressures. And though Hugh's family and Helen's family belonged to the same clubs, Mr. Shipley thought Mr. Ordway stiff, and Ed could only imagine what Mr. Ordway thought of Hugh's father, who was evidently known for donating unknown sums of money to the country club each summer in order to keep the bar open just one hour longer each night. When Hugh *had* met the Ordways, at a graduation dinner held by the Mervas in their townhouse, it had evidently not gone well.

"J.K. and Susannah," Kitty's voice suddenly boomed. "I mean it."

The two children poked their heads out from under the blankets. The girl had wide-set dark eyes and black hair, and the boy was a freckly blond. "Aunt Helen," they cried, and when they emerged, crashing toward Helen in wet bathing suits, Ed realized they were younger than he'd thought.

"Start cleaning up," said Kitty. "Your granny is going to lose her mind."

"But we're cozy," said the boy.

"How old are you two these days?" Helen asked, in a vaguely disapproving tone, as if she thought she was supposed to help her sister but she wasn't sure how. She seemed shy with them, Ed noticed, and he wondered if Helen liked children, if she and Hugh had talked about such things. It was difficult to imagine Hugh and Helen outside the context of this past year, and he realized that when he imagined their life together he couldn't conjure up much more than train stations, airports, and good restaurants.

Even now, with their bags left lying in the entryway that was bigger than Ed's father's living room and kitchen put together, they were dawdling. They were talking to the children about the ins and outs of a morning spent at the very club that Hugh and Helen claimed to have no interest in returning to, without any eye toward the fact that the sun would be setting soon on this glorious day. Ed was anxious to take his bag upstairs and unpack and make the most of the hour or so allotted them before they were evidently expected for dinner. He wanted to dive into the sea immediately, but Hugh and Helen didn't seem to be in any kind of rush. When he imagined their life together, he pictured it just like this, and he wondered if limbo wasn't the state they both most appreciated.

"Who are you?" asked the girl.

"This is Ed," said Helen. "Ed Cantowitz."

"Go on, both of you," said Kitty. "Introduce yourselves."

"I'm Superman," said the boy.

"You?" asked Ed. "I thought I was Superman."

"No," said the boy, "you're not."

"Oh," said Ed. "Jeez. Look at you. Look at those muscles. My mistake."

"I'm Susannah," said the girl. "I'm going to be six."

Hugh shook the little girl's hand, and Ed was the only one laughing when Susannah said to her mother, "Hugh's not wearing rags."

"*What?*" said Kitty. "Why ever would you say that?"

"You said he was a—"

"Mother," shouted Kitty. And the children hid under the blankets again. "Mother, *please* come down here. The children want to apologize, and Helen and Hugh and Ed are here. They're *waiting*!"

When Mrs. Ordway entered the room, there was no question who it was, because not only did she command a remarkable authority while wearing a floppy hat and dirt-covered trousers but it was like looking at Helen a few decades on. Mrs. Ordway took her time removing her hat and placed it on an ottoman, one of the only surfaces not covered with blankets. "Helen," she said. And Helen gave her mother a kiss on the cheek before presenting her fiancé and their friend. "No girl for you this weekend, Mr. Cantowitz?" Mrs. Ordway inquired, with what seemed like naked suspicion.

"No, ma'am, I'm afraid not. Thank you for having me, nonetheless."

"Kitty dear," said Mrs. Ordway, in a tone that somehow managed to be both breezy and pointed, "with children it really is all about control."

"Yes, Mother," Kitty said, her effusive manner now replaced by something equally childlike but defeated.

"I'll see you gentlemen for dinner, then?" She offered a smile that Ed realized was so practiced that it approximated warmth without actually being warm.

"Where's Father?" Helen asked.

"Who knows?" Mrs. Ordway said. "*The Shadow knows.*" She smiled with that same almost-warm smile, picking up her garden hat but not putting it on. She began strolling off but turned around just as she hit the threshold. "Little monsters," she said in a singsong voice, "I know where you are hiding," which precipitated squeals and shouts as the children threw off their blankets to run after her, but she had already gotten away.

As it turned out, their bags hadn't been languishing in the hallway after all. They had been whisked away to their respective rooms and unpacked. Someone (who?) had unrolled Ed's two shirts and one pair of trousers and hung them in the armoire, and they seemed to have been steamed as well. His shoes and tennis sneakers (he'd never played tennis) were lined up under the bed. His swimming trunks were hanging on a jaunty nautical-style hook near the bathroom.

Genius!

He happened to hate unpacking more than packing, more than doing his own laundry or dishes, which was really saying something, as—left to his own devices—he peeled and ate hard-boiled eggs over sinks rather than—God forbid—involve a dish. And he now had one more reason to make money, because he naïvely hadn't even realized that having someone unpack one's bags was something that was, in fact, possible. Would he be expected to tip the staff at the end of his stay? He hadn't the faintest idea and was hesitant to rely on Hugh for answers, because he knew that Hugh would prefer to pretend that he wasn't benefiting from such services.

Ed took a shower and shaved very very carefully. He combed his hair and tried not to think about all of the rooms—especially the many important boardrooms on Wall Street that Mr. Guy Ordway walked in and out of on any given weekday. He tried not to think about how Ordway, by the time he was thirty, had single-handedly built a Depression-shattered investment firm into a legendary Wall Street powerhouse. Ed had promised his father one last summer of laying pipes in the ground, but in the fall he would be attending Harvard Business School and, after that, he knew there'd be no need to ever do physical labor, unless (in the hopefully-not-so-distant future) he was overcome with the urge to plant a tree on the lawn of his own second home. He'd never gone so far as to imagine what that fantasy might look like, but standing in this bedroom, with the rich wood floors creaking ever so slightly when he shifted his weight before the white-painted oval-framed mirror that hinted at the decades of guests who'd stood right where he stood while dressing for dinner, he saw this as a perfectly fine example of the direction his life might take.

As he often did when he was nervous, he repeated his father's creed in order to focus, in order to get himself in gear:

Don't fuck up. Don't fuck up, don't fuck up, don't fuck up. Don't. Fuck. Up.

He headed down the stairs, toward muffled conversation and clinking glasses, only to find two maids in white uniforms putting the finishing touches on the dining room table. When Ed wandered in, clearly lost, the older one directed him—brusquely—to the porch. Ed imagined Mr. Ordway was the type to pour his own drinks, the type who didn't limit industriousness to the workplace. He imagined this was a house where remarkable people often arrived for drinks at six. As he headed toward the porch, a brilliant orange sunset cut through the windowpanes and Ed's eyes went teary with allergies and terrific expectations, but as he mentally prepared a solid handshake for Mr. Ordway, the sun's glare subsided and he found the pink-cheeked children on Kitty's lap, Helen on Hugh's lap, and a cat snoozing atop Mrs. Ordway's. Rocking chairs faced the water. Nothing in the way of libations.

"We're waiting for Father," Kitty explained.

"I see," said Ed. He had the sensation that they were all simply playing a trick on him and that, at any moment, laughter would break out with a pop of champagne. He held his breath and looked around. Helen stood up and leaned against a porch rail. Hugh lit a cigarette.

"Beautiful evening," Ed offered.

"Isn't it?" said Mrs. Ordway. "I never tire of this view. Did you spend summers on the beach as a child?"

"Sometimes," said Ed, remembering noisy and crowded, beloved Nantasket. He fought the urge to smirk. "Sometimes I did."

Nobody moved. Sailboats bobbed in the silver water.

"So——" Ed began, but J.K. and Susannah hopped off their mother's lap and called out, "Captain!"

"Captain?" Ed asked.

"My husband," Mrs. Ordway explained, and she seemed half delighted and half perturbed by his entrance and its accompanying fanfare. "Darling," she called out, "you have broken your rule."

"What's the time, then?" he wondered, looking at his watch. He was shorter than Ed had imagined. "Oh, for Pete's sake." He scowled, as if not he but everyone else was late. J.K. and Susannah took turns hugging their grandfather. They each received a nickel and a pat on the head. "Well, then," he said, "go on."

The children were whisked away for their dinner by the frowning Mrs. Mulroney, and, as they all made their way to the dining room, Ed came up behind Hugh and Helen and whispered, "It's ten after seven. What happened to cocktails?"

"Father doesn't believe in cocktails," Helen whispered back. "Thinks it's a waste of time. I'm afraid he doesn't even drink. One martini a season—or so he says."

"So what's his rule? The one your mother said he broke?"

"If everyone isn't assembled on the porch or living room by seven P.M., dinner starts anyhow."

"Mr. Ordway," said Ed Cantowitz as they approached the table, before he lost the nerve, "I want to thank you for having me."

"Who are you?"

Everyone sat down—pulling out chairs and taking up napkins and muddling the sound of Ed's name.

The food was not good. The servants went around the table, ladling chilled leek soup, doling out overcooked beef and potatoes, green beans gone gray. When Mr. Ordway needed something, he never called out yet, within moments, one of three dour Irish women would bring whatever he needed. Ordway loved ketchup. It was brought out twice, each

time in a silver bowl with an accompanying tiny spoon, until Ed began
to crave it himself. He didn't know if he'd somehow be acting offen-
sively by asking for the ketchup, but finally he came up with the idea that
at least he would get the man's attention.

"Excuse me, sir," Ed said, after taking what he hoped was a tasteful
sip of wine. "Would you mind passing the ketchup?"

"You're a ketchup man, too, eh?"

Ordway made no move to pass the ketchup, but then a strange thing
happened. One of the dour Irish trio sallied forth with a little silver bowl
and spoon evidently just for Ed. He imagined that acquiring a job position in the Ordway household not only involved extensive hearing examinations and a willingness to press one's ears against doors but an
acute understanding that every desire, no matter how small, no matter
how barely articulated, was desire nonetheless.

"Thank you," Ed said, and the maid ignored him. "What a beautiful
spot," said Ed. "I can't get over it."

"We enjoy it," said Mrs. Ordway, before taking a child-sized bite of
beef.

"The house really ought to be reshingled," mused Kitty.

"Well, yes, it *ought* to," said Mrs. Ordway, "but it's too ghastly expensive. Tony told me what it would cost last season, and I tell you I
nearly fell off my chair." She raised her eyebrows, as if to implicate this
Tony. "Just ghastly."

"Kitty gave us a heck of a tour from the ferry dock," said Ed, "but
I'd love to see more of the island."

"Oh, we'll have a busy day tomorrow, don't you worry," said Helen.
"Ed likes to be busy," she teased.

"Nothing wrong with that," said Mr. Ordway, and, from the way
Hugh's smile tightened, Ed could tell he wasn't enjoying himself.

"How old are most of the houses here?" Ed asked quickly.

"Old," sighed Kitty, who was seated to his left, "terribly old."

"End of the nineteenth century," piped up Hugh. "So not that old,
really. It's all relative."

"True," Kitty said. "California-old, then. I absolutely love the houses here." She was drinking what looked to be a tumbler of scotch and seemed to be teetering right on the edge of wistful. Ed didn't know her well enough to know what might be coming next—whether wistful, in Kitty's case, preceded melancholy or hysteria or even glee. "I absolutely love the houses here," she repeated. "I wish I could get away with having a shingle-style house in California, but it would stand out in all kinds of terrible ways. We have a neighbor who has a true stone castle— don't get me wrong, I think it's a fun house, but in Southern California?"

"What does your house look like?" Ed asked. She was, he thought, practically begging to be asked.

"I tell you, there is nothing like these houses," Kitty continued, as if she hadn't heard him. "Though you can't see much from the road, of course. Some people turn up driveways to look, but, I don't know, I think it's vulgar to just go into other people's backyards."

"That's what sailing's for," said Mrs. Ordway, "seeing other people's houses from the water. Heaven knows it's not good for much else."

"I take it you're not much of a sailing fan?" Ed asked.

Mrs. Ordway regarded him. "I like sailing just fine," she said.

"Oh," said Ed, confused.

"But you prefer your garden," said Helen helpfully.

"And your birds," added Kitty.

Mrs. Ordway raised an eyebrow that seemed to signify agreement.

"Mother's an avid birder."

"Do you know the cranes have nearly taken over the salt marshes this year?" Mrs. Ordway declared with what sounded like sudden and wild enthusiasm. "I'm *very* pleased about this," she said. "The past few summers they were dying at an alarming rate. I said to Dr. Bernard, 'Those birds need an *autopsy*,' and don't think he didn't agree. One just had to wonder what the devil was happening."

Ed cleared his throat. "But they're back," Ed tried, "the cranes. That must be . . . a relief."

"Mmn."

Entering a conversation with Mrs. Ordway was like jumping into a professional game of jai alai, with the ball flying from every which way.

"Mrs. Ordway," Ed ventured, "I would love to see your garden tomorrow."

Mrs. Ordway answered with not much more than a faraway "Of course," and he could tell this bothered Kitty. It bothered her that Mrs. Ordway was preoccupied with what was happening at the other end of the table, where no one was smiling and Mr. Ordway was doing all the talking.

"When Helen and I were small," Kitty said, lowering her voice, "Mother taught us the names of all the flowers, how to pick rose hips and beach plums. How to turn them into jelly so that all winter long you'd have a bit of summer at the ready."

Why on earth was she telling him this? Kitty had pinned her hair up, exposing her freckle-scattered neck. She had a strong musky scent that was making him horny as hell.

"She taught us," continued Kitty, "how to pick honeysuckle. How to suck the sweetness from the stem."

Though he'd had only two glasses of wine, he felt slurry in his head and couldn't have been thinking clearly, because it suddenly seemed abundantly clear that Kitty wanted to sleep with him. Kitty Ordway James, eldest and married daughter of Mr. and Mrs. Guy Ordway, sister of Helen—

"Ed?" Helen said.

Ed looked at Helen for what felt like the first time since their arrival. She was flushed, as usual after having some wine, but there was something else. Something agitated. He often had the feeling that she was angry with him, but the one time he ever asked her if this was so, he thought she was genuinely hurt by the question. She was the most perplexing person.

"Well, hello," he replied. "Enjoying your *boeuf*?" He was playing the fool because he felt like one, because it was obvious he didn't belong here. There was a reason that people created clubs at which they dined and swam and golfed and danced with those most like them. He was not like these people. He didn't care about cranes. He understood that this was all some kind of fairy tale, complete with the frosty queen mother seated to his right, and who else could he be here—who, besides the fool?

And yet this queen had taught her daughters to suck honey from a stem. She likely had been just as lovely as her daughters before her grouch of a punctual and financially astute husband wore her down.

Who could be safe from such women?

Hugh? Maybe. Maybe Hugh. But Ed still had his doubts.

He drank a long sip of water and dragged himself from the petal talk, the musk, and the honey; he was light-headed. He needed to have a conversation with men.

"But it *is* an opportunity of a lifetime," Hugh was saying, with a tone that somehow didn't betray any tension.

"I just don't understand, Hugh. You are an intelligent fellow."

"Father," Helen said.

"Now, don't misunderstand me," Mr. Ordway said, leaning back in his chair. "I mean it when I say that I don't understand what he's doing. I only want to understand more. Where he is going. What he is doing. What he is actually *doing*. You are engaged to this man, are you not?"

"Sir," said Hugh, "with all due respect, I don't understand finance at your level, but—"

"But you *could*," Mr. Ordway suggested. "And if you are interested in the world, Hugh, as you say you are, I assure you there is nothing more powerful than currency as a means toward understanding, toward *becoming*, that man of the world."

"Helen," Hugh said. He shook his head.

"Father," Helen started.

Two maids appeared to clear. Mr. Ordway shooed them away.

"Young man," said Mr. Ordway.

Hugh nodded, sitting back in his chair, and Ed had to hand it to him: He looked relaxed as hell; he crossed his legs and pushed away from the table ever so slightly, as if to lay claim to even more space.

"If you are interested in Africa," said Mr. Ordway, "why not make yourself useful there? Some of these countries may have theoretically gained their independence, but don't kid yourself, there is much to be done in the way of creating anything close to functioning systems."

"Mr. Ordway, are you suggesting that I join the Peace Corps?"

"Good God, no."

"Then what?"

"I know in your book this is a dirty word, but there are *profits* to be made. And you are an American. You are not a colonialist. That could go a long way."

Mr. Ordway speared a piece of his meat and dipped it in ketchup. He took his time chewing. Just when Ed was wondering if Ordway might not be finished with this conversation, he leaned forward and lowered his voice: "I am suggesting you don't fritter your education and connections out in the desert, like some kind of . . . dabbler." His lowered voice came across as more aggressive; he may as well have been yelling. "I am suggesting you get a job. A man needs a job. I imagine that your father—though perhaps he may not be interested or . . . able to express these things—I imagine he might agree with me."

Hugh nodded again.

"How about you?" Ordway suddenly called in Ed's direction. "What are you doing?"

"Excuse me, sir?"

"This summer and beyond. Are you going to Africa with your best camera, too?"

Ed brought his napkin to his mouth a touch too carefully. He cleared his throat. "No, sir."

"Well, what, then."

Hugh said, "Ed's going to business school. Harvard."

"Let the man talk," said Ordway. "Though he's yet to bear this out, I have a feeling he's a talker. What do you make of Hugh's plans, Ed?"

Ed balled up his napkin in his lap, took a tactical sip of water. "What do I make of Hugh's plans?" Ed said, stalling. He looked at Hugh as if to say—what? *Help me out here?* "Well . . . Hugh is my friend, Mr. Ord-way."

"And?"

"And . . . our friendship . . . I'm proud to say, is not based on any-thing so banal as common interests." Ed laughed, but no one else did. Nobody was bailing him out. "Look, I respect Hugh's vision," said Ed. "He's—he sees things differently from anyone I know."

"Yes," said Ordway, "that's all fine. But what do you make of this . . . vision?"

Ed glanced at Hugh, who was focused on his plate with distressing intensity.

Ed cleared his throat several times and then made himself stop. "Like Hugh," he said, "I believe in equality." He wished that Hugh would stop looking so obviously grim, which was making him feel badly enough that he was fumbling and losing all sense of purpose. "Look," said Ed, with reinvested vigor, "I'm afraid my own interests are simple." He forced himself to look directly at Mr. Ordway, as if a direct appearance might make up for such a woefully inarticulate response. "I'd like to build a fortune."

As if summoned by the God of Awkward Silences himself, the maids emerged at once.

"Go ahead, then," Mr. Ordway grumbled in their direction. And in they pounced—clearing, bringing dessert plates. Coffee cups. Coffee. For Mr. Ordway, a tall glass of milk.

"Calcium," Mr. Ordway explained, as if this extravagance, above all others, called for justification.

Ed took a bite of something that looked like vanilla pudding and ber-ries but tasted far worse. What he would have given for an Oreo. He looked up at Hugh, who wasn't looking back at him. But Helen was. She was shaking her head, but she was also smiling. He had the distinct feel-ing that she was somehow feeling particularly fondly toward him, but he wasn't sure why. It was disconcerting. Ed turned to Kitty, and—flustered by her undiminished scent, by botching the opportunity to impress Mr.

Ordway, by the stream of alcohol that had more than made up for the forgone cocktails and the fact that Ordway was a teetotaler—he knocked her dessert fork clear off the table. Before he could stop himself, he bent down to retrieve it. It was while he was under the table that he saw something he would always remember—more than the view from the porch, more than Helen's head-shaking, unusually fond smile or even the sight of Kitty under the table, her legs amazingly parted and inviting him to look right up her skirt and see if *the carpet matched the drapes,* the glorious flame-red drapes—as the most significant sight of that weekend.

As it turned out, the Irish maids didn't possess excellent hearing and the Ordways didn't have more-innate timing than every other dinner table across America. They just had a little button. Right atop the table at Mrs. Ordway's spot. And as Ed was retrieving Kitty's fork, he spied the wire that led to that button, which would obviously be ringing in the kitchen.

"Leave it," Mrs. Ordway said.

"Yes, ma'am," said Ed, bolting upright. He felt as if he'd seen something he shouldn't have—not Kitty's glorious parted legs and (sadly opaque) white panties but *the button*—and of course this was absurd. It was only Ed who'd perceived the orchestrations of the evening as magical. This was childish thinking. Everyone at that table had known about the button. And now Ed did, too.

They talked as they rode bikes along that same narrow road, flooded with dappled sunlight. Hugh had a gift for maintaining focus regardless of interference—whether animal or car—and he called back and forth to Helen about John Profumo, whose scandal involving a showgirl had been—as far as Ed was concerned—more than sufficiently covered at the breakfast table. But Hugh and Helen had evidently been left unsatisfied; they seemed dedicated to outdoing each other in a contest of nonchalance.

"Commitment has to mean something," said Ed, before pedaling madly to pass them by.

On hearing their laughter, he'd gone red-faced, but he'd also felt victorious about passing. And he believed what he said. It irritated him that they were so casual about a married Member of Parliament carrying on with a teenager and so casual about their own plans. If Ed, by some means, in some otherworldly scenario, had been the one to put a diamond on Helen's finger, there would've been nothing casual about it.

As he pedaled ahead, he coasted down a hill so green he thought: *Ireland*. He imagined he'd go to Ireland one day and that by then he'd think: *Fishers Island*. He'd tell someone a story about this weekend; he wondered what it would be. He passed a pond, a graveyard, and three girls drawing in colored chalk on the road. Riding a shiny red bicycle—probably brand-new this season—a husky kid shouted, "I'm gonna beat you!" and—in an uncharacteristic move—Ed let him.

They arrived at the yacht club, and it was shabbier than Ed had anticipated. It smelled vaguely of floor wax. There were shelves full of trophies and cups in need of a polish and walls of framed photographs featuring rugged, triumphant men who looked nothing like anyone in his family. He followed his friends through the wood-paneled reception area and onto the dock, where Helen's red-faced uncle was dressed in worn-out tennis whites, looking as if he'd just finished three sets and run from the courts. "Wind's up," he said, while hurriedly shaking Ed's hand. "Haven't you been sailing before? Can't wear those shoes."

"Oh, we forgot to remind you," said Helen. "That's fine," she said. "You can go barefoot."

But Ed didn't want to go barefoot. His feet were pale and hairy, and it was still technically springtime. He felt such sudden rage toward the two of them for letting him wear the wrong shoes that he said nothing. He just tossed his shoes and socks in a heap before walking toward a gleaming sailboat.

"She's the best thing that ever happened to me," the uncle told Hugh. "Look at her. Forgive me, Helen, but she's in a tight race with you for elegance."

"She's beautiful, Uncle Larry."

Though he didn't like knowing nothing about what to pull or where to sit, as they pushed off into the whitecapped sea, Ed started to relax again. The gulls were hypnotic in their flight and the water was undeniably lulling, until there was such a great blast in his ear that Ed truly thought a bomb had exploded and was baffled as to why a bomb would be detonated right here off Fishers Island. He'd gone so far in his mind as to deduce that the high concentration of banking families and likely CIA operatives who called this island home might be the reason and, of course, there he was, stupidly thinking it was some kind of paradise. . . .

Hugh and Helen were talking, but he only saw their lips moving. He saw the sun still shining. But then he made out the thinnest sound of laughter, and when he saw Helen's uncle Larry right beside him (Larry, Ed had learned during the brisk business of untying the knotted ropes, had become an ambassador to Austria after winning some big case at a New Jersey law firm), Ed realized it was Uncle Larry who was laughing. Laughing and holding his bullhorn. Which, Ed also realized, had been sounded directly and intentionally into Ed's ear.

"Uncle Larry!" cried Helen. And before Ed could think too much about it, he grabbed for the bullhorn.

"Easy, now," said the Austrian ambassador.

"Give it," said Ed, ignoring the waves, which were increasing in size and tossing the boat side to side, or the fact that he knew nothing about sailing protocol. Maybe it was normal to sound a bullhorn in your guest's ear, potentially bursting their eardrum. Maybe it was, but Ed was so angry he didn't care. "Give it here, you bastard," said Ed.

And, amazingly, Larry did.

"Apologize," shouted Ed. "That was a rotten thing to do."

"Come about," called Hugh, and Ed knew just enough to duck down low while the boom swept over their heads.

"This is my goddamn boat," said Uncle Larry. "Who named you captain?"

"We're headed back now," said Hugh.

"Come on," cried out Larry, "don't be a spoilsport."

Seemingly out of nowhere, another sailboat sailed close by, and when everyone on that boat smiled and waved, Hugh, Helen, and Uncle Larry smiled and waved right back. Ed watched the boat sail off into the distance. The name was *Fifty-Fifty*. Ed wondered what it could mean.

As soon as the boat was gone, Larry spoke up. "I was just having some fun with your friend."

Nobody spoke.

Helen inched closer to Ed. The wind whipped her hair about her head. She was going to have a wrinkle shaped like the letter *V* between her brows someday.

Uncle Larry worked assiduously on coiling ropes. Then he and Hugh docked the boat in silence. *They're graceful,* Ed observed, without taking any pleasure in the observation. They each knew exactly what to do without speaking or even seeming to look at the other, and this was—for a few moments, anyway—enough to distract him from the ringing in his ears and from what he could have sworn were tears in Helen's eyes. He'd never seen Helen cry and couldn't imagine why she'd do so now.

"Can you hear me?" she asked.

"Don't worry," said Ed. "Clear as a bell."

"I'm sorry about my uncle," whispered Helen. "I'm really sorry."

Ed was struck mute by her obvious and touching concern.

"Did you hear what I just said?" she asked.

But Ed didn't answer, and she didn't ask again.

They went next door to a house full of pallid cousins, one thinner and paler than the next. They lunched on ham, olives, and not much else, before changing into their swimming suits and heading down yet another dock.

Kitty's children chased them, and before Ed quite realized what was happening, the cousins had pushed him, Hugh, Helen, and Kitty into the water. When Ed surfaced, he was startled, until he realized that Kitty was laughing and calling out, "Well done, you got us this time!"

Here was yet another tradition of which he hadn't been warned. He watched Kitty's children scream with laughter and run up the lawn.

"We'll see them over at the country club," Helen explained, a bit breathless from treading water. "Mother will take them."

"Are we swimming there?" asked Hugh. "God, this water feels good." And he dove under, a plodding crawl leading into a preposterously flawless butterfly.

"Just follow us," said Helen. "It's about a mile."

"I didn't know you were such an athlete," Ed cried.

"I told you we'd keep you busy!" And off she swam.

Ed followed at a distance with bursts of swimming, surfacing all too frequently to orient himself, to make sure he wasn't going too far out of the way. The water was bracing and he was grateful for it, pleased to do something that required nothing but skills he already possessed. He pictured his mother at Nantasket, in a worried stance with her hands on her hips, watching him from the shore. But right as he began to see what looked like a beach in the distance, he found himself tangled in what he was sure were water snakes, and he began to scream. He fought to get out, but they were everywhere. Ed had followed the others, so why wouldn't someone have called to him, warning him to turn back or at least to swim farther out to sea instead of hugging the coast? As he cursed the others and cursed himself, he bore his way through the slimy mess of snakes, hollering and splashing, only to realize that the snakes were not snakes, of course. They were seaweed. And as the seaweed stroked his cheeks and twined itself with his calves and thighs, he promised himself that, when he finally made it to that beach club, he would keep to himself just how deeply he disliked this swim.

By the time he broke free, his heart was pumping as if he'd come face-to-face with a shark instead of a goddamn underwater plant, but there he was, feet on warm sand, before a scattering of lithe men and women lounging on chairs or watching their children or reading the newspaper, and there were Kitty's children cheering (they were chanting his name!), and a brunette offered him a towel. There was beer, so much beer, and the beer tasted better than beer had ever tasted, even better than after he'd done nothing but lay pipes in the ground for eight hours straight in terrible heat, and by the time they all piled into someone's convertible, Ed had no idea what time it was, but the light had softened and Kitty and her children were all in the backseat with him, and he was drunk. He was drunk already and it wasn't even dusk. He would have thought four years at Harvard would have prepared him for this kind of pace, but at Harvard he hadn't been asked to swim at least a mile—most of it through seaweed—only to sit next to Kitty Ordway James and her damp red hair.

"What?" Kitty was smiling, her breasts *right there,* barely restrained under a navy one-piece, a towel wrapped around her waist.

"I didn't say anything," said Ed.

He sobered up long enough to take a bath in his room, long enough to manage with his cuff links and a tie, long enough to realize, with something of a shock, that he was having a really good time. He wondered if Hugh was having even a fraction of the fun he was having, and he realized that it deeply mattered to him whether Hugh was having fun. *I'll make a point to let him know this,* Ed thought, and then it occurred to him that he was not, in fact, yet sober. *Fifty-Fifty*: The boat that passed them earlier popped into his head. Was the boat jointly owned? Or was it a comment about odds? He realized that he was starving.

Sunset brought them back to the yacht club's dock, and he almost hoped to see Helen's jackass uncle. But instead of a sailboat, instead of competitive Larry with his sweaty tennis whites, a long shiny boat with a second story of varnished wood awaited. Ed stepped onto it, and when a fellow in a white jacket offered him a cocktail, he almost said to Hugh, *Now, this is more like it,* but he knew better; of course he did. He'd had to be more careful ever since they'd stepped off that ferryboat. It was as if the more superficial the environment, the more seriously Hugh took every last thing. What surprised Ed was that he didn't feel like pointing it out. He was always the one to push Hugh into talking about anything remotely personal, but for the past twenty-four hours he'd been less inclined to do so.

It might have been that there were too many stimuli here for such discussions. This boat had an *elevator*. He thought of that boy with his brand-new bicycle, the excitement in his voice. Ed wanted to ride this elevator up and down one more time and memorize the slight dip in gravity that occurred before the doors opened up to the staterooms. Instead, he followed his friends to an already crowded party. He listened as Helen explained how seven summers ago her great-aunt Mary had given a party right here and how everyone had arrived full of morbid sentiments, as it was generally understood that Great-Aunt Mary wasn't long for this earth. And yet she seemed to be going nowhere except Palm Beach each winter. She was one hundred and three and drinking champagne in a deck chair.

"All the women in my family are addicted to champagne," continued Helen, making her way through the crowd. "Aunt Mary claims my grandmother put it in my mother's baby bottle and that she did the same with us. Aunt Mary," Helen shouted. "This is my fiancé, Hugh Shipley."

The old lady stuck out her clawlike hand to Ed.

"Oh no," said Helen, "this is our *friend* Ed Cantowitz."

Ed took her hand. It was surprisingly warm.

"*This* is Hugh," Helen repeated.

Aunt Mary looked up and smiled. She'd lost her eyebrows, in addition to whatever tautness her skin had once possessed, but her cheekbones were prominent, her eyes bright green. Hugh gave her a kiss on the cheek.

"For a moment I thought you were marrying the Jewish fellow."

"Oh," said Helen, trying to laugh it off, "no, I'm afraid not."

"I'm sure you're a fine young man," the old lady said to Ed. Her voice was shaky, vaguely British. She was not remotely out of it, nor did she seem cruel. She only wanted to get it straight. Somehow, this was worse.

"I need another drink," said Hugh, leading Ed away. "I've about reached my limit," Hugh added. "I think there's a two A.M. ferry to New London."

But just as Ed was about to reassure Hugh that he was fine, just fine, he realized that Hugh might not be. That Hugh looked genuinely uncomfortable. Just as Ed was about to start in about the benefits of lightening up, Helen's father stepped off the elevator, and Ed watched Mr. Ordway say hello to each and every person, ghosting along the surface of the crowd like some kind of seriously skilled professional, more prophet than politician.

"Look at you," said Hugh. "You *like* him."

"I don't," said Ed.

"I think we may have come across the one thing we cannot beat to death with conversation," Hugh said. He lit a cigarette, and the heavy lighter fell closed with a snap.

"It's not about whether I like him."

Hugh took an unpleasantly long drag. "I know," he said as he exhaled. But he walked off anyway, halfheartedly shaking his empty glass.

Ed looked past the women with their newly suntanned arms and charm bracelets and the men with their starched crisp shirts. He looked past Helen in coral and Kitty in pink, and there was the water, so blue it looked black, with the sun about to offer up its last green flash. He found the moon full to bursting, but the sky remained light; it was, Ed remembered, the longest day of the year. The moon was closer than ever and there they were, right this moment, tilting toward the sun.

"You wouldn't know to look at it," said Mr. Ordway, who was suddenly right beside him, "but this place has been shaped by disasters."

"Sir," Ed said, shaking Ordway's hand. "Good to see you."

"All the trees on this island were destroyed by a hurricane. It was over a century ago."

"Is that right?"

"Can you imagine a force that strong?"

"Yep," Ed said, nodding, "I think I can."

"Another one blew through in '38, spreading seeds, returning all the trees." Mr. Ordway put his hands in his pockets. He shook his head.

Ed realized Ordway wasn't drinking anything, not even water, and that this was somehow unnerving.

"Is that right?" Ed asked. "After so much time."

"That a martini?"

Ed nodded again.

"Have them *wave* vermouth over the top of the glass. It's the only way."

Ed almost spilled his drink. "*Wave* the vermouth. I'll have to remember that."

"I get the feeling you're taking some notes."

"Maybe," said Ed, laughing. "Maybe I am. Did you grow up here, sir?"

"Oh no," Ordway said.

Ed waited. He knew better than to ask.

Ordway looked at him and then looked away. In that one small look, Ed knew he'd decided something.

"I grew up all over this country," he said, as if he was offering proof of something, but of what Ed had no idea. "My father was an itinerant sort. Minister. Bet you can't believe that."

"Well, it's not what I would have expected, but, sure, I can believe it. I can believe all kinds of things."

"My poor mother played the organ in one church after the other and never bothered making any friends. My father was a tough actor, if you want to know the truth."

"Mine, too," said Ed, and instantly regretted it.

"Is that right? Well, seems like you did fine to me." He shrugged angrily, as if speaking ill of one's father was his exclusive right. "My old man died at forty-seven, but before he died he also happened to teach me several things. Among them was this: It is just as easy to love a rich girl as a poor one, and if you're going to meet a rich girl, you have to learn how to dance. So I became a great dancer." He grinned. "And that's how I met Helen's mother."

Ed was sorry he'd interrupted. He wanted more than anything for Mr. Ordway to keep talking. "And where was that?"

"A woman like my wife doesn't wander into a church social in some Podunk town, now, does she?"

"I'd imagine not."

"I tell you, I was walking along the same miserable dirt road I always walked each morning to my miserable school and, on my life, a man offered me a ride. This man was wealthy and generous, and I owe my good fortune to him, God rest his soul. Was he idiosyncratic? Was he impulsive? You bet he was. But he was also shrewd. You'll think I'm pulling your leg, but by the time he left me in front of my miserable school, he'd decided to send me to boarding school."

"He was a quick study."

"Don't I know it." Ordway nodded. "So, you see, *that's* how I met my wife. Not directly, not at the school—which wasn't even on the East Coast, by the way, but on an island off the Washington coast—but it was through that one chance meeting. Mr. Ivry. I must have impressed the hell out of that man, wouldn't you say?"

"I'd love to know what you said in that car."

"I don't remember a thing, son. And don't think I haven't wondered." Mr. Ordway smiled at someone across the deck. His face lifted for a moment.

When a waiter offered a tray of cheese puffs, Ordway declined, and so—with a heavy heart—Ed did, too.

"So you made your way east?"

"Mmn," said Ordway, "something like that."

"Well, that's some story," Ed said.

"I also made my share of mistakes before I fully turned to God. Gambled my first earnings away like an idiot, and those were some significant earnings."

"Are you a religious man?" Ed asked, already knowing the answer.

"Of course I am," said Mr. Ordway. "Aren't you?"

"I—"

"Take my advice: no gambling."

"No," said Ed. "That's not for me."

"I didn't think so. You fellows are good with money. You don't part with it easily."

Ed forced a laugh.

"Unlike all the guests at this party except for that fellow over there, right there." He gestured with his drink toward the distance. "I didn't inherit my money. My wife's trust is not the bulk of my fortune and I know about work, so don't go thinking otherwise." Mr. Ordway's voice went cold. "Got it?"

"Got it," said Ed.

Mr. Ordway nodded. Then he walked away. Ed watched him greet a woman with a brooch pinned to her chest—a dazzling jewel-encrusted insect.

They were the last guests to leave Great-Aunt Mary's party. There were more martinis, and, at Ed's insistence, they rode the elevator up and down until he felt sick and agreed to leave. Hugh drove Kitty's convertible. "Where's your sister?" asked Ed. "She didn't say goodbye."

Helen extended her hand out the passenger side, stretching into the night. "Careful," Hugh said.

"My sister was bored," Helen said. And Ed had the distinct feeling that Helen wanted him to think Kitty was bored specifically with him.

"Oh," said Ed, looking up at the trees. "That's too bad."

"She gets very motherly out of the blue when she's bored at parties. As if her children have never stayed with a sitter before. *I have to go home to the children.* It bugs me."

"I think you're jealous," said Ed lightly. "Watch out, Hugh," he teased. "Helen wants a baby."

"Shut up," said Helen sharply.

"Easy," said Hugh.

"You just shut up about that," she said.

"I'm sorry," Ed said. "I didn't . . ."

They drove in silence.

The swollen moon lit up the roads and the lawns, and as they approached the darkened Ordway home, Helen decided it was time to play tennis. Hugh knocked over several golf bags in the mudroom while looking for rackets, and Ed tossed a tennis ball between his hands.

"Catch," he said to Helen, and she caught it. They tossed the ball back and forth. "I'm sorry," Ed said again. But she ignored him.

"You know," said Ed, "I still haven't seen your mother's garden. That's what I'm going to do right now." He started walking. "See you in the morning."

"Helen," Ed heard Hugh say, his voice laced with both impatience and contrition, "he said he was sorry."

Ed turned around, already in the middle of the lush green lawn. He looked at his friends. They stood together holding tennis rackets; it was two o'clock in the morning. Ed held up his arms as if he was surrendering. *I give up,* he mimed. But what, and to whom, was he conceding?

Mrs. Ordway's garden was unexpectedly wild. It was as if she had put her every last unacted-upon urge down into that soil. Every square inch was planted, there was little in the way of borders, and as Ed tried and failed to name most of the flowers, he felt those plants competing, acting out some kind of horticultural survival of the fittest. The garden was the opposite of peaceful, but he'd almost fallen asleep right there. The scent of something like rich white wine sent him down to the grass, before he picked himself up and made his way inside the house, feeling like a burglar. Though a hedge obscured the tennis court, the court lights were on, and Ed wondered if Hugh and Helen were keeping score or simply lobbing the ball back and forth, carrying on a conversation. Ed noticed the lights in the library, too, and wondered if Mr. Ordway—like his own father—prided himself on not needing to sleep. Ed needed sleep. Although he rarely admitted to doing so, he liked to nap daily; he was convinced it made him a more effective thinker.

It was still hot; he stripped, and after carefully hanging his clothes on the back of a wicker chair, he lay down in bed next to an open window, below a rotating ceiling fan. It was hotter inside than it had been all day. He closed his eyes and heard the ball bouncing back and forth on the clay court, the fixed and fretful rhythm. He thought of the garden and remembered—hydrangea!—the name of those fragrant purple blossoms. Somehow being able to identify that powder-heavy scent released him into the kind of slumber he hadn't had in days.

When Hugh shook him awake and tossed him his still-wet bathing suit, Ed said, "Let me sleep," but before he knew it his feet were in the grass, damp from the sprinkler, and he was back outside, in the dark. "What time is it?" he asked, but Hugh ignored him. Helen was ahead of them both, already down at the water's edge amidst the reeds and below the dock, where low tide revealed the shore.

"Come on," she said, and when Ed saw she was in her panties and brassiere, he pretended not to notice.

"Nah," Ed said, as Hugh dove in. "No thanks. I'll stand guard. I'll make sure you two stay safe."

When Helen laughed, he laughed, too, but it didn't feel like laughter. It felt like acute discomfort and awareness, and though he pretended not to notice the slope of her stomach, the high hipbones and thighs that were even more exciting than her breasts, he did nothing but notice. Those thighs held up her ample behind, a lushness that was always somehow unexpected on such a coltish frame. He was reminded of a giraffe; Helen the giraffe, passing through the African savanna. He had to close his eyes.

"Bye!" she called out, before diving under.

And when he opened his eyes to bright light and a bedside clock that read nearly 7:00 A.M., he knew he'd dreamed the late-night swimming and also Helen's body in her bra and panties, which would remain—as well it should—one of life's great secrets.

His pounding headache and unquenchable thirst notwithstanding, he gently showered, shaved, put on his clothes, and was looking forward to a moment alone. If coffee was available, that would be all the better, but mostly he wanted to sit on that porch, to be awake before the others, before the day—before his life—began.

But of course he wasn't alone. Of course Mr. Ordway was seated at the head of the dining room table, four different newspapers spread before him. Ed chose to say nothing, and this seemed like a sensible choice. When he went into the kitchen, Mrs. Mulroney was listening to a transistor radio, smoking a cigarette.

"What can I get for you?" she asked. But Ed could tell she wasn't about to exert herself for someone like him. She must have become practiced, over the years, in making such assessments.

Ed cleared his throat. "A cup of coffee would be swell."

She put out her cigarette but kept on the radio. It sounded like some kind of liturgy.

"I'm sorry to bother you," he said.

She waved him out of the kitchen.

When he approached the table, Ed decided to sit as far away from Ordway as possible. He didn't take a section of the paper, nor did he look at his host, but after Mrs. Mulroney appeared with a cup of coffee, Mr. Ordway pushed *The New York Times* in Ed's direction.

"Thank you," said Ed. He took a sip of coffee—weak but hot.

Ordway nodded. He was hunched over *The Wall Street Journal*, which was spread atop the table like an architect's drawings, secured at one corner by a silver bowl of ketchup.

Ordway cleared his throat. "When I come to Fishers, I know the paper delivery is unreliable. So I bring the whole previous week's worth. Do you know what was invented over a century ago Thursday?"

Ed prepared himself for a discussion on any number of potentially difficult headline-inspired topics: civil rights, the separation of church and state, the communist threat in Southeast Asia.

Ed shook his head. "No idea, I'm afraid."

"The donut."

"No kidding."

"Some son of a bitch made a fortune. Can you imagine? All because he had a craving, I presume." He shook his head. Ordway's plate of food—a poached egg and potatoes—was untouched.

From upstairs, Ed heard the muffled voices of Kitty's children and their footsteps followed by what must have been their mother's slower gait. "Get ready," said Mr. Ordway, "here they come." He folded up the paper and took a bite of eggs. "What are you eating?"

"Oh," said Ed, "I don't know. That looks awfully good."

"I eat it every day."

"Really?"

"Every day."

"Huh."

"One less decision."

"I see what you mean."

Mr. Ordway grinned tightly. "Listen—and I don't want to talk about this any further, not with my grandchildren bouncing around—but you'll come to work for me this summer."

"Sir—"

"It's done." He began stacking up the papers.

Ed thought of how, as far as he knew, no Jew had ever worked at Ordway Keller. But it wasn't a commercial bank (*No Jews*, his favorite economics professor had cut him off, laughing darkly, when Ed had broached the question of working for one), so he supposed it was technically possible. Then he thought of how his own father would react when Ed relayed this offer. "I—I'm afraid I have another obligation, sir." Murray Cantowitz had demanded one last summer as payment for Ed's (despite the scholarship) pricey undergraduate degree. "But thank you, sir. Thank you so much for the offer."

"Change it," said Mr. Ordway, as he drowned a fried potato in a golden yolk.

"But why would you want—"

"It's done," he said.

By the time the others made their way to the table, Ed was long gone. He was sitting in what was—at least for the next several hours—still his room. He tried, unsuccessfully, to knock his father's desolate face out of his mind. He'd made the bed even though he didn't have to, and he was sitting on that bed, with his suitcase packed.

Ed was thinking of something Hugh had told him soon after they'd met, not even a year ago:

People like my father—and I know this makes no sense—they actually have no respect for their own. The money gets passed down, and, with it, a deep mistrust. The money undermines every decision you make. They give you the money so they can say: What would you do without it?

Ed had not believed him. They'd argued about it, of course.

He looked out the open window; the sun was already blazing. He watched Mrs. Ordway lug a watering can clear across the lawn, and, recalling her garden (although it, too, felt like part of his unshakable, unspeakable dream), he could see why she would be motivated to water those plants on her own, day after day. He heard a tennis ball getting going again. Hugh's muffled baritone; Helen's silvery laugh. Back and forth, back and forth. New day, new game.

Chapter Six

Summer, Ethiopia

Dawn in Ciengach was muted, the sky not overhead but everywhere. It was like being deep down under the sea, and when Hugh opened his eyes, he was caught in a net, *just* able to make out the surface above—the silvery promise of light. For these first moments and before the true sunrise, Hugh could still see the previous night and its faded constellations. He was unaccustomed to such a view but also to this particular type of exhaustion. Sleeping on the hard desert floor was not entirely familiar, but he'd camped enough as a boy in New England that it wasn't entirely *un*familiar, either. Stranger still was that, after a lifetime of never remembering his dreams, for these past several nights one dream was more vivid than the next; they went on and on and were almost exclusively populated by his mother.

By the breakfast fire, Charlie Case stirred a pot of beans, and his codirector, Etienne Marceau—who had importantly secured funding from French television for this excursion—indicated with his pointy chin the coffeepot, the cups. *"Café?"* he asked Hugh, with what was either (Hugh could never tell) trepidation or disinterest.

"Oui," said Hugh gamely. He was nothing if not polite. *"Bonjour."* And then he was full of questions for Charlie Case, who—in addition to

being his filmmaking, world-exploring fearless leader—also happened to recently value morning conversations about dreams. Charlie had met and loved a Jungian in Los Angeles during his essentially unproductive meetings with the Hollywood producers, and well in advance of when the cows here began their daily bellowing and moaning (their eagerness to reach temporary freedom out on full display by precisely 10:30 A.M.), Hugh took Charlie (and, inadvertently, Etienne) through his previous night's mystery.

He could never relay his dreams without imagining Ed taking in Charlie's nodding and Etienne's furrowed brow, how Ed's wiseass face would surely twist into a grin comprised equally of disdain and good humor. Ed would have changed the subject by the time the god-awful coffee had brewed. *Boring,* Ed would say with a laugh. *Do you people hear yourselves? Other people's dreams?* Then he'd proceed to balk at the ensuing insulted response: *What. What?*

"They should have let you go to your mother's funeral," said Charlie, repeating his primary refrain before dipping a precious cracker in his bowl. He was a quick eater, always the first one finished, but somehow this seemed efficient instead of greedy.

"Probably," said Hugh, "because what I remember instead is a clown putting a bird on my head. That's probably where all those feathers are coming from—don't you think?—the feathers in the dreams?" He took his first bite of watery beans and tried not to wince.

"Ze bird on ze head!" cried Etienne, who loved this detail as if it were a famous scene from Truffaut. "And your nanny, Meez Peg? *Mon Dieu.*"

"She's what you call cold comfort," said Charlie.

"She was all right," said Hugh.

"They should have let you go to the funeral," Charlie repeated, squinting into the already blazing sun. "We're all so damn scared of death in the West."

"Well," Hugh said, squinting at Charlie, "that's because it's so damn scary."

On the way toward here, when the road looked downright tenuous and Hugh's head was pounding from dehydration so forcefully he couldn't even smoke, when his eyes were stinging with sweat and he was certain they'd made a wrong turn, they had—each of them—witnessed a lion rip off an antelope's head. Hugh had felt an icy fear that both surprised and shamed him. In all of his fantasies of coming to Africa, he'd never considered the *animals*.

"Although," Hugh continued, "a magic show seems an awfully macabre alternative to a funeral. When I thought about my mother afterward, I always pictured her being sliced in half. Do you know I pictured her in a box with the blade sawing through her?"

"Goddamn," said Charlie. He put down his bowl and spoon; he actually looked as though he might be sick. "You ever tell anyone that?"

"You mean when I was a kid?"

"I mean ever."

Hugh looked at Charlie—his bloodshot blue eyes and thinning brown hair—and he could tell that Charlie cared about him, about what he was going to say. And when Hugh shrugged and shook his head, Charlie put his hand on Hugh's back for a brief but certain pat.

With their tails swishing back and forth as young men ushered them to pasture, the Nuer's cows commanded their full attention. As the volume of the village rose in a specific drone of young men singing and beckoning and cows frantically baying, Hugh stepped on the embers, put out the breakfast fire, and followed Charlie and Etienne toward the cattle. He noticed how Charlie walked quickly and said nothing now, as if the conversation had finished hours ago. Charlie walked as if he wanted nothing more than to shake off not only Hugh but also Etienne, whose most oft-used expression was: *I wonder, Charlie.* Etienne said this the same way each and every time, with the very same puzzled pitch, as if asking a question was, in itself, a terribly novel idea. He was also fixated on dancing. On the Nuer dancing. Preferably at night. Preferably by firelight. The Nuer were known for dance, and it was dance he wished to film. From the time he met Hugh and Charlie at the airstrip in Gambela and throughout their blighted inferno-hot ten-hour ride in the loathsome Land Rover, Etienne never stopped his wondering: *if they will dance without rain, if it will be different, better, less filmic, more expressive.* Hugh wrestled between crazed laughter and the urge to holler, *WHY DON'T WE WAIT AND SEE?*

"I don't want to force—*n'est pas?*" said Etienne right then, gesticulating far more wildly than his tone, as if his hands were doing the real talking, "but, maybe—I wonder, Charlie—we might . . . begin to *promote* ze idea of dancing?"

Charlie didn't take his eyes off the cattle.

"I see," said Etienne, and he expertly—almost medically—wrapped his head in a scarf. "*Bien.* I will go and I will ask them myself." Etienne walked off, shaking his head and calling for Nhial, their patient interpreter, a lean man of thirty years who had—years ago—evidently gone to university in Nairobi. Despite Etienne's sense of urgency, Hugh had a feeling his first stop would be to secure their dinner source, as Charlie had been in charge the previous night and the scrawniness of the chicken had sent Etienne—who had actually spent years at a time living in the bush—into an out-and-out panic.

When the cattle and the young men and Etienne were all out of sight, the village took on a sudden and eerie quiet, punctuated by the sounds of women sweeping insects from their cool mud floors. Charlie sat in the dirt, with his legs crossed beneath him, and watched the absence of the cows in what looked like a kind of trance, and Hugh knew better than to speak to him. He knew to simply accept the Bolex camera (which Charlie seemed to enjoy rather formally handing over, as if trusting Hugh to use it was an official assignment) and to listen to his mentor, though Charlie rarely offered much in the way of instruction. "Well," Charlie said, before wandering off with his own, more-cumbersome Arriflex, which was more like a third arm, so deeply was it a part of him, "you might want to shoot some dung." And Hugh understood that he was supposed to make himself scarce until late afternoon, when the cattle would come flooding back. The cattle's cycle—back and forth from village to pasture, from freedom to tether—was the perfect embodiment of repetition in landscape, so strongly did it resemble a tide, and Charlie wanted as much coverage as possible. And though it seemed as if the cattle were slaves to this cycle, the Nuer people in fact revolved around them. The cows were sung to, blessed—all but literally worshipped.

Looking across the dusty expanse, past the wooden stakes now empty of cows—aside from one lone heifer who remained tethered and crying, presumably for its mother—Hugh saw a young woman emerge from one of the conical huts in the distance, covered in a worn brown sheet. She made her way slowly toward the heifer, carrying a slender jug. After approaching the calf, she held its face in her hands.

He had an overwhelming sense that he was about to do something shameful, like a wave of needing to relieve himself or maybe even vomit, but then he realized he was thinking of his own mother, although *thinking* was too precise—too sane—a word for what this was. How could he *think* about someone who was a mother to him as a baby, as a toddler, but who drank so much that there was no other conclusion but to think that she had been a miserable mother, a mother without hope or relief or joy, a mother who could have easily killed him each and every time they were left alone? He'd gone most of his life without dwelling on her absence and its cause, and now that he was as far away from home as he could ever get, he could not get her out of his head. And because he had only that one real memory of the fogged-up glass, even though she was in his head, he couldn't actually picture her. Genevieve Conrad Shipley. He'd been told his whole life not to dwell on such a troubled soul, and he had listened.

It did occur to him that his increasingly unquiet mind was punishment for not having given her the consideration she'd deserved just for bringing him into this world. Here—after all—here on this dusty patch of earth, life was lived for one's ancestors; every act of the living was meant—if not to honor and delight them—to appease them. It did occur to him that he was being haunted.

The young woman in the distance held her trusting calf's face. Then she gradually tilted back its head and slowly poured the contents of the jug down the heifer's throat.

Instead of the Bolex, Hugh instinctively took up his Leica, through which he'd done his best looking for years, memorizing every detail of not only Helen but Ed, too, of the weeds and flowers that littered the roadsides of, the snow and slush and evening lights of, the utter familiarity of Cambridge, Massachussetts. The woman with the cow called to mind an afternoon by the pond this spring: He'd been lying with his head in Helen's lap. She'd said, *Open up,* before putting a wine bottle to his lips, and the wine had slid down his throat. When he'd looked up at Helen, she was blocking out the sun; he'd snapped a picture. There were so many afternoons by that pond, in the townhouse; they rushed through his mind before he fell asleep. But now, as his subject was framed in this lens he knew so well, he had to turn away. The young woman was intensely beautiful. Her beauty wasn't shocking—on the contrary, these were overwhelmingly superb-looking people—but the effect of her beauty was. As she tended to the cow, as she'd let the sheet fall, Hugh felt as if he'd been kicked in the gut. She was bare-breasted and encircled in ivory at her arms and waist. She also was covered with oozing sores. He'd never felt so physically attracted to a woman and at the same time so repelled. Which was worse? The sheer fact that he was watching her at a distance, turned on like some pervert at a peep show? Or that he was repulsed? He honestly didn't know.

They'd known about the possibility of smallpox, but nothing could have prepared Hugh for the dominance of this disease. With one hand stroking the calf's neck, the young woman held it gently, and her expression was no less than adoring, as if only helping the calf could afford her some relief. Perhaps in an effort to distract from the powerful attraction he felt for this Nuer girl—whom he couldn't help but try to imagine free of sores—his Yankee brain conjured up Mr. Cantowitz. Right there in Ethiopia—*Hello, Mr. Cantowitz, it must be a hundred fucking degrees, yes, that's true*—Hugh remembered how Ed's father supposedly resented all the attention paid to children. Hugh wondered if there was some poor bitter Nuer equivalent who found himself wrestling with this: *What exactly is so great about these cows?*

He watched the girl and the calf until the girl walked off, huddled under her foul cloth, most likely toward the swamp—the only water source, where everyone in the village (including the interloping film crew) also procured their drinking water—to wash and ease her disfiguring sores.

The sun was high in the sky. He hadn't shot a single photograph.

He thought of setting off for the swamp but was plagued with the notion that he was observing what he shouldn't. He knew he needed to get over this—*obviously*—because why else was he here? Why had he put off marriage and refused to get a job, refused to begin—at the very least—a graduate degree? Why had he endured the dusty gutted roads in the overloaded Land Rover with the busted rear springs, lost muffler, and gasoline leaks? Why had he waited out the essential rebuilding of the vehicle every few miles in sharp, stultifying heat or sometimes in the pouring rain? Why had he waded knee deep in mud and cow shit as Etienne refused to speak English and then refused to speak at all while Charlie shouted every curse word he could think of at whoever challenged his ideas? Why had he risked his life hailing the gangster truck driver who—for a steep price—had dragged them to this very village? Why had he done all of this if not to watch?

The Nuer weren't afraid to watch *them*. With early evening came the dung fires, and with those first wafts of vaporous smoke came the crowds outside their tents. Their tents were—stupidly—brightly colored, and so even though they had originally positioned themselves at a respectful distance from the far-sturdier homes of the Nuer, those tents might just as well have been the circus. There was never any bartering, only yes or no. *Give me that flashlight* was a typical greeting. And despite countless warnings from Charlie (first by letter, then on Air Afrique, and throughout their cursed two-day drive from the airstrip), Hugh was polite to the point of sycophantic, and by the second nightfall he'd predictably given away his flashlight in addition to nearly all of his allotment of cigarettes for the following day. And since cigarettes were never requested by the Nuer, only demanded, and since at least once each day they were simply taken right from Hugh's pocket, Hugh was going to have a personal crisis if he didn't learn to say no.

Their most frequent Nuer visitors were unmarried young men just like him (though, en masse, far more confident), men who clearly had plenty of time to socialize and make demands. These demands were un-ending and there was never a moment of privacy, no matter how many times Charlie told Nhial and Nhial told the Nuer men that they would like a moment's peace.

"Please," Charlie had said yesterday evening, as they were gnawing on that scrawny chicken's bones. "Please, Nhial, I'm beggin' you. Tell them we'd like some privacy."

Hugh started giggling, until he was howling with laughter that even he immediately recognized as unhinged.

Charlie sputtered, "Why are you laughing?"

"Listen to yourself! We've come all this way to try to know them and you're shooing them away!"

"Go fuck yourself, Shipley," said Charlie, but he was laughing, too.

Nhial finally said a few words to the small crowd, and then Etienne whispered something to Nhial.

"Etienne?" asked Charlie, with a chicken bone between his teeth. "What are you up to?"

"I am only asking him," said Etienne, after an audible exhale, "about the possibility of a dance."

This only made Hugh laugh harder.

"Stop it," said Etienne. "You are acting like imbeciles."

"It's impossible to take a shit around here," mused Charlie. "Have you noticed that?"

Hugh nodded, laughing so deeply that he risked taking an accidental piss right then and there.

"The term *vanishing point* has a whole new meaning. I swear I walk farther and farther away every time."

"The Nuer have the advantage," Hugh managed to say. "No clothing to remove." He'd seen old men walk down dips in the landscape, crouching until they were invisible. He'd seen women stroll off toward the horizon, squatting behind a tree. And then there were those on the periphery of his vision, wavering in the heat like desert chimeras. These men, women, and children were usually alone and clutching their pox-fouled sheets. They'd emerged from houses only to wander toward the horizon, in search of a place to relieve themselves. They were searching, it seemed, for more than such a place; to see them pushing through their pain, pressing wretchedly away from their loved ones into the most barren places for *privacy*—Hugh's laughter took a sudden turn toward tears snaking up from his chest, tears starting before he even recognized them for what they really were.

"You okay?" asked Charlie. "You all there?"

"Sure," said Hugh, forcing a cough. "You bet."

The heat became oppressive. A couple of weeks in and the hills in the distance floated on the hazy air as Hugh took part in the daily struggle for subsistence: boiling water, filling bottles, securing food and firewood. Without a chair and table, these tasks—to say nothing of basic camera maintenance—were far more difficult than he would have imagined. The Nuer system of living seemed, by contrast, pretty much unassailable. Hugh looked out toward their homes: packed-mud floors swept clean or at least (mostly) insect-free, the insides kept cool by the slanting grass roofs, an opening to enter and exit. When the floodwaters came, the Nuer would leave all these homes behind, all the jugs and pots and utensils, returning only when it was dry to start up all over again. Hugh's eyes stung, he blinked away mosquitoes, and he realized he was looking for that same diseased girl. He'd become possessed with the idea of at least managing to preserve—if not the girl's life—her image, however devastated, in silver, on paper, on celluloid. When he'd asked Charlie about the girl and the calf, Charlie had told him that Nuer women poured water down calves' throats as much for personal pleasure as for the needs of their calves and that only women did this work; they had the softer hands.

Once he'd filled enough bottles of water, Hugh set off for the swamp. After two days of looking for her, he was becoming not only impatient but also a little bit desperate, so when a group of young boys approached him, arresting his momentum, he prepared himself for the onslaught of their demands, geared up for what he had come to perceive as a specifically Nuer wellspring of self-interest and a profound certainty of knowing exactly what they deserved.

But these boys weren't making material demands. All they wanted, for now, was his attention. Pointing grandly toward themselves, calling out louder and louder, as if they were seasoned vendors in a marketplace and not naked eight-year-olds, they presented miniature clay cattle. And their craft—if not their subject matter—was extraordinary. He touched the charcoal and ash shadings, the detailed udders, the pebble decorations hanging from little necks and horns, no different from the real ones in their fathers' world. As Hugh offered his sincere admiration, he recalled how Charlie, in one of his more loquacious moods, had once told Hugh about seeing Margaret Mead in a coffee shop on Manhattan's Upper East Side. She'd eaten a tuna salad sandwich and an entire pickle before Charlie—seated right beside her at the counter, drawing out his already drawn-out coffee-drinking—had screwed up the strength to introduce himself. They'd had, according to Charlie, a perfectly wonderful conversation. Mrs. Mead eventually explained how she'd never been psychoanalyzed, because she didn't need to be, owing to the fact that she'd lived a life of observing children. When this had struck Hugh as rather simplistic, Charlie had cocked his head in that quintessential way he had of making Hugh feel as though his skeptical response revealed nothing but Hugh's own personal flaw.

Now, instead of demanding payment for their miniatures, the boys only wanted Hugh to watch as they played. The boys called to him, pointed at their cows, and though Nhial wasn't there and couldn't tell him for sure, he knew they were saying, *Watch me.*

One of the boys pointed in the distance, past the dwellings and the dung piles, toward where some kind of galloping animal was approaching. Hugh's heart sped wildly, imagining the lion they'd seen on their journey, the lion and the decimated antelope, which suddenly seemed like nothing more than a very clear sign leading up to this moment, when he was going to be mauled. It was unlikely it would be here and not at the watering hole, though, and, in fact, as the beast drew closer, Hugh saw that it was not an animal at all; instead, it was a mother and father running and holding up a listless boy covered with smallpox blisters, his skin so rutted that it ceased to resemble skin. Hugh was ashamed in front of these parents, ashamed to be not only white but also so *big,* as if slightness would have canceled out his color. At least, being the only white man around, he should have had more—much more—than a medical kit provided by the Harvard infirmary. And he was ashamed of being ashamed. Shame was not active, and, more than anything right then, he wanted to get something done.

There was the child, afflicted with not only the blistery horror of severe smallpox (for which photographs had not prepared him) but also other horrors—pneumonia? *What would Ed do?* It came crashing forth, and though the thought was unquestionably irritating (because where was Ed? *Where?* Working for his future father-in-law, that was where), it also helped. Because Ed wouldn't have been ashamed, Ed wouldn't have been encumbered by doubt, and there was the child being literally thrust into Hugh's arms, and nobody—suddenly not even Hugh—cared about his qualifications.

With his fingers shaking, Hugh called out for Charlie, who was nowhere to be seen; he called out for Nhial and Etienne. He was the one with so little knowledge, and of course they'd come to him. He was finally beginning to understand that, through no design *whatsoever,* his appearance—fuck relativism, here was further proof of its stupidity—telegraphed strength to complete strangers. He took out the syringe he used to blast air at his camera lens and quickly filled it with water. "Don't worry," he was saying idiotically, over and over, as the parents stared at him, pale dung ash clinging to their frightened faces.

He alternated between chanting *Don't worry* and shouting *Charlie*, but he also managed to tear open the packets from his kit and force sugar and salt into the boy's blistered mouth. Hugh held this boy's head in his hands. His hair was bristly, his skin was no softer than the cracked desert floor, but the eyes sunken between swollen eyelids were pools of the warmest brown. Hugh looked into those eyes and didn't look away. He worked quicker. "Charlie!" he cried, as the child convulsed right in his hands, coughing and coughing like a dying old beast, as Hugh somehow managed to shoot the child's arm full of penicillin, after previously practicing only a handful of times on overripe bananas—just in case.

This did nothing. As he knew it would do nothing—even if it worked, the effect wouldn't be immediate—but even as he scrambled to do anything—right then he would have done anything—he called out for Charlie, as if Charlie could do something he couldn't. Hugh looked at the boy's parents. They looked back without much expression, including reproach, before taking the boy back to their home.

Hugh would go see them later. When the sun was lower in the yellow sky, when the dung was assembled in small fire pits and lit as the cattle came home, Hugh would go and see them. And as he knew that the cattle would be fed and brushed with ash at the end of this terrible ordinary day, as he knew that heifer who'd been braying would stop its complaining the moment it was allowed its mother's teat, he also knew—though of course he hoped he was wrong—that boy would be dead. Just as that girl would soon be dead. The one he'd remember—not because she was any more deserving than any of the others but because, my God, was she beautiful.

When Charlie and Etienne found him surrounded by children some time—how much time? He wasn't sure—later, Hugh described the parents and the boy, his own panicked ministrations.

"Where do they live?" Charlie asked.

Etienne went off to collect Nhial.

Hugh pointed.

"Well, c'mon, then," Charlie said impatiently, and—Hugh could tell—excitedly.

They arrived minutes later and found the mother stirring a pot with another child—a baby—balanced on her hip. She looked at them blankly, and Hugh could tell in this look that his prediction had been right and that the boy had already died. And if he was dead, then he was also already underground, as the Nuer liked to bury their dead straight-away and without fanfare. She was standing upright, stirring. The boy's father was on the ground, singing to his bull. When Charlie began film-ing, the man stopped and said something to Nhial.

"What is it?" Hugh asked.

If they were going to make pictures, the man had explained to Nhial, then he wanted to put on clothes.

"Clothes?" said Charlie. "But they don't wear clothes."

"Well, he wants to wear clothes now," said Hugh. "Maybe they make him feel better. I don't know," said Hugh, shaking his head, "more regal."

The man returned, wearing khaki pants at least four sizes too large and a pink plastic belt.

"Regal?" said Charlie.

"Who cares if he's naked or not, Charlie?" Hugh said.

"I care," said Charlie. "I do."

"You do."

"That's right. And *you* should."

"His kid just died."

"You want to make films, Shipley? You want to capture something real? Or you want to sit around and talk about your dreams all day?"

"Fuck you," Hugh heard himself say. He said it reflexively and quietly—so quietly that he wasn't sure that Charlie had heard—but he'd never said such a thing to anyone, ever.

"Tell him," said Charlie to Nhial, "tell both of them, first of all, that we are sad for them. We are sad their son has died."

Nhial told the parents, who remained impassive.

"Now tell him that, after we make these pictures, we will bring them medicine, coffee, soap, and a goat."

"Jesus," said Hugh, "that's the package? That's the going rate these days? Why aren't we vaccinating all those who don't have it?"

"We can," Charlie said, Arriflex on his shoulder, ready for the OK to start filming. "We can do that."

"Why do you say it like that?"

"Like what?"

"Like it won't make a difference."

Charlie rubbed his face with his hands, as if he could wash this aggravation away. Nhial and the woman were still having words. What little light was left in the sky was starting to fade. "Because it won't. We won't. This is smallpox, Hugh. It has not been eradicated. And we have limited vaccine. Who're gonna be the lucky ones?"

"The children, I should think."

Charlie nodded. "Yes," he said, "of course. You want to choose which ones?"

Nhial gave Charlie the go-ahead, and Charlie began to film. It was quiet, aside from the man singing to his bull and the baby whimpering on and off.

"A dance is certainly unlikely these days," mumbled Etienne.

"I'd say so," said Hugh, biting the inside of his mouth, but this time not from laughter.

Long after the father stopped his singing, Charlie filmed the mother, still stirring, for a good ten minutes. Then he thanked the woman; he put the camera down. She took his hand and Charlie took both of her hands and they stood together.

The man rubbed white dung ash over his face and teeth. Hugh still had no idea why the Nuer did this, but their teeth were among the whitest he had ever seen, so they were clearly doing something right. Maybe they saw the dung as a cure-all, a natural extension of their cows. The father nodded; the mother nodded. They went inside their hut.

"Etienne," said Charlie quietly, "beginning or ending a film about Africa with dancing *is a cliché*. A fatal cliché. Look at what is happening here, and give it a rest. Would you please?"

Etienne was shocked, however briefly, into silence.

When Charlie and Etienne began to shout at each other in earnest, Hugh brought Nhial to the opening of the hut. "Tell them I want to give that baby a vaccination," he said. "Do they know what that is?"

He was welcomed inside immediately. It smelled putrid. When he stuck the child's arm with the needle, Hugh didn't expect to feel much besides an overwhelming helplessness, but he didn't feel helpless. He felt devoted. When he was finished, he started for another hut with small children.

"You've got to get your head on straight," said Charlie, catching up with him.

"My head is on straight," Hugh said. "I can do this. Even you said so."

"Hugh," Charlie said, raising his voice.

It was dark now. Hugh hadn't realized just how dark it was, but as Charlie stood still, he was nothing but a silhouette against the vast ink sky.

"At least wash your hands," Charlie said, calm once again, "and do this in a more organized way, during daylight, and not from some kind of juvenile fantasy."

Hugh stopped suddenly and, as if cooperating with Charlie's description, kicked at a patch of sand. "These people are stuck," said Hugh. "We're filming their deaths and they're stuck between the Arabs and the pagans and they aren't even in their own country anymore and they have smallpox and who even knows what other kinds of plagues—"

"These people have a life that makes sense," said Charlie calmly. "They happen to have supreme self-regard. We—" He stopped himself, and Hugh realized Charlie's breathing was labored. "We are all fragile," he said.

"But—"

"There's meaning here."

"There are cows," said Hugh. "There are very beloved cows. But they are still *stuck*. And you're concerned about whether or not a man who just lost a child is going to look authentic to white people paying good money to see an authentic film about Africa."

Charlie didn't answer for a good long while. "Yep," he said. "That's true, too." Then he walked away.

"Charlie!" called Hugh, but Charlie didn't turn around. "Hey, Charlie—it was you who kept asking about my goddamn dreams! You think I wanted to talk about all that crap?"

Charlie finally stopped. When Hugh caught up with him, Charlie firmly gripped Hugh's shoulder and said, "Yeah," and Hugh could tell Charlie was tired of him. "I do think you wanted to talk about all that crap. I think you were dyin' to. And I don't blame you."

"Don't patronize me," said Hugh.

"Then stop askin' to be patronized. We're here to make a film. I let you come along—"

"You *let* me come?"

"I let you come," he repeated. "You are a promising photographer and good company. And—not insignificantly—you were able to pay your own airfare. But you are not here to force me to defend my methods or provide moral instruction. Got it?"

Hugh nodded.

The dung fires were still burning. If he wanted to film anything, Hugh suddenly realized, it was only this: the smoke. The way it rendered everything—the conical huts and cattle horn spires, the dark tall slips of men and women, everything he had come here in order to understand—impenetrable.

The next morning he was awake before Charlie and Etienne. The sky was pale and his body ached from the hard, cracked ground. He'd spent the better part of the night giving a small girl fluids and injections, only to watch her die, too. The coffeepot smelled of cow piss, and he knew that even with double their daily allotment of beans, the coffee would be revolting. He would never talk about his dreams again.

Still.

When Hugh saw that rising sun, it was so orange, so enormous, and the light it cast was so brilliant and warm, that—contrasted with the gray-brown landscape—he could feel nothing but this: Here he was, alive.

And there was also this, Hugh thought, inviting her in, all of her—long fingers, breathless laugh, flushed cheeks, a loose strand of pale hair stuck to her lips—

He didn't miss her.

Chapter Seven

Summer, New York City

They weren't allowed to use the word *deal*.

Forget about shirtsleeves, they weren't allowed to go without jack-ets, not even with this terrible heat, this goddamn tremendous fucking heat (*goddamn* and *fucking* apparently being not nearly as vulgar a word as *deal*), not when it was in the nineties during some point of each day, not with the accompanying 98 percent humidity and the air-conditioning system that was on the fritz.

They weren't allowed to grow a beard, wear cologne, or eat garlic during lunch. They were not allowed to smoke cigars.

When he passed through the lobby's marble vestibule on the third Monday morning in August and entered the sparkling chrome elevator, it was all Ed could do not to ask Mr. Grisby, the elevator operator, what he made of Ed's new sartorial choice. After making the decision to branch out style-wise, he'd eaten so little that he'd lost a good ten pounds, deposited a month of paychecks, and, over the weekend, had walked all the way to Brooks Brothers and bought a blue-and-white seersucker suit.

When the elevator doors opened, he appreciated the fresh flowers in the entryway as he kept an eye out for Mr. Ordway, just as he'd done each morning for a little over a month. And just like on all the mornings preceding this one, there was no sighting. During his brief tenure at Ordway Keller, he'd had no real occasion to speak to the great man. Ed reported to Mr. Jack Stone, director of research, who took an eternity to explain even the simplest of concepts and, in addition, employed solely chess analogies, which meant that Ed spent his nights studying up on the rules of a game in which he'd never managed to be interested. As Stone droned on, Ed always thought of Hugh, who was fairly addicted to chess and would have known what the hell Stone was getting at. Hugh had done his best, on several occasions, to teach Ed how to play, but Ed could never get past being bored. It was nearly evening in Ethiopia. He could not remotely picture what Hugh was doing there.

He took in the room, which, first thing in the morning, never failed to impress. It was a sea of mahogany desks. Only Mr. Ordway and Mr. Keller had offices. Everyone else was out in the main room, all within earshot of one another. He thought about how Hugh would react to this room, housed in a former squash court with little to no ventilation, with décor consisting of severe antiques and paintings. He couldn't picture Hugh's life, but he did keep up imagined conversations.

Your workplace is giving me anxiety is how he imagined Hugh would respond. *Anxiety and a double migraine.*

Come on, Ed would say, *don't all these old hunting paintings make you feel like going out and conquering something?*

He wanted to tell Hugh just then that someone could make a fortune selling this kind of décor to the educated average Joe, who was smart enough to know that dead pheasants and dark wood meant not that you gave a shit about hunting but that, if you could somehow possess these images (home products, hunting-influenced sportswear), they would signify wealth and class and . . . being an authentic American.

Since Hugh was, of course, not there, Ed reminded himself to jot down that idea when he arrived at his very own (at least until Labor Day) mahogany rolltop desk. He sketched out his ideas in green felt-tip pen on a yellow legal pad, usually on the subway—in motion, which was where all his best ones began.

"Good morning, Polly," Ed said expansively. "Good morning, Bess."

"Good morning, Mr. Cantowitz."

"Any news about the air-conditioning?"

"'Fraid not," said Polly.

"Terrible heat," said Bess.

He was usually the first to arrive, and he relished the moment. Polly was an apple-cheeked brunette with green eyes, who couldn't have been much older than he was. She always brought the same thing for lunch—cream cheese and cucumber on rye—and ate at her desk. He was often tempted to ask her to join him at the diner around the corner, just for a change of scene.

"If you don't mind my saying so, Mr. Cantowitz," said Bess, "that's a smart suit."

"Why, thank you, Bess."

As he arrived at his desk and sat down for the morning, Ed actively willed himself to forget that Helen's father was his boss and that Hugh was living in the bush and that, even when Hugh eventually returned, Ed wasn't sure they'd have anything to talk about ever again, especially because Ed *was* working for Helen's father, whom Ed knew that Hugh—though he wouldn't, of course, *just come out and say it*—officially despised.

Each time he laid out his papers—his *Wall Street Journal,* his *Financial Times*—each time he licked an ink-smudged finger to turn a page or outlined a number or a phrase in his green felt-tip, he thought of Guy Ordway sitting at the breakfast table, eating buttery eggs. He thought of the sky through the trees, those sharp blue angles, clean white cotton sheets. But by the time he progressed to making his phone calls, he forgot about Guy Ordway and Fishers Island and all he thought of was earning the confidence of whomever was on the other end of the line. He tried to picture the eyes of the fellow to whom he was speaking and to always get straight to the point, and it appeared that his tactics—lack of small talk, tendency to skip the salutations before launching into the matter at hand—were working. It seemed to Ed that with each phone call, he was accumulating notice from the investment funds. *What are you working on?* said Ed, first thing. And they were talking.

Most of the time, Ed forgot about how he'd broken the news of the Ordway Keller offer to his father and how his father had hollered about betrayal for a good twenty minutes before Ed had called him an uneducated bully and they hadn't spoken since. He forgot he was the only Jew in the office, forgot about how more than once he'd returned from the john to hear a peal of collective laughter peter out or how, upon returning to his desk after lunch, he heard that moon-faced Parker Earle say cheerily into the telephone, "I couldn't agree more! Absolutely! This is why one doesn't want *too* many Heebs as friends!"

Ed forgot everything besides his ultimate goal: to distinguish himself. And after being at Ordway Keller for about a month, he knew that if he wanted to distinguish himself in the long term, he could not focus solely on the established companies that Ordway Keller handled, not where the majority of these well-bred gentlemen who'd be arriving any minute from Greenwich and Darien and the Upper East Side and sitting at desks all around him were already connected, those who would be content to discreetly negotiate their clients' mergers and tinker with their financial strategies. Ed knew that his strength lay in knowing— *really* knowing—that the past was no guide to the future. Opportunity rested in thinking about Americans and how they were changing and how change would affect their decisions. He knew that decisions started small, but he was sure if he could just understand how certain decisions were made, he could excel at buying and selling stock and he would be indispensable.

Ed knew this, but it didn't change the fact that this was his first job that didn't involve laying pipes in the ground, he had yet to set foot in a business-school lecture hall, and—most important—Guy Ordway was his only connection, and a tenuous one at that. He also knew that, before distinguishing himself as brilliant, it would go a long way in this old-line world to distinguish himself as distinctly genial and conventional. Here at Ordway Keller, the first task he laid out for himself was to consistently listen to Jack Stone, which was much *much* harder than it seemed when he wrote this directive in green ink on yellow lined paper each morning on the subway. *LISTEN TO STONE* (or at this point: *LTS*) meant that—in addition to suffering through the pointless chess analogies—Ed had to complete the endless daily loop of life as an associate junior analyst. Jack Stone asked him to do something and he did it. Phase one.

This was difficult.

Because after only a week of commuting from the Upper West Side to the Financial District and seeing how many men and women wore office attire on the subway—even when it was just after dawn—he became convinced that factory jobs in the United States were overwhelmingly giving way to office jobs and that there was a fortune to be made in office products and office furniture. He became convinced of the urgency of this situation and how much money there was to gain.

Also, art. During his first weekend in town, when he went to the Museum of Modern Art, he was shocked at the lines to get in. And since he knew from his excellent liberal arts education that displaying art on one's walls in order to display personal wealth was, in fact, a Jewish phenomenon begun by the Rothschilds in the 1700s, he liked the notion that during this most cruel twentieth century, when so many art collections—so many legacies—were ripped off lavishly papered walls, some Jews would acquire all over again and, in doing so, they would triumph. Upon achieving that first, significant deal (already inflated in his mind to mythic proportions), he vowed to enter the art market and buy something important, preferably a painting—brightly colored.

He'd run the art idea by Ira Gersten, a sportswriter he'd met outside the YMHA, who, unlike Ed, was primarily an enthusiast (*Great*, he said in response, while vigorously nodding; *that's terrific*). Ira looked decidedly disheveled, but Ed had assumed he was wealthy because he was also unlocking a beauty of a car, and who had a car in New York City? But when Ed admired the gleaming black Chrysler Imperial and told him about his own green beauty back in Dorchester, Ira had volunteered how he'd put himself through Columbia University by working at his uncle's Chrysler dealership out in Oceanside. "I've always loved cars," said Ira.

Sometimes life was really that simple.

Because, by the end of their first conversation, not only had Ed made a fine friend but he had borrowed Ira's Kelley Blue Book, and after a week of sleepless nights comparing the prices of the used cars sold at auction in the States to the recent market-share values of Chevy, Ford, and Chrysler, quarter by quarter, Ed had come up with this: They were all the same-quality car and they were all worth the same figure, more or less, at retail. But—and he'd been over it countless times—it seemed that Chrysler was selling, used, at three hundred dollars less. Which meant—it was obvious, wasn't it?—that Chrysler was going to be more popular with a conscientious consumer. Time to buy Chrysler stock. Time to explain this personal theory to a significant financial institution. Phase two.

When he wasn't working at the office, he was perfecting this theory or tagging along with Ira to ball games (a highlight being two weeks earlier, when—clearly under some nostalgic spell of the Yankees winning in the eleventh inning, after forsaking baseball for years—a sassy older broad extended a Labor Day weekend party invitation to Ed and Ira both). His life: baseball and numbers and subway tokens. Numbers for hours on end; rows and rows of numbers that represented companies' lifeblood, which only reproduced in his head when he finally walked away for the day. The women on the subway rocking side to side, reaching up for straps to steady themselves, reaching and revealing—against their silky shirts—the intimate glory of sweat stains. In his minuscule rented room—so tired he could barely bring himself to read the evening paper or even work himself into a frenzy about the parade of women who rode public transportation in this city—he fell into a crushing sleep.

The longer Ed had the car theory, the more clearly he recognized its excellence, but he also kept checking it again and again—not only for fissures but also for the unacceptable discovery that someone else had already thought of it. It was, needless to say, distracting. He was almost hesitant to share it with Ordway (Ed had no trouble imagining him listening intently and advancing him not an inch within the company), but the longer he sat on it, the more acutely he felt that he was in no position to do anything with his own idea. He had a little less than two hundred dollars to his name, and—up until this point—the extent of his relationship with a bank had been accepting a free pen when, upon graduation, he'd opened an account at Cambridge Savings Bank.

Listen to Mr. Stone. Ed repeated this to himself as Stone approached and dropped a sheaf of annual reports and 10-K statements on top of Ed's desk.

"Mr. Stone," Ed blurted out to Stone's back, as he hadn't so much as paused to say hello.

When Stone turned around, Ed couldn't help but notice that it was a particularly athletic move, as if Stone had suddenly shed twenty years and was in the hallways of his alma mater.

"Did you play ball?"

"Did I what?" said Mr. Stone.

"I was just wondering if you played ball. Y'know, in school."

"As a matter of fact I did. I was a three-year varsity letterman." Though he finally grinned, he seemed determined not to show his teeth. "How did you guess?"

"The way you turned your foot. I'm good like that."

"What can I help you with, Ed? I'm backed up at my own desk, you see."

"Of course, sir. But I have an idea. An idea I'd like to share with you."

Jack Stone didn't even ask him to explain. He simply raised his thin ginger brow. He listened as Ed explained his car theory, but he never quit looking skeptical.

"Cantowitz," he said, "this sounds like a marketing ploy. And this is not a marketing firm." He said the word *marketing* as if it belonged in the same category as the dreaded *deal*.

Ed knew better than to argue. There was no arguing here, as far as
he could see. That would only serve to make things worse. And so he
simply shrugged and said, "Mr. Stone, thanks for listening," and silently
applauded such deep self-restraint. Because now he was absolutely certain that Jack Stone possessed a limited intellect and that it was likely
the room and the street were full of fools like this. He wanted to prove
his correct assessment and his clearly superior intellect, but—most
crucially—he wanted to speed through this portion of his life, when
someone like Stone was his superior.

As Ed approached the elevator after sundown, he was sure he was
the last one to leave the office, and he checked his wristwatch, exagger-
ating the motion so that he might admire the cuff on his seersucker suit,
which had not needed a stitch of alterations.

When he heard the voice behind him, he was so shocked he almost
hollered.

"My daughter tells me your friend Hugh has yet to make it to Paris."

Bastard, he thought. *You scared the shit out of me.*

"Is that right?" asked Ed, feigning indifference. "Good evening, sir.
I haven't heard from either of them."

"No?"

"I doubt there are postcard kiosks where Hugh is working."

"Working," scoffed Ordway. "No, I suppose there aren't." He shook
his head vigorously. His face turned distinctly pink. "Do you think he
actually had the gall to stand her up?"

"No," said Ed quickly. "Absolutely not."

"Of course," said Mr. Ordway. "Of course not. But it doesn't look
right. It *does not look right.* You understand?"

"Is Helen—" Ed began. "Is everything okay?"

The elevator doors opened and there was Mr. Grisby, who'd likely
sat inside that elevator all day long, going up and down.

"What do I know?" muttered Ordway. "Do you think I understand
any of this?" He coughed, and—after overdoing a smile for Grisby—
Mr. Ordway took his voice down. "Do you think I understand why they
are individually gallivanting around different continents? Why she is set

on hitching her future—not to mention her family name—to a man who has displayed not one sign of normalcy? Do you think I have the faintest idea of what is going on here? My daughter tells me nothing."

"I imagine," Ed tried, "she's . . . swept up." He knew he sounded foolish, but what in God's name was he supposed to say? He wanted to keep his head down and to not fuck up; he wanted to devastate every powerful man he encountered with his excellent judgment. And though he'd tried—of course he had—to picture Helen *gallivanting* right down the boulevard, like any number of French actresses against whom she very much held her own (his basis for comparison based solely on the limited films he'd attended at the Brattle with Hugh and Helen), this was difficult to picture, because Paris may as well have been the Ethiopian desert. As much as his personal universe had widened—*he was living and working in New York City*—his vision had also narrowed. He knew how he needed to live right now in order to get ahead, and as the U.S. embassy was exploring alternate leadership in South Vietnam, and while Dr. King may well have been rehearsing his *I Have a Dream* speech, Ed scoured 10-K forms and read annual reports from early morning to well past any sane person's dinner hour. When he was tempted to sleep an extra fifteen minutes or leave the office a little earlier, he only had to picture his father's expression of absolute disdain.

"Paris," said Ordway, as the elevator doors opened. "My wife prevailed on this matter. I can't say I approve."

"No?"

"I was there," he said, shaking his head, as they stepped into the empty, gleaming lobby. "In the service," he added, as if the service itself was a filthy movie.

"I didn't realize you'd served, sir."

He nodded, looked at his watch.

"Army?" Ed asked.

"We had a telegram from my daughter this weekend," Mr. Ordway said irritably, as if he'd wanted to say this all day long and Ed had somehow prevented it.

"Really?" said Ed.

Mr. Ordway put his hands in his pockets. He carried no briefcase; for all Ed knew, there was no wallet in Ordway's pocket. Maybe, for the truly wealthy, common currency was actually unnecessary.

"Apparently your friend Hugh Shipley may be arriving in Paris this week."

"Well," said Ed lightly, "that's good."

"*May* is a month between April and June. *May* has no meaning to me. Do you understand?"

"Of course I do," said Ed.

Mr. Ordway shook his head and opened the door. The night was still hot, but the darkness itself was refreshing.

"Get some sleep," said Mr. Ordway. "From what Jack tells me, you're going to need rest one of these days."

"He's told you I'm a hard worker?"

"I don't need Jack Stone to tell me that," said Mr. Ordway, with a laugh. "Why do you think you're here?"

"I—"

The blast of a gunshot rang out suddenly, and both men flinched.

"*Goddamn it,*" said Ordway, visibly rattled.

"It was just a car backfiring," said Ed, the words tumbling out. He wasn't sure why, but he was in an instant rush to reassure him.

"Of course," said Mr. Ordway. "Of course."

More distressing than his urge to reassure Mr. Ordway, like every other toadying underling in town, was the image of Jack Stone's athletic little pivot.

Ed thought about telling Mr. Ordway about it now, how he'd been shot down by Jack Stone—erroneously and *stupidly* shot down. He imagined explaining his theory and how the look on Mr. Ordway's face would shift from mild interest to deep fascination. Ordway would take him uptown in his limousine; they'd stop at his club for a celebratory drink. By tomorrow Jack Stone would be gone.

But before Ed could make a decision, Mr. Ordway gestured to his driver down the street, dismissing Ed with a nod.

"Well," said Ed, "good night, then."

But right before he reached his driver—who was standing at attention, waiting to open his door—Mr. Ordway turned around. "Oh, and young man—"

"Sir?" Ed realized he felt less tired than he usually did at this hour, and he attributed it all to his brand-new seersucker suit.

Mr. Ordway cleared his throat, looked Ed up and down. "This is not the Kentucky Derby."

As Mr. Ordway climbed into the backseat of the car and the driver closed his door, Ed willed himself not to betray one iota of a reaction. It was a great suit. He looked sharp. He knew this. He even thought Polly had lightly blushed when she'd bid him good morning. But as he pictured that dark-wood office full of navy jackets, he also knew that the suit would hang in a succession of closets until he made real money. Then he'd wear it as a rich man, every summer, every chance he got. Even after he could no longer button the tortoiseshell button, because he'd eaten too much expensive food over too many years, and even after his inevitable discovery that the sight of Ed Cantowitz in a seersucker suit was, of course, just as foolish as Guy Ordway clearly thought it was.

At the tail end of August, Ed broke his finger by slamming it in the passenger door of Ira Gersten's Imperial. He didn't realize it was broken until the following morning, a Monday, when it was swollen and black and he called Ordway Keller and told Polly not to worry but he was taking himself to the emergency room. Bellevue was crowded with crying babies and knife wounds and such misery that Ed almost left without registering. But his finger was throbbing, so he sat in that waiting room for the entire morning, between a Negro reading charismatically aloud from a Bible while holding a long-ago melted chunk of ice in a dish towel to a nasty cut on his cheek and a flushed old geezer who kept repeating, "Jesus Mary and Joseph." It was like some kind of mixed-up house of God, and—at his most bored and agitated—Ed almost belted out the portion from his bar mitzvah that had mysteriously stayed in his head all these years and emerged (not comfortingly) during times of great stress, but he only kept his head down and waited.

By the time he'd been splinted and released and showered and changed, it was well after lunchtime. He ate a banana, swallowed four aspirin, took the A train downtown, and—as he struggled to both keep his finger elevated, as the beleaguered resident had suggested, and to not feel like a total schmuck with his bandaged hand held aloft—he greeted Polly and Bess, nodded at the others in action, engrossed on their telephones, and made his way to the rolltop desk that would soon be a summer memory.

He scanned his new pile of annual reports and 10-Ks, began imagining the appropriate steps toward one day acquiring his own company with its own 10-Ks—one that manufactured car parts, perhaps, maybe a retailer; why not Chrysler?—and, just as he was about to get up to take a piss (he usually waited until he could barely keep it in, so pathologically did he loathe wasting time), just when he forgot to elevate his finger and the blood rushed to it with one great painful throb—

"*Bonjour,* " said a familiar voice.

"Oh my God," he cried. Very polished, very suave.

Helen stood beside his desk in a yellow suit, holding a white leather purse with both of her hands.

"What are you doing here?" he marveled.

"I had lunch with my father."

"Look at you!" He sprang to his feet and—poking his hand in the air as if halfheartedly hailing a cab—initiated the most ungainly hug in the history of the embrace.

"What happened to you?" she giggled.

He was laughing now, too, and not quietly. He was especially cognizant of two things: that they had an audience, and that if he didn't get to the john soon, he was going to cause even more damage to himself than a broken finger. "C'mere," he said. He ushered her away from the desks and toward the flowers. "You look great," he said, "really great."

"No," she said, shaking her head. "I'm too skinny."

"How was Paris?" he asked. The pressure on his bladder was terrible.

"Paris was awful."

"Only you could possibly say that and still make it sound like you had a ball."

"No, really. My boss was always trying to feel me up, my apartment was so hot I couldn't sleep, and when I can't sleep, I lose my appetite. Can you imagine being in France with no appetite? Oh, and Hugh never arrived. He's evidently on to relief work. Says he's done with being an observer, which I suppose might be a very good thing. But what about you? That pretty secretary told me you went to the emergency room. I think she likes you, by the way—"

"Shh—"

"Don't worry, she can't hear me. I'm telling you, she seemed awfully concerned."

"I slammed my hand in a car door."

"Oh for God's sake. How?"

"Helen—"

"Was it a taxi?"

"No—Helen—"

"Were you drunk or something?" Her eyes widened. *"Were you with that secretary?"*

"Listen—I'm so sorry—but I have to excuse myself."

"Oh," she said, "oh, of course." She pushed the elevator button, and he realized she thought he was trying to get rid of her.

"Helen," he whispered, "I have to use the bathroom."

She smiled as if he'd just told her his biggest secret. "Well," she said, with a flourish of a throat-clear that—for a brief moment—reminded him of her father, "as it happens, I have to run to an appointment uptown. Let me buy you a drink later. Seems like you kind of need one. There's this new place that I read about. Or, actually, my sister read about. She's always reading about places in *The New Yorker* and telling me to go. Poor Kitty."

"Kitty reads *The New Yorker*?"

"Will you meet me at Grand Central?"

"Where are we going? I do have to get up for work in the morning, you know."

"The bar is at the station. Apparently it's done up like an old train car. Edwardian."

"Nifty."

"Just be there, okay?"

"See you at seven," he said, before nearly sprinting down the hall.

The Grand Central joint was too dainty, the lace curtains and delicate glasses made him feel even more ungainly than he already felt with his broken finger, and by the time the check had arrived and Helen waved it toward her, Ed was antsy as hell. "I'll let you pay this one time," he said bitterly.

"Of course you will. I already insisted."

"But no more after this."

"We're not on a date," she said, finishing off her sidecar, ice clinking in the glass.

"I know," he said.

"So you don't have to impress me."

"It's not about that. Just—"

"What?"

"Forget it."

"Come on, you hate when I do that," she said. "Ed?"

"Listen," he said, "I'm going to stop being a pill."

She looked a bit too relieved to hear it. Though she'd repeated how excited she was to have a real adventure, how Paris had been a disappointment and didn't count, and how wonderful Hugh had sounded during their one phone conversation, how *inspired,* Ed knew she was anxious about her current plan to meet him in Nairobi, a plan she had yet to tell her parents about (though she was booked on a flight leaving in less than one week's time), and he knew that it was somehow up to him to reassure her, when of course he couldn't possibly do that. Even if they'd finally set a date (this January; winter wedding, Connecticut), they still weren't married, and, besides which, what was Hugh really doing over there? And what was Helen Ordway going to do in Nairobi?

Ed looked around. This room was full of ladies. He had a feeling he was sitting in a place popular for resting after the exertions of shopping, for sipping while waiting for husbands. One husband walked in the door just then and tapped a woman's shoulder. She let her crisply folded newspaper fall to her chair as she stood to kiss him.

"Have you thought about what you'll do once you get there?"

Helen shrugged and stood up. "Let's go," she said. Sometimes she was so decisive, and it was always a surprise. "And no more talking about money. I want to see you plenty before I go. We can't let Kitty down, now, can we? This is the greatest city in the world and you're my favorite friend in town, *and* you have a broken finger. Okay?"

"Okay," said Ed. "Hey, okay."

From different bars, every evening that week, they wrote postcards to Hugh. They wondered if he'd ever receive them. Ed discovered that a brandy Alexander was nectar of the gods. How embarrassing, they both agreed; he couldn't exactly take a girl out and order himself a brandy Alexander. They ate Chinese food for dinner, little dumplings and noodles and cold, weak beer. They walked and walked, earning the understanding of how each neighborhood in Manhattan fit together.

Helen: "If you could live anywhere, where would it be?"

He pointed at an apartment on Park Avenue—limestone adorned with a broad navy awning, white-gloved doorman standing by.

Helen: "Typical."

But he could tell she wasn't disappointed.

And then their last night, Friday: something called lobster fra diavolo, someplace in Greenwich Village, his mouth afire but, for the first time, not minding such a kick, in fact suddenly understanding why people liked, even loved, spicy food. Bottles of Chianti: first to toast to Helen's trip, to her reunion with Hugh, and then to dull the diavolo, and then because the owner brought them a dusty bottle they had to try and also some kind of pastry exploding with cream. Next door down a narrow stairwell: horns, a snare drum, and a tall regal woman, her big eyes closed, singing, *Ill wind*—sequins over skin like sparkles on tar, those glitter-city streets—*ill wind, no good.*

Helen nudged him awake when the set was over, with a touch that knew unexpected sleep called for tenderness. As she took a cigarette from a familiar silver case, Ed reached for the matchbook between them. He struck a match and she leaned forward; he'd never found a ritual so reassuring.

"To be honest," she finally said, "I was a bit nervous that we'd run out of things to talk about."

"When?" He was tired and finally felt it, all those long days, all that working and not sleeping enough; he just wanted to put his head down on a cool dark surface, this table between them, the floor at Helen's feet, or maybe the singer's bare shoulder in the corner; she was having a drink and smiling like there was no trouble, never had been.

"We'd never spent any time together. Without Hugh, I mean."

"I think we've done okay," said Ed, still looking at the singer.

"Then," she said, "would you mind looking at me while I'm talking?"

He twisted up his mouth and tipped his chair back precariously. He did what she asked. Her lipstick was worn off and she looked mussed up and radiant, like it was dawn already and everything had already been done, every last shameful thing, and these terrible constricting necessary clothes were strewn across an anonymous floor. "What time is it?" he asked.

"One," she said, biting her lip.

"Hey, what's wrong?" There was a green light above the doorway next to the stage, and when the singer passed through it Ed wondered about what went on behind that door. He also realized that he didn't care nearly as much about anything else as he cared about Helen. Ed looked at her through the cloud of smoke.

"I'm worried," Helen said. "I guess I'm worried."

"Okay," said Ed. "What about?"

"I want to tell you something."

"So tell me."

"I'm not sure I should." She glanced up at the low ceiling. "But now I have to. Don't I?"

"You don't."

"Thank you."

They sat in silence while the voices all around them grew louder, anticipating a second set.

She stamped out her cigarette. "I had an abortion."

When she found a suitable lack of anything judgmental in his expression, she continued. "It was when Hugh and I were, you know, it was in boarding school. Or right afterward, at any rate. I had an abortion."

"Does he—"

"Of course he knows." Her face and neck flushed so quickly, it was as if—by his asking that question—Ed had lit a flame.

Helen took up another cigarette and Ed took up the matchbook. How he wished he enjoyed smoking.

"At the time, I didn't tell him. I guess I disappeared."

"You did?" said Ed, suddenly angry on Hugh's behalf. "He must have been devastated."

"I guess," agreed Helen. "That's what he's said."

"But . . . ?"

"It's hard to picture Hugh devastated. Isn't it?"

He had to nod. "I'm so sorry," he said. "I mean I'm sorry that you were . . . in that position."

Her face softened considerably. "Thank you."

"Helen," Ed asked, "are you pregnant?"

She shook her head. Then she inhaled softly, the red cigarette tip barely drawing.

"Then . . . ?"

"I'm afraid that Hugh doesn't—that he doesn't really need people around him. Does that make any sense? Sometimes I imagine being with him and he isn't there somehow. I'm afraid," she admitted. "I'm afraid of being alone."

"Well, then, you won't be," he said.

"You think that's how it goes?"

"I do. You'll get what you need."

She smiled. "I love that about you."

"What."

"You are just the most convinced person."

"Not the most convincing?"

She cocked her head and narrowed her eyes, as if she were trying to see right through him, and for one disorienting moment he was afraid she could. "That, too," she said. "You are mighty convincing."

"See," Ed said, leaning forward, "you're feeling better already." Her neck and cheeks were still hot, still pink. "I can tell."

"D'you want to know something?"

He nodded slowly, unnecessarily.

"That summer when it happened, I went to stay with my aunt for a while. She lives in this old harbor town in Connecticut; austere and completely depressing. Or maybe it was just my mood." She laughed tightly. "Anyway, black mood or no, you can stroll into the town square and see not a soul, even in the middle of the day. There was a man who I imagined was a war veteran—he had one leg and the rest of him was very upright, but he seemed like a vagrant somehow. I would always pass him everywhere—in the morning when I went to buy bread, in the evening, along the shore, he was always there, and do you know what? Even though he had to have been at least forty years old and he was half decrepit, really unkempt, he looked just like Hugh, like Hugh gone mad and lame. I kept trying to avoid him, but there he was wherever I went." Helen was looking past him, and he imagined her gaze traveling past the door to those narrow stairs, up the stairs, out into the streets, over the bridge, and onto the expressway, right onto that hulking jet plane.

"Hugh's fine," he said.

"I know that."

"He's fine."

She nodded. "He never told you about his mother, did he?"

"Well, I know that she died, if that's what you mean. I know that he barely remembers her."

"And do you know how she died?"

Ed shook his head. He realized he had no idea.

"She drank herself to death. Or at least that's what they told him. Who even knows how she did it. Who knows. That family somehow manages to keep everything very very quiet."

"All he's said is that he can't remember her. And that his aunt May was there."

"Well," she said, "that may well be true. His aunt is a lovely person; I've met her several times. But think about this: His mother drank so much for the first five years of Hugh's life that she died from it. Granted, she'd had a long head start—she was forty-three when she had Hugh, you know—but those first five years of Hugh's life: Those were the years that did her in."

Ed heard clicking, and it was as if, for a moment, he was back in Adams House, waiting for Hugh. There was the familiar sound of the record player in the background—click and pause, click and pause, the moment before Hugh took time to change the record, no matter what kind of rush they were in. Ed recalled not so much the music, though the choice almost always surprised him, but the silent moment before hearing a brand-new sound. Debussy, Ravel, Bill Evans, Roy Orbison; Ed remembered names but at that moment could conjure nothing but the clicking. Then he realized his own jaw was clicking, over and over again.

Helen's stem wrists and lily hands lay on the table and he touched them, covered them up, as if this was a test and he was hiding his answers—his precious answers—as if all he needed was right here, and there was his breath, fast and tight, then rushing forward.

"Hugh's fine," he said. "You both are." But *Jesus* is what he thought. *Jesus Mary and Joseph.*

———

He slept later than he'd wanted to, almost late enough to miss Ira's ride to East Hampton. He'd been looking forward to this day out of town for weeks. A beach still sounded great—less so a party—but he was focused on the sea, how (despite having to keep his bandaged finger dry) it would clean him up, clear out his head, and offer some perspective. He knew he needed distance: from his room and the familiar innards of the city—the underground sausage smell and nuts for sale and soda sweating into flimsy napkins discarded underfoot; that subway going and going and going—but most importantly from this past week; the nights had felt too important. He had climbed that narrow stairwell behind Helen before the second set. He had memorized her as if she were yet another piece of crucial information, and—after Helen tried and failed to light a cigarette, sending them both into drunken peals of laughter— Ed had hailed her a cab. What a rushed and completely (could there be any other kind?) anticlimactic goodbye.

"What's eating you?" asked Ira, during a stretch of no traffic on the expressway. "You were the one who was late. You should be groveling."

"I'm working on it. I'm getting ready to grovel."

"Okay, then. Wouldn't want to rush you. Wouldn't want to be *vulgar*."

"What the hell d'you mean by that?"

"You spend nearly all of your time around a bunch of tense WASPs."

"And?"

"You're not afraid of it rubbing off on you?"

"No," Ed said. "Christ, Ira, no, I'm not. I'm trying to work a god-damn *job* is what I'm trying to do."

Ira nodded, focused on the road.

"What."

Ira shook his head.

"Just say it."

"I only wonder how you can stomach it."

"Stomach *what*."

"It doesn't bother you that they see you as—well, you know—that Harvard Jew that Ordway hired in order to make his company some real Jew money?"

Ed shook his head. "No, it doesn't. Not for a second. Now would you please back the fuck off?"

Once they'd made it past the many houses and gas stations and out-croppings of stores and new construction, they were surrounded by farmland, and it was calming him down.

"Hey, I'm sorry," Ira said.

"No, it's fine."

"I am sorry."

"Okay."

"It's just that you've been an ass since you got in the car."

"Yeah, well." Ed put his good hand out into the air, feeling the speed, the hot breeze. "An old friend was in town this week. I'm afraid I'm paying."

"I thought you never went out during the week."

"It was a really good friend."

"From Boston?"

"That's right," he said, watching the fields, orderly green rows of crops about which he knew nothing, "an old pal from Boston." He thought of how he'd accused Hugh of keeping Helen a secret, and now here he was doing the same. *What is it about her?* He put this question to himself, downright resentfully, and came up with only this: She made him feel strongly that there would never be enough of her. What crumbs there were inspired the most basic of impulses: to hoard.

"Okay, let's get ourselves together, man," urged Ira. "Do you think Dick and Sarah go inviting everyone to their house?"

"To be honest, I guess I did."

Ira laughed and drove faster, but it still wasn't fast enough. It was good, Ed knew, that he wasn't at the wheel.

As they approached the house, Sarah—the sassy broad from the ball game—and Dick waved them into a field where a shingled farmhouse had been freshly painted white. It was an all-American vision corrupted or perhaps made more spectacular by the sight of their hosts, clearly eccentrics (he'd somehow missed this at the ball game—Dick had been wearing a baseball cap at the stadium, and now his hair, revealed, was a white nimbus, a true Einsteinian spectacle). "Welcome," they cried, offering booze and snacks and inflatable balls and towels and girls out back. He'd never been in such a house. Paintings and sculptures covered every available surface. Abstract oils hung beside seashore watercolors, wire and metal sculptures sat beside enormous bowls of lemons (they had a thing for lemons), and books and books were not only on shelves but stacked on the floor and tables. There were collections: Hotel ashtrays, fountain pens. A bright yellow telephone. He wanted to call Helen just to hear her breathe, just to hear her shout, *Who is this?* into the silence of the telephone line. But Helen was on the way to Idlewild, on her way to the other side of the world, and instead of calling Helen he was telling Sarah how pleased he was to be here.

"It's the end of summer and you're terribly pale," she said. "Poor dear, it isn't right. Especially with your wonderful olive complexion. Why, I bet you are as dark and regal as a Negro when you put in the time."

Ed wasn't sure what to say to this, but he understood he was supposed to flirt with her, that this was what she wanted. And she was easy to flirt with, decades ahead of him and nobody's fool in an orange caftan, with tits still saying hello.

"Come," said Sarah, taking his arm and leading him out toward the back of the house. Through the screen door he saw figures in shadow against the bright sun, figures that, when Sarah opened the door, came to life in a dizzying array of mostly young people in various states of summer undress, playing badminton and croquet, or mixing themselves drinks, waving away barbecue smoke while puffing on cigarettes. And there on line for the barbecue, waiting patiently with an empty paper plate, was a girl he knew. There was Polly—Polly from Ordway Keller!—so out of context that at first glance he thought she was someone from Dorchester. She evoked that same familiar response before he realized it was a new and still-mysterious familiarity, because all he knew was what she ate for lunch and how she answered the phone with the slightest of accents that told him only that she wasn't from New York or New England. "Polly," he cried out, "hey, Polly," and Sarah looked delighted.

"You know each other!" cried his host, and immediately glided away, calling out gaily to someone named Armande.

"Mr. Cantowitz," said Polly, blushing all the way down to her chest, which was—bikini top!—on full display.

"Ed," he said. "Please, call me Ed. I mean, take a look around you."

"Okay, then," she said. "Ed."

"Some party, huh?"

"They're very social," she said, before blushing again. "I mean, obviously." She smiled.

They stood together in silence, in grill smoke, and when it was Polly's turn at the grill she chose a frankfurter, and Ed had one, too. Her nose was upturned and seemed permanently sunburned, which was actually very pretty and made her look like a kid. He hadn't noticed this at the office, and he wondered if she covered it with powder. They drank spiked lemonade and ate frankfurters and told each other knock-knock jokes. At the beach they rode waves, and when Ed wanted to get out, Polly stayed in and swam some more. He watched her. The sun was just warm enough on his salty skin; the spiked lemonade had taken the edge off the previous night.

"You're some swimmer," said Ed, handing her a towel. She shook water from her ear.

"I grew up in Florida." She shrugged. "Not much else to do."

"That sounds like the life."

"It's all right. I like it better here; there's more going on." She sat down beside him. "How about you?" she asked, running her hands over her hair. It was such an unexpectedly confident gesture. Her back was strong; as she lifted her arms, he saw the small muscles moving. He also thought of Helen on Fishers Island and wondered if he'd ever get over that dream of his, the dream that began something inside him that was, in fact, terrible. Though he'd been living with that feeling for longer, it was far less recognizable than this, right now, by the sea. He felt as if he should touch Polly, and he did; he could.

"I like you," he said.

Which might have changed his life for the better, might have brought him to Florida during the winters to eat fried-fish sandwiches, to drink fresh orange juice, to tour, along with her beloved father and brothers, the local military base—all of which Polly had described to him over the course of this lovely day. But: During the evidently annual viewing of Dick and Sarah's travel footage, projected on the white shingle of their farmhouse, Polly had leaned over, smelling of melted butter, and whispered rather sheepishly, "I'm staying with a girlfriend's parents."

"Oh." He watched their hosts on safari, doing a lot of pointing. Elephants crossed a muddy river; hippos meandered like cows.

"They're, um, expecting me back before eleven tonight."

"Sure," said Ed, suppressing a scowl. "Of course."

"But I can give you a ride to the train station."

"Thanks," said Ed. Ira had one-upped him by scoring an invitation to stay with a girl in the Springs. "Yeah, that would be swell."

A wildebeest stared straight ahead in Africa on Long Island. Ed kept expecting Hugh to wander into the frame.

He may or may not have ended up with a better life if Polly had been an easier sort that night or if (as he'd briefly considered) he'd slept on the beach, alone. But instead, when he finally arrived back in the city, when he exited the subway after an epic ride on the Long Island Railroad and an A train that stalled twice in the tunnel, when he stood on the pavement and faced the sirens and the heat (which was so much hotter, even after dark, than it had been all day), and when he climbed the stairs to his rented room in the dingy hallway, with the broken overhead bulb and yellowing brown-striped paper, he saw something he'd never thought possible, and that was Helen sitting outside his door. Helen with her legs akimbo, with her head thrown back as if she'd been sitting for hours, as if she'd been waiting. For him. For hours.

"What happened," he found himself whispering. He was already on the floor with her, relieved that in the deepest chamber of his secret heart, he was, in fact, miserable at the thought of Hugh dead.

She looked at him, and he suddenly knew that Hugh was not dead but that they were going to kill him. They were going to kill him as he touched Helen's smooth pale cheek, tentatively at first, and then not tentatively at all, as his hands—they were everywhere—her shoulders, her lips; he had to force himself to slow down as there was Helen's head—silk hair, heavy skull—the full weight of it pressing down like an offering. They were killing him as he pushed down on the endless length of her, taller than he was and so much lighter, down into the linoleum of the hallway floor, right outside his door. In the hallway they killed him quickly at first, horrified at the intensity, the ugliness that was present, that had been there all along, pushing and pushing at both of them, making clear that if they didn't get rid of it, get rid of it fast, it was going to kill them all. He picked her up off that floor and took her long thin fingers in his, gripping as tightly as he could, bringing her inside his room. As the door closed, he was up against it, as she gripped at his coarse and stubbly neck—fever-hot from all that sun.

He tried to look at her, to comprehend and to even stop himself from going any further, but when she looked right back at him he could do nothing but kiss her, and when he kissed her he knew he would never stop, not even for one moment.

"I couldn't go," she said; he could hear her breath. And that's when she took off her clothes. She did it quickly, as if she'd been ordered to. He was too shocked by this, and by how much he wanted all of her, to do anything but stare. Then he got on his knees and took her hipbones in his hands. They fit there perfectly, two ivory-handled pistols. "I can't go," she said.

"I know." But he didn't, he hadn't.

By the time he was aware of anything beyond her body, the light was seeping in through the dirty windowpane. He gripped her and she was still shaking, they both were. "Say yes to me," Ed whispered. "Please say yes."

"Yes to what?" she said. She was breathing in his ear.

"Just yes," he said. "Just say it."

And she did.

Part Two

1970–1983

Chapter Eight

Dar es Salaam, Tanzania, 1970

When Hugh arrived for the third evening in a row at the New Africa Hotel, Bihlal and Patrick were on the roof and already laughing too hard. As they knocked back Kilimanjaros along with the journalists, the politicians and the would-be politicians, the gangsters, the priests, and the refugees, they looked out over the rooftops of the city; they tipped their faces to the dusky sky with its promise of accompanying breeze, and as Hugh approached Bihlal and Patrick, as he inserted himself into this familiar tableau of men conspiring over alcohol, he hoped that Patrick would at least give him a *hint* of what was going into his goddamn assessment.

"Evening to you, monsieur," said Patrick from Liverpool; he was in Dar es Salaam representing the British Christian charity that had been among the very first to take interest in Hugh's fledgling clinic. This sounded official and fair, but there was nothing remotely official about Patrick. It was here at the New Africa that Patrick met Bihlal even before paying a visit to Hugh's clinic, and everything that had transpired since—every meeting and quasi-meeting—had been dictated by Bihlal, who not only had the distinct advantage of being able to instruct Patrick (who valued a true African Perspective) where to eat and drink and (perhaps most usefully) use the bathroom, but was also profoundly charismatic—even Hugh couldn't argue with that—someone of whom it could be said: *He showed me a very good time.*

This scene was not what Hugh had pictured when he met Michael Shannon at a French journalist's dinner party nearly five years ago. Shannon was in possession of a dry wit, a bottle of malt liquor, and—significantly—a medical degree from Trinity College Dublin. What's more, he already had a modest facility up and running. Within a month, Hugh had made a verbal commitment to Shannon, and within a year—between a combination of funds from Hugh's trust and various loans (like the one that Patrick would or would not make sure was renewed during this visit)—Hugh had refurbished the clinic and had taken on every administrative duty, including (he hadn't entirely thought this one through) fund-raising.

"Evening," said Hugh, shaking their hands.

"We were not certain you were going to come," said Bihlal.

If Bihlal was a fixer or a journalist or even a politician, his befriending Patrick would have fit in fine with Hugh's agenda—would have even taken some of the pressure off—but Bihlal was from a village fifty kilometers outside the city, and he had his own fledgling clinic to fight for (or so he said—Hugh wasn't convinced). He, too, wanted Patrick's dollar, and these evenings were starting to feel more and more like a competition for Patrick's attention, which, it should be said, was usually focused on Yvette, the stripper from Zanzibar whose nonstop smile seemed alternately sweet and sinister; she performed each night—more or less—at ten o'clock—give or take several hours.

Bihlal clapped his hands together before waving over someone from the bar. Hugh couldn't see the bar—he'd intentionally sat with his back to the action—and when a girl approached and said hello, ostensibly to take Hugh's order, Hugh looked up and caught his breath.

Her expression—almost imperceptibly—shifted from irritation to amusement.

"No." Hugh looked away immediately and addressed Bihlal directly. "I know what you're up to. Really, now. No."

"Can't you order a drink, mate?" said Patrick. "Any harm in doing that?"

Hugh's face burned as he ordered a beer, but she didn't walk away.

"Come on," muttered Patrick. "You've done nothing all week but drink your beer and look mournful."

"This is not true," said Bihlal. "He also runs off to piss all the time like a German."

"I run a clinic," Hugh said to Patrick. "You are supposed to give me something to work with."

"And we are giving you something to work with," said Bihlal, as Patrick stifled an idiotic giggle. "Here is Aisha."

And Aisha, she only smiled. Her teeth were white and small.

Ridiculous, Ed would say, if Aisha were an actress playing the part of this waitress. In the dark, in the Brattle Theatre, he'd attempt to whisper: *You think a girl who looked like that—I don't care where, this is 1970—you think she wouldn't have better opportunities?*

Hugh smiled back at her. What Ed wouldn't have understood was that there were plenty of girls in East Africa who were just as lovely as Aisha. He had ceased being surprised by the beauty; only the poverty continued to shock him. When he'd arrived in '65, the country was still celebrating its recent independence, and the mood was buoyant. President Nyerere's *Ujamaa* blended Soviet socialism with African rural life, and Nyerere's faith in his people's traditions was undeniably stirring. But, like so many promising ideas, President Nyerere's *Ujamaa* didn't seem to be working. His particular repudiation of capitalism was resulting in plummeting agricultural output and countrywide disillusionment, or—as Charlie Case liked to call it—*the big fat LOS* (Losing of Steam).

Sometimes Hugh would lie in bed at night in his rented house near Ocean Road, watching the shadows from the palms and banana trees play upon the mosquito netting, and he would try to imagine what the sleeping arrangements looked like inland, on the dirt-dust floors, under barely-held-together roofs of the African quarters, which were of course farthest from the ocean and its accompanying breeze. Unlike so

many impoverished African villages created haphazardly (if inge-
niously, with the most inconsistent of scavenged materials) on the out-
skirts of a city, these African neighborhoods in Dar es Salaam had a
schematic appearance—almost insidiously so. The sand streets were
straight, the housing Soviet-style, with at least one family to a tiny
room, with eight or ten rooms to a cement block of a building. And
while one could not exactly say the people had prospered, God knew
they had found a way to multiply, and so, when he couldn't sleep, he
often tried to mentally diagram how so many people slept (and obviously screwed) under one roof. How anyone negotiated even the most
basic of bodily functions.

We all have the same body: Hugh always came back to this.

The privileged pretended it wasn't true, that human beings were
accustomed to different circumstances and thus had different needs, but
of course this was a lie. After everything he'd seen in the past several
years, nothing was truer than the fact of the body and its needs. He'd
realized soon after his limited foray into filmmaking that he was too
overwhelmed by the corporeal to transcend it and make it artful. Focus
on the physical, he'd reasoned again and again, and progress—relief—
will certainly follow.

While walking through the slums, he would often step in sewage and
think how children played in those waste-laced streets. He was still surprised by this. One of his first mornings in Kariakoo, when he was still a
new face, he'd walked with the intention of gaining a modicum of trust
in order to tell people about the clinic, and while he was walking, a
woman thrust a baby into his arms. She hollered: *Take him. Take him far
away.* Her eyes were feral, and before he'd come up with a response,
several women came and took the baby and—muttering, scolding—led
the wild-eyed woman back into her clay hovel.

"Aisha," said Hugh. "That's a lovely name."

"Thank you, sir. A Kilimanjaro?" she asked. "Like your friends?"

He nodded and she set off for the bar; Patrick and Bihlal tracked her
every move.

"Can you believe?" said Bihlal.

"Wow," said Hugh, knowing his sarcasm would not be registered. "Patrick, listen, I'm afraid I have to just go ahead and ask you: Do you plan on doing any actual observing while you are here? You do have to write something, you know."

"No one will read my assessment," said Patrick, draining the last of his beer. "I will type it up—beautifully, to be sure—and it will sit on a shelf at the mission office and a copy will be sent to headquarters in London, and no one—I mean literally no one—will read it."

"Well," said Hugh. "Thanks for your honesty."

"Right, then," he said, swallowing a belch. He gestured to Bihlal.

"Patrick is coming to my clinic tomorrow," said Bihlal, a slow smile spreading across his face.

"But you haven't even spent a single day at this clinic, *my* clinic, the one you are actually here for."

Patrick didn't look up from rolling—with great precision—his next cigarette. "What are you so worried about?"

"How can you ask me that?"

"You needn't worry," said Patrick, with a dismissive jerk of his chin. "You and the Irish doctor are doing excellent work."

"Well, yes," Hugh said, trying not to sound indignant, "as it so happens the incidence of malaria is down more than ten percent this year. But don't you want to see for yourself?"

"He is telling you that you will get your money," said Bihlal. "I would not quarrel with this if I were you."

"Hang on, then," said Patrick, striking a match on the matchbook with only one hand. "Before I put anything in writing, I think Hugh should agree to go with the girl. Have you had a look at her, mate? What I mean is: Have you had yourself a really good look?"

Hugh shook his head. He asked, "Why don't *you?*"

"Can't," said Patrick. "Not anymore, anyway," he corrected. "But you, *cowboy,* " he said, stressing the word *cowboy* in an atrocious American accent, the way he often did with what he obviously saw as particularly American words. "You're a young man."

While certainly not wanting to contemplate it, he was unclear whether Patrick—in saying *can't*—had been referring to fraternizing with local women or to the sexual act itself. Hugh was still shaking his head when Aisha returned to the table with his drink.

"You must be thirsty," she said. "Even the wind is hot."

"When I do not have visits from good people like you, people from excellent and fine organizations, I am weeping," said Bihlal, after they'd each had their fair share of lager. "I am crying like a child."

"Why are you crying, mate? You have a good life, good wives," said Patrick, hoarse by this late hour. "What about your clinic?"

"I do not own my land," said Bihlal. "And without land here, you are nothing. Less than nothing. But you know this," he said, smiling. "You've been listening to me each of these evenings, all of this time. Correct?"

"Correct."

"Do you know that when nobody comes—do you know what I am doing? I am collecting wood. I am selling this wood. To buy rice! I tell you, I am crying."

Hugh fought off his own requisite groundswell of sadness—good ol' drunken sadness. The sadness for others was always so much more accessible, so much clearer. Here he could identify infinite pain and frank inequality and the face of every bloated-bellied child with yellowy eyes. Here were poverty and its twin, poor health. Here was the sadness of remembering those Nuer babies with smallpox, years ago now, those men and women and children under those pox-foul sheets, who still seemed far better off than those here in Dar. Bihlal was a king compared to all of them. And compared to Bihlal, Hugh was . . . ? He was a sap, of course; a guilty white sap of a man, drinking his mushroom-y dirty-sock-smelling beer until it felt as if he were floating on the bitter pale foam of it, up up up, and steeling himself against his urges to give Bihlal everything in his pockets, against spewing promises to wire money the very next day into a personal account. And the more Bihlal talked, the more Hugh was fairly certain that there was no clinic fifty kilometers away, and, even if there *was*, Bihlal probably swept its floors and prepared its limited medicines. No, Bihlal was, most likely, a well-meaning con artist, and even if Hugh did empty his pockets right there, Bihlal would be right where he started in one or two months' time.

And Bihlal—he was anything but stupid—he probably knew this, too.

By the time the stars were diamonds in the sky, Hugh agreed they could use his Land Rover (bought in '65 from a bitter Brit, finally headed back to Surrey), which was parked across from the hotel. Aisha sat beside him, Patrick sat in the front seat, and Bihlal drove them all toward what was, according to Bihlal, *premium lodging quite near—very near—to my clinic!*

They sped through grassland, between trees whose branches reached every which way and looked, tonight, like broken parasols missing their shades. They sped over paved roads that turned quickly to unpaved roads that Hugh knew to be reddish and rutted, where one could only drive fast for fear of getting caught in the ruts. And when they arrived at the cement block without windows, at the choked weeds in cracked earth, he felt farther away from Dar es Salaam than he had ever been, even though he'd driven as far as Uganda many times throughout the year, and here he was smashed and exhausted and who knew precisely where?

A yellow light signified an entrance. Bihlal spoke to a man in a djellaba, who handed the three men three keys. Were they really going to see Bihlal's clinic in the morning? From the way that Bihlal spoke to the man in the djellaba, from the way the man in the djellaba was grinning, Hugh did not believe so. Tobacco and bleach wafted through the vacant hall.

"Thank you, my friends." Bihlal clapped the two men on the back. His room was evidently on the first floor.

"Good night."

"Good night."

"Good night."

"God will bless you."

"Don't be so sure," said Hugh.

Patrick laughed.

"Please, my friends," Bihlal nodded toward Aisha, "have no doubt."

"Good night," said Hugh again. "Thank you," he said, though he wasn't sure why.

Patrick climbed the stairs with Hugh and Aisha. They climbed in silence, and when Patrick opened a door on the second floor, he entered without so much as an attempt to kiss Aisha's hand. "I'm knackered," he said, and went inside.

On the third floor the hall light was broken. Hugh felt his way along the walls; the rough concrete lightly scraped his palms. "I'm over here," he said.

"Here?" she whispered.

"Closer."

He felt her reaching for him, but when her hand brushed his hip she immediately pulled away.

He opened the door to the room, turned on the light, and instantly regretted doing so. The dark had suited him, but—then again—he really wanted to look at her.

When she closed the door, the world—magically and conveniently—disappeared.

"Hello," he said.

"Hello," she said. "You look very tired."

"You don't," he said. "You never do."

"May I have a drink of water first?"

"Aisha, please," he said, not even concealing his irritation with her obsequiousness. "You know you never have to ask me something like that. I have told you and told you. You may do whatever you please."

She took up the jar that sat on the metal table and poured water into two glasses.

"Tell me," Hugh said, accepting his glass, though he made sure not to drink from it. "How is your father?"

"My father is the same," she said. "The money for the treatment—we were all very grateful to have it."

"I'm glad," Hugh said, before glancing away. "And I'm sorry."

"For what?"

"I'm sorry he isn't healed."

"Yes," she said, "of course." She pursed her full lips and nodded.

"I am," Hugh said.

"Yes, all right."

She sat down on the bed, atop a pilled orange coverlet, under the weak lightbulb, and when she sighed (lightly—but still) he knew she wasn't going to give him what he really wanted: the absolution for being unable to change not only her fate but the fate of her entire family, which he knew she viewed as one and the same. She grinned in the same way she had at the bar, when Bihlal had—unaware of their acquaintance—made his crass presentation. It was, then and now, as if she were not only a stranger but also a mother, and Hugh—slouching down in his chair—was a tiresome child, and she was going along with his tedious game of pretending only because that's what was expected of women, all women, when faced with a tiresome child.

"Aisha," he said.

He didn't apologize for pretending she was a stranger in front of the men. And he wasn't wholeheartedly sorry; Bihlal and Patrick—they'd needed something from him, too. They needed him to be the naïve one, the young one whose mistakes weren't grave as yet. Hugh had been unable to meet her gaze, had been unable to even ask her for a beer, and now, after riding through the desert with her thigh and shoulder touching his throughout the journey, with her sweet onion sandalwood scent right there in the car, he still couldn't look at her, not straight on. He glimpsed her in flashes—the brown skirt too warm for this temperature. The high, shining forehead. The otherworldly smooth skin. And he noticed, as he always did—before his overwhelming need erased the possibility for such sane observation—her stillness. Her stillness that brought forth his loneliness like an equal trade, and with the clarity of a runner gunning toward the finish, her stillness unnerved and undid him, until he came close to leaving the miserable room, thumbnail bitten to the quick.

But then she lay back on the bed and he came to her, and when she continued to say nothing and that nothing became silence—devoid of ethics or currency or the existence of before and after—when it was there, the blank silence, save the hum of the generator and the odd truck passing on the byroad, he touched the top of her tautly braided head and asked her to take off her clothes.

He clutched her from behind and didn't last long. As usual, he had the fantasy of being invisible and watching her pleasure herself or even do a series of mundane activities (prepare tea, sweep the floor, scratch an itch) rather than his actually being there and taking any kind of charge. Afterward, as always, she insisted on washing him. She led him to where a showerhead sprayed into a small cement room. She took the bleach-rough cloth between her hands and stroked and scrubbed Hugh's back. She didn't seem to be in any kind of rush, spoke of one day studying in London. She marveled at the beauty of his chest hair, which never ceased to amuse him. He turned his face to the nozzle, and the pressure was just strong enough. She'd begun to hum, and the tepid water drowned out her meandering tune.

He left an envelope full of enough money for Bihlal and Patrick to hire a car, whenever it was that they eventually awoke, and, after dropping Aisha off at a safe distance from her family's home, with a pocket full of money of her own (if my father sees your car, he will have you killed, she'd calmly informed him), Hugh continued on to Ocean Road. Night still clung to the sky. Hugh had trouble shedding Aisha's touch, Aisha's voice, and the haunted feeling to which he was already somewhat ac-customed. He convinced himself that his sense of being both haunted and more alive—which had started when he'd arrived on this continent as a devotee of Charlie Case—was at least part of why he had never really left. Oh, he'd been *back*—a few weeks here and there to reinstate his visa, have a job interview in D.C., see a doctor about his stomach (which had never been the same since dysentery four years ago), and spend one summer vacation. But it was always for a distinct purpose and never more than a month, and it had always made him feel out of sorts and yearning to return.

Yes, he'd wanted to make a contribution to a postcolonial system; yes, he was deeply disgusted with the proliferation of poverty and disease in the world, and both were more than plentiful here. But he'd also found several bureaucratic avenues while on this continent that allowed him to avoid being drafted to Vietnam, plus he had no interest in being anywhere near his father, whose own disgust with Hugh had evidently not dimmed with age. *I love Africa,* Hugh had written years ago to Charlie Case. *One reason for this may very well be that, here, there simply is no concept of time.* And Charlie had written him back, from Harvard, where he had started his very own film department, despite continuing to insist that he was not an academic. *Shipley,* he wrote, *you're not an African, so African time hardly applies to you. Don't get in the habit of justifying your own laziness. That's a deadly one, especially in an expatriate.*

After, when Aisha's arms were around him and he was a safe distance from his own life—he didn't give a good goddamn how pretentious it sounded; he wasn't planning on saying it aloud, for Christ's sake—he felt closer to the dead. He felt the burden of his own insignificance, and this specific bewildering weight gave him a simultaneously disconcerting and reassuring charge. And though he knew he had to stop these visits to Aisha (he wished he could convince himself that this last one didn't count; he hadn't sought her out, he really hadn't), he wasn't totally convinced he would ever stop, now that he'd begun it. He knew, too, that it wouldn't always be Aisha. He couldn't even allow himself that particular romantic delusion.

It had been more than a year since he'd met her at the clinic where she'd come with her father—a tubercular, pneumatic tyrant. Among

Hugh's various administrative duties was managing the line of miserable souls, often deciding who needed to see Dr. Shannon immediately.
When Hugh met Aisha and her father, he knew her father did not qual-
ify to cut in front of the others—due to the fact that his demise was already in full swing. This kind of judgment was precisely what Hugh was
supposed to be able to handle, but Aisha had taken Hugh's hand and
asked him to move her father past three truly sick children—who Hugh
knew were not only more critical but also had the potential to bounce
back—and right to the front of the line. Her voice had been low, it was
a voice that meant business, and Hugh decided the old man was as deserving as anyone else.

Who was he to judge, after all?

As he drove now, in the middle of this moonless night, he felt the
intestinal twitch (a souvenir from his bout with dysentery), which meant
he was soon going to need to relieve his bowels. He hoped—he even
prayed—that he'd make it to his house. His intestinal disasters, his dif-
ficulties swallowing—he had not pictured any of that when he aborted a
promising career as a photographer. He had made choices. This was all
a choice; he knew this. He also knew he hadn't sunk the bulk of his trust
into renovating and restructuring and running a health clinic for Afri-
cans who couldn't afford their local hospital in order to spend his life
alternating between rushing to the bathroom and fawning over dark
skin, leaving money on dressers and in shoes.

But there he was—exactly right there—in the middle of the night.
He drove faster, passed through the mercantile neighborhood, with the
closed-up shops of Indians, Bangladeshis, Pakistanis, and Sri Lankans,
the signs in Hindi, the smells of a thousand spices and their vats of
starchy rice, all wafting through Hugh's open window. He recalled a
time when the most exotic place he had ever driven through was Blue
Hill Avenue—only miles from his childhood but a world away—when
Ed probably had no idea that Hugh was having to refrain from acting
too eager, too thrilled.

He crossed the bridge to the other side of the lagoon, and there the air underwent a drastic change. The wind still carried the faintest trace of burning garbage, but as that smell faded, as he heard the waves lapping against the seaweed-choked and salt-whorled cliffs, another smell—saline, floral—arrived in its place. Here was moonlight on purple bougainvillea, blue jacaranda, and flaming red hibiscus. Here were porches, gravel driveways, a wandering peacock; here was a parked Mercedes. Here it was—good fortune—contained and severed from the rest of the city. And as he drew closer to the street where they'd lived for more than three years now, his insides sprang into coils like the insides of the mattress he'd laid on with Aisha, the rusted metal poking now and again through cheap, hard foam. His stomach churned as he tried to remember whether he'd gone through all of the antacid in the medicine cabinet.

The house was dark, but the too-bright streetlight meant to deter bandits was illuminated, and it filtered through the curtains that his wife had so carefully (*obsessively*, he'd argued) considered—brightly colored batiks chosen from a stall on Uhuru Street, from the most convincing of vendors who'd shouted and whistled for his *mzungu* bride. There were crumbs along the countertop of the small kitchen; a cluster of red ants was arduously clearing them away. He wondered, briefly, what she'd eaten to leave such crumbs and if it had been her whole dinner. He imagined crystallized honey on crumbly bread—the swallowing again and yet again, waiting for the taste to improve.

He turned on the bathroom light and relieved himself, checked his stool as Shannon had taught him to—for irregularities, for darkness—smirking as he always did, because he remembered Raoul Merva telling him a story about how, as a young man in Hungary, he'd suffered terribly from insomnia, until one summer, when he'd been working on a dairy farm (*I'd been using my hands*, Raoul had solemnly explained), he'd begun to give some thought to feces, about why, as human beings, we are so afraid of our feces. Perhaps, he'd mused, these thoughts had blossomed because he'd grown so fond of the cows, who (he'd clarified) really knew how to take a shit. Raoul told Hugh with considerable pride how one evening he'd had enough of fear. "My friend," he told Hugh, "I relieved myself in the shower. And I looked at it. And do you know what I did? I picked it up. I picked it up, and I held it in my hands." Hugh nodded and nodded until he couldn't hold back his laughter. He'd laughed until it became clear that Raoul had something more to say. "Since that day, I have slept like a baby. Since then," said Raoul, "I am not afraid."

Hugh smirked because he remembered what it felt like to be that young and laughing and because there was nothing funny about shit these days; nothing funny about shit at all. A few chalky antacid pills remained, and he took one with a tall glass of water, wincing, as he always did, when he felt the pill go down. He turned off the light and went into the living room, sat for a moment on the green couch that looked comfortable and cheerful but was in fact punishingly hard. Hugh glanced around. He could be anywhere. The house looked the way he imagined an army barracks house might look, like the home of some poor drafted son of a bitch heading from Texas to Saigon, with the scared wife sleeping in the lumpy bed, praying for a safe return.

The draft, argued Ed, *unifies a country. Certainly you're not saying that anyone really deserves a special exemption?*

It was a stupid argument, one of their many, as neither one of them thought the war was just, and frankly—for different reasons—neither one of them was going to fight in it (Hugh wrangled himself a job as a Peace Corps evaluator, while Ed remained in school as long as possible—there were somehow always more classes in which he apparently *had* to be enrolled—before finally enlisting in the reserves). But their conversations had become increasingly polarized during the few times they'd seen each other over the years, and the war, the draft—it was an obvious place to start. Ed believed in the draft but not the war, which Hugh argued meant that he couldn't believe in the draft, because how could he support a draft for a war in which he did not believe?

It was like that.

It was—during the few times Hugh had been through New York—two quick drinks and one long lunch, over which they had their final blowout three years ago, over the goddamn Middle East.

All Hugh had done was bring up a *New York Times* editorial he'd read that morning in the gastrointestinal doc's office, which had questioned the wisdom of Israel's annexation of Jerusalem's old city, and Ed—who'd seemed agitated upon sitting down, who frankly had not seemed remotely relaxed with Hugh since they'd said goodbye at the ferry dock in New London after that awful Fishers weekend at the Ordways'—became suddenly enraged. He'd broken down the history of the Jews: their expulsion from every country after committing the sin of success, their near extermination, the subsequent allowance (*thank God*) by the rest of the world for—finally—a Jewish state. When Hugh tried to maintain that, though he was not arguing with Ed's position (he really wasn't!), Ed had to admit that this *allowance* had not exactly been established with much concern for the existing indigenous Arab population, Ed grew silent and twitchy.

Hugh said, "Listen, you're upset. I understand it's emotional."

"I'm not emotional," said Ed. "Listen, you know what? We don't have to agree." He picked up a toothpick, turned it over in his hands.

"We never have," said Hugh. He'd smiled. He'd tried to catch his friend's eye, but Ed was looking at the maître d', signaling for the check.

Ed shrugged. "I just think, y'know, why force it?"

"What are you talking about?"

The maître d' brought the check, and Ed slapped down his credit card.

"Let me," said Hugh. "You paid last time."

But Ed shook his head.

Hugh nodded. "I hope we can chalk this up to another chapter of a lifelong argument."

"Look," Ed had said, squinting out the window at the streets of Manhattan, where he so obviously belonged now. "We're old friends," he'd said, still not looking at Hugh. "And old friends?" He shook his head. "They usually grow apart."

Now he tried not to wake his wife as he moved the cloud of netting aside and climbed into bed. He tried not to shift, not to breathe. He could get a few hours' sleep if he didn't wake her. If he did wake her, they might get to talking, and when they talked at this late hour, neither one could go back to sleep. Sometimes it was nice—she'd make coffee with hot milk, maybe they'd fool around—and sometimes it was not. Sometimes she decided they needed to figure out their future straight-away in that one sleepless moment: when could they move, if maybe Hugh should go back to school, if maybe she *could* give in and have a baby after all, even if they stayed right where they were.

"That you?" she murmured.

"Maybe," he said.

Recently Helen had been talking in her sleep, and he often tried to engage her in conversation. Sometimes he told her about these noctur-nal exchanges and always portrayed a funny scene, but, in fact, his mo-tives were not as lighthearted as he described; he knew what he was really doing was trying to catch her in the middle of something—he wasn't sure what, but in the grip of a secret life is what he'd begun to suspect.

"*Maybe* it's me," he said, smoothing the blankets on top of her hip. "And maybe it isn't." He heard her quietly snoring again and was strangely disappointed.

When he thought of Ed these days, as he was doing just then, it was usually because he craved his opinions, the very opinions against which he'd always fought. He knew he was thinking of Ed because of what he would say if he could see him now, in bed with Helen, after coming from Aisha. Leaving aside the impatience, the arrogance, and the aggressiveness—Ed was the most loyal guy he'd ever met. That Ed had essentially dumped him as a friend somehow didn't disrupt this idea. Hugh still saw Ed as being loyal to his own beliefs, loyal to his feelings of disconnection, to the idea of friendship as being something true, something you feel or you don't.

When he'd told Helen about that awful lunch in New York, she'd seemed oddly relieved, as if she'd secretly been thinking that Hugh's friendship with Ed had been doomed from the start. They'd even fought about it; when Hugh accused her of never having liked Ed, of even looking down on him, she'd grown furious—she'd even cried. Hugh ended up apologizing; they'd hardly spoken of Ed again.

But now he pictured the Cantowitz arguing style of sitting up straighter and straighter, of posture improved by ire, and for some reason—at this late hour, at this very moment—picturing this friend who had written him off over a stupid political argument *that hadn't even been an argument* strangely made him feel—if not exactly better—somehow more authentic. He'd valued the obvious differences between Ed and him and still frankly revered the idea that people could, in fact, come from wildly different worlds, completely disagree, and still remain true friends. The funny thing was that he knew this guiding principle separately rankled both Ed and Helen. He knew they each pegged him as a bit phony, too cerebral or worse.

"Where were you?" Helen asked suddenly, and Hugh could tell that she was no longer sleeping.

"The clinic," he said, pulling her close.

"Mmm," she said, yawning. "What time is it?"

"Around five."

"Hugh?"

"Yes."

"Someone spit on me today."

"Someone spat at you?"

"A woman. I didn't have any money on me. I went into my purse to give her something, and when I couldn't come up with something, she spit at my feet."

"Helen—"

"I was angry, Hugh. I didn't recognize myself. I wanted to spit back."

"Oh, Helen," he said. "Oh, no."

A mosquito dove into his ear and—defeating all previous attempts at quiet—Hugh slapped furiously before bounding out of bed for the badminton racket, purchased for this specific purpose. *From China, my friend*, the Hindu had said. *Superior choice for killing mozzies.*

"It's dead," said Hugh. "I got him."

"I hate it here," she said. "I really do." She put her ankle over his. "You're the only person I know."

Chapter Nine

New York City, 1970

Armed with two summers at Ordway Keller and an MBA from Harvard Business school, Ed (with no small amount of fear and exhilaration) turned down a more permanent offer from Guy Ordway himself, and—with the conviction that too much history haunted both Ordway Keller's stodgy protocols and his own unpleasant memories—took up with three other upstarts, three other men equally lacking in heritage but who'd convinced him to join a brand-new securities firm; they had scraped together enough money (primarily from fathers-in-law) to pay for a seat on the exchange.

Hy Bechstein was incontrovertibly fat and had paranoid fits, but his knowledge of companies was exhaustive. Ed couldn't figure out how he'd acquired so much information, and, if Hy had any net worth whatsoever (he didn't; they'd each disclosed their bank statements at the start), Ed would have assumed he'd hired a pack of spies. It was as if he personally went to every targeted factory and boardroom daily; he had a nose for opportunity. It had been Hy's idea to buy the black-and-white marble notebook from the office supply near the A train and have each partner record his business at the end of the trading day. When Steve Osheroff (handsome, from Larchmont, nothing exceptional upstairs) had laughed wryly at this idea (Steve was the only one among them who

could actually pull off *wry*), Hy stood his ground with such conviction
and such an impassioned speech about fairness that Ed and Marty Rabb
(stutterer, number cruncher) were awed into rare silence.

There was a frenetic quality to each day in their Broad Street office,
which suited Ed, an urgency that put him at ease. The days were so intense that he'd even given up coffee for two years now, as he'd often
drunk untold amounts and had become so jittery by the end of the day
that once he got into a screaming fight on the subway with a putz who
refused a pregnant woman a seat. In their office, even the details of lunch
were treated with serious consideration, and there was an open competition over who could a) buy it cheaper (or better—bring it from home),
b) get it over faster and waste less time on eating, or c) book more
lunches out with potential clients and get better tables at top restaurants—
La Grenouille, Chambord, 21. *Who won lunch?* was decided with an afternoon Cert. Marty was addicted to them, went through rolls at a time,
and each day at four o'clock he peeled one individually out of its
gold-wrapped tube and placed it on the winner's desk. Each day's lunch
had to produce a winner; failure to reach consensus was not tolerated.

"When articles are written about Cantowitz, Bechstein, Osheroff,
and Rabb," said Steve, while rolling a Cert around in his mouth, "they'll
talk about the importance of healthy competition."

"When *books* are written," said Ed, "because you'd better believe
they will be, they'll just say we were four Jews obsessed with money and
food."

"That's fine by me," said Hy.

"M-m-me, too," said Marty.

Ever loyal to his first great idea, Ed became the resident expert in following all things automotive, and his first substantial record in the
black-and-white marble ledger was getting the Boston Mutual Funds to
invest in auto-aftermarket securities. He'd convinced them with his
well-honed used-car theory and with his hard-earned statistics about
automotive parts. Ed convinced them that these many manufacturers

were compelling—even necessary—securities investments. There were, in fact, more than 150 million cars on the road these days.

I don't see that number dwindling anytime soon, Ed had said, leaning back in his chair, after at least a full hour of leaning forward. *Do you?*

He spent much of his day organizing a travel schedule for himself, as he was more or less constantly visiting dealerships and factories, and this suited him fine; he liked traveling. Having been particularly affected by Albert Finney's roadside blonde in *Two for the Road,* he liked the fantasy of meeting women in transit (a fantasy that had, sadly, remained just that). Also, he liked having excuses to indulge his cravings for Ring Dings and Wise potato chips each time he stopped for gas. He wasn't crazy about being at home. His apartment was a boxy one-bedroom far east on 74th Street, with more or less zero personal touches besides a framed Mondrian poster from the Boston Museum of Fine Arts gift shop, acquired during his first year in business school. He'd taken a date to the exhibition and—in a fit of excitement about both Mondrian and the date—bought the poster with every intention of giving it to her, but the relationship had fizzled by the time he'd picked it up at the framer's.

He was the only bachelor in the firm. The others all had wives and children and mortgages, while Ed's only responsibility was to look in on his father now and then, to make sure he was still washing, eating, breathing. He followed enough companies in or near Boston that he could usually check in on him during one of these trips, and it never failed to amaze him how much the neighborhood had transformed. Ed could always tell when the high school was about to let out for the day, as the vendors along Blue Hill Avenue would suddenly rush to take their goods from the sidewalk stalls, head inside, and lower their metal grates. Once or twice Ed saw what happened if they didn't take this precaution: overturned fruit carts, clothing thrown into the street. The avenue be-longed to these furious kids now, and to be an old Jewish man living in Dorchester these days was to fully embrace one's obstinacy. To hear his father (boastfully) tell it, groups of black youths, with knives in their pockets, dared him only to look at them wrong.

But as much as his father was apparently hated, he had also (and only

God knew how) managed to ingratiate himself to Mrs. Darrence, the black woman whom Ed employed to clean his father's apartment. It wasn't uncommon for Ed to stop by on a weekday afternoon and find his father and Mrs. Darrence watching a game show on television. Once, Ed found Mrs. Darrence's kid there, too, jabbing his adolescent fist toward the TV in what had to have been the most informal boxing instruction Ed had ever seen. His father harshly criticized the boy over the noise of the game show, but neither Mrs. Darrence nor the boy seemed offended. Ed became accustomed to his father's maid looking him over with undisguised disapproval, sucking in on her teeth if Ed—during one of his many stabs at conversation—raised his own voice to his own father in his own childhood home.

Ed of course wondered if Mrs. Darrence was getting more money from his father or if his father might even be *involved* with her. Ed sometimes walked into a room of angrily raised voices, but the content always proved to be the unforgivable shortcomings of others. Often others they'd seen at the supermarket. Or on the television. Ed had never heard such shouting. Despite the fact that her paycheck came from Ed, Mrs. Darrence did not hide her belief that Ed was an ungrateful ass.

He liked bringing people together and he realized he was good at it, focusing more and more on deal-making, beginning with his connections from those summers at Ordway Keller and calling them up—*What are you working on?*—sticking his nose in a few western corporations, and eventually investing in companies whose need for capital was critical. He got a thrill from being the touchstone for so many moving targets; sometimes he imagined the meetings were movie shoots and he was the director. Not that he wasn't preoccupied by the numbers but, just as seriously, he considered the chemistry of the players: who was insecure, who was bombastic, who needed Ed's lighter touch to set the deal in motion and bring the story to life.

Since deal-making sometimes involved dinners with wives and since

Ed didn't have a wife or steady girlfriend, he often brought the best-looking date he could find to accompany him during these evenings, earning him what seemed to be a combination of some resentment and more than a little respect. Usually it was right before dessert that the wife to his right or left leaned in and charmingly inquired why he wasn't married. Usually the wife in question was flirting or he told himself she was; either way, this question always made him feel as if he was a catch and that the state of his bachelorhood was troubling to someone other than himself—not that he would ever admit that this aspect of his life wasn't exactly by design.

Since his first summer in New York, when Helen Ordway stripped him of every shred of confidence in his impulses and his judgment, Ed took out girl after girl, but never for long enough to find out what any of them was really like. He came to see his subsequent parade of dates like the reams of paper that covered his desk on any given day, even Saturdays, even Sundays, now that the nation, too, was having a fit of insecurity and stocks were truly sliding. Ed was coming to see that girls were like numbers, and numbers didn't lie, but they also never represented the whole picture. It was the numbers he pursued harder now, taking the time to visit the companies, going past the statistics to meet the people behind them, investigating the complexities of what made a company undervalued or overvalued, and never taking any one person's word. But with girls he stayed on the surface, hardly putting in the time. By the time one girl was reapplying lipstick beside him in a banquette, he was looking in her compact to see who might be reflected from one table over. *Onward and upward,* Hy liked to say. *Boy, do you have the life.*

But he knew that Hy didn't mean it. Ed knew that Hy's idea of a great time was to stop at the nursery off the parkway and buy plants for his half-acre backyard in White Plains, where his beloved wife, Franny, let his two chubby girls draw with crayons on the walls. "I tell her—go on and let them. They'll be artistic!" said Hy. "Because we won't live in this house forever, am I right? I tell them that soon enough we'll buy another house. And before we leave? We'll repaint!"

Though lately even Hy's confidence was wearing thin. Wall Street was suffering, firms were reporting losses due to paperwork confusion, and Cantowitz, Bechstein, Osheroff, and Rabb (though doing respectably) were not exempt from danger, as they were dependent on a clearinghouse to process their paperwork and their clearinghouse wasn't able to keep up with their needs. Apparently their little firm represented a disproportionate amount of business for their overloaded clearing broker, and Ed took it upon himself to meet with the head of the company, an old blowhard named McKay, whom he despised on sight and who treated Ed—over the course of a tense dinner—as if CBOR's huge volume of activity was somehow suspicious, too aggressive, as if their very rapid rise was in itself an affront. And when Ed had the nerve to explain that the clearinghouse was stuck in the past and to say, *One day you will thank me for saying this: Invest NOW in the technology you so sorely need to keep up with the present, and you will own the future,* McKay asked for the check, nearly grabbing the waiter's arm, he was in such a big hurry to leave. *So we need our paperwork processed regularly,* explained Ed. *Is this really too much to ask?*

When, by the following month, their clearinghouse dumped them as clients, and when Ed's personality was cited as the deciding factor, he spent one brutal and completely sleepless night in the office (leaving only to eat an enormous diner breakfast at six A.M., watching the street come to life beyond the smudged window) and greeted Hy, Steve, and Marty as they came through the door, demanding they hear him out before making any calls.

"We can have our own processing facilities," he blurted out. "We can do it in-house and save boatloads."

"W-w-where," demanded Marty.

"I ran the numbers. I've been over it all night. This is a good thing."

"A good thing," repeated Steve. "Pardon me, but a good thing, my ass. And you're ignoring Marty's excellent question," said Steve. "Where, Ed? Where indeed?"

"We'll need a bigger office," Ed said, as if it were perfectly obvious. "You didn't think we'd stay here forever, did you?"

"I didn't think we'd be dumped by our clearinghouse due to your *personality*. Did *you*?"

"Come on," said Ed, "the clearinghouses are hopeless. You gotta trust me."

Hy cleared his throat. Up until that moment, he'd been scarily silent. "We'll bring in an expert," he finally said. "We'll double our daily business. Say goodbye to your home lives. Marty will be in charge."

"Thank you," said Ed. "Thank you, Hy."

"The justice department is raising questions about the whole . . . overarching . . . fixed-rate fucking *system*," said Hy. "The SEC will soon be up our ass anyway, we're already under attack, and now *this*?" He loosened his tie. "I'm not speaking to you unless I have to."

Ed was watching coverage of protests in D.C. when the phone rang one evening, and soon after answering he knew that the fever pitch of the teeming crowds plus the phone's somehow particularly urgent ring would always be sealed in his memory. The governor of Ohio said something equating the protesting students with brown shirts and communists and vigilantes, and the networks were playing it again and again, and when Ed finally picked up—"Hello?"—there was Guy Ordway's voice, deep and immediately recognizable, even though Ed hadn't—up until that day—ever heard it over the telephone. His first awful thought was that something had happened to Helen. "Sir?" he asked foolishly. "Is everything all right?"

"We need to talk," he said. As if it hadn't been more than six years since they'd done so, since Ed had turned him down after summer number two and Ordway had refrained from shaking his hand after a particularly chilly goodbye.

"Are you watching the news?" asked Ed, prolonging the moment when he'd hear something truly terrible and understand why Ordway had called.

"No," said Ordway. "This country is a disgrace."

Only Ordway could somehow intrude upon his evening and then make such a statement sound as if Ed was personally responsible for the state of the fragmented nation.

"Sir," said Ed, picking up a cushion and slamming it against the wall, "what do you want to talk about?"

"Just business," he said wearily. "I'll pick you up at your office tomorrow at six."

"You don't even know where—"

"Six," said Ordway, and he hung up, leaving Ed to feel a strange combination of relief mixed with disappointment and curiosity. He watched a replay of a clip from just days ago: Nixon defending his decision to invade Cambodia. The president trained his beady eyes at the camera; every now and then he consulted a piece of paper, held between two steady hands.

On the following unseasonably hot spring day, the kind of disorienting weather that creates instant drama, Ed was in the office by eight-thirty and Hy was already there; the phones were ringing. Ordway Keller was going under. One of the oldest firms in America, underwriter of many of the largest and most reputable companies in the country, exquisitely jump-started by Mr. Guy Ordway in the 1950s—its problems were now insurmountable. Evidently they'd had their own paperwork disasters along with the rest of Wall Street, and—according to Hy's various sources—by the time Ordway finally agreed to implement anything close to a modern computer system, the bedrock was so shattered that the firm had lost more than five million dollars at the start of the year. Unbeknownst to Ed, the office had already drastically shrunk, and still they'd continued hemorrhaging money at an alarming pace.

As Hy spat out the information as fast as he could speak, at first Ed was simply relieved. He was relieved not to have stayed in that death trap, and he spent a good couple of minutes inwardly praising his instincts. But the more he heard—over the phone from others, and every several minutes from a very keyed-up Hy—the more he realized that since Wall Street firms were affiliations and the New York Stock Exchange was essentially one gigantic affiliation, if a weak link was a big weak link, the whole system could potentially collapse. And since any special trust set up for such disasters had to already be pretty depleted during such a fragile time, it alone could never cushion the fall of such a giant as Ordway Keller.

"They'd found a way out," declared Hy, who was holding an enormous cheese Danish in one hand and a phone in the other. When he hung up the phone, he hung on to the uneaten Danish. "You'll never believe this," he told Ed, at the end of a particularly long phone call.

"Out with it."

"There's a group of Texans who agreed to put cash into Ordway Keller in exchange for a huge interest rate and stock options. Everything was all set, but then one of these guys—real hard-nosed type, I guess— began to suspect Ordway Keller was misrepresenting how bad the situation was and he flew up, arrived at Ordway Keller, and wouldn't budge until Ordway showed him the most recent results, which were basically clouded up with all kinds of crap. This guy—"

"Named?"

"Zimmerman."

Ed raised his brow.

"Nah—he's probably a Kraut. Anyway, this guy is enraged. Not budging. Wants to sue Ordway Keller on top of everything, even though, at this point, there's at least thirteen million of theirs all mixed up in Ordway Keller. He's on a rampage. Uncovering all kinds of missing assets and debits and, oh my God, what a fucking mess."

"That's why he called me," said Ed. The sun was blazing in through the window so brightly, he had to turn away.

"What are you talking about?"

"Ordway," said Ed, suddenly needing to sit down. "Ordway called me last night. We're robust," he said, nearly shaking with astonishment. "We're clean."

"Are you fucking kidding? For a merger? We're unknown."

"Not to him." Ed grinned. "Remember I turned down his offer, and it was a good offer. I bet you he knows all about us. I bet you he's been following us from the start."

"That," said Steve, "and—let's be honest—the more-prominent firms probably turned him down."

Holding the Danish with great and unmistakable authority—as if he were Moses with the Ten Commandments—Hy Bechstein smiled before finally taking a huge bite. His mouth was full, but Ed heard his every word. "I am so fucking happy."

Early August, seven years after his first summer working at Ordway Keller, Ed sat with Hy, Steve, and Marty across from Guy Ordway and more than one hundred of his subordinated lenders, including the furiously white-haired, red-faced Donald Zimmerman, at the Metropolitan Club on East 60th. The building was imposing, the room was frigidly air-conditioned, and there was a lovely breakfast spread that even Hy did not touch. Ed and his partners had learned their nickname among this crowd, most of whom had never before heard of their firm:

Corned Beef On Rye.

Even Ed had to admit it was clever. He looked them all in the eye—the widows, the retired Ordway Keller partners, the sons and grandsons—and when they looked back at him, he could read their thoughts:

This? This is our legacy? But they also looked stunned and weak, and Ed almost pitied them their helpless expectations.

He hadn't yet looked at Ordway. He was almost afraid to see him act grateful, and he felt simultaneously dizzy and angry, and suddenly he realized he was thinking about Helen witnessing her father like this, Helen whom he had vowed never to allow into his thoughts other than as a correction, a way to stay clear-eyed through life. He was thinking of Helen as he listened to a Keller—great-great-grandson of the original company's founder—comment on CBOR's proposed acquisition, and Ed could not take in a word. He was only able to focus on avoiding Ordway's eyes, and since he could not stop thinking of Helen, Ed was so overcome—so unexpectedly thrown off balance—that, after years of abstention, he drank a whole cup of coffee; he needed something bitter, something strong.

The news here at the Metropolitan Club just got worse and worse, with a call-in from Chicago's board of trade demanding Ordway Keller transfer all of its customers' accounts to other firms within forty-eight hours. The pièce de résistance was the announcement by Donald Zimmerman that he would not sign an agreement promising not to sue CBOR, even after the crisis committee chairman of the Exchange gave a stern speech about the very real possibility of at least two hundred securities firms collapsing based on his singular decision and gave Zimmerman a hard deadline. The merger had to happen in two days.

But when the two days passed and the chairman and chief executive of the Exchange telephoned to let Zimmerman know that he was still the only one standing in the way of the merger with CBOR, Zimmerman's lawyer called back and said he was unable to discuss the matter and that he was away on business. The Exchange hastily extended the deadline until nine-thirty the next morning, and when Ed got the word that afternoon, he told Hy they were going to Dallas.

"Are you nuts?" Hy asked.

"Are you?"

"How the fuck are you going to get there on this late notice?"

Ed was already dialing. "We're chartering a plane."

"Chartering a plane," said Hy. *"Chartering a plane?"*

"Teterboro Airport," Ed said to the operator. He wrote the number down.

"Fine," said Hy. "Okay, fine. FINE. Fuck." He slammed his fist on his desk. "I'm calling Franny."

When the evening brought fog and pouring rain, they were stranded for hours at the airport, and by the time the plane actually took off at two

A.M., they had each rehearsed their arguments so many times that the reasoning had started to seem thin. But the good news was that, after using nearly twenty dollars' worth of quarters alternately telephoning the Dallas office and the crisis committee, they had finally located Zimmerman, and he'd agreed to meet Ed and Hy at his offices as soon as they touched down.

At four A.M., on the Dallas tarmac, against the washed-out oil-spill sky, and after more than two sleepless nights, Ed insisted on stopping for coffee and a donut. At the moment he had zero interest in eating, but he doubted Hy would put up much of a fight about stopping, if he mentioned the donut.

"What if he changes his mind?" hollered Hy, as they scrambled into the taxi. "No coffee."

"We're stopping," said Ed, and then to the driver: "I'm sure you know a place to get a strong cup of coffee, am I right?"

"We're not stopping," hollered Hy. "You want me to get a burned tongue right now? You want me to spill coffee on your shirt?"

"You can wait in the cab—"

"Not happening," said Hy, and he gave the driver the address.

When they approached the office complex and took in the metallic-gray high-rise, Ed saw that Zimmerman Enterprises was just as free of personality as he had expected. When the security guard let them in and led them through the halls, the blandness was increasingly intimidating. The blandness seemed to say: *I need nothing other than to complete the task at hand.* It was still dark when a nervous-seeming woman in her fifties showed them to the conference room, and when she flipped on the fluorescent lights, a galaxy of colors flitted across Ed's vision. It took him a second to realize Zimmerman was already in there and that he'd been sitting alone in the dark. He was no longer florid, but he looked angry and tired; from his pale hair to his pallor to his steely demeanor, the man was a study in gray.

Ed stepped forward, offered his hand to Zimmerman, and Hy did the same. Zimmerman's youngish attorney rushed into the room and shook hands. When they all settled into their chairs again and silently prepared for what promised to be a protracted debate, Ed saw their reflection in the dark wall of the windows, and what he saw there—aided no doubt by the greenish light—were four ghouls. Four men with hollow eyes and bright white shirts; four souls sitting around a table, looking haunted and hungry and waiting to be served.

Before anyone else had the chance to do so, Ed stood and launched into his primary plan of attack. He used every ounce of his intensity to break down what would happen if Zimmerman didn't change his mind. "This isn't about saving Ordway Keller," said Ed. "Not anymore. In fact, forget Ordway Keller."

"Believe me," muttered Zimmerman, "it's my greatest wish."

"There will be such a massive crisis of confidence in the very idea of investing. All kinds of firms will close—responsible firms with whom you've done business for years—and thousands of investors—responsible investors!—they'll all be completely destroyed."

"You think I haven't considered this?" barked Zimmerman. "You think I don't know? Young man, this is what happens when men are deceitful. There are consequences for everybody—simple as that."

"It's hardly simple, sir."

Zimmerman looked as if he'd tasted something rotten. "Excuse me?"

"Has it occurred to you, sir, that Wall Street—based on your one decision over the next few hours—might be taken over by the banks or . . . *the government?* That, based on your decision, we might be delivered into socialism?"

Zimmerman laughed, but Ed could tell the bit about socialism had rankled.

"Mr. Cantowitz, I have written off this investment. I have already written it off as a total loss."

"But you don't have to," said Ed. He said it more quietly, more intensely.

"You don't," added Hy.

The woman who'd shown them into the room stuck her head in and said, "Sir, Will Baines is flying in. He's on his way from a meeting in Chicago."

"Thank you, Gloria."

"Y'all need anything?"

Ed made a silent prayer for food and hot coffee, but Zimmerman dismissed her.

"Will Baines won't convince me, either," said Zimmerman. "Thinks just because we went to school together . . . Goddamn fool for signing the agreement. He was swindled same as I was."

"Maybe you should listen to his reasoning," said Hy.

But Zimmerman didn't even answer. He stayed firm as the sun rose, exposing flat highways and other homely office buildings in the distance. He held steady as a fellow Texan, now a top man at Lehman Brothers, called in several times over the course of the morning, urging him to sign. He did not budge as they all descended ravenously on the breakfast trays when they finally appeared or when the big guns were brought in via phone conference, in the form of every major player on Wall Street. Even the trucking suppliers for Zimmerman Enterprises were calling in, offering heartfelt speeches of their own. Ed frankly didn't understand how one man could hold so true to his stubborn opinion, and he started to think about his father up in Dorchester, his father who would always be his father whether or not this deal went through.

Hy was wiping sweat from his brow and eating everything in sight and once in a while giving Ed a look that said, *What the fucking fuck do we do now?*

Things took a surreal turn when one member of the crisis committee in New York apparently had not only tremendous chutzpah but also one hell of an eleventh-hour connection, and Gloria once more stuck her head into the room and said, with notable grace, "Sir, President Nixon is standing by."

And Zimmerman closed his eyes. He calmly shook his head.

The room, for the first time all morning, fell silent. Ed looked up at the clock, at the minutes ticking by. There was one half hour left. Back in New York, Ed knew, the floor would be packed with young brokers ready to kill one another, with older brokers worrying over unstable hearts and agitated ulcers, as everyone waited for the trading to start and for word to come.

Ed took a slug of coffee and looked across the table at Donald Zimmerman. "Donald," Ed said. These raw and terrible hours had worn down any doubts about being on a first-name basis, but even saying his name felt like a calculated risk. "May we go into your office and speak privately?"

"Ed—" attempted Hy.

Zimmerman pushed back his chair and stood up. Ed followed him out to the industrial-carpeted hallway and into his spacious corner office. Zimmerman was a man with stooped shoulders, probably not any younger than Ed's own father, and Ed wondered if he had children. *I'm exhausted,* thought Ed. *But he's more exhausted.*

"Donald," said Ed. "I want you to listen to me very carefully."

"Son, I've been listening," he said wearily.

"This is different," said Ed, and his coffee-laced heart started to pump wildly. "You're a Jew," he said. He waited a moment for the incensed reaction, but—as he'd expected—it didn't arrive. "You're a Jew and so am I. I am not speaking to you as someone invested in this deal. I am speaking to you as someone who knows what's going to happen if there is a disaster as momentous as everyone is predicting."

"Okay," he said. "I'm listening."

"The story," continued Ed, "is going to go like this: One stubborn Jew brought down Wall Street. A Jew brought on a second Great Depression. You know I'm right. You know it." He fixed his gaze on Zimmerman and willed himself not to blink. "We have already lost so much, sir," Ed said, and—taking his voice down—added, "I beg of you: Don't do this."

When—after what must have been a good two minutes—Donald Zimmerman finally nodded, when he sat behind his desk and grabbed hold of a blue Bic pen, Ed ran out of the office and into the conference room, where he grabbed the telephone as if it was a lifeline. He called their trusted floor partner on the Big Board, the one they all owed big-time for that first successful year of CBOR's shaky existence. "Get the order tickets printed," Ed told him hoarsely. "CBOR–Ordway Keller."

"You serious?" the floor partner whispered.

"Very. The deal is done. Oh, and one more thing: Do me a favor and don't hang up the phone."

Ed stayed on the line as the news spread throughout the floor. He would never forget the sound. It sounded like being at a stadium, a boxing stadium: a slow and ruthless roar.

Chapter Ten

New York City, 1971–1972

Since that fateful day when Donald Zimmerman folded and the Ordway Keller deal was done, Cantowitz, Bechstein, Osheroff, and Rabb went from having five thousand accounts to fifty thousand.

They'd also found their blueprint for success.

Ed's Dallas vision of four ghouls around the table turned out to have been something more prescient than the mere hallucination of an exhausted man. For what catapulted CBOR–Ordway Keller to the big leagues of Wall Street, and what would necessitate not only a Beverly Hills office but fifteen others throughout the country, was that they capitalized on the deaths of once-powerful firms; they listened for the struggling, wheezing last breaths and moved in like surgeons or vultures, depending on one's perspective. One could (and Ed did) argue that what they specialized in was facilitating graceful exits; they preserved shreds of dignity, upheld fading reputations.

He'd also persuaded enough traders to buy shares in CBOR–Ordway Keller that he was, officially, a big shot. Ed had acquired not only the legitimacy of history but enormous capital through the initial public stock offering, once the SEC finally allowed it. But these were volatile times, and his success did not change the fact that the markets were sluggish and investors were more or less consistently bowing out. Nothing was a sure thing. And because Ed still lived in his boxy impersonal apartment and he spent all of his nights either at the office (now in Midtown) or at increasingly frequent business dinners, life had not changed nearly as much as he would have imagined.

At thirty he was also officially "still single." The wives at business dinners who asked if he'd like to be set up now did so with a slight note of annoyance, having set him up so many times already, with less than spectacular results. Ed knew that the unwritten rule of dating was to act at least a little bit flirtatious, even if it was clear at the evening's start that there was not a prayer for romance, and he also knew he wasn't one to live up to his end of the bargain. He thought that wasting someone else's time was downright deceitful, and because Ed would have absolutely preferred an honest assessment of what his own chances were, he figured it was only fair to share his own appraisal. He'd once suggested to a date that they leave it at drinks and not proceed to dinner; he'd expected that she'd agree and that they'd shake hands and say goodbye, full of relief. Instead, the date had started to tremble, before telling him tearfully that, for his information, he was ten pounds overweight.

Rude was a word that had reportedly come up. Also: *Who does he think he is?*

His best blind date thus far had been described as "a powerhouse PR gal, divorced, no children, attractive Jewish brunette." Their phone conversation was brief, no last names were mentioned, and when he walked into the Oak Room (her choice), there—laughing from the first moment, saying, "Come *ON*! You've got to be *kidding* me!"—sat Connie Graff. "This is ridiculous. You're not going to believe this, but I thought I was meeting someone named Fred." She was the picture of New York chic, in a black pantsuit, thick hair upswept with a heavy tortoise comb. Her face looked slightly different and, though he wasn't absolutely certain, he was pretty sure it was her nose. She'd had it done; it didn't look phony at all. She looked so great that he was surprised how enthusiastically she leapt up to embrace him. He hadn't seen her since she'd left Cambridge, engaged.

"Tell me everything," she said, while simultaneously waving over the bartender.

"Well," said Ed, "what you see is what you get."

"In that case, I see an expensive Italian suit and . . ." She tilted her head. "Someone's been jogging."

"Tennis," said Ed. "I've taken up tennis."

"I bet you have. And don't kid yourself, because of course I already know about your wild success. I know all about it. Ear to the ground and all that. Hey," she said, her brown eyes shining, "congratulations."

"Thank you."

"No, really. You've done what you set out to do. How often does that happen?"

"Okay, but what about you? I hear you're a force. *Powerhouse* is actually how you were described."

"Though," said Connie, after some modest and satisfied smiling of her own, "if you recall, it's not exactly what I set out to do."

"So what happened with the dentist? Son of a bitch got your virginity, I suppose."

"He's a dermatologist. And he did; it's true. But I have to hand it to you—you gave it a noble effort."

"Good old college try." Ed drank the last of his beer. "Maybe that's where that dopey expression comes from. Connie, it's so good to see you."

And despite one quick kiss later that evening that neither of them would ever mention, they quickly settled into the kind of fast friendship that can mysteriously and quickly transpire between two equally busy people who never have time for anything or anyone. That they were not dating seemed a mutual certainty, though Ed couldn't exactly say why. Connie was funny and smart and attractive. They coveted the same real estate, ate the same food, wanted the same two kids, and neither was stuck on having boys or girls or both. They even talked about how neither of them had any interest in moving to the suburbs when those fantasy children arrived and how Manhattan was the best place they could think of to raise children. Throughout the month of September they had dinner most nights and met up at open houses each Sunday (Connie was looking to buy a condo), which was routinely followed by Chinese food at Ed's place.

"This is a fabulous table," Connie said, while pausing her thorough gnawing on a sparerib. She was an enthusiastic but extremely careful eater; he could tell she relished each bite.

"Really?" asked Ed. "I had no idea." Connie had the ability to render something or someone *fabulous* or *ridiculous,* and once she'd said it he was rarely able to look at something or someone the same way again.

"Of course," she said. "It's great design. You can't argue with great design."

He'd been toying with the idea of buying something bigger, with a glass top, but he didn't mention it. This white square Formica table that he'd bought at a thrift shop on West 23rd Street? It would not be going anywhere—not for a good long while.

"The dermatologist left me," said Connie, as if she'd finally decided to respond to a question Ed had asked over a month ago.

"Yeah," said Ed. "I was beginning to get that feeling. I was hoping it had been you who'd done the leaving."

"Thanks. But, you know what? It was a long time ago at this point. Bastard's remarried. Three kids."

"Connie, I have to tell you: He wasn't in your league."

She smiled uncharacteristically shyly. "Come on, you never even met him."

"I could tell," Ed said. "Guy was a zero."

"He was!" Connie said. "He really really was! But listen to this: I truly thought if I didn't get engaged before I was twenty-two, then what was the point of having moved to Boston? What was the point of having gone to college? Can you imagine? And now . . ."

"What?"

"Oh, nothing."

"Out with it."

"I'm afraid I'm not going to get to have kids." She coughed, and Ed realized she was tearing up.

"Oh yes, you will," Ed said.

"You sure?"

"Of course I'm sure."

"Okay, then," she said, taking a sip of beer.

"Okay."

"Thanks for saying so."

"No problem."

Ed looked out the window at the bright lights of Manhattan. The sound of an airplane flying overhead, sirens blaring—it was all muted through the thick glass. Connie cleared their plates and put them in the sink. She ran the faucet. He could almost imagine that she was his wife. During the day he looked down on the treetops of Central Park; this room was flooded with so much light that sometimes it felt as if he was living in a terrarium, but now the dark night made that vision impossible and the view seemed downright desolate.

"I bet Helen Ordway has kids," said Connie, turning from the sink. "I bet they're beautiful."

Ed shook his head.

"No kids?"

"Nope. Not that I know of."

"But she married Hugh Shipley, I bet."

"Yes," said Ed. "That she did."

It was three more Sundays before Ed finally told Connie what had happened between Helen and him, to which she replied:

"Are you *insane?*"

"No," said Ed, opening another beer. "But I was for a while there."

"I bet," she said, nodding.

"For a while, I really think I was."

"That bitch," she said.

"No," said Ed. "It wasn't like that."

"Oh," said Connie, raising one eyebrow, the way she did sometimes; Ed could never tell if she was aware of doing so. "Oh, okay." When Connie bit her lip, Ed knew that she was practically begging him to notice how she was, in fact, refraining from offering an opinion.

"What."

"Of course."

"*What.*"

"She got to you. You thought you loved her, that you really loved her, and she left you with nothing more than a clichéd note on a pillow." Connie waited for Ed's reaction, but he didn't know what to say. He had never told anyone about what had happened with Helen, and the shock of his confession was distracting.

"It was only a couple of nights," he said. "That's nothing."

I'm so happy, Helen had said on their second morning. He remembered the yellow sheets, the promise of a perfect day; they'd drifted back to sleep. She was gone only hours later.

He'd torn up the note she'd left him, with the words *I'm sorry* in her always-surprising handwriting, which leaned to the side as if the words were all windswept, like her hair that night after the jazz club: windswept and, yes, drunk, too, just short of falling down. He'd torn up the note and immediately regretted having done so. As he recalled that windswept hair and how she'd tried to light a cigarette backward and how her face had never been more intent, he remembered, too, how she'd seen the comedy in the backward cigarette immediately, how all week long she'd laughed harder than he'd ever seen her laugh. He'd even gathered the pieces of the note from the dust-coated floor, dumbass that he'd become.

And as if the note had not been enough, as if Ed might have, in fact, been in danger of missing the point, Helen also telephoned him from Idlewild, before she boarded her plane. She hadn't been crying or pleading or sweet. She'd told him simply that she'd made a mistake; they had both done something awful.

"That's why you're different," said Connie now. Her dark hair, he noticed suddenly, was oddly unruly—loose from any barrettes or tortoise combs. To Ed's surprise, he realized that she looked better this way.

"I'm not different."

She leaned across the table, taking both of his hands. Her nails were unpolished, her olive skin was smooth. "You're heartbroken."

Ed shook his head, but he wondered, for the very briefest of moments, if this was why he was still unattached at thirty.

"But you are," she nearly whispered.

Your heart is fine, he'd said to Hugh, and, most important, he'd meant it. He'd never had a friend like Hugh, someone he'd loved like a brother, with the genuine depth of feeling that didn't need much else, including like-mindedness. And yet he'd betrayed Hugh horribly, in the very worst possible way. He'd known it would be up to him to distance himself, to do his duty and lose touch.

And he did. It was easy.

He'd read about their marriage in the papers. How they'd shockingly eloped in Africa, and how apparently—and Ed thought it was telling that neither of them had ever mentioned this, not even as a joke—Shipleys and Smythes (Mrs. Ordway's family) had been marrying since before the Civil War. He had cried—wept, really—when he'd seen Helen's bridal photograph in *The New York Times*. She must have flown in and had it taken; surely she would have done at least that for her furious parents. It was so stiff and so unlike her, similar to how a corpse could never look like a living soul (and leave it to him to think of a bride as a corpse—God, he'd gotten morose). The first wake he'd ever attended had been for his favorite secretary's mother. He'd stood with Hy Bechstein at some funeral parlor in Queens, and upon seeing how that poor woman's skin looked no more alive than clay, Ed had said: *The Jews have the right idea on this one, don't you think? Get it done in twenty-four hours, thank you. Plant me like a goddamn tree.*

Connie pulled her hands away, and when she did, he felt the strangest sense of betrayal. As if Connie's hands, in fact, belonged to him. He looked beyond her, beyond the windows, as if the city itself could offer succor. "It's raining," he said.

"Look at that."

"You thought she was a bitch?" he asked.

"Oh, yeah," Connie said.

"But she was your friend."

Connie nodded, almost sadly. "*Kind of.* She was kind of my friend. She wasn't exactly the type to stay up late telling secrets."

"Were you?"

"No, I guess not. I think we both wanted to be that type, though. Maybe that's why we liked each other."

"Hmm," intoned Ed. He had no idea what Connie was talking about. "You think I'm different from back then?"

She nodded in that semi-sad way again.

"How?"

"Ed, it was almost ten years ago," she said, suddenly dismissive. "We are who we are."

"That was a fun time, though," said Ed. "Wasn't it?"

He never asked Connie to accompany him to various business functions; he didn't want to complicate matters by confusing their comforting routine with something that seemed like a real date. But Hy took a table at a Sloan–Kettering benefit, and the thought of someone's wife inquiring, between a too-cold iceberg wedge and medallions of overcooked beef, why Ed had not asked her too-good-for-him-anyway friend out on a second date inspired Ed to ask Connie Graff to join him.

He picked her up in the marble lobby of her building, on an unseasonably warm evening, and when the elevator doors opened and Connie stepped out, he felt a sudden and very real urge to tell her to get back inside the elevator. With him. He was always a sucker for a dramatic dress, and Connie was wearing a silver cocktail number, cinched in at her small waist.

"You look dynamite," said Ed.

"You do, too," she replied, before smiling at the doorman. "Don't wait up, Rodrigo," she said lightly, which made Rodrigo—who resembled the great Tito Puente—chuckle.

"This him?" asked Rodrigo.

"Rodrigo Vasquez, meet Ed Cantowitz," she said, and Ed shook his hand before Rodrigo opened the door for both of them, ushering them out into the warm night.

"Well, you two seem to have a cozy routine," said Ed. "Cab or walk?" he asked.

"Have you even noticed my shoes?" she asked.

"I'd been focused a bit higher." He shrugged, sticking his hand out for a cab.

"You never surprise me," she said, smiling.

"You make that sound like a good thing." A cab swerved over to the curb.

"Well," she teased, "who's to say it isn't?"

Ed opened the door and shuffled across the black vinyl seat first, the way Helen had taught him to; Helen, who, after he'd held open the taxi door for her that first evening together in Manhattan, had corrected him. *The polite thing to do?* she offered, once she'd told the driver their destination: *Give the lady the shortest distance to slide.*

Shouldn't I hold the door open, though? he'd asked.

She'd shaken her head, though not—he'd noted—without a note of apology for pointing out this gap in his knowledge.

And now here he was, nearly a decade later, still . . . what? Wallowing?

What's wrong with you? He could almost hear Helen hiss at him now, as the taxi driver slammed on his horn. *You're perfect for each other!*

That evening, as if guided by something that he could only later (graspingly) identify as inevitability, he took Connie in his arms on the dance floor at the Plaza. She smelled like cherries and baby powder. When they didn't say a word to each other as they danced to the swooning music, when they danced a waltz and then a fox-trot so blatantly well together that not only Bechstein but also Steve and Barbara Osheroff told them so, Ed put his hand on Connie's neck and said, "What do you say we get out of here?"

She smiled, almost primly.

Her apartment was closer and, because they had not stopped kissing since they'd gotten into the taxi, proximity was a deciding factor. Ed briefly wondered about Rodrigo seeing him and disapproving, then banished the thought as ridiculous (who cared what her goddamn doorman thought!). He told himself that Connie was no longer a virgin, for God's sake, and was more than capable of making her own decisions. He was definitely attracted to her—he would not be burrowing his nose in her powdery neck if he were not—but part of his urgency was rooted in the fear of stopping. He knew he feared stopping and becoming too conscious of what he was doing. He feared knowing with complete certainty that he was making a choice. But he was also dead sick of feeling this way.

"Whoa," said Connie, "easy, tiger."

Ed forced a laugh.

"You're not drunk, are you?"

"Yes," he said, "I am."

"How drunk?" asked Connie, pulling ever so slightly away.

It was cool inside Connie's apartment. She didn't turn on the lights or ask him if he wanted anything to drink. She only walked toward her bedroom, and he followed. Streetlights streamed through the windows, allowing Ed to see her perfectly made bed. For a moment he only wanted to lie down and fall asleep. He turned her around so that her back was facing him and ably undid several tiny buttons along her spine. *She's too thin* is what he was thinking, as he removed her silver dress. But she turned around and her breasts were in his hands and they were heavy and perfect, and she reached up for his shoulders as they fell onto the bed in their underwear.

At some point she ceased being the Connie he'd always known—flirty and reassuring—and transformed into someone just as plainly voracious as he was. He remembered the nights in his dorm room when he'd consistently tried to get her to take off her shirt, to at least let him *see* her breasts if not touch them, and how Connie had only blushed and left, time after time. She hadn't retained any vestige of modesty, and he was not only surprised at this but also, oddly, proud of her. As they lay next to each other afterward, it wasn't awkward at all; he draped his arm over her smooth skin. She really was too thin—so much slighter, somehow, than she seemed in daily life. He wondered if she'd been dieting; he made a mental note to tell her to eat more.

"Listen," he said. "I'm playing tennis early in the morning and I really have to win this time; last week's match was shameful. And how can I get any sleep with you in the bed or even the goddamn building?"

Connie laughed. "Go home," she said.

He kissed her. "You're terrific."

"Ed," she said, "if you don't call me, I will never forgive you." She was smiling, but he knew she meant it.

"I'll call you before I head to the courts."

"Too early," she said, climbing back under the covers. "Call me after you win."

He made it neither out of the elevator nor past Rodrigo's silent but obvious appraisal before the panic set in. He fought against the tightening in his chest, assuring himself that he cared deeply for Connie, that he'd enjoyed the time spent together in bed, and he had no good reason to feel anxious. And maybe if he'd decided to take a cab home, the panic would have ceased by morning. He would later realize that this was not the first time his life had nearly taken a drastically different direction with regard to the opposite sex. If he had taken a cab or even a different route home, maybe he would have had a good night's rest, aced on the court (he really did have a game; he hadn't lied about that), and gone to bed with Connie again, even nightly for the rest of his life.

But it was a warm fall night. The medians on Park Avenue were still choked with blooms. And even if he *had* left Connie's place in order to get sleep the night before his Saturday tennis game, Ed—while tired—was equally restless, and he decided to walk home. And maybe it was due to having just had sex, or the waves of panic that followed the sex, but his senses were heightened; he had the distinct sensation that he was either being watched or that he needed to pay attention. He wondered, almost idly, if he was about to be mugged. Or maybe hit by a bus. He stopped for a moment and closed his eyes, trying to get ahold of himself.

When he opened his eyes, he walked west, and—seemingly a direct answer to the question: *What requires my attention?*—there appeared an expensively dressed young woman who was, improbably, sitting on the steps of a magnificent townhouse and rubbing her foot.

"Shit," she muttered. "And how can I help *you?*"

It was true: He'd been staring. She had gorgeous legs and was in a bad mood; he couldn't help himself. "I should be asking you that. Can I?" he asked. "Can I help?" There was, he reassured himself, no shame in being chivalrous. It was late; maybe she was in trouble.

"Cruel shoes," she said. "Fucking cruel. Expensive, too."

"I'd imagine," he said. He thought of Connie's beaded high heels and how, at the Plaza, she'd twirled with such grace. "Beautiful and painful all too often go hand in hand."

"And you're a philosopher, too," she said, with far too much sting for any healthy man's ego. He had begun to suspect he was not a healthy man.

"Not at all," he said. "I hate philosophy. What a colossal waste of brainpower. Are you coming from or going to a party?"

"Coming from. It was actually a dinner." He noticed that sizable diamonds were in her ears and encircling her wrists but—surprisingly—there was nothing on her fingers. "You?"

"Charity ball."

"Mine was a sit-down dinner. No one was looking at my feet and I shouldn't have bothered with the shoes. I do realize that."

"You're probably right," he said. "But I understand the impulse."

She stopped holding her foot quite so desperately. "What impulse?"

"Extravagance."

"Huh."

Her change of expression was no less palpable or uplifting than a pleasant shift in the weather. She was young. Her clothing and her jewelry had made her seem older at first. What did she look like? She had brows much darker than her dark-blond hair, and this, combined with a truly aquiline nose, gave her a slightly serious and exotic air, even though she had distinctly adorable dimples. Her lips were so full it was distracting, and her skin was a rich person's skin, which Ed had noticed was different somehow. Sightings of a woman like this all alone in the city—not just a beautiful woman but a clearly wealthy one—always gave him the feeling of glimpsing a rare bird in its natural habitat.

"Would you like me to hail you a cab?" he asked.

She began to laugh. "No," she said, "that's fine. I live here," she said, glancing up the stairs of the townhouse. "I just wasn't quite in the mood to go inside."

"Oh," said Ed. "In that case—"

"I'm kidding," she said, shaking her head with—again—annoyance. She put on her shoes, wincing as she did so. "Buy me a drink?" she asked.

Did she frequently ask strangers to buy her a drink? Was she a crazy swanky nymphomaniac?

He sort of hoped so.

Miraculously, there was a burger joint with a decent bar right on the corner. Then they talked until the bar closed, and he did finally hail her a cab.

While the cab waited—he was about to kiss her—he noticed her lips were the same size on the top and the bottom, like two perfectly even rose petals. And as the streetlights shone and the cabbie's meter ran, it seemed to Ed that her lips were like one of those glass flowers in the Harvard Museum of Natural History, and he was one of so many gawking tourists, marveling at how something so delicate and intricate could, in fact, be made of glass.

But she wasn't made of glass. Nor was she a Manhattan princess, nor was she (as far as he could tell) a high-society nymphomaniac. She was

Jill Solomon, a whip-smart third year law student at Columbia University, with a job waiting for her at one of the top firms in the city. In addition to intensive studying—and evidently going to dinner parties—she played tennis three mornings a week and she really liked to win.

She wasn't nearly as young as she looked, but she was still six years younger than he was.

And she was Jewish.

When he did kiss her, those lips were soft, almost passively so, but then she whispered goodbye and, astonishingly, gave his ear a little bite.

So. Jill Solomon?

For the first time in years, he found himself having an inner dialogue with Hugh Shipley.

Yes, said Ed, *Jill.*

Who is she?

She's . . . powerful.

Sounds kind of frightening.

She isn't, though, not exactly.

Okay.

Okay?

Maybe she's—

What—out of my league? Is that what you're suggesting?

I'm not suggesting anything like that. What is it with you? What league? Why do you always think in terms of leagues?

Because it works like that.

I disagree.

Fine. I feel like if I devote my life to her, I will, somehow, stop orbiting and finally land.

Okay.

I want to land.

Right.

Do you know what I mean?

I think so.

So what are you not saying? I feel like you're not saying something.

Fine. What about Connie?

I feel terrible about Connie.

No one's asking you to feel terrible.

She's terrific.

She is. I always loved her smile.

There's no accounting for desire. We want what we want. Isn't that true? Hugh?

Here is what he actually said out loud, if not exactly to anyone else, each night of that life-changing week: *I'm sorry, Connie.* He practiced saying it as he fell asleep, but still he hadn't told her. He'd called that Saturday morning as promised—after he'd played (though lost) his tennis game. He told her how much he enjoyed not only the night's unexpected turn but also the dancing. But he also told Connie that he had to go into the office that evening, which was only the first of the lies. He lied to Connie Sunday through Thursday, claiming office disasters of epic proportions, blaming Hy for everything. And every evening— Monday through Thursday—he took Jill to dinner. Each night after dinner they made out on the sidewalk with progressive intensity, so that by Thursday he nearly forced himself into her taxi after she was already inside it.

"Get out," said Jill, breathing heavily.

"Where to?" the cabbie said.

"Get out," she repeated, but this time she wasn't kidding around. "Just a minute," Jill said to the cabbie, before telling Ed to get his own cab. "There is no way I am sleeping with you tonight," she said. "Do you understand?"

"I do," he said. And he got out. "I'm in pain," he said.

"I know," Jill replied, before giving the cabbie her address. "You came of age in the 1950s, so I know you know how to do this. Go take a shower," Jill said. And, with an additional quiver of cruelty, "Oh, and I forgot to mention: I'm leaving town for the weekend."

———

On Friday morning he'd been expecting calls from at least a handful of bad-tempered executives. CBOR–Ordway Keller had coped respectably during a grim couple of years, but since both underwriting and brokerage commissions had leveled off, and because volume levels were low, the daily atmosphere in the office was more tense than ever. The CBOR–Ordway Keller Midtown office had intentionally kept the same open layout as their Broad Street one, so privacy did not exist, and therefore when Ed picked up the phone and heard Jill Solomon's voice, he knew better than to draw attention to his immediate elation. It was generally understood that the men in this room had all kinds of pretend conversations in order to save face, usually with their wives. He'd once caught Hy saying: *All right, honey, I'll see you this evening, then,* after it was clear to Ed—who'd heard Franny screaming on the other end of the telephone—that Hy's wife had already hung up.

Although Jill had certainly cleared whatever plans she may have previously made this week in order to see Ed, and she was likely staying up studying into the morning after he'd seen her home, she had yet to call him—he'd simply telephoned her home each day until she picked up. And since she'd told him she was leaving town until Monday, he was doubly shocked to hear her voice. So when she said, *Hello, how's Wall Street treating you today?* he stifled a broad smile.

Then he glanced out the window at the 59th Street traffic, at Hy huddled over papers and Steve on the telephone and Marty pacing back and forth the length of his desk, and Ed realized he was not entirely convinced that Jill would have said yes to any kind of date with him if he wasn't a part of this world. He had seen when her eyes lit up (the time he met Johnny Carson, had chartered the private plane) and where they lost their focus (his steamfitting summers, the woes of Blue Hill Avenue). This was not college, where potential in itself was some kind of currency, now it was the money that mattered. His money enabled him to attract a woman like Jill. It was an ugly thought, but it wasn't a deluded one.

"So," said Jill, "I hope you don't subscribe to the effortlessly-whip-up-something-marvelous school of entertaining," she said. "Because I'd love to make you dinner tonight."

"Really?" he asked softly. "I thought you were leaving for the week-end."

"I was," she said, "but I decided to stay."

Maybe he was being a little reductive about the money. He sat down and then stood up again. "I'd love to come to dinner."

"Good," she said. "I'm more of an I'm-panicking-and-so-you'd-better-panic-too kind of hostess. Just a warning."

"Due diligence?" he said.

"Something like that."

"Any other warnings?"

"Let's see . . . no."

"That sounds like a qualified no."

"And it is."

Ed recalled her skin, her lips, and her insistence on never being in a room alone with him. While waiting for her coat at the Four Seasons, with the coat-check girl on an absurdly long break, Ed had kissed Jill's neck, and when she let him, he'd tried to put his hand beneath her blouse. She had not smiled when he whispered: *I'm not sure if you're aware, but there's a sexual revolution going on. Even uptown.* She had, in fact, swatted his hand away.

And now she was inviting him to her apartment.

"Wait a second," he said, "is this some kind of dinner party?"

She laughed.

"What."

"I guess you'll just have to take that chance, now, won't you?"

He stopped at Connie's apartment on his way home. He didn't know if she'd be there, he wasn't even sure he wanted her to be, but when a doorman—not Rodrigo—told him that he could go up, Ed knew what he had to do.

Connie was too smart for the bullshit he'd been offering, and though Ed knew this, he wasn't sure if she might play a little bit dumb for the sake of believing in him. He knew if she did that, he was going to have an even harder time coming clean, and so, when she greeted him coldly, he was relieved.

"Connie," he said, going in for some kind of clumsy embrace, and she turned toward the kitchen before he had to decide what kind.

"I'll get you a beer," she said.

"That would be terrific." He tried not to sound too grateful.

She brought him a bottle, even though she knew he liked his beer in a glass, and he took a sip, stalling. "Let's sit down," he said.

"Fine."

Her couch was beige suede and he ran his finger one way, then another, creating and erasing the same wobbly line. "I love this couch."

"Ed," she said. "Please."

"Connie, I—"

"Just be a man and say the words, Ed. We'll both still be sitting here after you do."

"You're right," he said, sitting up straighter. "We will."

"You met someone else."

"I met someone else. How did you know that?"

Connie just looked at him; her face was not hardened, she had the nicest-looking freckle on her neck, and for that moment he was fairly sure he was making a mistake by closing this door. But then—as certainly and inexplicably—the moment passed.

"I know you met someone else because I know you," Connie said, not unkindly. "I know you bolted after what happened between us, and I know that you would have done anything to find someone else so that you wouldn't have to be totally alone when you backed out of this."

"No," Ed said, "I swear that isn't how it is. It's been one week—less than a week. How could I have—it was just the strangest circumstance—"

"I don't want to hear it."

"Okay," he said. "Fair enough."

"Don't call me for a very long time, okay?"

"If I don't call you for a very long time, do you think we can be friends again?"

"I doubt it," she said.

"That would break my heart," he said.

"Your heart is already broken," she said, with a tone of pity that he'd never quite shake. "Remember?"

That same evening, the first Friday in November, he approached Jill's address, and he noticed the russet trees and the one denuded ginkgo with its fan-shaped leaves fallen to the sidewalk. He noticed the relative smoothness of the concrete, fouled only by a smear of dog shit. He noticed two teenage boys—one carrying a basketball—hustling at a good clip. The air felt cleaner somehow, and he wondered if it had rained while he'd been in the shower. He checked to make sure of the address, even though it had long ago been fixed in his brain, and as he walked soberly up the stairs, he realized this townhouse was, in fact, a more modest version of the one Jill had parked herself outside only one week ago. He'd brought her a bottle of Bordeaux, which now seemed unoriginal. Shouldn't he also have at least brought some flowers? She was making him dinner. It was autumn in New York.

He was greeted by a taller, darker, boy version of Jill, wearing jeans and some kind of shirt that suggested a life of picking fruit and sleeping in one's car. "Howdy," he said. "Ed?"

"Howdy . . . Jill's brother?" asked Ed, extending his hand.

"One of them."

"How many are there?"

"She didn't tell you?" he asked. "Talk about insulted."

Jill came forth in a red apron and kissed Ed on the cheek. "This is my kid brother, Mark," she said. "He's a junior at Columbia, and when he's not smoking grass, he shows up, sniffing around for food."

"Nice introduction," said Mark. "Though," he said, stifling a laugh, "basically true. And, by the way, we do have an older brother, too. Don't forget Jeremy."

"No," said Jill. "Of course not."

"And Jeremy is . . . ?" asked Ed lightly.

Jill took an audible breath. "Jeremy lives somewhere in Canada after dodging the draft but won't tell us where. Our parents' nerves are shot. Soooo . . . you look great," she said. "You didn't have to wear a suit, you know."

"Well, you didn't give me much to go on: Is it a party? Is it just us? And, look, given the option of being overdressed or under, you know I'll choose over. You've figured out at least that by now, I'd imagine."

"Yes," said Jill. "Yes, I have."

"Take off your tie, man," suggested Mark.

"No thanks," said Ed.

Her apartment was the first floor of this townhouse, and with its fireplace and French doors and garden, it reminded him of Boston, which he almost said but didn't. He didn't want to talk about that time at the Mervas', even in the abstract, even just to compare the houses. He tried to imagine describing that time in his life, the time spent with Hugh and Helen, but any description, he knew, would only serve to scrape away its clarity; words would dilute the meaning. Mark turned up the hi-fi until the apocalyptic tone of the Doors threatened to bring down Ed's mood. Mark was excitedly recounting how Jim Morrison's death was obviously not from natural causes, and Jill—who was disconcertingly well informed—was disagreeing. Ed was eating all the cheese. He could barely recognize the music of the Doors, let alone have any kind of conversation about its members. They drank the bottle of Bordeaux. When Ed asked Mark what he was studying, he answered vaguely that he wasn't so sure anymore. This wasn't what Ed had pictured when he'd set out for the evening. About an hour in, Ed took off his jacket and tie; he rolled up his sleeves. He had to physically readjust himself in order to continue paying attention.

But then Mark said, "Okay, I'm taking off. I volunteered to be part of a psychological study. I really dig the grad student, so I figured it couldn't hurt my chances with her. Do you think that's unethical?"

"Yes," said Jill. "Definitely." Jill's laugh was kind of loopy, and Ed had no trouble imagining her as an adored older sister, an excellent audience from the start.

"Ed," Mark said, clapping Ed on the back, "you'd better hope that chicken isn't underdone, man."

"That was one time!" said Jill. "You're so ungrateful," she said, "and you smell, Mark, you really do."

She walked him to the door, where there was some mumbling and giggling before Mark was gone, and—nearly simultaneously—the record finished and Jim Morrison blessedly stopped singing. Ed closed his eyes, relishing the silence. When he opened them, Jill was standing in the doorway. "Long day?" she asked.

He sat up straighter. "Is anyone else coming? I hope not. You are very distracting in that apron."

She smiled graciously. She was obviously used to compliments, had learned long ago how to properly accept them. "Mark seems like a hippie, but he's only into free love for himself. He insisted on checking you out. I apologize if it was obvious."

"How did I do?"

"Shit," she said, "I forgot to set the timer. How long do you think you've been here?"

"About an hour and a half," he said.

"You sure?"

"Ninety-five percent."

"Good enough for me. Let me set it now and then I can put the rice on."

He followed Jill into the kitchen and watched her baste a chicken, set a timer, measure out cups of water, rice. Her movements were intermittently languid and erratic. Salt was overpoured. A pot's lid went clattering to the floor. She struggled with a corkscrew and, when finally victorious, spilled some of the newly opened wine. Ed noticed, too, the silver art deco containers for coffee and sugar, dahlias overflowing from a bright-green vase. There were three framed black-and-white photographs on the wall next to the stove: a bridge Ed didn't recognize, a set of train tracks, and something that looked like undulating sand, shot up close. The blacks of the images were so deeply black, and the whites had so many subtle changes, they almost looked iridescent. "Those are something," Ed said. "Do they have a story?"

"Oh, I guess so. I mean, I took them. The bridge is in Prague, which I really loved. The train tracks are in Germany, which—for obvious reasons—I did not love, but I couldn't stop taking pictures of those tracks; I took way too many. Then I had to print all the negatives, and now I can't bring myself to throw any of those prints away, no matter how lousy the shot."

"That makes sense."

"What does?"

"That you want to hold on to them. Why *not* hold on?"

"Well, first of all, there's something obviously morbid about them, and second, they take up space."

"People keep things for far less valid reasons."

"Like what? What do you hold on to?"

"Me?" He thought about the pieces of Helen's note, collected, taped together, and sealed in a manila envelope three times their size. He thought of the yellowing receipts and cocktail napkins and books and books of matches; he thought of how the one photo he had of her was also of Hugh and him. "Oh, I don't know. I'm just talking."

"You're good at talking," she said, "aren't you?"

He looked at Jill and tried to tell whether or not she was making fun of him. Her face was a beautiful blank. Her cheeks boasted *nearly* invisible fine white fuzz; he'd identified this—yet another of her more lovely and original aspects—when, bathed in the last of the setting sun, she'd opened the first bottle of Bordeaux. "I can shut up when I need to."

"I know," she said softly. She refilled their wineglasses. And even though there was more work to be done, more basting and stirring near the hot stove, she took off her apron. She was wearing a silky navy dress with a splashy print. One strap fell off her shoulder; she let it stay there.

He felt a tightening in his chest, but it wasn't panic, not exactly. It was helplessness. He held himself back from her and, for a moment, resented that he had to.

"Tell me about the last photograph."

"Oh, it's just fabric from one of my dresses. I'm not sure why I took that one, but it's my favorite."

"Mine, too."

"Really?"

He nodded. "I thought maybe it was sand, that you'd taken it somewhere in the desert. These are really very good; ever think of being a professional photographer?"

"Nope," she said, without hesitation.

"Well," he said, smiling—because he appreciated her self-knowledge, her unabashed confidence—"anyway, they're very good."

"Thank you."

"When did you do all the traveling?"

"After I graduated from high school. My grandparents took me. It was their gift. Jeremy had gone with them two years before I did."

"How terrific."

"I know," said Jill. "I know. I always felt so bad that Mark never had his chance to go. I even go as far as to think maybe he'd be different. . . . I don't know; they were both sick by the time Mark graduated. Anyway, it *was* wonderful. They spoiled me."

Ed shook his head. "You don't seem spoiled."

"I don't?"

"No. You seem . . . impressive."

"Thank you."

"Even your apartment. This is a real home," he said.

"As opposed to a holding pen?"

"You know what I mean."

"I do. Of course I do."

She sat down in one of the rattan chairs, looking briefly disoriented.

"Jill?"

"It was my grandparents' place until they died. One after the other, my grandmother first. I was in my last year at Vassar, and before my grandfather died, I promised him I'd keep this place up beautifully, that even while I was in law school, I'd keep it just so. And he told me no—don't worry about keeping it like anything. Just make it yours."

"I can't imagine," Ed said, and what he was thinking was how he couldn't imagine having so much so early on—not only the European tour and charming inherited apartment but also having such kindness—from anyone aside from his mother. "I can't imagine how much you must miss him."

"I do," she said, rising to choose a wooden spoon from a drawer full of only wooden spoons. "Anyhow, I hate how most girls think of their homes as holding pens until married life. Even girls with their own money"—she paused to taste a simmering sauce—"like me."

They stood in the kitchen and Jill held his gaze, waiting—he supposed—to see what he'd say in reaction to her candor. He took her hand and held it, listening to the stove fan and faint sound of traffic. "No one's like you," he said, suddenly serious, even somber.

"Aw," she said, "you're so sweet."

"Sweet?"

"Sweet."

"You sound like you're talking to a puppy or a kid."

"That's ridiculous."

"It's not. I'm not ridiculous."

"I never said you—"

"You are impressive. I am crazy about you. You are seriously god-damn impressive to me. Do you hear me?"

"I hear you, but come on," she insisted, "you said something sweet, did you not?"

He swallowed his urge to continue this. He told himself to let it go.

It was hot in this kitchen, he'd been on display for the deadbeat brother, and Jill hadn't even reassured him of the kid's approval. Why should he have been on display like that? The two of them chattering at the front door, so obviously about him?

"Why do you like me?" he asked. Suicide.

But, somehow, it wasn't. She didn't look uncomfortable. Instead, she put her arms around his neck as if they were about to start dancing or—it did occur to him—boxing. They were exactly the same height.

"I'm not sure," she said, looking at him dead-on. "Maybe it's your appetite."

He held himself back from questioning this or from asking her for more. They were close enough that for one near painfully fine moment he could feel her long lashes brush against his cheek. When she kissed him and he realized that her initiative surprised him, he felt slightly stung at the realization and so continued holding back, until he realized that she was being—for the first time all week—utterly straightforward.

"Oh," he relented. "My God." Then he pulled her to him, hard.

Four months later he married Jill Solomon at her parents' club in Scarsdale. He insisted on marrying her as soon as possible, and she was charmed by his insistence. She also had no interest in fighting her mother for a year over wedding plans. Ed maintained that any friend who showed up clad in a tux would automatically be made a groomsman, but there were no surprises. Ira Gersten made noise about flying in from Chicago, but evidently there was a Cubs game that needed his analysis; *new pitcher,* he'd solemnly explained. Ed's groomsmen were Bechstein, Osheroff, and Rabb—the same hardworking and irritating men with whom he spent his days and nights. Plus Mark Solomon. Ed had asked Jill's brother, who'd cleaned up for the event and, standing next to poor Marty Rabb, he looked like Peter Fonda at the Oscars.

Neither Connie Graff nor Jill's brother Jeremy was in attendance.

And Ed wasn't sure what he was expecting, but, even though they hadn't been invited, and even though the last he'd heard they were living in *Bongo Bongo* or wherever Hugh could play out his own do-gooder story and Helen could stay remote, wherever they could rebel against their class but have each other as a reminder of that class, he still found himself surprised and even briefly miserable when he looked beside him before saying his vows and he didn't see Hugh Shipley, who—Ed didn't care how many years he lived in the bush—would always look at ease in formal attire.

His father sat in the front row, grousing about something—the rabbi? The room's temperature? The first thing he said when Ed and Jill collected him at Penn Station was, "What makes you so lucky?" When Ed smiled and tried to hug him, he started coughing and complaining about New York City filth. Over the course of the next two days he'd gone on to complain about Ed's future in-laws, how they were snobs (which they were), and generally whatever unpleasant thoughts happened to rise to the top of his forever-mysterious consciousness.

As Ed stood now before Jill, as he took in her lace veil and long eyelashes, he had flashes of her miraculous body shrugging out of a wet one-piece bathing suit, a month prior, in Barbados (he'd surprised her with a weekend getaway), and how she'd let that wet suit fall to the floor. His mind rested on her tan narrow feet with their red-painted toenails and how those feet cradled his head as her eyes closed, as she lifted her hips up and up below him. As he half-listened to Jill's brother Mark reading an unfamiliar poem about fire, as the rabbi chanted blessings in Hebrew before talking at some length about the meaning of home, he also tried not to think about how much he wished his mother were here, not *in addition to* but *instead of* his father.

But then the rabbi pronounced them married and he kissed Jill Cantowitz. His bride. He smashed the wineglass to bits and found himself, finally, smiling.

They danced their first dance. "Have you ever really listened to this song?" asked Jill.

"Of course," said Ed, kissing her.

"The lyrics are actually a little creepy. *Someone to watch over me?* By the way," said Jill, in his ear, "I hope you're grateful I took your name."

Ed put pressure on her back, just as he'd been taught to years ago by a confident Dorchester girl whose name now sadly escaped him. "I am," he said, "tremendously."

———

That December, during the heaviest snowstorm of the year, Jill went into labor, and by the time their daughter was measured and weighed, the sky was pale gray and eerily calm. She was a big baby, with a shock of black hair and round dark-blue eyes. When Ed held her for the first time, he thought he might faint from terror, but instead he told Jill how happy he was. "I want another one soon," he whispered. "Don't you?"

"Very funny," she said.

"I'm wasn't being funny."

"Shh," she said, marveling over his shoulder and staring at their daughter. "Isn't she pretty?" Jill was holding a glass of champagne. She had given birth not two hours before and yet she looked impossibly the same as before she'd been pregnant; not an ounce of extra softness remained. Her hair was pulled back with a wide white headband; she'd hastily applied some lipstick and powder for pictures, and the effect was oddly theatrical, as if she might be an unhinged dance teacher.

"So pretty," he said. "She looks like you."

"I don't know about that. I see a bit of Cantowitz already. But she also kind of looks like a papoose. Did you call your father?" she asked Ed, and Ed said no, but he would in a minute.

This conversation came and went for hours, until finally he walked down the hall to the pay phone.

"Pop," Ed said, "it's a girl."

As Murray Cantowitz wept through various attempts at language, Ed fed the phone more quarters. Finally his father coughed into his voice, the one that Ed knew and expected. "You name her for your mother?"

"Middle name," Ed managed. He was unprepared enough for the strength of his own feelings, but for his *father's?*

"Not good enough," his father said.

As he smoked a cigar outside New York Hospital with Hy, Ed couldn't stop thinking of Jill in pain. She'd refused the drugs, maintaining she could do without them. She yelled: *Please stop fucking asking me if I want the fucking drugs.* And when he stopped asking? *You motherfucker,* she'd screamed and screamed. *You have no idea.* She kept saying that: *You have no idea.* She also looked gorgeous. He knew he was supposed to say that no matter what, but he was so awed by her strength and . . . and . . . *grandeur* as she pushed, and her breasts were huge and her dark eyes were glittery and he remembered what a physical force she could be, before she'd stopped being remotely in the mood to sleep with him, which had happened fairly soon after conceiving.

You motherfucker.

Ed knew it was childbirth and that—God bless—it was certainly not unusual for her to swear like a sailor, but he also knew—even if it was just for that moment—she'd looked at him and she'd meant it.

"Congratulations," said Hy. Bastard had tears in his eyes.

Ed wanted to talk about his daughter's perfect eyebrows, how she had a tiny auburn patch in her shiny black hair, how her hands were the most elegant he'd ever seen, complete with long pink nails.

He wanted to say her name: *Rebecca Dorota Cantowitz.*

He wanted to ask Hy how to be a father, because all he could think, all he'd been able to think for months now, was: *Don't fuck up, don't fuck up, don't fuck up.*

What Ed talked about was the weather. *What a goddamn glorious day. Have you ever seen a storm like that. Would you look at that pearl of a sky.*

Chapter Eleven

Port-au-Prince, Haiti, 1982

The house in Haiti never felt like theirs. Her father called it excessive; her mother called it beautiful. Her parents drank before dinner.

Look at this veranda, said her mother. *Look at this shade of yellow.*

Helen, was what her father replied. As if to say, *Stop.*

Oh, come on, her mother said teasingly, *it's not as if it isn't falling apart. You can always take comfort in that.*

It's just a bit much, her father concluded, with a shake of his head.

When else will I get to live in a gingerbread house perched on top of a hill?

You come from a house like this, her father said.

Not like this, her mother said.

Yes, her father said, *like this.*

As for Genevieve, she was almost eleven and she loved the pool. She loved the feeling of being underwater so long that her eyes stung and her fingers pruned, and Maude would bring her a cloth and press her eyes tight and hold her so close, warming her up like a baby. She loved telling Maude to close her eyes and cracking an imaginary egg over her fuzzy cocoa hair. She loved the quiet that came with this daily afternoon treat: Genevieve and Maude and a fluffy white towel. She was so lucky, such a lucky girl. She couldn't remember a time when she wasn't acutely aware of her own good fortune and when this knowledge didn't feel—just a little bit—like a sinking stone.

Here was the bad part about swimming: Their house and pool were on top of a hill, and past their house—deep in the pine forest—there was also a public water pump. Most days while Genevieve was having her swim—no matter how Maude and her mother tried to time it—a group of kids dressed in rags, really poor, a few her age and older, too, would walk up their hill, balancing buckets on heads, and they would rap at the iron gate with sticks. They would rap at the gate and call out—*tifi! tifi!*—which she knew meant *girl;* four boys, one girl, rapping and rapping until she had no choice but to come up for air. But that wasn't the worst part. The worst part wasn't that they looked angry— angry with *her*—and that they didn't have shoes, or that she had the feeling she was doing something she shouldn't be doing by swimming, by even breathing. No, the worst was seeing Maude yell at them. *Ale! Ale!* Maude shouted, and, when they wouldn't go away, she rapped right back at them with the stick she always carried with her in case of taran- tulas and rats. Sometimes she grazed their knuckles and Genevieve cried "Stop!" but Maude just ignored her and yelled until those kids ran off, and then Genevieve didn't want to snuggle with Maude in the towel.

And then one day Maude went to check on the bleaching sheets, and Genevieve was not to jump into the pool until Maude came back. She sat on the edge of the chaise longue, waiting with her towel in her one-piece yellow bathing suit that had come from Grandmother at Christmas. And though she knew her mother was within earshot, having lunch with Ma- dame Richelieu on the veranda, and she knew that not only Maude but Arvede in the kitchen and William in the garden knew she was right there by the pool, she felt not only alone but invisible. As if her pale white skin had been, each day, growing paler and paler and leading up to this moment, right now, when she was no more than a ghost.

When her tormentors arrived this time, she didn't hide or scream. She drew her towel around her and stood up. She'd practiced the line in her head each night before sleep: *"Kisa ou vie?" What do you want?* But as she approached the gate, they didn't stop banging and she said nothing, ran up the stairs to the veranda, and approached her mother and Madame Richelieu.

"Bunny," said her mother, not quite smiling, taking a sip of white wine.

"May I have five gourdes?"

Her mother laughed lightly. "What do you need?"

"Nothing. I just want to copy the palm trees on the bill."

"Oh, good," said her mother, "you're drawing again," as she searched the pockets of her white cotton pants. "Simone, did you know that Genevieve's an artist?"

"*Oui?* Oh, I have one," said Madame Richelieu, handing over the crumpled bill. "*Mais, ma chère,*" she said cautiously, "I give you ze gourdes, you show me ze drawing. *Oui?*"

"*Oui, bien sur,*" and "*Merci, Madame,*" said Genevieve, darting off before they had any more to say.

She stood between the house and a fat banana palm, and for a moment she could see all of them but they couldn't see her. The kids weren't rapping with their sticks and yelling anymore. Instead, they were laughing and chanting something she didn't understand to the meanest-looking boy, who wore a cutoff T-shirt that said FLORIDA IS FOR LOVERS. But the boy didn't look mean right then. He looked embarrassed or maybe even happy. The youngest boy was picking his nose; the one girl—weighed down by big boobs, though she looked not much older than Genevieve— was hunched over and biting her nails. When she stepped out from behind the palm fronds, their rapping and yelling started up once more. The boy looked mean again, and he called out the loudest. Genevieve's face burned as she approached. Rotten fish and pigeon beans, iodine; a sick, sweet hint of warm Coca-Cola. There it was: the smell. That smell would stay lodged in the mysterious part of the brain that was forever linked with fear and desire. She would forget the T-shirt and the girl's frighteningly large breasts, but she would never forget that smell, present only in the one moment it took to thrust five gourdes through an iron gate.

———

Her father spent his days at a health clinic. Before leaving home in Dar almost a year ago and flying across the world—away from the comforting scent of dust and sand and burning trash, away from the school that she hated and her best friend, Emme Wu, whom she loved—her father had explained to Genevieve how, because of the evidently excellent job he'd done running the clinic in Kariakoo and because of Dr. Shannon's success rates with malaria, he'd been asked to come to Haiti to assist one of the clinics here.

Her mother had joined her in crying, but Genevieve knew she was also relieved, because one of the conditions of their relocating was that they were going to have a much nicer home and have more help than her father had ever previously allowed. Genevieve's most vivid experience of school was how her mother had spent each morning instructing Genevieve not to eat anyone else's lunch, not to drink from anyone else's cup. But her mother had also grown attached to the women in a nearby village, who credited her with personally lowering the infant mortality rate ("I did next to nothing," her mother admitted to Genevieve, seeming more angry than proud. "I hydrated the babies, like any fool with a medical kit."), and she often used this very example of getting too much credit for doing too little.

If her mother spoke passionately about what a sorry state of affairs both Tanzania and its foreign aid were in, she spoke just as passionately about how irresponsible it was to raise a child the way they were raising their daughter. *Plenty of children are raised here,* said her father; *And plenty of them die,* said her mother, *and plenty would leave if they had the choice, before it came to that. It's not as if you have an embassy post, or even a stable position. . . . Shannon is kindhearted, but he drinks too much. . . .* And on and on—Genevieve heard them through the thatch screen that created the two bedrooms. These conversations usually ended with the obvious example of how Genevieve had, in fact, almost died from dysentery (and was medevaced to New York) at two and a half years old, after one of the many rainy seasons. *She doesn't remember it,* said her father, more than once. And Genevieve wanted to say: *Yes, I do. I re-*

member the iced oatmeal cookies and the television. I remember Grandmother's freckled hands and Grandfather's glasses of milk. But Genevieve knew—even at age ten—that these were not the memories that her father wanted to hear.

Her mother seemed to love her father best when she greeted him at the end of the day. She kissed his lips in the doorway; her hand grazed his bearded cheek.

"Jesus," her father said, shaking his head. "Like they really needed this on top of everything else."

Genevieve wanted to wrap her arms around his waist, but something stopped her.

"Jesus," her father repeated. "Hi, bunny," he said sadly. "I mean, did anyone think about how bad it was going to look?" He started to laugh, and Genevieve realized he'd gone to the hotel before coming home, the one where, once in a while, the two of them had Papa Days and she swam and he drank and waded into the pool and pretended to be a monster.

He kicked off his boots now, into the corner, where a fake pug sat as a doorstop, and he was still laughing. Her father rarely laughed when he was happy. When her father was happy, he was quiet; he petted her head and gently held her neck as if she were a dog. Genevieve went to the drinks table and poured her father a whiskey. She did it like he'd taught her, measuring the amount carefully by the size of her own thumb. It had recently occurred to her (and she was sure it was not lost on her father) that as she grew so did his drink. "I mean," he said, "did anyone think about the public-relations disaster of trying to sell this idea to the people? Forget about the actual folly of what is going on here. Forget about the enormity of this mistake. We'll kill your black pigs and we'll replace those black pigs with light-colored pigs and also mixed-race pigs—just like the Haitian elite?"

"You said the replacement pigs *thrive* in tropical countries. You had me read pages and pages about *feed conversion efficiency,*" her mother said, before shaking her head. "You used this experiment as a way to convince me to move! You can't come home like this every day."

Her father walked over to the open window and took a breath, as if he was literally breathing in that particular air. "I know," he said, clearing his throat. "And I know what I said."

"Papa," Genevieve said, handing him the glass, "are we moving again?"

"Do you want to?" he asked bitingly, accepting the drink. "Where d'ya want to go? The Congo? Oh, look—it even rhymed."

"Stop," said her mother, "just stop it."

"I'm sorry," said her father. "Thank you for the drink, bunny." He looked at both of them for a moment as if he was dizzy, as if he'd forgotten what he was talking about. "I need to think."

"Please do that," her mother said. "But so you know, unless you can come up with a radically better plan, we are not leaving that clinic and this house before you said we would. There is constant change and then there's plain instability, you know?"

"Maybe I should go to medical school," he said, obviously not serious.

"Maybe you should."

"Maybe we should just buy this goddamn clinic. Is that what you want?"

Every now and then her father made mention of a mysterious source of money; he talked about it as if it were poison, threatening to kill their family. This is how Genevieve learned they weren't poor. In Dar, they lived in a house that could fit in this one's kitchen, and her father regularly fretted over wasting energy and water and buying too much at the market. Once he had started crying because he found a crisper full of rotten, obviously forgotten vegetables. He'd acted like their lot was no different from that of most of their neighbors.

But then they'd left Dar es Salaam. They'd boarded a jet plane. They moved into a new house, a big one, in a new country, with Maude and Arvede and William to help take care of everything. Genevieve almost asked how it was possible, before realizing the answer was already clear. It was also clear that her father had made these concessions to her mother and that he would have been happier to live the way they always had, the way her mother called pretending.

"Are you hungry?" her mother asked him now, more gently.

"I could eat," her father said. "Bunny," he said, sitting down at the table, "what did you do this afternoon? Get in a good swim?" No matter how he felt about their new living situation, about the big house and the help, no matter how he might have disapproved of the swimming pool, Genevieve also knew that her father loved how she loved to swim.

The boy and the yelling still rang in her ears—*tifi, tifi*. Maude's stick. She wanted her father to know about it, yet she realized she was not only afraid but also ashamed to tell him.

"Show us the drawing, why don't you?" said her mother, bringing out a tray. She poured drinks and lit a candle as if she were sleepwalking, and they all sat in their usual seats. Her mother always lit candles for a dinner table and set out cloth napkins, even if they were having only bowls of rice and scrambled eggs, which was often the case, especially in Dar es Salaam, where she'd had some bad experience with meat early on and was always reluctant to buy it. And because Genevieve was a notoriously particular eater, it was even more important to her mother that—no matter if Genevieve's tastes were baffling and even disgusting—she sit down to a civilized dinner. If her mother was going to give in and allow Genevieve her shredded cheese mixed with shredded coconut or her beloved ketchup on rice and spaghetti, if Genevieve was going to hoard her best friend Emme's salty-sweet dried squid for special treats (dried squid for which Genevieve traded her cheese sandwich at school, despite all of her mother's warnings), well, then Genevieve was going to learn impeccable table manners; she was going to learn the art of conversation.

Genevieve watched her own glass; a drop of wine spread through water, and she thought of cleaning watercolor brushes, how fast the glass went gray.

"The drawing?" asked her father.

"Oh, it didn't come out good," said Genevieve.

"*Well,*" said her mother.

"It didn't come out *well,*" said Genevieve.

"What did you draw?" asked her father.

"Nothing."

"It wasn't nothing. It was the five-gourdes note. The palms."

"What a good idea, bunny."

She shrugged.

"What's the matter?" her father asked, and she could hear that some part of him was annoyed.

Her mother bowed her head in her customary moment of silence before offering any food. She'd started to meditate with Madame Richelieu and Madame's two friends, and sometimes Genevieve found her mother sitting on the living room floor with her legs crossed, the way Genevieve had learned to sit in kindergarten.

"Why don't you have some tomato salad, bunny?" her mother asked, upon opening her eyes. "Maybe some fruit?" In addition to the table manners, her mother believed in a daily salad, but she always offered it casually, as if she didn't care what Genevieve did or didn't eat.

Genevieve's face burned the way it had earlier, when the boy was yelling through the iron gate and she'd thrust the money through. She hadn't yelled, *Come back, come back, I'll go get more—I can.* "I hate the swimming pool," said Genevieve.

"You do?" they both said. She couldn't remember when they'd ever responded in unison.

"I want to go back," said Genevieve. She pictured the oil drums in the field abutting her father's clinic in Kariakoo, how nearly every evening one of the neighbors would throw garbage or paper scraps into those drums and set the pile on fire. Genevieve remembered the dogs barking at the curls of smoke, how the burning created a shimmery haze, and how—on these evenings—even if she was at the clinic, where there were plenty of other upsetting distractions, the sunset was always like magic.

"We can't," said her father. "You know that." He put down his fork. "What happened today?"

"Nothing," said Genevieve. But she knew she'd cry if she didn't tell him, and this she didn't want to do. "It was just those kids."

"What kids."

"Oh, Genevieve," said her mother, "you didn't give them the five gourdes?"

"What kids?" said her father, more agitated.

She let her mother explain.

"Hugh, please, you already know about the kids. They walk to the well in the forest. I wish we could simply open the doors here and not worry about—"

"Christ," said her father. And then to her mother: "Would it have killed you to tell me earlier?"

"Tell you what exactly? Look around, why don't you."

"Stop," Genevieve suddenly shouted, "don't blame Mommy. It was me. I was afraid. I thought if I gave them money—"

"This is what you should do," he said calmly. "The next time they come, you should tell Maude to open the gate."

"But Maude said—"

"*Open the gate, Maude,* that's what you say. And of course you say please. Say please. Make sure Maude is with you. Ask them if they'd like to eat something."

Her mother pushed her chair away from the table. She stood up, smoothed her pink shirt and white pants, and went out on the veranda. Genevieve knew she was lighting a cigarette, even though she'd recently vowed to quit.

"They're kids?" he asked Genevieve.

She nodded.

"Any older than you?"

She shrugged.

"I'd try that first," he said softly. "Call me crazy," he said, in a raised tone that was obviously meant for her mother, "but I'd try that."

———

Her father told bedtime stories. He spun tales about a king whose house was so big that he couldn't find the bathroom, who was so used to servants that he didn't know how to make himself two slices of buttered toast. "I can't find the bathroom," her father would say in a high, sort-of-British voice. "I believe I have taken a wrong turn. Dear Jeeves, can you please point me in the right direction?" And Genevieve would laugh and laugh and her father would lie beside her, his big feet hanging off the end of the bed.

Her mother told stories, too.

"Tell me about when you and Papa got married," said Genevieve. She wanted that one tonight.

"Well," said her mother, lying on her side, "I was in New York."

"Paris hadn't worked out," Genevieve said.

"No," said her mother. "Once you take a job typing, you never stop typing. Remember that."

"I will." A gust of wind slammed the broken window frame at the foot of her wicker bed. "I hope Papa fixes that soon."

"I wish he'd let Arvede do it."

"But Papa likes to fix things."

"And how long has the window been broken?"

"Since we moved in."

"That's right," said her mother. "That's right." Her mother turned onto her back so they were side by side, staring up at the ceiling. "Anyway, I was in New York."

"And you were supposed to meet Papa in Nairobi, but you missed your flight because you'd been out the previous night with Aunt Kitty, who was visiting."

"Mmm," her mother said, closing her eyes. "I let Kitty take me all over town to these different places that she'd wanted to try. I kept thinking: *This will be the last place, this will be the last song,* but I didn't go home. I couldn't, somehow."

"Because you were having so much fun."

Her mother reached under the covers and held Genevieve's hand. "So much fun."

"And you missed the flight and Papa was waiting and waiting and he got so worried, and by the time you got word to him that you were coming but it was going to be another day or so, he had decided you'd thrown him over for another fellow."

"He was jealous," she said. She kissed Genevieve's hair, her eyes, her nose, her cheeks. Then she brushed Genevieve's bangs off her forehead until Genevieve began to feel sleepy.

"When you arrived in Nairobi he picked you high off the ground, which isn't easy because you're so tall, and when he finally put you down, *you* said, 'Let's just get married here,' and he said, 'Yeah, okay.' "

"Right," her mother said, laughing, "just like that."

"And you got married in a garden."

"We did."

"That priest did it—"

"—Father Emile."

"But neither of you was a believer."

"That's right, bunny," her mother said; she always smiled when Genevieve said that. "Your father liked Father Emile, though; he listened to your father and helped him figure out what he wanted to do with his life. And he was a really good cook. For both of these things, I was truly grateful."

"Papa decided to take that job with the Peace Corps."

"Mmn."

"But first you went to Lamu for a honeymoon."

Her mother was nodding and stroking her hair, watching her fall asleep.

But she wasn't going to fall asleep. She wasn't even thinking about her parents in love on some faraway beach, an image that usually made her happy.

Genevieve was thinking of this afternoon and how of course those kids had all grabbed for the five-gourdes note and of course the meanest boy had gotten it. He muttered something before picking up his bucket, and they'd all shot off, laughing—of course they did—but Genevieve had burst into tears anyway, not even having had the satisfaction of understanding what the boy said. What she'd really wanted, what she had always wanted, was for them to stay; she wanted them to like her.

Her face went hot, even as her mother continued to stroke her hair, and she thought of the clinic here, where her father worked and where her mother also volunteered. How before each of Genevieve's visits, her mother spoke quietly about what Genevieve might see. It was worse here, in Haiti. She knew her mother tried to steer her away from the worst sights, but there was no way to do this, and this was what her mother eventually said, in a tone that conveyed that *this* was the point of Genevieve's visits, the fact that there was no way to protect her. Genevieve was thinking about how she'd gone from dreading those trips—the open sores, ever-present flies, the saddest smiles she'd ever seen—to craving them. What Genevieve wanted, what she always wanted now, was to see. Last week at the market with Maude, she'd seen a goat's head severed from its body. Maude tried to shield Genevieve's eyes, but she'd shaken off the smooth, pliant arm and drawn closer to the sound of the bleating and of course the sight of blood, spraying into the air and trickling through the ground, touching the tip of her left Tretorn in a stain that she was convinced would never bleach out. But it did bleach out. And now those Tretorns looked the same as before, which was much scarier than the stain.

She wanted to see everything. She thought if she could really look at it all and not turn away, if she was able to never flinch from the orphans and the crowds that mobbed them in the streets anywhere outside their home or the embassy or the hotel, then she might understand it somehow, and the severed goat head, the blood, the orphans, and the crowds—they would become a part of her, and maybe if they were a part of her, then she could somehow conquer the god that had created all of this misfortune. She imagined there had to be two gods. Because the other god had somehow—up until now—kept her not only safe but lucky. It's not that she wasn't grateful.

But she knew that wasn't how it worked. At least according to her father, there was no counting on God—her father had made that very clear when she'd made friends with some missionary kids in Dar es Salaam (Father Emile aside, he thought religion was *a load of crap*)—but, still: She couldn't help wanting to believe. She wanted the suffering to be a part of her like blood, not separate like a view, like *the* view from this house—her house now—that overlooked the mountainside. The gates protected her, but they also did not. She was, as Maude often told her, a clever girl.

"Mommy?" Genevieve called out, as the window banged. The room was pitch dark and her mother was gone.

Mwen genyen match la.

That's what the boy said when she'd handed him the five gourdes. When she'd reached through the gate and he'd grabbed it. *Mwen gen-yen. Match la.* His eyes were bright and his fingers were filthy.

I won the game.

No, you didn't, she wanted to say. *Look at you.*

And now, as the wind rattled the broken window that she knew Ar-vede would end up fixing, she heard someone else's voice; whose? Hers. It said: *You can't just pay them off.* And also: *You can't just let them in.*

Chapter Twelve

New York City, 1982–1983

Ten years later, Ed, Hy, Steve, and Marty were still equal partners.

The financial system was changing, and CBOR–Ordway Keller had to either be at the forefront of change or perish. *End of story,* thought Ed. *The. End.* The future was not about retail and the individual investor but about complex conglomerates. But for all of his meticulous research, for all of his powers of persuasion, none of his partners was entirely convinced. They were all wealthy men now, each of them argued. Why topple this improbably strong, once-scrappy boat? This boat that had managed to sail—without ever (more or less) hitting a squall—all without one official captain? They had remained an egalitarian firm, had maintained their open floor plan. Hy often told Ed that—although they'd more than made it through the grim years of the early 1970s—they should always limit financial risk and never put net worth on the line. Which, Ed argued, was at best too conservative and, more accurately, a total failure of imagination.

When employees complained several times about not being able to follow Ed's increasingly complicated and risky trading positions, Ed tried and finally failed to remain calm. *You can't follow my positions well enough to sell them to our clients?* he yelled. *Take a night class, okay? That isn't my problem.*

Despite the warnings from his partners, despite their firm belief that what he was after was nearly always too risky and hopelessly complex, he continued to seek out the highest of all high-profile conglomerates, many of whom he knew from his earliest days while working for Guy Ordway and whom he'd carefully cultivated over the years. He began to sit down these top men, one by one, poised to underwrite a new venture. Through polite brunches in Greenwich and drinks at the Racquet Club, he maneuvered.

And Jill was this close to making partner.

The Cantowitz family did not see one another terribly often.

One autumn weekend, Jill and Ed headed out of town for separate meetings, and Solange—the Cantowitzes' workweek live-in from Haiti—along with Solange's vast extended family, hosted Rebecca, now almost ten, in Brooklyn. On Sunday night, after Ed and Jill made a point to come home and have sex before venturing over the FDR and the pitted BQE (*you'd think New York was a Third World country,* they agreed), they arrived at Solange's run-down Victorian, which would—Ed noted—look great with a new coat of paint. He'd send over their painter; Jill repeatedly told him that he insulted people by making such gestures, but he'd been poor once, too, and was more than willing to take that chance.

Solange answered the door and Jill nearly jumped into Solange's arms. She could be so unexpectedly affectionate. "How did she do?" Ed asked.

"Mr. Cantowitz," said Solange, "she an angel."

They followed Solange to the basement, where a pack of children was navigating boxes and broken toys, in the throes of what looked like a fairly organized soccer game.

Rebecca called out, "Hi, Mom! Hi, Daddy!" She was dribbling. She was also wearing a see-through synthetic pink dress; her hair had been elaborately styled and she was wearing bright lipstick.

"Hi, honey!" cried Jill. Then she whispered, "She looks like a hooker."

"A very athletic, very happy hooker," Ed whispered back.

They stayed for coconut cake—it was Solange's cousin Antoine's birthday—then they made the trip home to their classic six on Park. It seemed awfully quiet in the car.

"Rebecca was happier in that house," Ed said later in their dark bedroom, while lightly scratching Jill's back.

"Solange and her family are from the Caribbean," Jill said. "Don't you know they are a naturally happier people?"

"I'm serious," said Ed.

"So am I."

"No, you're not," he said, kissing her neck.

"Okay," she said, sitting up. "For God's sake, of course I'm not." She flipped on her reading light. "Listen. You need to listen to me, please. I do not want to have another child."

Ed turned on his reading light, and the room was shockingly bright. "I just don't understand," he said, launching them into this, their most consistent fight: *How Could You Not Want to Give Her a Sibling?* The consistency of their positions was almost comforting. They could argue for hours. "You love your brothers," said Ed, as if this was a new insight. "You love Mark more than you love your parents."

"How can you say that?"

"Well, isn't it true?"

"Do you want a boy?"

Funnily enough, she'd never asked this before, and he couldn't help being impressed with her new line of questioning.

"Is that why you are so insistent?" She could tell he was impressed and she relaxed against the headboard, looked up at the ceiling. "If you want a boy," she said with striking serenity, "just admit it, and this will all go a whole lot easier."

He couldn't help but laugh. "Who are you? The Godfather? What are you talking about? Jill, I just want another baby. A *sibling*."

She crossed her arms and shook her head.

"Do you know what I did in Switzerland this weekend?" he asked, while looking up at the ceiling.

"Do I want to know?"

"Stop it. Do you?"

"Sure. What did you do in Switzerland this weekend?"

"I had dinner with a billionaire at his house."

"Nice?"

"There was a tiger—a real live tiger—roaming around the property, like a guard dog."

"That's completely bizarre."

"It was, it really was. And that's how I spent my Saturday night. Away from you. Away from Rebecca. And I do sometimes have to wonder, Jill—I mean, I do sometimes wonder exactly how it is we're spending our time. How we're spending our lives. In the big picture. Because Rebecca's going to be a teenager before we know it, and—"

"So did it work? Did the tiger intimidate you? Why else would someone do something so crazy?"

Ed shook his head. He wasn't giving up, but for at least a few minutes he'd try to let it go. "I felt sorry for the guy."

"Maybe that's the point of the tiger—to lower the guests' defenses." She faced him, lying sideways, her head propped up by her hand. "Were your defenses lowered?"

He shook his head while fingering her nightgown strap, sliding it off her shoulder, then back up again.

She looked at him and was about to say something. Then she changed her mind.

"What?"

"I just would have assumed, with the way you dote on Rebecca, that she's more than enough for you."

"You say that like it's a bad thing."

"No, I'm not."

"But you're implying it."

"Exactly who is going to be here to take care of this sibling?"

"Well." He sat up. "You, at first."

"Aha. Me. I don't know if you noticed, *honey*, but I'm working to make partner. And I'm very very close."

"And then Solange. Solange will. She told me she will."

"What do you mean she told you? You *asked her?*"

"I asked her hypothetically."

"Hypothetically."

"Hypothetically."

"Good night," said Jill. She flipped off the light and arranged herself in a tight little ball, the way she seemed to do only when she was furious. On other nights she sprawled out, leaving him very little space.

"Jill," he said. "Jill, please."

She sat up; then she looked at him piercingly. He realized it had been a good long while since he'd had that kind of attention from her. "I want you to listen to me," she said, and he could see her tawny chest rise and fall. "I do not believe that the sun rises and sets with you."

"I—"

"Do you hear me? That was your mother, Ed. Your mother was a selfless woman. And that is not me."

He was too stunned by her control, by her heavy breathing, to say much of anything.

"Do you understand?" she asked. "Does that shock you?"

Whether it was her message or her sheer intensity he couldn't parse out, but he kissed her and she didn't stop him.

And then one day, not long after Rebecca turned ten, Jill announced that she'd had her tubes tied, and Ed was so angry that he insisted on taking Rebecca to Disney World for the long Presidents Day weekend without Jill, who relented far too easily as far as Ed was concerned. "You get to go on a special trip with Daddy," she exclaimed, and Jill's secretary booked her a separate ticket so quickly to visit her brother Mark, now living in Madrid, that Ed was convinced his wife had already planned that trip to Spain, even before Ed's Big Disney Revenge.

He instructed his secretary to organize the most over-the-top itinerary possible. So when they arrived at the Polynesian Village and Rebecca didn't beam like those kids in the advertisements, and when, in fact, she noted that everything was smaller than she expected, Ed suggested they head to the Tambu Lounge, where they spent more time than most families having their own special cocktail hour, ordering drinks that arrived in hollowed-out pineapples.

"Did you know," Ed said, sucking down his big fat alcoholic drink through a straw, "that John Lennon officially broke up the Beatles right here?"

Rebecca shook her head.

"It's true. He came here with his son, just like I'm here with you. And he signed the paperwork."

"How do you know that, Daddy? Do you even own any Beatles albums?"

"Oh, y'know, I read it somewhere."

"That's kind of depressing, don't you think? Imagining John Lennon doing that?"

"I guess," Ed admitted. "Though there's a saying: All great things must come to an end."

"Yeah, I've heard that one. Anyhow, now he's dead." Rebecca was sitting perfectly straight. "I still can't believe that man shot him."

"I know, honey. It's awful," he said. What the hell was he doing—bringing up John Lennon not twenty-four hours into her first trip to Disney World?

Her expression was deadpan. It often was. When Rebecca was a baby, they'd worried about that poker face, her infrequent smiles and cooing, but when she hit toddlerhood and Manhattan's private-school entrance exams for four-year-olds, she answered *every single question* correctly, and it was clear that all that time she had simply been watching. "Little Buddha," Jill's brother Mark called her, which Ed knew was meant kindly but which he still found profoundly irritating.

She'd inquired, not infrequently, when she was three years old: *Daddy, if there are seven days in a week, when do the days end?* And then, with that furrowed delicate brow: *When is the end of days?*

"You okay, honey?" he tentatively asked now.

"Yeah. I was just thinking, my favorite fruit is now pineapple."

"Pineapples are good," said Ed; his sense of relief at the conversation's downright jaunty turn was intense.

"You don't eat enough fruit," she said.

"I eat fruit. I eat plenty of fruit. Which one is your second favorite?"

"Oh, I don't know. Probably an apple."

"But you can get an apple all the time. Apples are boring."

"Plenty of places an apple is special," she said. "Plenty of places people are so poor there's nothing to eat."

"Well," said her father, "that's true." He realized he felt ashamed and that she had, more than anyone—more than even his father ever had—the capacity to shame him. "But, sweetie," he said quietly, "we're at Disney World. I kind of thought that we could talk about stuff that wasn't . . . y'know . . . so real."

"Okay." She nodded, then sat up even straighter and, assuming a pose that looked eerily like Jill's, she said, "But you know what? I don't really want a brother or sister."

Ed sucked too hard on the straw and the cold liquor pierced his head. "How can you not want a brother or sister?"

He was hoping, of course, that she would say something like, *I don't want to share you with anyone,* but instead she looked at him with quiet frustration and said, "I don't know, I just don't."

"Well, would you like another virgin lapu lapu?"

She shook her head, then: "You'd better make up with Mom."

"I know," said Ed.

"Her work is very important."

"Very," said Ed. *This is what I get,* he thought, *for sending her to that school.*

Jill had been more flexible about (or less interested in) the details of Rebecca's education, but Ed had felt strongly that they should send Rebecca to the *best* school in the city: a single-sex environment, a tradition of academic excellence, staffed with faculty that would challenge and ultimately mold Rebecca into the kind of Radcliffe girl who had so intimidated him when he arrived at Harvard as a freshman. But now that his daughter was—at ten years old—well on the way to becoming that girl, Ed was a little afraid of his daughter's self-possession and had the distinct feeling that the school's philosophy actually boiled down to a staunchly feminist version of noblesse oblige.

Rebecca had her picture taken with dopey Minnie Mouse and conceited Snow White and self-righteous Cinderella, filling her head with all kinds of beautiful bullshit; Ed got buzzed and bloated on lapu lapus and piña coladas, and by the time they were back home he was less angry than sad and he apologized to Jill, who seemed awfully restored by her quickie trip to Madrid. She was clad in her white terry robe and, due to her post-flight skin regimen, her face was a mask of alien green.

"Give Mom her present," said Rebecca.

Jill opened up the chocolate-covered coconut patties that Ed had remembered she'd told him about—how she'd loved them as a kid, how they'd been a once-a-year special treat when the Solomon family vacationed in Miami. Ed and Rebecca had searched at five separate stores. "Wow," Jill said, upon seeing the candy box. "Thanks, you two. Did you have a great time?"

"We did," said Ed. "Didn't we?"

Rebecca nodded, still watching Jill. They both were.

Jill smiled as if something smelled bad. "What?"

Ed tried to keep it light. "I think we're both just wondering if you recognize the significance of your gift."

"Of course I do. I ate these as a kid. It's so sweet of you. But I ate so much in Madrid—I've never eaten so much meat—that right now I also need these like I need a hole in my head."

"That's a terrible thing to say," Ed shot back. He felt his throat constrict and his face go hot; his back begin to sweat, and he thought he might actually cry. He knew he was being overly sensitive and that her humor had always been on the dark side, but that expression? *A hole in my head?* In response to his attempt to fulfill one of her childhood desires? "How can you say that?".

"What?" said Jill. "I really do appreciate the thought."

"Funny way of expressing it."

"All I'm saying is that they're fattening. That's all I'm saying."

He swallowed, hard. "Right."

"Ed," said Jill. "Please don't do this. We're all home, together. Thank you for the candy."

"They're the exact same chocolate-covered coconut patties that you loved when you were Rebecca's age. You told me you loved them and I remembered. I remembered the brand."

"And I'm thanking you," said Jill, as if he had turned some danger-ous corner and she wasn't going to let him take the two of them along. "Rebecca," said Jill, "let's get ready for bed."

"I wish you could just be a little more sentimental," said Ed.

"I know," she said. "I know you do."

Rebecca's eleventh birthday: a sleepover party at the (Jaffe designed) East Hampton house. By Sunday morning, Amanda Cohen was recov-ering from an evidently upsetting outburst; every minute or so Rebecca asked her if she was okay. Danielle Alfano and Eleanor Bliss had seemed like nice enough girls, but apparently, according to Jill, they'd stopped speaking to poor Jennifer Moore, whose steady work as a child model (in addition to a partial scholarship) helped her single mother pay for the private girls' school where these alliances had been formed. Danielle and Eleanor had accused Jennifer of "being conceited," which (again, according to Jill, who seemed concerned but also kind of jazzed) was perceived to be among the worst accusations among girls this age. Then there was Lauren Sealove, who didn't go to their exclusive school but who was Rebecca's best friend from Hebrew school and whose parents Ed pictured as sanctimonious if not socialist. Though the kid had done nothing but wear torn jeans and ask Ed if he liked his job, Ed didn't trust her. The first time Rebecca went to Lauren's, Ed asked his daughter how the apartment was, and Rebecca said: *You wouldn't like it.*

Eleven years old and already full of subtle implications.

Ed had forgone his Sunday ritual of reading all of his papers in order to make the girls chocolate chip pancakes, but as the girls were barely speaking, due to the evidently rigorous and emotional demands of a slumber party, they were each (aside from polite Jennifer Moore) sulking over the pancakes, and it was all Ed could do not to shake every one of them.

Jill had become their translator. "This is totally normal," she whispered to Ed, while he was getting dressed and puzzling over what had gone wrong with his daughter's party. "And believe me," said Jill, "it's only going to get worse."

"Are they leaving soon?"

"The parents are picking up in twenty minutes. Rebecca's going over to Lauren's for the day."

"The socialists have a house in the Hamptons?"

"Renting," she said. "Sag Harbor."

"Ah."

Ed emerged from the bedroom. "Girls," he said, planting a kiss on Rebecca's head, "it's been a pleasure."

"Have fun, Daddy," said Rebecca.

"Have fun, Mr. Cantowitz," echoed several of them, and they ceased being mysterious and frightening and returned to being children.

"Hey, thanks," said Ed. "I'll try."

Hy not only knew how to fly his own helicopter from Westchester to East Hampton and back, but he'd always been an on-time guy, a guy who even Ed, who counted on no one, could count on. But now, with a perfect blue sky for today's third flying lesson, Hy was late and hadn't called this morning to confirm their weekly appointment. Ed waited for Hy in the empty lot (a barren potato farm), which was walking distance from Ed's home. Ed did forty push-ups in the tall dry grass, and after Hy still hadn't arrived, he did an additional forty sit-ups; he threw in some jumping jacks (God knew he could use them). But as the sun inched behind the clouds and the morning turned to afternoon, the air grew hotter, the sky went dull, and Hy still didn't appear.

When Franny had bought the lessons for Hy's fortieth birthday five years ago, Ed thought his friend an unlikely candidate for piloting. Ed assumed he'd take a few lessons and leave it to the professionals, but Hy took to the skies and went on to get his license. He also became an enthusiast—donating flying lessons to every auction that asked, extolling the wonders of floating through the clouds, the virtues of bypassing traffic. By the time Ed asked Hy for flying lessons, Ed was so deeply troubled by the management of their company, by their collective inability to agree on most matters, that unfortunately these lessons were little more than an excuse to align himself with Hy, with whom Ed had every interest in continuing to work. He believed that—despite their frequent disagreements—it was Hy and he who were silently loyal to each other. Osheroff was so smooth that if he had any brains he'd be dangerous, Rabb knew the numbers but lacked any creative vision, but Hy still inspired him—there he was in the air! The man was flying his own chopper!—and Ed had every intention, during today's third lesson, of making this clear.

After the initial windswept chaos and the handshakes and good-to-see-yous, Ed strapped on his helmet and seat belt and they were both ready for takeoff.

"Remember," said Hy, over the *budda budda budda* of the blades, "acceleration, elevation. Deceleration, descent."

"Got it," said Ed, as his legs began to sweat.

"What else?"

"You never stop flying a helicopter until you land."

"Good boy."

"What are you doing?" Ed asked.

"Accelerating."

"We're going up?"

"We're *accelerating.*"

"Not sure I'm ready."

"Sure you are. Pull up on the collective."

Ed took the throttle between them and did as Hy instructed. "We're rising," said Ed.

"Elevating," said Hy.

Ed looked out over the flat planes of Long Island, at the green farm-land and blue ocean, at the patterns of how they came together and how they stayed intact. Suddenly he knew that it was time to speak his mind. He felt the sense of urgency that was his comfort zone, and he also felt that if he didn't say it now, he somehow never would, or that if he waited, the sense of urgency would turn inward and become something else, something depressing.

"Hy," Ed hollered, "I'm terrified."

"Don't worry, I'm right here. I'm not gonna let you fuck it up. You think I want that?"

"I'm not talking about the helicopter. I'm not talking about the les-sons. I'm terrified about our operation. Our lack of shared vision." Ed shouted to be heard above the din of the propeller. "Do you know what I mean?"

Hy might have nodded; Ed wasn't sure. The only thing he was sure of was that Hy was, in fact, going in for a landing—*deceleration*—and Ed asked, "Is there a storm coming?" but he knew there was no storm even before Hy shook his head.

"Are you okay?" shouted Ed. He should have waited until Hy had a plate of clams in front of him before bringing up something like this. Last time, they'd landed near a clam shack they both appreciated, where Ed bought Hy all the fried seafood he wasn't supposed to touch after his heart scare the previous year.

"I don't think you're ready for this," said Hy. "I thought I'd teach you the basics of hovering, but it really is the hardest part."

"Sorry," said Ed. "I'll be more focused next time."

"Sure," said Hy, "of course."

Ed knew better than to talk anymore. Hy was focused on landing.

"Feel that? That's where you feel the urge to pull way up on the col-lective," said Hy. "Don't," he said.

"What happens if you do?"

"You don't want to know."

They made contact with the ground, and Hy rolled the throttle to idle and the engine spooled down. Neither of them spoke as Hy's hands remained on the controls until everything stopped moving completely.

"*Baruch HaShem,*" muttered Hy.

"*I'll* say. I can't believe you have the stomach for this."

"Y'know what?" said Hy, almost severely. "Neither can I."

Outside, the day had changed. As they disembarked, the wind slanted the tall dry grass and Ed could smell a fickle sky. How it was, in fact, getting ready to rain.

"Listen," Hy said, shaking his head as he planted his feet in the dirt. "I'm not supposed to tell you yet. Not for a month at least. But I can't take it."

"You've been acting strange all day."

"I'm telling you, I can't take it."

"Hy?"

"We put it to a vote."

Ed's stomach lurched. *"What vote?"*

Hy faced him now, mitts on his hips, looking Ed straight in the eye. "As you say," he adjusted his stance, "there is no consensus. This is because there's no concrete leadership."

"I agree." Ed nodded. "I agree completely."

"I think you'll also agree that only two among the four of us have leadership potential."

"Of course," said Ed. "You and me, Hy, like Rockefeller said—"

"An extrovert and a driver."

"That's right, and don't kid yourself, Hy—we can do it. We need to stop hedging and begin to truly use our resources. We need to restructure and pare way down. Shift the focus, I'm telling you. Deals like the one I'm working on."

"Even though I told you—we all told you—it was too great a risk."

"I'm telling you, Hy—"

"And I'm telling *you.*" At first Ed thought he was imagining it, but by the time Hy said, "You're out," the sky had turned dense and gray.

"What are you talking about?"

"We have different philosophies."

"What different philosophies? What the hell are you talking about? *You already put it to a vote?*"

"Listen—"

"WHAT."

"There can only be one leader. Ed, with you, nobody ever knows what they're going to get."

"That's bullshit! *Everyone* knows what they're going to get. That's exactly why we've made the money we have. That's WHY. Because I tell people the goddamn truth!" He turned away.

"Ed," said Hy, "you are a remarkable salesman. Phenomenal. The best I have ever seen. But you are not a manager."

"Right," he said. A *salesman?* "Fuck it. If it's over, it's over. That's one thing I know."

Ed noticed, abruptly, that the field was littered. He'd never noticed the litter until now—beer cans and cigarettes, what looked like torn-up work clothes. He imagined the strips of those work clothes and those empty beer cans all mixed up in the landing, blown up and caught in the tail. He wanted to turn around and tell Hy about the litter, to warn him for the next time, but he knew there wouldn't be a next time, and this knowledge prompted him to want to promise Hy they would all suffer horrible losses if they went through with this and that they'd better believe Ed would fight it. Instead, he just turned away and started walking, then running, until he was sprinting through the grass so fast he had shooting pains in his chest and calves, and still he didn't stop. The rain was falling now, but it was a light rain, so much lighter than the dark sky had suggested, and shouldn't the sky split right open? Shouldn't it all fall down?

By the time he burst through the door to his house, he let himself imagine that it was Helen he was searching for, Helen he had married, and that it was—in fact—Helen who was the one always angry at him for petty reasons and that his real wife—dazzling mother of his only child—was someone he admired only from afar, someone he'd passed by one night off Fifth Avenue and fantasized about over a lifetime while having sex with Helen, his wife. He could even imagine Helen's clothes—

increasingly plain over time: pastel shirts, khaki skirts—strewn on the bathroom floor, clothes that Jill would never wear, let alone throw on the bathroom floor; he could see Helen's cheeks, flushed—and they were always so pink in his mind, so heightened, embarrassed, amazed.

"What happened?" cried Jill. He grabbed his real wife and she said, "Watch it."

But he didn't watch it. He pressed her onto the eggshell-colored living room wall, held her there until he got himself aroused and he couldn't stop himself from yanking off her tennis skirt, tugging the elastic from her long thick hair.

"What's with you?" she demanded.

"You're sexy," he muttered.

"I'm what?"

Ed shook his head. "Can't you just let something happen?"

"Yes," she said pointedly. "I can."

He backed away from her. Her impatient tone was so familiar. Why? What had he done? "What's that supposed to mean?"

"It means—Jesus, Ed—you're out of breath, you're slamming me into walls. It means, *what happened?*"

He turned from her, and as he sat down on the couch, tugging at what thankfully remained of his own hair, as he continued to think of a way to phrase it, all he wanted was for Jill to sit beside him, to ease this moment of telling her what Hy—whom she had never trusted—had told him.

The rain fell onto the roof, patterning the windows and the skylight.

As Jill looked at her watch, his mind cast about for comfort, and there was Provence when Rebecca was one—it had rained then, too. There they'd seen the French countryside through rain on windshields and windowpanes. But his most vivid memory was not of the rain, or of any châteaus or excellent wine, but of sitting with Jill in a rented Peugeot on the side of an ordinary road. On the way to a Michelin-starred restaurant, Rebecca had fallen asleep in the car, and rather than try to move her inside and cope with the potential consequences of her interrupted nap, they'd both agreed to let the Michelin star go, and, instead, they bought sandwiches at some kind of gas-station café. He remembered the slightly soggy baguette, the ham and cheese and butter, and how they'd eaten in silence. Only it wasn't the same as silence, because they were listening to Rebecca sleep.

Then, over the sandwiches and lemon soda, Jill had told him more about her late grandparents, whom—up until then—Ed had mostly heard lovingly described as cunning enough to have (on limited funds) bribed their way out of Vichy France and into New York at precisely the right time. As the rain fell in sheets, Jill told him about these grandparents, a pair of Russian peddlers who'd made it to Paris on sheer dint of will, who'd spent summers on Lake Gérardmer selling embroidered linens to tourists, and who—later—loved to see their granddaughter dressed beautifully; how they'd enjoyed sitting on park benches and telling her these stories; how neither of them had ever seemed bored.

"Ed?" Jill demanded now. She was gripping her car keys and the heavy Cartier key chain he'd once given her for Mother's Day.

He wanted to say, *Please come here,* but instead he said, "I wonder where Rebecca is."

"She's eleven," Jill said. "It's rain."

"That's what everyone said when she was a baby. When she and Solange were caught in the park."

"You weren't crazy to worry then, okay? Is that what you want to hear? You were not crazy to worry. Do you want to hear that not only should you worry now but that I should worry, too? That we should all be just as worried as you?"

"Her fever was so high she had to be hospitalized. All I'm saying is that I wasn't overreacting."

"All you're saying is that you were right."

Please sit, he wanted to say. *I'm in real trouble here.*

But she didn't sit; she was late for a doubles game. He knew without asking that she assumed the rain would clear.

And so he didn't tell her.

Part Three

1988

Chapter Thirteen

The Woods and the World

Forget about her dorm—small white clapboard house, quiet roommate from Ohio—and forget about her classes (excellent, she had no complaints): Rebecca met everyone through smoking. The Pines. The River. The Mountain. The Tree. The Watertower. The air growing cooler; sunlight streaking through the black-green trees. There was a place called Canfield, a clearing in the forest. Kids sat around, facing an ancient Pepsi can nestled in the dirt, as if it were a mesmerizing bonfire. Dan, her best friend from home, had warned her to stay away from DHs (*Dirty Hippies,* he'd deadpanned; his older sister, Adina, had spent four years on this very campus and then chose to attend Santa Cruz, based on the "clothing optional" clause in the literature), but there was Rebecca, one month into boarding school, sitting on a log. There she was accepting a light from Brian, the Dirty Hippie King.

There was Rebecca Cantowitz chatting with Ariel, fat and beloved, who ate green apples while she smoked. There she was with a girl named Merry (weirdly pronounced Murray, like Rebecca's grandpa), who was frequently tripping on acid; Merry took Rebecca's hand and said, *Your lips are like a baby's lips,* and Hassan laughed because Rebecca so clearly had no idea what to say. Hassan was six foot five and perpetually slouching; it was hard to see his eyes through the thick glasses and mass of black hair. He hung around Stephan, Mike, and Josh, who each wore flannel shirts and had more or less sandy hair, more or less lanky good looks. They laughed without making much noise and rarely spoke to anyone besides one another and Chris Huang, who, for some reason, was referred to only by his full name.

She had found them all on the very first day of school, because she'd followed a tall girl with white-blond cornrows, in an electric-blue dress, across a covered bridge. When the girl turned around, she looked Swedish or vaguely elfin. Her eyes were light green.

Rebecca took a calculated risk. "I'm looking for a place to smoke."

"Oh, Lord," she said, in a way that made Rebecca want to laugh. There was suddenly nothing Swedish or elfin about her. "You freaked me out. You look so serious. I thought you were going to start reciting poetry or something."

Rebecca kept silent but finally said, "What are you talking about?"

"You're new, aren't you?"

Rebecca nodded.

"I'm Vivi," the girl said, more as an explanation than introduction. She'd resumed walking and led Rebecca into the woods.

When they'd arrived at a thick cluster of pine trees, Brian was playing hacky sack with particular flair, as a tinny recording of what Rebecca was pretty certain was a noodling Grateful Dead guitar solo played from a boom box. And even though Rebecca disliked hacky sack and thought "Uncle John's Band" was profoundly grating, she couldn't take her eyes off Brian's glossy brown hair, his almond eyes, his skin so freckled it looked tan. Vivi approached Brian, who didn't stop *hacking*, and for a second Rebecca locked eyes with her and saw that Vivi was seriously pissed. Whether she was pissed because Rebecca had been staring or she was just that angry with Brian had been unclear.

"Where are you from?" asked Ariel, while lighting Rebecca's cigarette. Her nails were bitten down to the quick.

"New York."

"City?"

Rebecca nodded.

"I'm jealous," she said sweetly. "Stephan's from Manhattan, too." She took a big bite of her green apple. "If I lived there? No way I'd leave. You have a good summer?"

"Uh-huh, sure."

"What'd you do?" asked Stephan, who had evidently been listening.

"Um," said Rebecca. She was unreasonably nervous. "I went to Greece? My dad took me." She looked at some leaves in the dirt, looked back up at Stephan. "It was beautiful."

"I bet," he said, and she could tell she'd sounded too serious. "I bet it was." Stephan didn't look like he was from New York, or at least her New York. He was (as her mother would say) rough around the edges. He was smiling maniacally.

Rebecca reminded herself that he was no real renegade; none of them were, because they, too, were students at this very same prep school, which counted among its alumni not only two U.S. presidents but (more excitingly) not one but two stars of *Fatal Attraction*. They, too, had written those essays and been interviewed. "How about you?" she asked Stephan. "What did you do?"

"I sold acid in Washington Square Park," he said.

"Oh." Rebecca nodded, trying not to look unsettled. "How was that?"

"I'm just kidding," said Stephan. He was laughing.

"I know," she said. "I know you are."

"I was a camp counselor in Mount Kisco."

"Right," she said, "okay." She smiled vaguely. "Thanks for the cigarette."

"Where are you going?" somebody asked, but she was already gone—shoes shuffling through the dirt, heart in her throat. *Relax,* she scolded herself, *please oh please—for the love of a perfectly nice place to smoke—would you please learn to relax!*

She *would* relax. It would take about a month and a half. She spent at least a small part of each of those days in the Arts Center courtyard. Though "aggressively modern" (as her mother had observed), the building reminded her of the ancient amphitheaters she'd seen with her father in Greece. Their hosts, the Barkopolises (who, according to her father, "owned Athens"), brought Rebecca and her father to their summer home near Delphi for a weekend. Rebecca was the youngest guest by a good thirty years. And yet, as she'd watched her father drink ouzo among the men and women, who must have smoked two packs of cigarettes a day, as she'd watched them all dancing nightly, often with underwear atop their heads, she'd felt much much older than any of them. She'd also spent most of the trip trying to discover if her father was having an affair with someone and so approached every remotely attractive, raspy-voiced woman as a potential enemy. Rebecca not only listened with spylike intensity to every phone call but also scanned every story her father told for innuendos. She finally decided that it really was only her mother who'd done the cheating. Which hadn't made her feel any better.

This modern–ancient Arts Center was the sole reason she'd agreed to apply to boarding school at all, even though she had little to no interest in theater and only a general interest in visual arts (she took pictures of buildings that she liked, but she often forgot to develop the film—did that count as an interest in the visual arts? How about hanging out on the steps of the Metropolitan Museum?). She'd seen that pale colossal building, its shaded courtyard, and agreed to apply to this one school, where—after learning to relax—she now spent most of her free time not exploring photography or theater but rather sitting in the woods and staring at the trees, the sky, Brian, a soda can.

I don't know what it is about boarding school, her friend Dan had warned, *but I swear it's, like, relatively preppy arrival, followed by quick descent into patchouli cloud.*

I hate the smell of patchouli.

Which is one of the reasons I'm guessing you come right back. You'll be one of those kids everyone talks about senior year. Gone but Not Forgotten.

Right, she had said. Gone but Not Forgotten. She'd thought of her parents living not only without her but also without each other.

———

Her mother was (in her own words) not much of a phone person; she preferred to send little gifts, which were usually nothing Rebecca needed or even wanted but were somehow always the very things that elicited compliments: yellow alarm clock, Japanese notepad, fuchsia fingerless gloves. But—at his request—she called her father most nights, from the telephone closet off the small dorm kitchen. Before calling, she rummaged around the freezer for a frozen sesame bagel (kept in a plastic bag on which she'd written *CANTOWITZ* with a thick black Sharpie); she toasted the bagel until it was soft and warm and brought it into the phone closet, closing the door behind her. She and her father usually talked about her classes, her grades, what the dining hall served; he had a weird fondness for institutional food. They talked about the places he traveled for work. On Memphis: *It would be refreshing to live there; I wouldn't have to socialize with anybody.* On the many Mexicans in Arizona: *The hair! These guys put my hair to shame!* Over the course of the phone conversation, she nibbled on the bagel in the phone booth, making it last until they said goodbye.

And now, after dialing and hearing the first ring, Rebecca could picture how whatever her father was doing—watching the news, reading an article, writing himself yet another Post-it note to leave around the apartment—he would not be able to *stop* doing it until at least the fourth ring. That she knew her father this well flooded her with sudden warmth, but when she heard his voice—always somewhat annoyed—saying, "Yes?" (one of the few words that displayed his Boston accent), she jumped right in:

"You know," Rebecca said, "you don't *have* to answer the phone."

"What are you talking about?"

"You sound so put out when you say hello. Do you not want me to call so much?"

"That's ridiculous."

"Okay, then."

"Highlight of my day. Okay?"

"Okay, right. Highlight of your day."

"How was the calculus exam?"

She chewed on her bagel, took her time. "A," she said.

"That's my girl."

"I studied." She shrugged. "How's the used-car business?"

"Very funny."

"Well, that's what it is, isn't it?"

Her father had been buying up Japanese and European car dealerships all through the South and the Southwest for a couple of years now. His constant travel was one of the reasons cited when he and her mother had brought up boarding school. After Uncle Hy (whom she hadn't seen since she was eleven but still thought of as Uncle Hy) had betrayed her father and the company had basically kicked him to the curb, he'd sold his shares and decided to focus on what he best understood. His goal was to create an auto group and take it public, which, as he'd explained to Rebecca—over a late lunch at the Harvard Club one winter's day after shopping and seeing *Dreamgirls* on Broadway—had never been done before. Shopping bags had surrounded their table, dead animals were mounted all over the walls, and she'd had a tough time concentrating on what he was saying. Rebecca remembered nothing of the conversation, but she remembered very clearly that he had wanted her enthusiasm. Also: The early sunset had cloaked the nearly empty dining room in sadness. At the time, Rebecca attributed this sadness to the plot of *Dreamgirls* and how the fat girl who could really sing got kicked out of the group, while the gorgeous skinny one who was only so-so at singing became a megastar. How it was, of course, based on a true story.

"So," her father said now over the phone, crunching on what she was sure were ice cubes from a cobalt glass filled with Diet Coke, "your mother still saying that I'm a used-car salesman?"

"No," she lied.

"Let me tell you something. When you are a stock analyst, you are always an outsider. Always. And I'm only so interested in being an outsider."

"Huh," Rebecca said.

"What. What's that *huh* supposed to mean?"

"I don't know, Daddy. You always seem to kind of *thrive* on being an outsider."

"I'm talking about my profession here, sweetie pie. My profession. Quit analyzing me."

She waited for him to ask if she missed home, if the kids at school were snobby or messed up. He never asked about her friends or potential friends and she never brought anybody up, because he always zeroed in on their flaws, and even if Rebecca was sure he was wrong, she would, in time, become unable to disregard his comments. Her father would no doubt describe her friends from the woods as a bunch of scuzzy dead-beats. She cared too much what he thought.

"Until you are the owner of companies, you don't understand the necessity for all kinds of knowledge. All kinds. Not micro but macro. I'm telling you."

She heard a group of girls laughing in the common room. They'd asked her to join them—they were eating cookie dough—but she had declined in order to call her father; he'd insisted she "keep him posted." If he was so insistent on these phone calls, she thought, shouldn't he be answering on, say, the second ring?

That day at the Harvard Club when her father had explained his new venture, Rebecca had thought her sadness was about the dead animals on the walls and the fact that a leopard who was once alive and darting across a savanna had encountered a New York Harvard man who'd wanted to shoot it dead. And how proud that Harvard man must have been. That was what made her really sad: imagining his pride, his twin-kling smile, and how all of his friends must have clapped him on the back, saying, *Well done!* As if his accomplishment was something other than killing living beauty. She had thought her sadness was about *Dreamgirls* and the sudden clarity with which she'd begun to see that most of her favorite childhood tales followed a similar story and were always letting us know that the pretty girl, no matter how dopey, *does just fine,* as her father liked to say.

"You know, you looked really pretty when we dropped you off at that school," her father said now. "I thought to myself, those prep school boys aren't going to know what hit 'em."

That day at the Harvard Club, she hadn't known yet that her parents were finished with each other. In a way she wished she had. Because that's what the sadness was really about, even though she wasn't aware of it then. When they finally did tell her, last year, she became fixated on the fact that her parents had known their marriage was over and that they had *planned* on telling her—for how long? After they'd lied to her about loving each other, she felt she would never believe that anything was entirely true.

But despite all this, and despite her father's exhausting combination of overbearing interest and total remove and how strange she still felt about living away from home, and despite the fact that her mother already had a boyfriend (*David*) and probably had for longer than she admitted, Rebecca was oddly okay right then, in the phone closet, with her bagel nearly gone. Though *okay* wasn't the right word. She was overcome with a distinct weightlessness, as if she were looking down at this phone closet with the phone numbers and the Rilke and Patti Smith and Fleetwood Mac quotes scrawled on the wall, and not only could anything happen but nothing really mattered all that much; no one scenario was better than the other.

"You there?" her father asked.

"I'm here."

"You're pretty quiet."

"I am?"

"You know what I would have given to have gone to that school?"

"Now are you trying to teach me about rhetorical questions?"

Her father laughed and she could picture his broad smile, the very one that always made her at least marginally happy.

"Daddy, you know I've spent some quality time with Grandpa. Of course you would have killed to go away to school."

There was a friendlier silence between them then, and, after she'd eaten all but the very last crumb of her bagel, her father said, "Rebecca?" And just as she'd known he wouldn't answer the phone until the fourth ring, she now knew what was coming. "It'll all work out. Okay? Your head is on good and straight."

And—as more than one friend from home had started to point out toward the end of last year—she really *was* straight. Even square. Each friend who'd remarked upon this had done so with a perplexed tone, and Rebecca attributed their confusion to the fact that she was the first of her friends to take up smoking, way back in eighth grade. She knew that, even though she hadn't done it to impress anybody, she'd commanded an early authority that had been conflated with rebellious behavior. And she knew, too, that her new friends from the woods must have been seeing her in that same rebellious light, as each time she ventured into those woods and lit up, she was, in fact, breaking a major rule. There was—as stated in the school's "Student Contract," which she perversely enjoyed reading over and over—NO SMOKING ALLOWED ANYWHERE.

But she wasn't rebellious. She was a virgin. She had never been drunk. She had never smoked pot. She'd declined all invitations from her old friends, who had—over the course of the previous year—started going to Au Bar and Nell's to flirt with married cokehead bankers. She wasn't rebellious; she simply liked smoking—preferably by herself. She'd logged hours on the roof of her building, in Dan's mother's garden, by the boathouse in Central Park, and in diners while she was studying. Solange had moved back to Haiti at the start of her freshman year of high school, and Rebecca missed her even more than she thought she would. She missed eating Jell-O with Solange and watching *Dallas* together; she missed her beautiful singing voice and how she made up all kinds of lyrics to songs she didn't know (the Eurythmics: *Sweet dreams are made of cheese*; Men at Work: *You better run, you better take the bus*) and how she could laugh about Rebecca's mother and father without ever seeming as if she didn't like them. The only upside of Solange being gone was having the apartment to herself and wandering through the rooms—windows all open no matter what the weather—like the star of her own hollow art film. To remove the tobacco smell, she ate peppermint patties, rubbed her fingers with orange oil. Her father, she knew, might literally have a heart attack if he knew she smoked. His cholesterol was high, which was not exactly shocking. He wasn't fat, but he wasn't exactly what he called his "fighting weight," either; he alternated between trying to diet and absolute overindulgence. He had taken her to Paris last spring and she'd watched him devour foie gras and steak frites and all kinds of brains and cream and butter and duck fat—usually during one meal—washed down with red wine. He was hardly a shining example of healthy habits, and yet whenever he saw anyone smoking (which was, of course, a ubiquitous sight on the streets of Paris), he offered his standard remark to whoever was in earshot: *What kind of idiot would smoke these days?*

She liked smoking because it gave her companionship, because it relaxed her, because it—ironically, she knew—helped her remember to breathe. And it wasn't only on campus where she wasn't allowed to indulge in or—*face facts*—maintain her nicotine addiction. If a teacher saw her smoking off campus in the town's crappy diner—*if they caught her as far away from here as Central Park*—that teacher could turn her in, and she would be suspended. And she had zero interest in being suspended. She wanted to go to Columbia University. Being in Manhattan for college was one of the reasons that two years at boarding school didn't seem so terrible.

But here she was, breaking rules, hiking toward the Tree, which had evidently been struck by lightning years ago and left to rot on its side, in an abandoned field. In the past—before the two schools merged and went coed—this field had belonged to the girls' campus. In the future—it was rumored—the Tree would be gone and the field would become faculty housing. But for now it was a perfect playground: Two people could comfortably fit inside the sideways hollow, and it sustained a crowd on its trunk and surviving branches. Since it was a chilly October weekday right before dinner and the Tree was a weekend place (it was a hike to walk there and back from the main campus), it wasn't unrealistic that Rebecca expected to have it all to herself. But when she approached, there was Vivi Shipley: laid out flat with her eyes closed, as if she were on a cruise.

Rebecca climbed up to the highest branch. *Just us chickens,* her father would say. But Rebecca didn't say anything. She looked out at the weedy field, at the pine forest where the path to campus began. Midway through her cigarette, she wondered if Vivi was sleeping.

"There's something wholesome about all these spots," Rebecca mused.

"Wholesome?" Vivi said, still not moving. Definitely not asleep.

"You know—the fresh air, the grass. Sometimes I find pine needles in my pockets."

"You ought to campaign," said Vivi. Her voice, Rebecca noticed, had a certain *full* quality to it—not quite accented, but almost—and Rebecca tried to put her finger on what it reminded her of.

"For what exactly?" Rebecca asked. "Smoking outside?"

Vivi laughed, still on her back. Then she sat up, looking drained. Rebecca realized she was stoned. "I don't know. Maybe you can make a million dollars hawking soap on TV. Maybe you can raise money for my father's clinics. That would be good. My father runs health clinics. I'm just saying." Vivi focused suddenly on Rebecca. "You have a face you can trust."

"Really?"

"Maybe not," she said. "But I trust you."

Old movies, thought Rebecca. That's what Vivi's voice reminded her of. The way Americans spoke when life was reflected back in black and white. But she didn't seem to be putting it on—if anything, she seemed to be somehow at odds with her natural elegance.

Vivi picked off a slice of bark, flung it far away. "I've trusted you since I saw your expression that first day of school, when I was about to lay into Brian."

"You did? What did I look like?"

"You looked at me as if to say: *Don't.* As if to say: *Just walk away.* And I did. Such a better tactic."

"Huh," said Rebecca. "Well . . . I'm glad."

"Do you trust me?"

"What?"

"Do you trust me? Like, instinctively."

Rebecca nodded.

"No, you don't." Vivi smiled, as if this wasn't such a bad thing.

Rebecca looked at her and, instead of maintaining that, yes, she did trust her, she jumped off the tree branch, landing on both feet. "What does *trust* even mean?" Rebecca asked. "I'm not sure I really trust anyone. I think I'm like my father that way." And it was only as she said it that she realized it was true. "It's ingrained or something."

"So . . . your dad's suspicious?"

"I guess. I don't know." She didn't know how to explain either of her parents. She'd wrongly assumed that one of the perks of boarding school would be that she wouldn't have to. Her father was suspicious and demanding. Her mother was doting. Her father was generous. Her mother was selfish, a total bitch. Her father took her to every museum he could think of. Her mother went to theater and symphonies by herself. Her mother was the smartest, most beautiful, most kick-ass corporate lawyer working in New York today. "My whole family is totally bourgeois. Let me tell you, nobody is running health clinics. Actually, to be honest, it's way beyond bourgeois. You don't even want to know. By the way, Monsieur Simonet seems to *really* love saying that word. There was a girl in my class who didn't know what it meant, and when she asked, he nearly fell out of his chair, he was so excited to tell her. He promised we could have a screening of a movie called *The Discreet Charm of the Bourgeoisie*. Isn't that a great title?"

"Who'd never heard the word *bourgeois*?"

"Oh, I don't remember her name," she said, feeling suddenly protective of Allison McEvoy from Maine.

Vivi stood up on the tree so that she was towering above Rebecca. She was wearing a long flowery dress over a brown turtleneck. On anyone else, the whole outfit would have looked downright puritanical, but on Vivi it looked like she was the lead singer of an original band. She squinted, as if she was trying to make a decision. "I slept with him, you know."

"You slept with who?"

"Monsieur Simonet," she said. Then she jumped off the tree and landed clumsily, brushed dirt and leaves off her dress.

"You did?"

"I did. He was . . . disappointing."

Rebecca's heart was beating fast, but she wasn't exactly sure why. She'd assumed Vivi hàd slept with plenty of boys, probably even some men. "But—"

"*What*—I'm seventeen."

"Oh, sure. I mean, of course." Rebecca lit another cigarette.

"So I actually do want to know. When you said your family was *way beyond bourgeois*? What did you mean?"

"Oh, you know," she said, taking a long exhale, "the whole culture of spending, of constant accumulation."

"You mean—you're rich?"

Rebecca blushed and undid her scarf, which suddenly felt as if it was strangling her.

"I just want to hear about New York," said Vivi firmly. "The whole package."

"Why?"

"This might sound weird to you, but everything there seems so . . . clear."

Rebecca squinted at Vivi. "Did you really sleep with Monsieur Simonet?"

Vivi started to laugh. "No; I was kidding about that."

"Screw you!" Rebecca said, but she was laughing, too.

"Sorry," she said, "but I've only slept with Brian. At least in terms of here, where the pickin's are—in my humble opinion—pretty slim."

"Is Brian your boyfriend?"

"Well, not right now, but it's been kind of on and off with us since pretty much the first day of freshman year."

"Do you fight a lot or something?"

Vivi shrugged. "He repulses me."

But Vivi's repulsion clearly meant something more than repulsion, and it was something Rebecca knew that she herself had never felt.

Rebecca's eighth-grade year had been the zenith of not only her popularity with but also her own interest in boys. She'd wrongly assumed that she'd go from being asked out for pizza after school and playing a bit of Truth or Dare in the Meadow to having an actual boyfriend one of these days. But freshman and sophomore year had each passed by uneventfully, without so much as even an *unrequited* love, and she'd spent the better part of this past summer by herself, mostly reading or writing anti-apartheid letters to corporations, urging them to divest from South Africa. She'd gone to exactly one party at a loft in SoHo, where a boy from Collegiate went from trying to kiss her in the stairwell to telling her that she was *dead inside* by the time they made it to the roof. The sky was murky and violet; it was a hot summer night and the boy was cute; there was nothing wrong with this boy. Did she take a step closer, as he obviously was challenging her to? As Vivi certainly would have done? No, she did not. Instead, she'd countered: *I am not. I am totally not dead inside.* She'd proceeded to hold forth about how she just so happened to be consumed with important issues. The boy had leaned on the roof's railing. He'd asked her, sincerely, what could possibly be more important than desire, and she had lectured him on how all anyone cared about was pleasure and consumption and it was making her sick. And she hadn't stopped there. She'd gone on to outline the horrors of apartheid. As if they weren't obvious to anyone with half a brain. Especially to a boy whose father was (she later found out) a famous civil rights lawyer and whose mother was black.

"So," Rebecca ventured, wrapping her scarf around her neck one more time, "are you and Brian . . . y'know . . . these days?"

Vivi shook her head no.

"I thought you were serious about Monsieur Simonet."

"Oh my God, Rebecca! *You* want to sleep with Monsieur Simonet," cried Vivi. "You want to have French teacher sex! And by the way," she said, openly looking Rebecca over, "you totally could." She chanted, "Simonet, Simonet, Simonet," as she ran down the hill.

Rebecca didn't run but instead walked slowly, savoring her last few delicious puffs before tearing her cigarette into strips, the way she'd learned about in history class. *Soldiers did this,* Mr. Marshall had mentioned, *in order to leave no trace,* and Rebecca had felt as if he were speaking directly to her. When Rebecca didn't run, Vivi turned around and backtracked. Rebecca noticed how Vivi's grace was tinged with something awkward, as if she'd grown up quickly and was still figuring out how to catch up with her own range of motion. Though she'd noticed this before, it surprised her.

"Okay," said Vivi, "so what I mean about New York—at least bourgeois New York—is this: It just seems like there are the schools and the restaurants and the hotels and traditions, and it sounds as if everyone follows the same basic social rules. Or at least tries to."

"I have to tell you," said Rebecca, pretty certain that Vivi was being at least slightly patronizing, "I don't really get what you're saying."

"Come on, yes you do. I can tell you do. And you think I'm being condescending, but I'm not."

Rebecca shrugged and kept walking. She stuck her hands in her pockets, looked straight ahead toward the cluster of pines. She found herself testing Vivi, seeing how far she could push her before she looked the way she had that first day—with her green eyes narrowed and her rangy body tense.

"This idea I have of New York—it must come from my mother and her stories," Vivi continued, and they were walking together now, down the dirt path, and it felt good to be moving. Rebecca had no idea what Vivi was going to say and how, in turn, she was going to respond. She knew if they became real friends, this novelty would wear off and that she'd know what to expect from Vivi, and part of her wished they could skip this preamble. She wanted to be able to instinctively figure out when Vivi was stoned, and how often, and whether or not these kinds of conversations would happen during the times that Vivi was also sleeping with Brian. The wind was picking up.

"Did your mother live in New York?" asked Rebecca. The sky shut down the last of its lights; outside Manhattan, night seemed to come out of nowhere.

Vivi shook her head. "She just thinks it's the greatest city."

"I do, too," said Rebecca.

"You'd love my mother, by the way."

"Where did you grow up?" She remembered someone saying something about Vivi and Africa (about the cornrows?), but Rebecca couldn't remember the specifics.

"Tanzania, then Haiti."

"Wow."

Vivi nodded. "I think I'm lucky. But you'd be amazed at the questions some people here have asked me."

"Like what?"

"Like, *Did you have elephants in your yard?*"

"Come on. Nobody asked you that."

"Oh, yes they did. I'm used to it now, and, no offense, but Americans are pretty ignorant."

"Not to generalize," said Rebecca.

Vivi smiled. "You know what I mean." Rebecca couldn't help but feel just a little bit special, the way that Vivi was excluding her from the ignorant majority. "Both my parents are from here, so I'm technically American, I do realize that. And I've been at this school for almost four years, so if I wasn't American before, I certainly am now." She smiled sheepishly. "It's so funny, because I remember when I was in primary school, in Tanzania, I used to play with this American girl and we'd talk about how much we missed American things. I remember saying how much I missed cheeseburgers, although I'd never actually had one."

"Do your parents ever talk about moving back?"

"My mother did when I was little," Vivi admitted. "But she's very adaptable. She loses herself in the present. She meditates a lot—she has for as long as I can remember—so maybe that's why. But she has a thing about New York. She always said that if she could have more than one life, she'd want to live in Manhattan."

"How about you?"

"Oh, I want to live lots of places, though I'm not in love with the idea of men having more than one wife, which was the norm everywhere I looked, growing up."

Rebecca couldn't help but smile.

"What."

"But not really," Rebecca said.

"What do you mean, *not really?* I'm a jealous bitch."

"I mean, where did you go to school? And you probably knew some missionaries and embassy people, didn't you?"

"Jeez," said Vivi, sounding—if anything—impressed, "someone's been paying attention in world history. Okay, so not *really,* but let me tell you, you can feel it."

"Do you think it affected your father or something? Did it make him, you know, want more wives?"

"No," said Vivi quickly. "My father adores my mother."

"And she adores him?"

She nodded. "I know," she said. "It's rare."

"I don't know if my parents ever adored each other."

Vivi stopped walking. "Well," she said, "I bet they adore you." The lamps along the campus path all lit up at once. "Voilà," Vivi said. "I love when that happens."

Over peanut butter, granola, and honey sandwiches (they made it to the dining hall as it was closing), Vivi talked about her mother and father as if they were characters in a movie, a timeless classic of family solidarity, romance, and adventure. Only after Rebecca pushed for something not so perfect did Vivi acknowledge that, okay, sometimes her father drank too much and, yes, at times her mother could seem a bit . . . far away, but these admissions only made the Shipleys sound more intriguing. And when Rebecca skipped studying in the library for the first weekday night since the beginning of school in order to go to Vivi's room—a single in a turret above the infirmary—Vivi showed Rebecca her family photos, bound in a large black sketchbook. The room smelled like some kind of spice (not patchouli) and was adorned not with van Gogh or Pink Floyd posters or photo collages but an African batik and a sequined cloth embroidered with a two-tailed mermaid. Above her cluttered desk hung a map of the world with an intimidating number of pins stuck into all the places she'd presumably been. There was writing in the sketchbooks, too—entries that Vivi obviously didn't mind if Rebecca read as she sat on the floor, on what Vivi described as a Muslim prayer rug. As Rebecca turned the pages, Vivi narrated as if this was a book that someone else had put together and that she and Rebecca were—just then—discovering for the first time.

This is when I was a baby and we lived with my grandparents in Connecticut—I'd been airlifted out; I almost died. Here's the first time I had my hair braided. The lady couldn't find rubber bands; with black hair they just burn the ends, so she tried to burn bits of rubber onto my ends. What a disaster. When I came home and my mother saw my hair, I was so afraid she was going to lose it—she loves my hair—but she just laughed. Here's my mother with our best friend from Haiti. We became so close, but I always called her Madame. Her house looked like the one in Scarface. *There were men with guns who patrolled her roof. Haiti's poison, its corruption—it's everywhere, you know?*

Rebecca did not know. She did not know about Papa Doc or Baby Doc or the *Tonton Macoute* or the time that Vivi and her classmates had to go to school in secret because it was too dangerous to be anywhere except houses under embassy protection. She did not know that Haiti was the only country to have been born from a slave revolt or what it was like to have parents who thought nothing of flying in a single-prop plane over Lake Tanganyika to show their daughter 18 percent of the world's freshwater supply.

It was unnerving the way Vivi never complained about her mother and father during any of her many anecdotes. Rebecca wondered if this was what happened when your parents did irrefutably cool things like move to Tanzania in the 1960s and Haiti in the 1980s. How could you roll your eyes at opening health clinics and ministering to the poor? You couldn't. Or at least Rebecca couldn't. Much of the time, Rebecca walked around thinking about other people's pain. In European history class, Mr. Marshall started the last class by writing numbers on the board. *What's with the numbers?* called out Sean Riggs, who still hadn't removed his well-worn baseball cap. *Death,* said Mr. Marshall, sitting on his desk. *First World War.* And though Rebecca didn't think of herself as much of a cryer, she'd been suddenly overcome by those numbers and had felt as if she had a choice between breathing and crying or not breathing at all. Those numbers—they somehow made more of an impact than any books she'd read or photographs she'd seen. But what could it mean, other people's pain? And what good was feeling for others if there was no way to actually contribute—forget about contribute—if there was no way to literally remove their pain? She'd excused herself to the bathroom and wept in a stall. Wasn't all this endless feeling, those tears, weren't they just another kind of consumption? If she ever met Vivi's father, this was something she wanted to ask him. And had he chosen his work based on his inability to only *think* about pain anymore?

One of Vivi's biggest themes of the evening was how her dad believed in forging one's own path in the world; he believed in what he called *leaving the camp.* Evidently he had been expected to go into business or law and instead he'd chosen to serve the Third World. He'd made a career choice of setting up health clinics (he wasn't even a doctor, didn't even have that title to appease his family), and his work, these choices—it was all completely impressive.

"Hey," said Rebecca, "it's nine. I have to go sign in."

"Okay," said Vivi. "This was the best day."

Rebecca was so surprised by this assertion that she just nodded. "Good night," she said. "See you around." As she was closing the door, she became convinced she'd somehow sounded rude. "Um, Vivi?" she asked, standing in the doorway. "Do you want to come to the city next weekend?" As soon as she'd asked, she instantly regretted it. "My dad's going to be out of town."

Sending Vivi to boarding school was, evidently, the most difficult thing Vivi's father had ever done, because *he* had gone to boarding school—to *this* boarding school, in fact, before it was coed—and had hated it. He'd agreed to let Vivi go only because she frantically wanted to and because the options in Haiti were—even he had to admit—pretty limited. Her father had warned Vivi about the kind of kids she'd meet at boarding school, the types of ostentatious houses to which she'd be invited. And since Rebecca knew that she was (at least on paper) one of those kids, and since she herself disapproved of her own upbringing (had she and most of her classmates really needed Louis Vuitton purses at the age of thirteen?), she was embarrassed for Vivi to see where she'd grown up.

Still, once she'd put together that Vivi's grandparents were, in fact, most likely rich themselves (they lived in Connecticut and belonged to a country club that didn't allow Jews), Rebecca often found herself searching for holes in Vivi's stories, and the whole chronology confused Rebecca so thoroughly that she wanted to ask Vivi to write—along with the one Rebecca had suggested for Vivi's European history exam—a timeline of her own life.

And Rebecca could never quite tell if Vivi truly shared her father's disdain for ostentation. She seemed awfully interested in every detail of Rebecca's former Manhattan-bred classmates—their clothes and country houses and vacations—but every now and then she'd make some kind of cutting comment about unnecessary displays of wealth. Rebecca couldn't tell if Vivi might not be more than a little covetous along with being disapproving or if she simply enjoyed reveling in the fact that her father was right. That people really did live this way.

They rode Amtrak through Connecticut, through industry swathed in green. At Penn Station they bought cigarettes and giant salty pretzels, that they ate during the cab ride to Park Avenue. When they arrived at the familiar awning, Sal, Rebecca's favorite doorman, was on duty. She was so happy to see him that, though she'd never done it before, she gave him a hug.

"This," said Vivi, "is swank."

Sal laughed. "Oh man," he said. "Right?"

"Sal, this is my friend Vivi."

He gave Vivi's hand a good shake. "I've known this one—what?" He nodded at Rebecca. "Ten years? Since she was practically a baby. You girls be good, you hear me? Your father know you're here?"

"Of course," Rebecca lied. "You know me, Sal. I'm the last good kid on Park Avenue."

He said, "I'm telling you."

Though it had been only a couple of months, Rebecca had the feeling that when she opened the apartment door everything would be changed, but she was wrong. Nothing was different. The wall of Picasso sketches, the red Rothko, the gray Knoll couch, the white Eames kitchen table where she'd done her homework for years—all there. The photographs in their silver frames still stood staring on the piano. And the view from the fourteenth floor—overlooking the trees of Central Park, the way she always knew the beginnings and endings of seasons—the view was intact.

Vivi took off her blue cowboy boots, slid in her socks across the dark-wood floors. She touched the couch, the dove-colored cashmere throw, a row of leather-bound book covers, three crystal vases, the Giacometti on the end table. And then, looking suddenly kind of raggedy, as if she could use a shower, Rebecca's friend pressed her face against the thick glass windows. Vivi stood like that, frozen, looking out over the treetops. After what felt like the longest silence that had passed between them aside from that day at the Tree, Vivi asked, in a near hush, "Why didn't I come here sooner?"

Rebecca laughed and—with a distinct feeling of relief—collapsed onto the gray wool couch. She kept her eye on Vivi, who, after continuing to pick things up and put them down, finally sat down at the piano to play. When Rebecca immediately recognized Vivi's piece as the only one her mother ever played, she almost told her to stop. She could picture her mother tugging off her rings and saying, *Chopin Prelude Fifteen,* as if Rebecca should pay attention. But Vivi played the piece faster than her mother ever did, and Rebecca had to fight the urge to tell Vivi to slow down. *Think of a dark and wooded path,* she wanted to say, *a cool stream of water in the shade.*

"That was nice," Rebecca said instead, after Vivi had finished. "Who taught you to play?"

"My father," said Vivi. "There was this old hotel with a piano." She seemed less proud than sad. She stood up and started to look at the pictures, zeroing in on the coarse-looking man and smiling plump woman standing in front of a tenement—

"My grandparents," Rebecca said.

"Which side?"

"My father's," said Rebecca. "Dora and Murray. Never met Grandma Dora. Really wish I could have."

"And old Murray?"

"Tough customer."

Vivi looked silently at Pigtailed Rebecca, Ballet Rebecca, Awkward Bat Mitzvah Rebecca, Beach Rebecca held by her very tan father in swimming trunks, shielding his face from the sun. The pictures of her mother were gone.

"You were a seriously cute kid," she said.

"Thanks," Rebecca mumbled.

"Your dad looks kind of tough himself."

"My dad? Yeah, I guess. A lot of people say that. But, y'know—he's a businessman. He's not *that* tough. Hey, what are we doing tonight? We have to do something."

"Of course we do," said Vivi. "Who's showering first?"

"There are four showers," Rebecca said, laughing. "Here." She walked Vivi through what she still thought of as her parents' bedroom, into the art deco bathroom that opened into what used to be her mother's dressing room, which was now her father's study. "You can have the nicest one."

When Rebecca returned, wearing outfit number one—black REM concert T-shirt, black miniskirt, black combat boots—to get Vivi's assessment, she found Vivi, still in a towel, sitting on her father's desk chair, reading one of his many yellow legal pads.

"What are you doing?" Rebecca snapped.

"Relax," said Vivi, "I wasn't snooping."

"What are you doing, then?"

"Um," she laughed in that sudden way of hers that seemed to indicate contrition, "snooping?"

"Get dressed, okay?" Rebecca said, not bothering to ask Vivi's opinion of her clothes. "I want to get going."

"Are you wearing that?" asked Vivi.

It was a good two hours before they went anywhere, which didn't matter, because the club where Vivi's friend was DJ'ing was way downtown and didn't even open until eleven. It was in a warehouse, the music was rap, and there were shared urinals and people much older than Rebecca and Vivi, one of whom was speaking French to Vivi, shrieking happily over the music. There was a silver flask of tequila, proferred by (according to Vivi) Suzanne Vega's brother. There were bottles of beer drunk quickly and the relief that she was finally—at fifteen—drunk for the first time. They met a guy, a friend of the shrieking French woman, named Jean-Loup Wolf, who was American and tall and so untouchable that Rebecca found herself laughing hysterically over his name out of sheer awkward desire. His lips were full and his hair was so thick and so gloriously unwashed and he was wearing some kind of silky shirt that looked . . . elegant. Loup *means wolf in French!* she whispered dumbly, and, *Jean-Wolf Wolf,* she kept saying to Vivi, but Vivi wasn't beside her anymore. Vivi was standing in front of Jean-Wolf Wolf, and then, within seconds, she was perched on top of a railing, her legs wrapped around his waist. They were kissing and Rebecca was watching. She thought, *What is she doing with her hands? I have to remember to do that.*

Vivi and the wolf walked over; his arm encircled her shoulder. "We're going to Jean-Loup's." She said his name with a strong French accent.

Rebecca followed them outside.

"I'll give you rides on my bike," he said, pointing to a gleaming motorcycle. "One by one."

"Thanks," said Rebecca, quickly sobering up. "But I can't ride on a motorcycle."

Vivi quickly took her aside. "You're kidding," she spat.

"I am definitely not kidding. They are death traps," she muttered back. "Besides, look what you dressed me in!" Rebecca yanked down the black Lycra minidress that Vivi had found in a ball at the bottom of her closet, which Rebecca had previously worn only once, in the sixth grade, when she was a cat for Halloween. "There is no physical way."

"You have to relax," said Vivi.

Rebecca shook her head. "Just give me the address and I'll meet you. That is," she hesitated, "if you want me to."

"Of course I want you to." Then, in a brighter voice, meant for Jean-Loup: "It's no big deal. She has a thing about motorcycles."

That night in Jean-Loup's apartment was the first time Rebecca saw a bathtub in a Lower East Side kitchen. It was the first time she smoked pot and sat outside a bedroom talking to a sexually ambiguous guy, while Vivi was inside a bedroom, making time. The friend, Tad, was nice. He was even kind of old-fashioned, dressed in a clean white button-down shirt and black trousers. He offered to make Rebecca a cup of hot chocolate. He asked her if she'd seen any John Waters films, and when she said no, he popped in a VHS tape and they watched *Pink Flamingos,* which was, without a doubt, the most disgusting thing she'd ever seen. He told her that trash could be beautiful, even violence could be beautiful. She told Tad that she was feeling a little freaked out and he said sweetly, *Okay, I understand—you are a lovely girl.*

By the time Vivi emerged from Jean-Loup's room, the light outside the window was silver.

"I must have fallen asleep," Rebecca whispered. She was lying on the couch, still in the Lycra dress, covered with a soft blanket. She looked around, but Tad was gone.

Vivi knelt beside her; her face looked red and raw. "Are you okay?" Vivi asked.

She nodded. "Are you?"

"Absolutely." Vivi smiled. "Let's go."

They walked to a diner and had coffee ice cream sodas for breakfast. Vivi didn't tell her any details and Rebecca didn't ask. They watched the sun rise over the East River—gray and platinum, blue and gold—until it was a new day.

In November, in the Arts Center, Vivi showed Rebecca a series of self-portraits.

"You have no face," said Rebecca.

"It's supposed to symbolize my shyness."

Light poured in through the skylights of the painting studio even though it was wet and rainy. "Okay . . . but you're not shy."

"Secretly."

"Secret shyness? I don't know, Vivi. . . . You might need to learn to paint your features."

"Just because your own shyness is so obvious—"

"Hey, I managed to meet you on the first day of school, didn't I?"

"Doesn't count," said Vivi, still scrutinizing her canvas. "I was the one who introduced myself. You were following me, but you never would have said anything."

"See—you're not remotely shy. And you think everyone is following you."

Vivi shrugged.

"You *do*! I swear I've never met anyone more . . . confident."

Vivi started to laugh and shrugged again. "I'm just willing to see what's right in front of me."

"Like what?"

"Well, let's see. Off the top of my head? Okay." She took a dramatic breath. "Nobody really looks like me. I am not as smart as you. Smartness is overrated. Also? My friends from freshman year? Not my friends anymore. Not sure when that happened, maybe it was my fault, but, whatever—there's nothing there now."

"Does it bother you?"

She nodded. "I'm sentimental."

"*You?*" Rebecca wasn't being sarcastic, but as soon as she'd said it, she realized that of course Vivi was sentimental. She'd just never thought of her that way.

Vivi blushed, and her face was so deeply, so unexpectedly red—it was almost uncomfortable to watch. "Oh, and here's another thing. This painting? Bad. And," she took a generous pause, "every painting I've ever made is bad." She chewed on the end of one of her cornrows, which she did only when deliberating. "I'm going to stop painting and try photography."

Rebecca looked at Vivi's painting. It wasn't good. Nor were her grades. But instead of noticing all the various ways in which the painting was lacking or thinking that Vivi should have gotten her grades up last spring in order to get into a better college, Rebecca found herself impressed that Vivi could move on so quickly, that she didn't cling to the idea of making the painting better, that she cared more about expressing herself than she did about her college placement. Part of Rebecca's inability to try even the most minor of creative endeavors (like baking a long-promised coconut cake for her friend Dan's birthday last August) was that she knew she'd never know when to let the idealized version go. She knew she'd be up all night baking that stupid cake, convincing herself that she could make it better than it could ever actually be. "I think," said Rebecca, "this is a good call."

"Okay, then, we're in agreement there," said Vivi, still focused on the canvas. "I totally suck as a painter."

"No, come on—"

"What are you doing for Thanksgiving?"

"My mother's boyfriend's beach house. Remember?"

"Oh, right. What's it like?"

"I don't know." Rebecca shrugged. "Decorated?"

David's house in Southampton was exactly the kind of place that Vivi loved hearing about. But Rebecca did not tell her about the antique Mercedes convertible that was used just for going to the beach or that there was a whole other "cottage" for the year-round chef. She did not share how, during her last visit during the summer, every morning there was a newspaper for each and every guest—the sections already separated and neatly stacked alongside the breakfast spread. She did not mention the breakfast spread—the baskets of croissants and pastries and bagels from E.A.T., the platters of smoked fish and exotic fresh fruit and made-to-order omelets. Or how there was a giant Calder mobile on the lawn leading to the clay tennis courts. Or that one of her early memories was of her father taking her from the Museum of Natural History straight across town to the Whitney, where he pointed out *Calder's Circus* and told Rebecca he preferred Calder to dinosaurs. Rebecca did not tell Vivi how her father would have been so jealous if he saw that Calder—maybe even more jealous than if he saw her mother kissing David—because her father wanted to own what he loved.

"Is that where you want to go for Thanksgiving?" Vivi asked.

"Sure."

"Really?"

Rebecca pictured the white four-poster guest bed and how she knew she'd have trouble sleeping under the same roof as her mother and David. She already knew that she'd long to feel close with her mother and yet would barely be able to look at her, forget about touching her, not even a hug goodbye.

"No," Rebecca admitted. "That isn't where I want to go."

"So come with us instead."

"To Haiti?"

Vivi shook her head. "We're going to Anguilla."

"Your family goes to *Anguilla*?"

"My aunt Kitty is a decorator, and she's doing up a house there. She's done a bunch of these houses in the Caribbean and then she sells them at a gigantic profit. Mom gave her the idea. My father totally disapproves and thinks it's obnoxious and that she's ruining the island's integrity, but he's coming anyway. I think he feels bad about disappointing Aunt Kitty. Plus my cousin J.K. is in rehab—poor J.K.—which is really expensive. I had no idea rehab was so expensive. Did you?"

Rebecca shook her head. She looked over at a still-life display; a white sheet was crumpled at the foot of a table. She felt like pulling that sheet over her head and waking up with Vivi's family in Anguilla, where nothing was remotely familiar. People adored one another and stayed married, and made even a trip to rehab seem okay. People spent their lives working with incredibly poor and sick people, got paid next to nothing, and vacationed in Anguilla.

"I can't come," said Rebecca.

"Why not? I just invited you."

"But—"

"I really mean it. You're invited. I understand the importance of an invitation."

"Huh. I find that hard to believe."

"What does that mean?"

"I think you probably walk through a whole lot of doors without an invitation. In fact, I bet your un-American globetrotting life is like one big fat American game show. What's through door number one? The Caribbean! Oh, wait, what about door number two?" Rebecca knew that she was being more than a little confrontational, but she wasn't exactly sure why. She waited for Vivi to take offense, but Vivi only began to place her canvases alongside other painted canvases, under a sign cheerfully labeled: FEEL FREE TO PAINT OVER!

"You're invited," said Vivi definitively, with a somewhat eerie disregard for Rebecca's rotten behavior. "You should come."

Chapter Fourteen

NYC/Velocity

During a fit of Zionism combined with a feckless desire to rid his collection of a Philip Pearlstein (the model looked like Jill), Ed had donated a painting to the Tel Aviv Museum of Art. He had learned for the first time of Jill's struggles with fidelity, and though it was several years before they actually signed divorce papers, he'd thought of that painting's journey to Israel as representing the bitter end of their marriage. He went as far to picture himself as the painting: crated up, stuck in limbo, waiting to emerge. He should have, in fact, held on to the Philip Pearlstein. If he still had the Pearlstein he would be able to sell it along with the rest of his collection in the coming year (if it came to that—which it could have).

It could, in fact, come to that.

However.

Having made the donation, he received invitations to anything remotely suggestive of contemporary art or Israel, and, over the past few years, he'd taken to attending one event per week. Though he hadn't finished packing and his flight was in the morning, and though he'd never previously been to China, he was far too socially careful these days to miss an event for which he'd RSVP'ed. He abandoned his suitcase and his checklist and strolled over to Roseland on a late October evening. As a kid, fall had been his favorite season—he loved returning to school—but as an adult he found it disheartening. It was getting dark earlier now, and the air was crisp; everything was beautiful in that sad kind of way that he absolutely fucking hated. A party was what he needed; he needed to feel like a sociable person, which—for him— entailed talking with people who didn't know him yet. He heard the swing band, the muffled chatter, the clinking glasses and silver, and as he entered the room, the first two people he saw—the very first two, as if this all were nothing more than one of his ridiculous Ziegfeld-style dreams—were Ted Kennedy and Connie Graff.

They were dancing. Teddy twirled Connie, who was wearing a low-cut red taffeta number; they were both laughing. It was still cocktail hour, and they were the only ones cutting a rug. Teddy was very red and very large. He had a presence. It didn't matter that his dance moves weren't terribly fluid. He was a friend of the Jews. Ed swiped a glass of champagne. A toast-and-salmon canapé. He didn't know whether to laugh or leave, but he couldn't take his eyes off the senator and Connie. He watched them through a fine rendition of "I Get a Kick Out of You," and, when they were finished dancing, Connie whispered something in the senator's ear and—to Ed's great surprise—they came right over.

"Ed," Connie said.

He kissed her on the cheek. She smelled citrusy, metallic. One of her diamond earrings nicked his cheek. She made the introduction.

"Senator," said Ed, pumping his meaty hand. "Good to meet you."

Ed asked how they knew each other, and Connie and Ted Kennedy had a good laugh. Finally Connie offered, "Oh dear, that's a long story, but we met while vacationing. If you can believe it, I stumbled down a rocky cliff, and who helped me up but this fella. Imagine my surprise. Teddy's good in a crisis, I can tell you that."

Ed was not only afraid that Connie had made a tasteless joke but that the senator was actually going to laugh in response. But then Ed realized she was being completely serious. To Connie, he was not the Kennedy who killed a girl; he was the Kennedy who was her friend.

"You know I came only to dance with you," Ted said, kissing Connie's cheek. "Pleasure to meet you, Ed."

"Next month," Connie called after him. "Don't forget."

"You look terrific," said Ed, the minute Kennedy walked away.

"Thank you." She smiled broadly, but it didn't feel as if she was smiling. Her teeth were very white. "And thank you for coming."

He must have looked confused.

"You might want to read those invitations more carefully from now on." She waited a moment, but he was still too disoriented to rescue her. "I'm co-chairing this event."

"Oh," Ed stammered, "oh, but of course you are. I only meant—"

"Save it," Connie said, still smiling. "You remain in the running for the world's worst liar."

This awkward encounter was nothing if not proof that he never should have gone out the night before such an important trip. "Fine," he said. "You're right. I somehow missed your name on the invitation."

"It doesn't matter," said Connie. "You're here."

"So . . . you invited me?"

"Not exactly. But I did consider that you might be here this evening. Please, Ed, don't look so terrified." She flipped her thick hair behind her shoulder. "It's good to see you."

"You, too!" And, quickly, because he'd finally found something to say: "I see you had the good sense not to cut your hair."

"Sorry?"

"All the women I know seem to be doing that these days. It's good to see your hair, that's all."

"Thanks," she said, with a note of bitterness so faint he almost missed it. "I'm glad you approve."

With Connie's one bitter note, he felt officially nervous, and it galled him. "I do," he said, not backing down. "I definitely approve."

The band stopped playing and a bespectacled gentleman took the podium. "Good evening," he said, and, aided by a thick Israeli accent, his bespectacled-ness seemed less professorial and more edgy, avian. "I hope you all can—like the song that was played by this . . . very nice band—forget your troubles and . . . get happy."

A polite laugh from the crowd.

"I know many of you still feel the sting of last year. But as we say in my country: *Yihyeh beseder.* Everything will be just fine. I can tell who is Israeli by those of you who are laughing. Because"—he squinted out into the crowd—"you know that we say this in opposition to reality. We say this as things get worse." He smiled, this charmer of a positivist, and raised his glass.

"Great motivator, this guy," Ed whispered to Connie. "Who is he?" But she said nothing in return, and Ed felt like the class screwup—trying to impress the straight-A girl with his lame quips.

After thanking all the appropriate people and saying something minorly uplifting about art, the Israeli finally left the stage.

"What I don't understand," said Connie, "is money."

He was surprised by her digression; she'd seemed so doggedly focused on the Israeli's introductory remarks. "What's to understand?" Ed shrugged. "It's gone. Boom. That's why they called it a crash."

"But all the money all those people invested—including yours truly, of course: Where did it all go? I mean, literally, where did it go?"

"You see that candle?" said Ed. He pointed to one of the cocktail tables. "You see how it burns down?"

"Well," said Connie, "I've never understood candles, either." She suddenly seemed a little woozy, as if the energy she'd expended thus far in being friendly to Ed had already worn her out.

"You wouldn't be much of a pioneer woman."

"What?"

"You know—candle-making. They all had to do it, those women."

"I would have been a fabulous pioneer woman. You should taste my meals these days."

"I hope you haven't forsaken Chinese takeout. I think of you every time I eat General Tso's chicken, you know."

"I heard about your divorce."

He nodded. *Fair enough.*

"I was sorry to hear it." He was no longer surprised when anyone knew. "I was sorry," she repeated.

He must have made a terrible little grin, because Connie said, "Oh, come on. You think I'm still upset at you for dumping me in the early seventies?"

He started to laugh like an idiot, because what else could he do? He *did* think she was still upset about it. And—what a schmuck—he did not want this belief taken from him. Not tonight, not right now.

"Poor guy," she said. She swiped a glass of champagne from a passing waiter's tray. "You were a mess then."

"Yes," Ed said, because he owed her that acknowledgment, even if he wasn't sure how true it really was. He didn't remember himself as a mess. He remembered a youngish man with more options than he had at the present moment.

"I do hope time has healed that wound." And, with a meaningful look, she took a sip of champagne.

"What wound?"

"Helen," she said.

And it was as if the collective Cold War nightmare suddenly culminated in a nuclear white-flash instant. It was that intense, that unreasonable, as Connie said her name. He felt dizzy and nauseous, and when he remembered he was holding a drink, Ed sucked down nearly all the bubbly, his nostrils tingling from the rush of it.

"Don't worry," she said. "I never told her."

And Ed was sure Connie could somehow feel the velocity of his heart as it dropped straight into his bladder, as, simultaneously, he dropped to the floor outside his rented room, where Helen was sitting, waiting for him. Waiting. For him. He was sure Connie could also feel the sheer curiosity pulsing at his temples, his chest, and—most insistently—his prick. Ed wondered if Connie was as surprised as he was by just how forcefully such insinuation had affected him. In a weird way, in a generous way, he wanted to let her know. *Connie, you have thrown me.* But: "Oh, right," said Ed. "Of course."

"Of course?"

"Time heals."

"Well, good," she said. "I'm glad."

It was as if he were rooted to the wood planks of the floor, as if the adjacent socialites and art lovers and and politicos and all those years and people and countries and all that money coming and going and the very real threat that his company was failing and unable to meet its monthly commitments: It had all been nothing more than distraction from this story, the one about Helen, the one about that morning at the Y when she was sitting in the hallway, waiting. He knew this wasn't true. He'd been crazy about Jill—certifiable. And he knew that his love (puny, feeble word!) for Rebecca was sometimes more than he thought he could stand. But at that moment it was as if Connie—in an attempt to take him down—was intentionally projecting an air of familiarity, and her plan was working. He felt weakened by her proximity. Connie's straight nose and white teeth drew him closer and closer with their promise that all problems had corresponding concrete solutions, and goddamn if he didn't feel as if none of his relationships were as real as what came before having an income or an apartment—not to mention a wife and child—before the president was gunned down in Dallas that November and Hugh and Helen were together somewhere in Africa, which may as well have been the moon, and there was nobody else he wanted to call.

"So you and Helen," managed Ed. "You're in touch?"

Connie waved to several couples and fielded three sets of air kisses before answering. "Well," she finally said, "back then, after you and I were—" She interrupted herself here to indicate Ed with her champagne glass, as if to imply disappointment itself. "I wrote to her. I reached out. I just—I don't know why."

"I'm surprised."

"Well, we *were* friends, Helen and I."

"Yes, but—if I recall—you didn't exactly have the nicest opinion of her. You told me she was—"

"I remember what I said, Ed."

"What did you tell her?"

"Ed?" she said firmly, "I remember everything. I remember how I felt about Helen Shipley, and I remember how I felt about you."

"Oh," he said, and though taken off guard by her sudden candor, he was also distinctly relieved. "Me, too." He remembered Connie's warmth, her humor; he remembered her sophistication, which had always seemed slightly studied somehow. He remembered her breasts, too, and how the rest of her felt too slight, and how this slightness was the sole quality she'd possessed that made him feel nervous. He remembered the sense that, while he was in her company, she was always looking out for him, and he remembered thinking that she, Connie Graff, was the woman he was supposed to end up with. And it was exactly this sense that he had turned from. He remembered when he'd turned from it—from her; it had felt, with its requisite bit of pain, exactly like freedom.

"She wrote back immediately." Connie nodded, her words now stripped of their sparkly surroundings. It was a voice that belonged to the middle of the night, when trappings no longer mattered. "For a while there, Helen wrote all the time. She wrote about five letters to every one of mine." And, as if she realized that she'd come across as boastful, Connie added, "She was lonely, obviously."

Ed followed as she inched farther and farther from the center of the room in a kind of thoughtful silence. They brushed by several potted palms. Older couples strained to hear one another above the cocktail music; dinner would soon be served. Connie was no longer fielding waves and air kisses; it seemed as if people knew to stay away. Ed and Connie drifted to the periphery of the party, though they never did sit down.

"Did you—" started Ed. "Have you seen them?"

"I saw her that summer. She came to visit her parents. Hugh didn't come. Helen—she seemed okay. A little worn out, a little overwhelmed, but, then, she had some trouble after the baby was born."

A baby? They had a baby? They stayed together and had a goddamn baby? "What kind of trouble?"

"She was never the most perky person, *obviously,* but . . . I think she took a bad turn there for a while. God knows what it was like where they were living. Hugh always had some kind of punishing—or self-punishing—streak, don't you think?"

"Hugh didn't like being rich," said Ed. "That's what I think."

"But I think it went further. I don't know. She was very tight-lipped about their living conditions—I got the feeling that she was always holding back from telling me the real story. She was protective of Hugh; you know how that is."

"How what is?"

"You know—being married. People turn private."

"They do?"

"Oh, stop it. You know what I'm talking about. She didn't want me to think badly of Hugh."

"Why would you think badly of him?"

"Ed."

"Fine."

"Stop digging."

"I said fine."

"I mean it."

"Okay," he relented. "Go on."

"I don't know that there's anything more to say. It was as if she made some kind of decision. I started to hear less from her, she seemed more settled, and—" Connie abruptly stopped talking.

"What."

"You didn't know they had a child?"

He shook his head and thought about Helen pregnant, about Hugh holding their newborn, and he wanted to sit down. He wanted to lie down. Had he really not considered this possibility? He must have considered it. He'd considered everything at one point or another. Hadn't he?

"You looked so . . . crushed when I mentioned it."

"I'm not crushed," he said, with an attempt at incredulity. "Of course I'm not."

"They have a daughter."

"Oh," he said. And then, because he couldn't stop himself, "I do, too."

"I know," Connie said softly.

"You do?"

She nodded.

"And how about you?" he asked.

"How about me?"

"You're wearing a ring."

She smiled, and it was such a relief. He'd forgotten her real smile. "The man who spoke at the podium? That's my husband, Micha. We have a boy and a girl. They're eight and ten."

"That's terrific," said Ed. "Just terrific."

"It's the best," she said. As if to say: *The rest of this conversation has been meaningless.*

"I'm going away for a couple of months," he found himself saying. "But when I'm back, maybe we can get together."

"Where are you going?"

"China," he said. "I'm leaving in the morning."

"Really. Where in China?"

"Shenzhen. I'm flying into Hong Kong. But maybe when I'm back we can—"

"Well, safe travels." She smiled. "Our friends just went—adopted the most delicious little girl."

She caught someone's eye in the distance and began nodding and laughing, and he was jealous. He was jealous in a way that the younger man—so full of options, so full of himself—never could have understood.

That night he poured himself a glass of Diet Coke, sat at his desk in near darkness, and, under the one desk lamp's bright yellow light, the conversation with Connie and its sense of timeless urgency faded away. He was relieved that this was possible. He was relieved, too, to be able to focus on his legal pads and on his (thus far) relatively private potential disaster. He could not comprehend his interminable (why not just name it?) obsession with Helen and—in a different way—Hugh. He could not comprehend the fact of their parenthood or their enduring marriage. He could not exactly comprehend the demise of his own marriage, either, or the fact that his daughter was not somehow down the hall in her oddly spare bedroom, eating orange sections between bouts of sulky letter-writing. He could not comprehend any of this. But here at his desk, by the light of his stainless architect's lamp purchased at the Harvard Coop in 1961, he could begin to think straight. And as he sat with his head in his hands, all that remained were these two facts: He was in trouble, and he had a plan.

When Hy and the others ousted him, Ed had convinced Wells Fargo to loan him twenty million dollars. Twenty million—by talking. The fact that the company he built with this loan could easily turn enough profits to make the monthly payments was something he'd never seriously doubted, and for years he'd been correct. But after Black Monday, one year ago, after his net worth plummeted, there was not enough money to pay the employees of those one hundred forty dealerships.

Ed's company was in the process of filing for Chapter 11.

And he had sent his daughter away.

Looking up and out the window, he imagined the treetops of Central Park, though he was, of course, met with nothing but his own reflection. How many times had he faced himself like this? The glaring white of his unbuttoned shirt, the blue glass sweating on the desk. But he once flew to Texas in the middle of the night and, based on his powers of persuasion, he'd saved the fate of Wall Street. He had been that man, too. And the fact was (he sat straighter now) that once the company filed for Chapter 11, it would be absolved of debts and interests until there was a hearing in front of the judge, and, with the help of his most excellent lawyer, this hearing could take up to four years to sort out. He could buy himself four years. For all that he wanted to pull off, he needed those four years, that same excellent lawyer, and a telephone.

He also needed capital.

He took one last awful slug of Diet Coke and crunched down on three fat ice cubes.

What he was going to do was not legal, and he could, in fact, go to jail. It was not as if he didn't grasp this. But he was also convinced that if he followed these plans, written out nightly with his green felt-tips on his yellow legal pads from the very first step to the very last, if he annotated these plans with questions that diminished daily with his ever-increasing knowledge—if he stuck to his plan, one step at a time—everyone would come out on top.

He called Rebecca on the dorm phone. It was late, but those kids never went to sleep on a Saturday night before two A.M. After several rings, a girl answered, called out for his daughter, and then told him to wait, that she'd go find her. Though he had, in fact, seen where the dorm phone was, he could picture neither the room nor the comings and goings of so many teenage girls. What he pictured—and what he knew was patently incorrect—was some kind of nineteenth-century warren.

Moments later another one came on the line. It was not uncommon to hear several chirpy voices before finally hearing Rebecca's. "Mr. Cantowitz?" said this one. Her voice was uncommonly mature.

"Hello," he said.

"I'm Vivi," she said. "I've heard so much about you."

He hadn't heard a thing about this Vivi. "Nice to meet you over the phone," he said. "Seen my daughter around?"

"She's taking a shower right now. We went hiking—"

"It's past midnight."

"Right, but—I mean, you know, earlier today. At any rate, she's in the shower. Is everything okay?"

"Everything is fine," said Ed.

"Good," said the girl. "Listen, don't worry, I'll tell her to call you right back."

"Okay," said Ed. Was this girl on drugs? What was with the hiking and the shower? It was all a little overexplained.

"Okay," said the girl. "I'll be seeing you."

"Where?" asked Ed.

"I don't know," said the girl, and she started to laugh. "I just mean, you know, generally. Good night, Mr. Cantowitz."

"Good night."

He never heard from Rebecca that night. They spoke briefly before he left for China, and when Ed asked about the girl he'd spoken to on the phone, his daughter didn't say much. She'd always been very independent, never too focused on her friends.

Chapter Fifteen

Caribbean Queen

They took a plane to St. Maarten, where they loaded up on *céleri rémoulade*. "Nobody wants cheese in this weather," said Vivi's father, and then, when he went across the street to the liquor store, Vivi's mother picked out hunks of Brie, Gruyère, and, after some deliberation, Roquefort. She bought two days' worth of baguettes, quail eggs, sliced ham, seafood salad, two big bars of Toblerone. Rebecca split off, wandering through the *épicerie*, only to come upon Vivi's mother holding two jars of jam, staring into the small selection as if she'd lost all train of thought. When she saw Rebecca, she smiled, pushed a stray hair out of her eyes. "Strawberry or raspberry? It's always a paralyzing choice."

"I know what you mean," Rebecca said.

"I'm getting both," she said, her eyes widening, as if this were the definition of decadence.

"Aunt Kitty said we have to try the marinated artichokes," said Vivi, approaching with a container.

"Well, we can't let Kitty down," said Vivi's mother, and for another second she looked kind of absent. "Now, can we?"

The shopping trip had a vaguely illicit feeling, and Rebecca had the sense this had something to do with Vivi's father. As if they had to gather everything not only before the ferryboat was leaving but before he could say no.

Rebecca offered to contribute money for the groceries, and Vivi's mother shook her head. "I don't think so, sweetheart," she said quietly. "But thank you."

It had been easy to get permission. Her father was in Asia for the month of November. Several years ago, he had spent a month in Japan. He'd met with Mr. Toyoda (still no word on why they changed the *d* to a *t*). All she remembered about his reports was that the all-important luncheon with Mr. Toyoda had been followed by an excellent lemon meringue pie, that Mr. Toyoda had been—even by Japanese standards— short and uninterested in talking about business, and that he'd had an excellent tan. Now her father was doing *something big* in China. She'd always had a hard time keeping his business dealings straight, and since she'd never spoken less to him than she had during the past few weeks, it was even harder still. The time difference made it almost impossible to remember when to call him, and each time he'd called her, she was never in the dorm. They'd managed to have one longer conversation, during which he relayed, apropos of nothing and strangely excitedly, that he didn't believe in trust funds, because people who worked in banks were essentially stupid, and that he was going to put all the dealerships he owned—all that land, all of it—in her name. Eventually, he'd hastened to add. There were, of course, some kinks to work out.

Rebecca had not brought up the invitation to Anguilla.

She was experiencing, for the first time, an upside to her parents' divorce.

Since the trip fell during her mother's vacation time, Rebecca was able to avoid the gauntlet of her father's decision-making. Before saying yes to anything, he always thought of every possible negative scenario and managed to ask more questions than her mother could even begin to imagine. She knew if she consulted with her father about this trip, he would come up with hypothetical, frightening Caribbean scenarios that, in the moment, Rebecca would deride as being absurd and then—after hearing them—would be unable to shake.

As for her mother, she'd happily taken Vivi's parents' phone number and promised to call them immediately. "No fair," her mother had teased. "You're going to Anguilla before me? David was planning to take me to Malliouhana in February."

"Well," said Rebecca, playing along, "I'll do some reconnaissance for you."

Within days, her mother had bought the round-trip ticket and FedEx'd two black one-piece bathing suits (the only kind Rebecca ever wore), a lavender sarong, a check for spending money, and an array of Clinique sunscreen. *Happy Thanksgiving and Bon Voyage!* said the note, in her mother's stylish script. *I can't imagine you'll miss my marshmallow yams. P.S. I spoke with Vivi's father on the phone. He and Dad were in the same class at Harvard and they were friends! I'm sure they'll want to catch up, but (have no fear) I told him that Dad was away until December. How typical is it that I never once heard of him?!*

Rebecca ran from the mailroom, across the athletic field, into the infirmary, and up the two flights of stairs to Vivi's room, where, totally out of breath, she held out the note for Vivi to read.

"Yeah," Vivi said, "I had a feeling."

"You did not. You said you *doubted* they knew each other."

"I know I did, but I was lying. I'm a little bit psychic and I thought we knew each other in a past life or something, but I guess this is the reason."

"You believe in past lives?"

"I certainly do," said Vivi. "*What?* Don't look at me that way."

Her mother and David took Rebecca's trip as an opportunity to go to Palm Beach that Tuesday morning, opting out of Thanksgiving altogether, and Rebecca spent one night alone in the apartment (smoking!). Some of the art was missing. Her father had mentioned that the Picasso drawings were being reframed, that the Stella was being restored, but several other pieces were also gone. These pockets of space adorned with empty hooks inspired her to take some photographs. She knew that by the time she developed the film these empty spaces wouldn't be nearly as interesting to her, but she took a whole roll of film anyway. And while taking a taxi to JFK Airport at six o'clock in the morning on the Wednesday before Thanksgiving, where Vivi and her parents were waiting to meet her, it was those empty spaces she continued to see whenever she closed her eyes.

Mr. Shipley had notably thick wheat-colored hair that reminded her immediately of Stephan and Josh and dozens of other boys she knew. He was deeply tanned, his face was engraved with complicated lines (especially around his light blue eyes), and he wore nothing like the semi-hippie exotic garments that Rebecca had imagined but rather a pair of khaki pants and a white linen shirt that her mother might describe as *way past acceptably shabby.* Mrs. Shipley, too, looked more ordinary than Rebecca had expected. She wore a denim skirt and a light-green V-neck sweater, but then, on closer inspection, Rebecca noticed a variety of necklaces laden with charms and lockets (even what looked like a tooth), as if there was a lifetime of stories lying right above her heart.

Vivi's parents each shook her hand, and Mrs. Shipley started to giggle and couldn't stop.

"But you're so much prettier than your father," said Mrs. Shipley, finally getting ahold of herself and suppressing her giggling fit.

"Agreed," said Mr. Shipley, looking away, smiling, and then right back at Rebecca. His eyebrows were flecked with gray, although his thick longish hair was not. "Good God."

Rebecca listened to the Cure on Vivi's headphones during takeoff. And when Vivi reached out for Rebecca's hand, because Vivi knew, without having to be told, just how fearful Rebecca was about flying, and when, before landing, Rebecca finally brought herself to look out the window and gazed at the turquoise water and toy-sized palm trees down below, she thought: *I did the right thing.*

The "villa" was built into a cliff, overlooking a beach shared with just a few other villas, and it was halfway through being renovated. The girls were assigned twin beds on the lower level, where the floors were crappy linoleum and needed a thorough cleaning, but outside the creaky sliding door lay the cement patio, the pool, and (down steep, narrow stone steps) the powdery sand beach, protected by a rocky cove. On the upper level, Aunt Kitty's work was in evidence. The master bedroom, one guest room, and a living room were done up in a style that Mr. Shipley (*for Christ's sake please call me Hugh*) derided as *Generic World Traveler* and that Rebecca couldn't help recognizing as strikingly similar to Vivi's room at school. The living room opened out onto a dramatic deck, where they would soon be eating.

While Mr. Shipley set off to dive into the sea, Mrs. Shipley asked the girls to set the table. She washed lettuce and chopped vegetables and toasted pine nuts quickly and efficiently. She arranged the salads in little bowls, doused the greens with oil and vinegar, and tossed it all together with her newly washed hands before sipping from a glass of wine. Mr. Shipley padded through the kitchen, soaking wet, wrapped in a towel. He swiped a carrot from one of the bowls, then another.

"Are you still appalled by staying here?" asked Mrs. Shipley, looking him over.

"Not at the moment," he said. "Are we eating?"

"We are," said Vivi. "So put some clothes on, Papa. For God's sake," she teased, "we have a guest."

It was the first time Rebecca had ever drunk wine with a meal, besides Manischewitz at Passover, and it was certainly the first time she'd drunk any alcohol while the sun was shining. After they'd eaten on the veranda overlooking the beach, Mrs. Shipley produced a pack of cigarettes and Vivi took one from her mother's pack. Mr. Shipley lit his wife's and then his daughter's cigarettes, before lighting his own.

"Would you like one?" offered Mrs. Shipley. And then, seeing Rebecca's hesitation, "Don't worry. We won't tell."

And so Rebecca took the cigarette, and Mr. Shipley offered up a light with his silver Zippo, and, as the sun bounced off the sea in a wine-buzzed glaze of gilded blue, it was impossible not to smile. She knew that smoking caused cancer and, at the very least, wreaked havoc on your complexion over time, but here was Mrs. Shipley and she had some wrinkles, sure, but she was also seemingly unscathed. She was—Rebecca realized only now—really beautiful. At first she'd seemed kind of wan, but Rebecca noticed she wasn't wearing even a stitch of makeup, and Rebecca wasn't used to seeing older women—aside from some of her teachers— go without. Also, she didn't dye her hair. It was part silver and part blond, and it hung in that same childlike silky way that she imagined Vivi's would without her cornrows. Mrs. Shipley extended her long arm off the balcony and let the cigarette burn away between her fingers. Then she closed her eyes and turned her face to the sun. Rebecca loved how Mrs. Shipley didn't say anything like *We know we should quit* or *I'm terrible.* There was no point in qualifying bad habits (Rebecca planned to quit smoking at twenty-one); if she was going to smoke, she was going to enjoy it.

"Tell me," said Mr. Shipley, squinting into the expanse of the sea, "where do you usually spend Thanksgiving?"

"Well," said Rebecca. She took a drag of her cigarette, which bought her a little time. "It's different now, since my parents are divorced. We used to have a big dinner at three o'clock in our apartment in Manhattan, with mostly my mother's family. Then we'd all go to the movies. It was fun," she admitted.

"How about your father's family? I met your grandfather, you know."

"You *did?*"

Mr. Shipley nodded. "In fact, I spent an afternoon at his house in Dorchester. He doesn't live there anymore, does he?"

Rebecca nodded. "He does," she said, softly. And suddenly she felt exposed, as if this were a bad dream and they all were, in fact, eating in Dorchester with her grandpa Murray and she was solely responsible for each step of the ill-conceived meal. "He won't leave."

"I liked him," said Mr. Shipley.

"You couldn't have," she said, rallying. "Nobody does."

"He was a rough character, I'll give you that, but at least he *had* character. It was only a brief visit, and, believe me, I know he had his short-comings. And of course he wasn't easy on your father."

"No," Rebecca agreed.

Not one of her friends had met her grandfather. She had no other family on her father's side—the older generation had all died off, and her father didn't stay in touch with his second cousins. Grandpa Murray didn't like to travel, and she had the feeling that this was a relief to her father. And here was Vivi's father saying he'd not only met him but he'd *liked* him? She pictured that dangerous neighborhood, that old house, which smelled of unwashed clothes, and how she was allowed to watch more TV there than anywhere else. Her father and her grandfather were always yelling at each other; had Mr. Shipley seen that?

And, as if Mr. Shipley understood how off-kilter this revelation had made her feel, he changed the subject entirely. "You've been to the Hamptons, I imagine?"

"Rebecca was supposed to go there for Thanksgiving," said Vivi, as if *this* was, in fact, the real coincidence here. "Her mother's boyfriend has a house."

"Is it true," asked Mr. Shipley, "that houses there are selling at an extraordinary rate?"

"I guess," Rebecca said. "I mean, I don't really know."

"People just buying houses and tearing them down . . ." He shook his head. "*Gut renovations* they're calling them. It's almost violent, isn't it?"

Rebecca took a sip of wine. "Like gutting a fish," she almost whispered.

"Do you know what happened to my father's house in Boston? Some perfectly well-behaved couple bought the old place—very good house, built in 1806 or something like this—and I'll be damned if not one week after the closing they didn't bring on the house-sucking machines. You know which machines I mean; they literally suck the life out of the house."

"Surely not *literally*," said Mrs. Shipley.

He ignored her: "Five dumpsters full at the end of the day." He poured himself the last of the third bottle of wine. He had, Rebecca noticed, consumed most of that bottle on his own. "They suck *everything* out. Really and truly. Vivs, what's that movie we watched in the hotel that time?"

"The Japanese one?"

"The one in the mall."

"Dawn of the Dead."

"Well, these gut renovations—I tell you, they remind me of those flesh-eating zombies—"

"Oh, please," said Mrs. Shipley. "You are not comparing renovating a home to flesh-eating zombies. Hugh, even for you—"

"Denying the fact that there aren't enough places to live," said Mr. Shipley, leaning forward, with his elbows on the table. "Denying the house and the house's own history? It is—I'm sorry, Helen—but it's hard not to see this as a nihilistic turn. Just a touch, you know? Something so empty . . ." He trailed off, and right as Rebecca thought he'd finished, he offered, "Those so bent on acquisition don't even examine what they are acquiring."

Rebecca realized that her head was in her hand and that she would be perfectly happy to skip the beach if it meant Mr. Shipley would keep talking.

"You know that phrase *Don't get me started?*" said Mrs. Shipley. "My husband never bothers with it. Have you noticed this yet?"

Mr. Shipley had seemed to become genuinely agitated during his rant—sweat was now noticeable at the temples of his craggy handsome face—and Rebecca worried that Mrs. Shipley's comment might put him over the edge. But, to Rebecca's surprise, he merely wiped his brow with the batik napkin and said, "Who's coming swimming?"

The beach—though right down below them—looked awfully far away, and Rebecca nearly asked if she could take a nap, but she didn't want to miss anything. She couldn't remember the last time she'd felt this way, and this acuity propelled her to clear the table, to wash the dishes and the wineglasses. She wanted to be helpful. She wanted to be—frankly—indispensable. Vivi, after she noticed that Rebecca was being awfully thorough, offered to dry.

"Lovely, thanks," said Mrs. Shipley, noticing Rebecca's efforts. "I'm off to my room," she said, before wandering away.

"Meditation," Vivi said quietly. "She's very disciplined."

When the dishes were done, Rebecca walked out onto the veranda to make sure the table was all cleared. She saw Mr. Shipley in the distance, climbing up the rocks. When he reached the top, he dove the great distance into the sea below.

"I can't believe he just did that," said Vivi. Rebecca hadn't realized she was behind her.

"I know," Rebecca said, her mouth still gaping open. She really was amazed. But, also, she would kill her father if he pulled anything like that.

They raced to change, suddenly in a rush to soak up the last good hour of daylight. And with the sand still holding the heat of the day, the girls ran down the stone steps and straight into the water, and Rebecca felt about ten years old. She was aware that—no matter how thrilled she'd been to sit with the Shipleys and partake of their wine and cigarettes and listen to what she knew both her parents would have seen as Mr. Shipley's ridiculous opinions—she'd been pretty tense. Now she let the water hold her, and she floated and floated until the shapes in the clouds had all dramatically changed; when she looked up, Vivi was out of the water, lying facedown on a towel.

"You asleep?" Rebecca asked, hopping up and down; she always got water in her ears.

Vivi turned to face her. She was wearing a purple bikini with gold stripes and had somehow already acquired a tan. "Let's put Sun-In in your hair tomorrow. I brought you some."

"My hair will never turn blond from that stuff. Do I really want reddish hair?"

Vivi twisted up her face. "Sit," she said, and Rebecca did. Vivi lifted Rebecca's dark thick hair and let it fall. "I think you do," she said.

"I could get used to this place," said Rebecca, stretching out on a chaise.

"You should come skiing with us sometime."

"You go *skiing*, too?" Rebecca realized she was still tipsy from lunch, but this was absurd. When she'd pictured the Shipleys, she'd imagined them only in health clinics, sweating and serious.

"We go about once a year—usually Switzerland. My dad worked briefly for the U.S. government, and we went to this ski resort that had been Hitler's country place, and we stayed at this hotel that was only open to military families—for dirt cheap, too. I guess after World War Two, the States basically took over all of Hitler's best spots."

"You stayed on Hitler's former playgrounds? That's . . . creepy. I mean, don't you think?"

Vivi nodded. "I think it is creepy but also kind of perfect. What better revenge? American families enjoying his favorite places?"

"But do you think most of the families even thought about it?" Rebecca looked out at the water. Mr. Shipley was swimming long laps beyond where the waves were breaking. He hadn't even looked up. "Do you think most military families think about the Holocaust, or do you think they're mostly, like, *Ooh, totally excellent powder today?* And how many of those Americans staying in the hotel are even Jewish? I couldn't stay in a place like that. I'd be too preoccupied with the past."

"Ever been out west? Like California or Arizona? Or, really, anywhere in America? Are you preoccupied with the slaughter of Native Americans?"

"That's not exactly a fair comparison."

"Well," said Vivi, before sitting up. "We don't go skiing there anymore, anyway."

"I'm just saying—"

"You don't think I know what you're saying? Did you hear my father at lunch? Believe me, his passion about home improvement doesn't begin to approach other, actual *human* injustices. Ask him about bigotry sometime. I mean it, go on."

"Do you think he's . . . too extreme?"

"No, I don't." She shook her head. "He's dedicated. I don't really know what I'm saying. But sometimes," she said, with uncharacteristic intensity, "I wonder what the point of ranting is. You know? What does it actually do?"

"But I wonder the same thing. What *is* the point?"

"You want to help people? Fine. Then help. And my father does help. I'm not saying he doesn't. And—listen—just because I skied at Hitler's former mountain getaway and I enjoyed it, it doesn't mean I'm empty-headed. Just because I'm not openly despondent over every single human-rights struggle doesn't mean I'm not deep."

"Who said anything about you not being deep? You are extremely deep."

"You don't have to go that far, but don't make that mistake about me. Okay?"

"Definitely not." They both lay back and closed their eyes. "So," offered Rebecca, "what do you do on these ski trips, anyway?"

When Vivi didn't say anything, Rebecca sat up and saw Vivi lying with her eyes still closed. She remembered that day at the tree; it seemed like years ago now.

"We usually hit the slopes around ten-thirty," said Vivi finally. "We have lunch at one-thirty, and that's . . . generally about it for the day. We're all pretty lazy about skiing. My mom and I usually crap out on the last day—sit in the hot tub, eat too much fondue." She opened her eyes and sat up, more animated now. "Do you know how to ski? I didn't even ask."

Rebecca nodded, tried to keep from smiling.

"What?"

"It's just that we start at about eight, break for lunch at noon—half hour, *maybe* an hour—and ski until the very bitter end of the day. My father doesn't have it in him to pay for something and not use it. And he's constantly paying! *And* we have a ridiculous amount of photos indoors in the ski lodge, which are always terrible because of the goggle tans, and then my father always insists on having one professionally done at the top of the mountain, where we have to do something stupid like stick our poles in the air."

"I want to see *those* pictures," said Vivi.

"One day," said Rebecca, taking a deep breath. The errant palms sticking out sideways, the pale-turquoise water, the white sand—it was all so beautiful. And then she realized, with an odd little twist of smug surprise, that this kind of beautiful was also boring. "Why do you think our fathers didn't stay friends?"

Vivi shrugged. "Who knows. They don't exactly have much in common, do they?"

"No, but—"

"I mean, I doubt they were all *that* close."

"What makes you think so? It sounds like they were. I mean, nobody meets my grandfather."

"I guess I think my mom would have more to say about your dad if he was a really good friend back then. She's opinionated, and my parents were definitely together then. They've been together since high school. I mean, maybe my mother didn't like him. Maybe that's why they didn't stay friends."

"Or maybe she did," said Rebecca, widening her eyes.

"Oooh . . ." said Vivi dramatically. "Can you imagine?"

Rebecca let herself. She let the image pass across the screen of her mind: tall, aloof, in-the-present-moment Mrs. Shipley and *her father*, kicking leaves in Harvard Yard.

"No way," said Rebecca. "Besides, even though your mom is so beautiful, she's not my dad's type."

"You know your dad's type?"

"Well, I know my mother. And, yeah, I think I do know his type."

"No offense, but I think my mom was probably everyone's type. You should see *those* pictures. And your dad . . ."

"What?"

"This is so stupid," said Vivi.

"What were you going to say about my dad?"

"Let's just ask them."

"No," said Rebecca, "I don't want to."

"Why *not?*"

Rebecca felt her chest and face flushing, and she became so flustered that she nearly shouted, "You're suggesting that my dad was some kind of loser."

"I'm not suggesting your dad was a *loser.* Rebecca! You're the one who said my mom wouldn't have been your dad's type."

"Okay, fine, but—I don't think he ever dated anyone who wasn't Jewish."

"Oh," said Vivi. "Well, okay, then! I guess this ridiculous hypothetical conversation can come to an end."

"Definitely," said Rebecca tersely. She stood up too quickly and got dizzy. The sky was easing into some kind of lurid pink. And then, even though she was suddenly chilled, she rushed into the sea, taking giant sloshing steps into that pale-blue water, which was—she now observed—the same color as Mr. Shipley's eyes.

Later that evening, Vivi shook her awake—when had she fallen asleep in the lumpy twin bed? It was pitch dark outside. Vivi picked out Rebecca's clothes, handed her a cup of strong tea, and they were all off to the home of a local musician named Maxy Max—a black man with reddish dreads and a graying beard, who wore sunglasses even though it was nighttime and who threw his arms around Mr. Shipley and began talking so quickly about what he'd been missing since the last time he came.

"I thought this was your first time here," whispered Rebecca, after the introductions.

"I guess not for my father," said Vivi. "He travels a lot. I lose track." They wandered off to sit on a big piece of driftwood. "How about this place?"

It was a gnarled tree house by the sea with a large deck. There had been some damage, said Maxy, during the last big storm. A beautiful woman reclined in a hammock. It was only on closer inspection that Rebecca noticed she was nursing an infant. A pack of children ran around chasing a chicken, while a couple of men smoked a joint by a bar. They laughed and one skinny man called out: *Getim getim gowon and get that nasty bird.*

Mrs. Shipley was drinking from a bottle of beer and talking to the woman in the hammock, whose dreadlocks were piled high atop her head. Rebecca heard Mrs. Shipley ask, *How old is he? Are you getting any sleep?* But because of the wind and the sound of the waves lapping onshore, Rebecca couldn't hear any answers. *Your fourth?* said Mrs. Shipley. Then: *Me? Only my daughter. Oh yes, just the one.*

They both watched Mrs. Shipley hold the baby boy. He reached up and grabbed Vivi's mother's hair, and as Mrs. Shipley smiled and smiled, Rebecca could not deny this unexpected thought: *She's sad.*

"You okay now?" asked Vivi.

"Yep," said Rebecca. "Totally fine."

"Glad to hear it."

"I'm moody," said Rebecca. "I realize that."

Vivi nodded.

"And you're not."

"No," said Vivi. "That's true. But I'm other things."

The girls watched Vivi's parents. They were laughing at something that Maxy had said. On the beach, two white birds poked around between the rocks and shells. A tree that looked like a giant gnarled bonsai appeared to be bending from a harsh wind, even though it wasn't windy. She wondered if the Shipleys even celebrated Thanksgiving, which seemed—at this moment—like a monumental waste of time.

"Maybe," said Rebecca, "we should try to get a beer?"

"Well, what do you know," said Vivi.

Down a dirt road, the car got stuck. The Shipleys were not fazed. Mrs. Shipley said, *Girls, out of the car,* and they got out, all set to push. Mr.

Shipley, at the wheel, didn't even take the cigarette from between his lips as he called out, *NOW*. The stars and the moon were so bright that it seemed as if there were streetlights, and as the car regained its momentum, Mr. Shipley sped over rocks and the girls jumped in, as if they were leaving a crime scene. He sped toward another outdoor deck, where there were so many bodies on the dance floor that it took a moment for Rebecca to realize they were the only white people on it. No island reggae here. No Jimmy Buffett. A shirtless black man rapped into a microphone over a dance-hall beat. His skin was slick with sweat. Everyone was sweating, and everyone was dancing, except for Mr. Shipley, who remained standing, a tall still tree amidst a field of waving, twisting reeds, and Rebecca was one of them.

And after the rapping stopped, the canned beat went on, the dancing went on, and Rebecca squeezed through the crowd, following Vivi and her parents to what looked like the back lot of someone's house (what, in fact, *was* someone's house). Mr. Shipley knew to knock on the door and order barbecue for four. They sat at a picnic table in a small yard strewn with plastic toys and the familiar sight of headless, naked Barbie. They ate chicken and ribs. They drank Carib beer. And when, after Mr. Shipley drove them home too fast, weaving on both the dirt and paved roads (*please oh please don't let us die*), they still didn't go to bed. Without discussing it, the Shipleys took the narrow stone steps down to the sea, where Vivi and her parents stripped to their underwear and rushed into the water, and Rebecca raced to catch up. When it started to rain, they looked out for lightning but there wasn't any; just rain—steady, warm, falling.

She woke up with a speeding heart, panicked over the fact that she had ridden in a car with a driver so obviously drunk, that she was, actually, exactly that stupid, and that her father had no idea where she was. She thought it was five in the morning, and when she looked in Vivi's bed and didn't see Vivi, she assumed that her friend had stayed up all night reading, as Rebecca knew she sometimes liked to do. But then she peeked through the blinds and saw the light flood in; it wasn't dawn light, not even close. She went up the stairs in search of—what? She wasn't sure, but it felt urgent that she find out the time, that she orient herself, that—

"Happy Thanksgiving," called Mr. Shipley from the kitchen.

"What time is it?" she wondered aloud, seeing the table on the veranda festively set, hearing the far-off splash of someone in the sea. She wandered into the kitchen.

"Oh, about noon, I'd say. Or nearly." Mr. Shipley was chopping mint; the scent hit her when she inhaled deeply—which she did when she was nervous.

He looked up from his chopping, took a sip of water. "How'd you sleep?"

"Um—really well? I have never slept past nine," she marveled, kind of proud of herself. "I mean never in my whole life. What are you making?"

"Sun tea," he said, playing with the chopped mint as if it were a pile of sand.

"The kind when you let it brew in the sun? Did you sanitize the jar?"

"Did I—what?"

"Sanitize the jar. You can get poisoned if you don't."

"Yes," he said. "I cleaned it thoroughly."

"Well, that's good."

He took another sip of his water and looked at her for a moment. "Aren't you funny."

"How am I funny?" Her face burned, but all she felt was vigor.

"How many fifteen-year-olds know that kind of thing?"

"I don't know," she said, trying with all of her might not to sound defensive. "My babysitter taught me when I was little. She was from Haiti, too—not *was,* she's still very much alive, thank God; she *is* from Haiti. I mean, not that you're really *from* Haiti. Anyway, she moved back there. She lives there now. Her name is Solange." As if he might go ahead and look her up? What was *wrong* with her?

"Is that right?" he asked, nodding toward the refrigerator. "Why don't you help yourself to some orange juice? Helen squeezed some this morning."

Rebecca did as she was told, and the juice was delicious. She drank it all and poured some more. Mr. Shipley stirred his tea.

"I always make iced tea when I'm on vacation, but I never drink it otherwise," he declared. "It's one of those things."

"Yeah, well, my father does that, too," she said, "but he eats donuts."

Mr. Shipley smiled, and it was a real smile, nothing like the tight grin that was, she'd noticed, usually skewered to his face. "There was this townhouse in Boston," he said. "It was Helen's cousin's house. In the end, it's a sad story, because Lolly later had a nervous breakdown, but during that time she seemed happy, or happy enough. She was so generous. And she made marvelous tea. It was always in the refrigerator. It was a reassuring sight, that pitcher full of tea. Who knows why? But I remember it better than any of the meals, and they were all excellent, too."

"That's so sad about Mrs. Shipley's cousin."

He winced. "You must call us Hugh and Helen."

"Really?"

"Yes. I promise. My God, were you raised well, though."

She blushed, finishing her juice.

There was the far-off sound of a squawking bird. Mr. Shipley mimicked the sound.

"So," Rebecca continued, in lieu of squawking right back, "do you have a Thanksgiving dinner?"

"Of course." He smiled. "We're from New England," he said. "Besides, I really am a fan of the yam."

"Me, too!"

"Well, then." He grinned. "We have that in common. And let's see what else . . . Do you know what you want to do with your life?"

"Actually, I—"

"I had no bloody idea when I was your age. Or when I was older, for that matter. I thought I wanted to be a photographer."

"I like taking pictures, too," she admitted. And she felt his interest; she wanted to keep him interested, to keep talking, but she didn't know what else to say. "But I don't want to be a photographer."

"Well," he said, "that's a very good thing to know."

"I think what I like about pictures is that they're proof." She waited for him to interrupt, but he just watched her. "My mother took these three pictures when she was a little older than I am, and they always hung in our front hall. And I'd always look at them and think: *This is what she saw.* Do you know what I mean? This is *how* she saw. And I feel like that taught me more about who she was than most of the pictures where she's smiling for the camera."

"That makes a lot of sense," he said.

"Plus she's really photogenic, so there are a lot of those."

"I'll bet. Is she an artist?"

"Oh no. She's a corporate lawyer."

"Is that right?"

Rebecca nodded.

"And your father?" he asked, leaning back in his chair. "What's he up to these days?"

"He was in finance, but he stopped doing that about five years ago. Now he sells cars—I mean, it's bigger than that. He owns car dealerships?" She heard how her voice went up at the end of her sentence in the way that her father hated, and she felt the need to cancel out that whiny imploring tone. "He's in China now. He's not going to believe all this." She gestured vaguely: to the two of them sitting in a kitchen, to the sunny world outside.

When Mr. Shipley—Hugh—took another sip of water, Rebecca suddenly realized that he was drinking vodka. And his ease with her, his smile, it all seemed a little different now. He was drinking straight vodka and it wasn't even lunchtime. But this was a vacation, wasn't it? And didn't he work under stressful and emotionally draining conditions? She thought: *If I had that job, I'd probably drink all day long, too.*

"Where're Vivi and . . . her mom?"

"You can say it, Rebecca, I know you can."

"You're teasing me."

"I'm sorry, but please. You can do it."

"Fine. Where are Vivi and Helen?"

"They went to St. Maarten to go shopping. They're on a mad quest for hazelnuts."

Rebecca realized that she was a little bit relieved. "Do you need help with anything? Any cooking?" she asked.

What she really wanted was to walk down to the beach by herself, and when Hugh shook his head, that's what she did. She put on her bathing suit and was grateful for the emergence of a big fat cloud, which kept the heat at bay. There were other people on the small beach today. Two girls lay in the wet sand on their bellies, and each one had an arm buried up past the shoulder so that, at first, they looked as if they were each missing one arm. One boy held a large shovel and finished burying a man's body completely; only his head was visible. It struck her suddenly that beachgoing—the ritual lying out with eyes closed, the burying of bodies—was a clear practice round for death, complete with the beckoning sea. She waded in; it was as warm as bathwater. She floated until she was salty and pruned, until she was once again so tired that she didn't have the energy to go back to the house for sunblock. She wrapped herself in a protective cocoon of towels and thought of her favorite children's book, *The Very Hungry Caterpillar*. The caterpillar eats his way through the journey—pickle, plum, salami, cake—never stopping long enough to see how anything tastes. Never stopping until he hides himself away, until he looks so remarkably different that, when people look at the caterpillar, they see only a butterfly; nobody sees the caterpillar anymore. This book was her favorite despite the fact that she was always aware how the next step for that butterfly was death. How there was nothing else left to become.

There was a buzzing in her head. She'd come back to the city, to construction on their neighbor's apartment. But how could they begin construction so early in the morning? She imagined—through the buzzing—telling her father about the noise, and how he would rail against the co-op board for allowing such nonsense. It was time for school—time to wake up. She felt the buzzing in her teeth and she realized, with a start, that she was underneath the mountain of towels, underneath the Caribbean sun. But what was the drilling sound? The girls with the buried arms were up, fully restored, playing in the water as if the sound wasn't there. The boy and the man were gone. Only the mound of churned-up sand remained. There was a path cut into the trees behind the beach and the awful sound took her up that path, to where sand turned into dirt and the temperature dropped. The path snaked alongside the house—it was maybe even on the same property— and the drilling grew louder. There was a shed shaded by trees.

When she approached, she saw that Hugh was holding a chair leg in the teeth of a table saw, and wood chips were flying around him. He was wearing goggles. There were stacks of wood all around the room. One dark chaise with scrollwork on its sides was the only finished piece. Hugh looked up and turned off the machine. The silence was delicious, though there was ringing in her ears.

"Christ—" he said. "You scared me."

"I did? I'm sorry. And I'm really sorry to bother you, but do you know how loud that is? Has anyone ever complained? I couldn't figure out what it was, and I followed the noise."

He took off his goggles and wiped his brow on that same white linen shirt, which surely he would retire after today. "I'm sorry for the noise. These house projects of Kitty's—she's done four now—have allowed me to indulge my interest in carpentry. They're usually half construction sites, and there's always equipment lying around."

"Have you been here—to this house—before?" Rebecca asked.

"Look at that piece." He pointed to the chaise, without—it had not escaped her—answering the question. "Can you believe how beautiful? I want to meet the man who made that piece. God knows he probably isn't earning what he should." A sweating plastic tumbler had created a puddle of water on the worktable. He leaned over and picked up the tumbler, but he didn't yet take a sip.

Maybe she was being controlling and uptight, but wasn't it just plain stupid to mix alcohol with amateur carpentry? There was a wall full of hanging saws, their sharp blades glinting in the shed's low light.

"Using my hands like this—it relaxes me more than any beach." He smiled tightly. "A man working with his hands in order to feel real. Do you know about that cliché yet?" He took a long drink.

She felt suddenly, painfully aware that she was dressed in nothing but a bathing suit. She stood up straight, as if posture might take the place of clothing. "I'm going to go back to the beach now," she said. "When do you think they're coming back?"

"From the hazelnut hunt?" He put the tumbler down. "Anyone's guess. But I'll use the saw sparingly," he said. "Almost done."

She went back the way she came; it seemed like a much shorter walk. On the way to the shed, she'd noticed nothing but trees and sand and dirt, but now there were two tiny orange butterflies, a wasp's nest, and clusters of wetly red berries, or flowers that looked like berries. She wanted to know the names of things. She wanted to be . . . specific.

On the beach, there was nobody left. She walked straight into the sea and swam underwater for as long as she could hold her breath. For her, this was luxury: no decision bigger than whether to be in or out of the sea. She kept her eyes open, and it was so clear—the tiny silver fish and the sandy bottom were the only reminders that she wasn't in a heated pool. Out of breath, she burst up through the surface, panting harder than she'd expected.

That's when she heard the screaming. Though she had never heard a person being tortured, this sound conjured that word—*torture*—almost as if it were a memory.

She raced out of the water, and even before she reached the shore, she knew exactly from where this noise was coming. This time—climbing the hill, the sand into dirt—it whizzed by like a view from a speeding car. Her heart was pounding, she was the only person in sight, her father didn't know where she was, and, in the doorway, she saw Vivi's father—she saw Hugh—holding up his hand: "I've cut off two fingers," he said. He'd managed to take off his shirt and wrap it around his hand,

and the white linen was already red. The cement floor was spattered with Hugh's blood. His face was pale as he said, very evenly, "Rebecca, you need to listen to me. Go get me a cooler full of ice and some plastic wrap. The cooler is above the refrigerator. Plastic wrap in the drawer. You need to run, because I'm losing a lot of blood very quickly."

"Shouldn't I call—"

"Go now," he said firmly. "Hurry."

She ran in a way that felt as if what she'd previously called running, up until this moment, had in fact been something else. She hoped Vivi and Helen had returned, but they hadn't, of course they hadn't. Of course it was only her, in a bathing suit, no time to change, no time to pull on anything else but Vivi's pink shirt with black roses, which she found draped over a kitchen chair, the chair she'd stood on to take the cooler down. After a slight hesitation (Vivi loved that shirt), Rebecca pulled it on; she slammed all the ice trays until the cooler was as full as it was going to be, which was not very full at all. She ran fast and awkwardly— holding the cooler and the plastic wrap—back to the shed, where Hugh was now sitting on a bench with his hand over a metal bucket. The sound of blood hitting the bucket was all she could hear. Hugh was even more pale; he looked as if he was getting ready to throw up, and she was shaking now, shaking and saying, "What do I do now, Hugh? Tell me what to do."

"Is there ice in the cooler?"

She nodded.

"Good girl. The fingers," he said. "I'm going to need you to pick them up. They are under the table saw. Do you see them?"

She did: half curled. Pale.

"You're going to gently put them on ice and wrap the ice in the plastic wrap. You hear me?"

She nodded. She crouched down and picked up Hugh's fingers and she did not throw up. She did not drop the ice or the fingers, nor did she have difficulty tearing sheets of plastic wrap. She closed the cooler. "Now what? Hugh?"

"I need that shirt."

"Vivi's?" she asked, lifting the hem.

He nodded.

She took it off, and she was once again wearing only a bathing suit. Hugh let his bloody shirt fall to the floor and she quickly turned her eyes away before seeing any gore. When she looked back, Vivi's pink shirt was turning red.

He rose to his feet. "Thank you, Rebecca. Can you do something else for me? I know you can. In fact, I'm positive you can. Because you are tough."

I'm not, she wanted to say. *You're wrong.*

"Pick up the cooler," he managed, and she did.

He was stumbling, leading her out of the shed, outside toward the road, where the garage was empty because Helen and Vivi had gone looking for hazelnuts. "You're going to have to drive," he said, leaning on the garage.

"There's no car," she said moronically, because he was, in fact, pointing to a motorcycle. "Oh," she said, "I'm sorry, but, no. I can't."

"Come on," he said, nodding to a hook just inside the garage. "There is the key. There is a helmet. Come on," he said, more impatiently. "I can't drive. I am starting to feel faint. But I can tell you exactly what to do."

"I'll call the ambulance."

"Forget it," said Hugh, "this is the way we're going to do this. We are not waiting for a bloody fucking ambulance—excuse me. Not here. Not going to happen. Come on now."

The motorcycle—amazingly—had a milk crate strapped to its back and had likely been used up until now for transporting cases of liquor. She put the cooler in the milk crate. She grabbed the helmet and the keys. "This is stupid—" She realized she was yelling and it felt good to yell. It felt right. "This is totally stupid. I can't drive a motorcycle. We are both going to die."

"You listen to me," he said gravely. "We are not going to die. Idiots can drive motorcycles, and you are a smart and able girl. It's all going to be fine."

"Fine? Are you kidding?"

"You need," said Hugh, quietly now, "to get on that motorcycle and drive me to Dr. Branford's clinic. It's a straight shot and he'll know what to do. If he isn't there, we need to get him there. And this is important: If I pass out—do not let anyone give me any blood. Do you understand me?"

There were vines crawling around a drainpipe. Gravel crawling with ants.

"Rebecca," he shouted. "Look at me. *Do not let them give me any blood*. Now get on."

She did. He sat behind her.

"Put the key in the ignition."

As she turned the key, he put his arms around her. The blood was all over her right away; Vivi's shirt was ruined. His concern over not having any blood transfusions, she reasoned, surely meant that he did not, in fact, already have AIDS. She felt the warmth, Hugh's warmth, his heaviness—she'd never felt anything so heavy—as he fell against her, as he clutched her, as he gave her precise instruction after precise instruction: *brake pedal, clutch, ignition switch, choke*. She thought, *He's right; I can do this*, and that thought lasted until she was driving. They were bobbing and swaying and Hugh was yelling at her to straighten, to relax into it, but the sound of the motor was drowning him out, and at some point she ceased to hear anything aside from the fuzz in her head, flosslike, an underwater silent hum. And then: Cruising. As if she'd been driving all her life. As if she'd grown up with a dad who, instead of forbidding her to ever ride a motorcycle, had fixed them up in the driveway—the fantasy driveway, the existence of which she could, right now, almost recall. As if she were really that girl, speeding up now, despite Hugh's yelling not to, speeding on a motorcycle to get where she needed to go.

She thought about AIDS, how her chorus teacher from the city was dying. She thought about how Hugh worked in a clinic in Haiti. How his blood was pouring out all over the place, and who knew if she had any small cuts, any open wounds. She did not ask if Hugh was all right. She was too afraid to do anything besides keep her eyes on the road and listen for instructions. The wind whipped at her hair, her eyes teared, but somehow she kept her focus. Hugh shouted directions, but it was straight, mostly flat, until a sharp turn took them off the main road (*Lean left,* growled Hugh, *really LEAN*) and up an unpaved path to a blue cement building. It looked more like someone's tacky house than any kind of clinic. There were a few cars out front, and she did her best to park beside them. She scraped her ankle, but it didn't matter; she couldn't feel anything. It took her a moment to realize that Hugh was leaning on her, trying his best to walk.

What happened next she would think about for years to come, but no matter how often she thought it over, she'd never remember what happened with any more clarity, any more sense or specificity. The doctor told Hugh to lie down on a table. *Your daughter can stay with you,* he said. Then he closed the door. The door was closed. It was a white room. It wasn't terribly clean. She stood across the room, leaning on the door.

The pain is really kicking in, he said.

I'm sorry, she said.

No, he said, *I am. I can't believe I made you drive.*

I won't tell my father, she said. And then she smiled.

Christ almighty, this hurts.

She came toward the table, stood behind his head. He looked up and said, in a strained voice: *You're an angel.*

Ha, she said.

You have a light coming out of the top of your head.

Hugh?

I never understood it, he said.

Understood what?

He started to cry.

Understood what, Hugh, understood what?

She put her hands on his bare shoulders. They were burning hot.

It's freezing in here, he said. *You know, your father always did love cars. Why cars and not motorcycles?* Tears leaking out his eyes, dripping into his sweat; his hand submerged in yet another bucket. Where oh where was the doctor?

What did you never understand?

He was my friend, Hugh said. Then he reached up with his good hand and touched her cheek. *I can't believe you're here.*

By the time Rebecca and Hugh arrived back at the villa, it was well after dark. She stood as Vivi and Helen embraced Hugh in the entryway. Vivi was hysterical. Rebecca stood there watching, until it felt unseemly to watch anymore.

She retreated downstairs, past the lumpy bed, past the patio, and down the stone steps. She stepped out onto the sand. She waded into black water.

The fingers couldn't be reattached. The way he'd sliced them had made this impossible. Hugh had managed—on Thanksgiving Day—to get a Boston surgeon on the phone, who, after talking with Dr. Branford, had confirmed it. There was no rush to be airlifted.

I'm such a fool, he'd said, when she came back into the room after the doctor had cleaned him up as best he could.

It was an accident, she said.

Yes, he said, with the kind of smile she'd only seen in movies, the smile of a man on painkillers. *But I'm still a fool.*

You are not, she said, and her voice, she realized, was fierce. *You're the opposite of a fool.*

The opposite of a fool? He laughed. *Well, how about that?*

———

She was a skinny furnace of a nervous girl. She broke out in hives with some regularity.

But once she'd gotten going on that motorcycle, she'd been in control. And not the kind of tense control she was accustomed to feeling, the kind where she held everything together by sheer effort and will-power. Even the doctor had been impressed. *Your daughter is extremely self-possessed.* Rebecca had waited for Hugh to correct him, to say, *She's not my daughter,* but he hadn't. He'd hardly been in his right mind, after all, and so it was Rebecca who had pointed out: *He's not my father.* And the doctor's expression had changed. It had gone from approval to . . . bemusement. It was only as she floated in the ocean now, as she looked up at the half-moon, that she realized why.

She woke up, shaking, in the middle of the night. At first she thought she was cold, but she was underneath two blankets and the air was warm. She thought she had a fever, but she felt fine aside from the shaking. And then she knew why she was shaking. She knew in her bones that Hugh was outside that door, and that he was there for her. She could imagine him sitting by the pool, his eyes bloodshot but focused. She knew he wouldn't come up to the sliding door—he would never—but she knew, if she wanted to, that she could go outside and he would be waiting. Her heartbeat was thundering inside her chest; it obliterated everything except her need to retrace the steps of the evening. She remembered that Vivi still hadn't come to bed by the time she'd fallen asleep. She remembered that she had fallen asleep thinking of three Shipleys locked in their embrace, which had been—for some reason—an unsettling image. She knew that Hugh would never come for her; she knew that he was there. That she thought so was outrageous; she knew that, too. She wasn't used to this kind of certainty, which followed not one shred of sense. Vivi was snoring faintly now from the other bed, and though seeing Vivi offered real relief, the shaking didn't stop.

She shook off the blankets and crept up the stairs. One light was on in the living room. She could see onto the veranda, where the table was still set for the Thanksgiving meal, and she walked out onto it, up to the railing, where she leaned as far as she could, farther than she probably should have—out toward the pool, the sea, the moon, the lights, into the warm night air.

She looked down, of course. There was no one out there. Or at least not anymore.

Chapter Sixteen

Shenzhen

Charcoal Armani suit and tie, buffed Gucci loafers, lucky briefcase from Milan, and yet Ed Cantowitz felt like no one so much as his daughter's old Paddington Bear. Watching Chinese pour onto the train with a seeming singularity of purpose that made his New York stride feel like amateur hour, he couldn't stop thinking of sad-sack stuffed ol' Paddington as the Hong Kong train pulled out of the station and blasted toward a former fishing village that had—evidently, before Deng's reforms—boasted not much more than some rice paddies and duck farms.

Shenzhen. Tax-free special economics, smog-ridden pit full of immoral engineers—that's what he was here for. He'd read on several leaflets in his Hong Kong hotel how Deng's opening-up policy was creating not only *fresh air* (ridiculous even as a metaphor) but also *earthshaking changes*. The Chinese, for all of their environmentally destructive, innovative, technological savvy, sure did cling to their time-honored images of nature.

As he looked out the window at a countryside of rubble, at one shockingly beautiful flash of painted aluminum fences—teal and yellow and orange and blue—at skinny trees and ghosts of mountains and streetlights under smog, he patted the thin sleeve underneath his shirt, which contained not only his passport and his visa and several thousand dollars and francs and not enough yuan (he would have to exchange right after clearing immigration) but also a notecard that the Hong Kong concierge had written out for him. *You need,* the concierge had muttered sternly, while inking Chinese characters. And not that Ed would know if the characters said otherwise, but apparently *Mr. Ed Cantowitz* in addition to the address of the Shenzhen Golden Canopy Hotel was printed there, in case he became lost (poor fat dazed Paddington) and nobody at this border crossing understood a word of his rudimentary Mandarin.

He smelled Shenzhen before he saw it. Something like every fetid canal he'd ever walked over—one night in Brooklyn, early morning in Amsterdam—or was the smell just a universal signifier of hasty construction, a rush to ignore what lies beneath so that the cream can rise? As the train came to a stop and the exiting commenced, Ed kept close check on his briefcase, kept his hand on his sleeve of goods beneath his shirt. After an impressively brief time at both immigration and customs, his confidence trickled back, and when he saw a mass of people lining up, he, too, fell in line. If Chinese after Chinese exchanged money and went on their way, why shouldn't he? He'd been told to expect currency swapping at the station, and who knew how long it would take to find an actual bank. So Ed waited his turn and stepped right up; a toothless crone did brisk business. He admired her square hands and utter absence of facial expression, her economy of movement. Ed handed over three hundred dollars in exchange for a fat sheaf of yuan banded by red rubber. He went to check through it but was hurried along by the woman behind him and by a man behind *her* issuing some kind of admonishment. And—quickly—in an unprecedented moment when sheer intimidation outweighed his careful nature, Ed shoved the yuan into the sleeve.

Then he went about finding a driver.

Cars flying past (right-hand drive, British style), no English anywhere, not even in the faraway vibrations of music coming from cars and buildings. No English in any of it, nowhere in the smoggy ether of activity, and when a car stopped, he presented his little card, which—the Hong Kong concierge was correct—he'd needed. He settled back against the dust-encrusted vinyl and asked the driver to please turn on the meter. But the driver pretended not to comprehend not only *what* Ed was saying but also the basic fact that he was speaking at all. He glanced out the window long enough to have the revelation that Shenzhen looked like Harlem in the 1970s, minus the excellent brownstones and glamorous Jazz Age residue. There was the same sense of impending disaster, even though the worst had surely already come to pass. The construction was rampant and defied any kind of logic. Cables swung above him and far into the distance. Bamboo scaffolding held up platforms of workers, all working on hulking monstrosities. The driver turned a corner and skidded toward a cement wall, before turning around once again. A car felt like a deluded way to move through a place like this. Where was his body armor? His jet pack? Where was his own fucking crane?

The hotel room, at first glance, looked like one of the many hotel rooms he'd inhabited while on the road in America, both in the early days with CBOR and recently, when nobody—including his daughter—had any real idea where he was or what he was doing at any given moment. She'd complained that he wanted to send her to boarding school because he was totally consumed with his work. He was indeed consumed with his work, but what she didn't know was that he was suddenly—after almost two decades of ridiculous success—simply trying to stay afloat. And while appraisers from Christie's had been evaluating his art collection, he'd been running around the country to all the godforsaken places where his dealerships were failing. They had failed due to mismanagement and—in one case—a manager's procuring of parts from a chop shop and selling the actual German factory parts out of his ex-daughter-in-law's garage. Those dealerships had failed and he couldn't afford to have any more fail, not when he'd lost a tremendous amount of capital on that blackest Monday and his company had to meet its monthly obligations.

While the auto group still looked reasonably profitable on paper, he had a window of time to accomplish several seemingly Herculean tasks. His company would file for Chapter 11. There'd be an interim president brought in to run the company, and Ed would make damn sure that this person could not afford to buy it. The company would continue to run, his thousands of employees would keep their jobs, he'd be investing his personal capital (thank you, Cayman Islands) into the Chinese economy, helping to make good on Deng Xiaoping's excellent proclamation that *to get rich is glorious.*

Though there were, *yes,* more than likely several steps that were not *entirely* legal—namely, using the offshore capital on which he wasn't even paying taxes in the first place—Ed was convinced he was doing the right thing.

Or, at least, he was doing the smart thing.

He would use that capital. At seven this evening, he would meet his contact (they'd agreed on the time and place during one brief and awkward phone conversation), who would hopefully be a trustworthy translator. He'd already taken several meetings in Munich and felt reasonably confident that not only was he close to acquiring the rights to BMW in Shenzhen but, just as important, that in this Chinese Wild West he'd be able to carry out his plan without the Krauts' crippling surveillance. He would pay whatever it took to whomever he had to, and he would use his personal, hoarded, illegal offshore capital and pray each night to a God in whom he believed for a life uninterrupted by prison.

He, Ed Cantowitz, would lease land in Shenzhen. He would import and sell beautiful Kraut BMWs.

BMW: a company that produced aircraft for the Luftwaffe, assisting in dominating the noxious skies of Nazi-occupied Europe.

BMW: Ed's future.

And so here he was at the Golden Canopy. A hotel that looked, on the surface, like a Holiday Inn—utterly impersonal, ugly in its sparseness, but admirable for its absence of any decorative strivings. But, of course, it wasn't a Holiday Inn. Not even one year old and the walls were already crumbling around the windowsills, the drywall falling in streams of dust onto the tile floor. He stared at the mushroomy walls and envisioned the copious amounts of sand mixed into the cement, the absence of necessary rebar. There was something odd about a Chinese version of a generically depressing Western-style business hotel, and this oddness *almost* saved the room from being more depressing. He took the brick of money from the crone, his sleeve of goods, his little card, and dumped it all on the bed. He stripped off his suit, letting his clothes drop to the floor that—after a half second of deliberation—he deemed no less clean than the bedspread, and he went to take a piss.

Water dripped from the shower nozzle, a steady syncopation—*Chinese water torture* came to mind—and something in the dripping conferred the instant realization that made him want to scream. He didn't scream. He ran back to the bed and ripped off the red rubber bands and, right there in his hands—of course—right between the top bill and the bottom, was not money, not yuan, but tissue.

All those Chinese lining up for the crone had surely been her employees. She probably paid each and every person in that crowd in order to draw in the single sucker of an American businessman.

He put his clothes back on. He felt vulnerable enough without being naked in addition. He lay down, tense from head to toe. He closed his eyes, taking deep breaths, or attempting to—because all he needed now was to have a fucking cardiac arrest in Shenzhen, China—but as he tried to think of his daughter, his heart sped that much faster. Because his daughter was not at home on Park Avenue, eating Häagen-Dazs at the kitchen table. No, Rebecca was at boarding school in Connecticut; he had sent his only child away. He'd suggested it because he knew he needed to be gone for most of the time now, and—more important— he hadn't wanted Rebecca to see him the way he knew he currently was on a daily basis: desperate and distracted. When he and Jill had brought her to school on the first day, when they had moved her into her little room in her little dorm with her music and her books and her pens and her pillows, he had driven away from that campus so fast that he'd gotten a warning from the crossing guard. Then, once on the road, he'd cried so hard that he had to pull over to the side of I-95.

Times had changed—they had changed tremendously—and he repeated this to himself now and again. Of course the school was different from when Hugh Shipley had attended—it was coed, for one thing; it had abolished chapel services, for another—but as Rebecca had been applying, as he'd seen the school crest on the brochure and every page of the application, Ed certainly remembered how Hugh had frequently referred to the school as *prison*. He had hated it with such a fervor, which—looking back now—had bordered on excitement. Oh, how Hugh had hated that school.

But Rebecca liked it—didn't she? Wasn't Hugh's alma mater, first and foremost, one of the highest-ranked prep schools in the country? Wasn't its excellence the main reason that Ed had suggested it? Still. He couldn't stop himself from flushing with shame when he imagined how Hugh would react if he ever found out Ed had sent his daughter there, no matter how excellent the education. Ed had, for the most part, stopped having conversations—real or imaginary—with Hugh, but this topic brought him back there, each and every time.

It still irked him that Hugh could believe he'd end a friendship over politics. It irked him—irrationally, he did recognize—that Hugh hadn't immediately understood why he would behave so terribly. Of course, more reasonably, he also wished that he could have simply gotten over what had happened with Helen and behaved like a normal human being. Couldn't he have made it with his best friend's girl and just moved on, like countless other men throughout history? Couldn't he have managed to have dinner once a year with them both, even though Helen had stayed with Hugh? Would that have been so terrible?

But, yes. Yes, it would have. His wanting to know about her—his wanting—would have gotten the best of him each and every time. He would have pushed and pushed until he ended up telling Hugh. And so—a fact he always came back to—he'd made the right decision.

Then, as now.

Before he plunged into some kind of seriously ugly mood, he picked up the phone to call Rebecca. Connecticut was twelve hours behind, and what did that even mean? He was pushing fifty. Shouldn't he be able to conceptualize time zones? His attention to concrete details was utterly required.

"Snap out of it," he said aloud. "Don't fuck up."

The phone rang and rang. The dorm phone. It was in a little closet and Rebecca never answered it; her room was way down the hall. It made him unaccountably distressed to imagine Rebecca making the journey from her room to the phone closet. When he pictured her face on that journey from her room to the phone closet, it was never happy. He wished he could call her on another phone, on a personal phone. He wished that each student—like mini doctors or corporate raiders—could have his or her own personal, portable phone. Jill had had sleek black phones installed throughout her new apartment. There was a phone next to her bathtub, so that she could answer it without even sitting upright. She'd told him this once this past summer, when he'd picked up Rebecca, and he could have sworn that she was flirting. He'd fantasized about getting in that tub with Jill—of course he had—hearing her sounds again, feeling her against him in some new impossible way.

He sat in his suit now, on the terrible synthetic bedspread, and that dorm phone rang and rang and he tried not to think of how Rebecca would be going to Jill's *boyfriend's* Southampton house. The house had a name—Gould Gardens. How pretentious was *that*? And what difference could it possibly make if—as Jill had obviously felt the need to point out—the name was meant to be tongue in cheek? He tried not to think about how, maybe even during Thanksgiving, Jill and the schmuck would announce their impending marriage. Where would Rebecca sleep then? When she wasn't at school and when she wasn't with him—where would his daughter be picking up the phone? Why wasn't someone picking up the goddamn phone right now?

He gathered his belongings and locked the door behind him. He'd be early for his meeting, but he went—where else?—to the Golden Canopy Hotel bar.

———

The bar was decidedly better than the room, and he was immediately buoyed by his swift decision, by his wisdom in choosing to get out of there. The right thing. Besides which, in addition to alcohol and music—whining Chinese music, but music nonetheless—there was a woman at the bar who was slim, with a curtain of black hair and an alluring birthmark at the corner of her mouth. Though she looked anything but cheap, he idly wondered, before taking a seat beside her, if she was a prostitute.

"This song," said Ed, to the Chinese woman. He assumed she didn't speak English, which made his attempt at conversation strangely easier.

She turned to face him, tilting her head in a question.

"What are the lyrics?" He knew he was talking for the sake of it, in order to feel less alone, but when she smiled and said nothing, he persisted yet again. "The song." He gestured vaguely to the ceiling. "What does it mean?"

Though her expression was unchanged, she seemed to listen for a while, and finally she said carefully, "I am in my car, Shenzhen. How fresh the night breeze, Shenzhen. How bright the flowers when I am running my car in the streets . . . through the sea of lights."

"Sea of lights," said Ed, making sure to hide his surprise at her fluency. "Running my car. That's nice."

"You like Chinese music?"

Ed shrugged. "I don't know."

She offered a grin. "You are honest."

"I am. And you?"

"I am an honest woman."

"Okay, then," he said, "can I buy you a drink?"

"Very well, but I am waiting for somebody. He comes? I go with him."

"Fair enough."

"You like whiskey?" she asked. "You like American Johnnie Walker? Suntory?"

"I'll have a Tsingtao, please." It seemed understood that she would be ordering for him; he wondered if she maybe even worked here at the Golden Canopy in some capacity.

The drinks arrived along with some peanuts; Ed scooped up a handful, more because they were familiar than because they were appealing. "So," he said, "are you from Shenzhen?"

She laughed, endearingly showing her gums before quickly covering her mouth. "Nobody is from Shenzhen," she said. "You must know this, no? Aren't you an American businessman?"

"I was just making conversation."

"Nobody is from Shenzhen. Nothing. Only trees."

"Why did you come here?"

"Why does anyone? Money."

"And are you finding it?"

She stuck out her lower lip, in consideration. "One day here a person barely survives, and another day, next day—rich."

"Sure," said Ed, "okay."

"Most important is how people react to these type of days." She took a slow sip from her glass of whiskey. "Reaction's important."

He took in her black crepey dress, her pale skin, bare hands, and minimal chest. Flame-red lipstick. "So do you work?" he asked.

She nodded.

"What is it that you do?"

"You guess?"

"No, I couldn't possibly. Let's see . . . are you a dancer?" he said, trying his hand at euphemism, which really could not sound cornier.

"Dancer? You guess very poorly." She shook her head, clearly displeased. "I attended university."

"Yeah? Where?"

Her face went a shade darker. "Wellesley," she said curtly, before taking another sip of beer.

"You went to Wellesley?"

She looked him squarely in the eye. "Yes."

"Wellesley in Wellesley, Massachussetts?"

"Yes."

"Like Madame Chiang Kai-Shek."

"Like her," said the stranger, with her first hint of archness. "But less good fortune."

Suddenly he felt off balance; what an idiot he was. He cleared his throat. "Ms. Li Huy Ying?"

She nodded, less confusedly than he'd expected.

He smiled. That they were both early for this meeting seemed fortuitous. There he was, already thinking like an Asian. "I'm Ed Cantowitz."

At dinner he declined the ox penis, which was cut in the shape of delicate stars, and stuck with something that resembled chicken in brown sauce. He drank several bottles of beer.

After the meal, she removed a cigarette from a black lacquer case. Ed reached for the matches on the table and scrambled to offer her a light. It had been a long time since he'd done that (any cigarettes he'd lit between Helen's and now were nowhere in his memories), and it felt as if he were playing a role in a school play. He expected she might laugh. She didn't laugh; she inhaled and exhaled.

He laid out what would happen if she made significant introductions (hefty bonus), came down with unfortunate sicknesses (he'd pay her up to a point), or in the unlikely case that she was overstating her abilities (they'd part ways swiftly and she'd forgo compensation).

"You know, businessmen typically investigate me more carefully," she said. "They ask what I know about the state of Massachusetts."

"Oh, I don't have time for that," Ed told her. "You come highly recommended. I want to get started. I've got a feeling you are very smart."

"I am," she said. "My name means intelligence."

He offered to escort her home and she said no, understandably not wanting him to see where she lived. They shook hands in the lobby of the Golden Canopy. That night he had no trouble sleeping. And when they met in the lobby the next morning, he didn't recognize her at first.

She was wearing a navy suit with a slit up the side of the skirt. Her hair was elegantly pinned up. And she looked more comfortable, as if this powerful presentation was her real self and the sexier version he'd met at the bar had been an odd trick.

She escorted him to meet the representatives of several generals, and in their bad suits, with their offers of tepid tea, these lackeys talked around issues, always arriving at the unsurprising conclusion that any decision must be made by a general. Ed imagined these generals sitting in canvas tents with side flaps, as if they were still at war. He imagined the waistlines bulging, the gold affixed to their teeth, and when—at their last meeting—he instructed Li to tell the representative that he wanted to meet with his boss, the lackey replied in harsh tones. Though Li was obviously not translating every last comment—and certainly not the comments directed toward her—Ed knew the stream of Mandarin was unfailingly vulgar. Each meeting led to another meeting. To more god-awful tea. The sounds of those chuckling lackeys would surely haunt him. He spent the days in such meetings and the nights at a club where early Frank Sinatra crooned from a record player no different than the one in his uncle Herb's basement.

"There is gambling," Li explained. "It is in another room."

Ed nodded, watching a stunning young woman at the bar. She was talking to a fat old bastard. Probably a general. "Blackjack? Poker?"

She nodded. "Chinese dominoes, too. But not for money."

"For what, then?" Ed asked, sipping his Tsingtao slowly. You always had to be drinking alcohol here. People became edgy if you weren't constantly on your way toward being soused.

"Guns, ammunition, and"—Li looked away—"visas."

"Visas?"

"People gamble for visas. Work visas for Hong Kong are important, very valuable."

This, then, was what Li was after. He understood, but he didn't let on.

"You'll tell me more about that," he said, taking a long drink and ordering another beer for him and another whiskey for Li. Ed had realized after the first night in the club that nearly everyone in the room spoke basic English.

"What more to tell?" asked Li, making him work for it.

"About the visas."

"Hong Kong work visas?"

"Yes."

She ran her hand along the table for one sustained moment. "Generals in each region—they can print visas," she said. "They can print whenever they want to. They have a printer."

"And you can just . . . pay?"

She nodded, but there was something more she wasn't saying. And because—right that moment—he felt gripped by an unfamiliar reticence, he didn't push her to tell him.

On the day the general agreed to meet Ed, Li took him to Xili Lake, where, after drinking three Tsingtaos from dusty bottles, he found himself agreeing to don a helmet and mount a horse. Never mind that the horses were emaciated and flea-bitten and that the helmets were old and obviously never intended for the purpose of riding. Ed and Li sat in their saddles, side by side. They shooed away flies. How were they supposed to act in this unprecedented context of forced leisure? The horses began to plod up into the hills. It was a silent ride, uneventful, until they came back to where they'd started and, without provocation, Ed's horse spooked and threw him.

He landed on his bony ass (the only bony part of him) and, when he realized he hadn't broken anything but that he was legitimately achy, to say nothing of embarrassed, he cursed the animal and rose to his feet, dusting off his clothes. The stable master's child toddled out, naked from the waist down, and began to pet the spooked horse. The stable master followed the boy, hollering, and Li dismounted amidst the chaos. She came to Ed's side, and he realized—not too late, thankfully—that this pathetic horse had actually given him a gift. "I think," he said, reaching out for her arm, as if merely to steady himself, "I think I need to lie down."

It all came later in a room that let in the moonlight. He would be grateful to the moonlight, grateful to find out that moonlight was, even in a place so deeply strange, still available free of charge. It may have been the dismal surroundings and the relative comfort of the room, but when it was just the two of them—Ed and Li—finally alone, he didn't waste a moment. The pathetic surroundings created, if not unprecedented passion, the unprecedented un-self-conscious expression of it. He'd never once thought of himself as anywhere near repressed, but years later—in fact, for the rest of his life—Ed would look back on that night at Xili Lake with a shudder of excitement that was, in the end, overshadowed by a lingering embarrassment at the noise that he'd emitted, that had sounded, even to his own ears, like some kind of terrible suffering.

After Li left his room at Xili Lake, Ed circled several notions, feeling wrong, all wrong, but unable to place precisely why. They had a more than pleasurable time together. She'd initiated it. He understood what she wanted—visas for her parents—and that, because of him, she was going to be able to achieve it. He thought he had done—and would continue to do—the right thing.

But his mouth tasted like blood. He briefly wondered if he'd cut his lip when he fell from that horse, or whether Li might have nicked him with one of her small white teeth.

They were strangers.

It always came back to knowing, to being known. To wondering over a gesture, whether she liked him or hated him and if it mattered. If it ever mattered. And this uncertainty, this familiar uncertainty in the most unfamiliar of places—it filled him with startling rage. He was pushing fifty, he was no exoticist; what the hell was he doing in this hotel room, in this corrupt and frankly preposterous situation? He bounded out from beneath the sheets, because being in bed suddenly disgusted him. Standing in the moonlight, which pooled at the foot of the bed, he imagined Li climbing the stairwell and finding her room. He imagined, with strange certainty, how she would watch herself closely while brushing her teeth, how she would brush her teeth quickly, like a child forced to do so, how she'd scrub her face with concentration. And he was glad that she'd gone. He wouldn't have wanted to see her like that.

It dawned on him that, because Shenzhen was twelve hours ahead of New York and that, though he'd been counting down the days, he'd missed a day—somewhere in there he had actually *missed a day*—he'd missed Thanksgiving. The guilt he felt over having not called Rebecca on Thanksgiving was out of proportion to how much she would care. He knew this, and yet self-loathing stung him as he shuffled back under the scratchy sheets and the nubby bedspread; he was riddled with sadness as he imagined her—someone's future stepdaughter—eating dark-meat turkey but mostly yams at an unfamiliar table.

He picked up the phone and placed the call. As the phone rang, he went over the time difference once more and realized, amazingly, that he was wrong *yet again* and that not only was it, somehow, the perfect time to call, but across the world, in a Jed Johnson–designed dining room suffused with the exquisite clear light of Long Island's East End, those staying at Gould Gardens would, in fact, be sitting down to eat. They would be turning their attention to the head of the table, to where his ex-wife's *boyfriend* would declare—while raising a glass—just how very thankful he was. Ed knew he would do this, because Jill had always complained that Ed never set the right tone for their celebratory meal, that he had always shied away from any kind of public gratefulness, which had shocked him because he'd thought of himself as grateful to the point of obsequiousness around Jill.

The phone rang and rang. No answering machine.

He hung up and redialed several times, his heart speeding up with his escalating ire. Wouldn't someone—Jill? *Rebecca?*—think to consider that the ringing phone might just be Rebecca's father, calling to wish his only child a Happy Thanksgiving? Wouldn't someone imagine how he might want to—yes—express his own particular gratitude?

As the phone continued to ring, the light in Southampton grew more and more celestial, the guests more fascinating, the décor and art more remarkable. As it rang, the air in Xili Palace grew staler and strangely cold. There were scratches on his ankle and on both of his knees; an inevitable bruise was forming on his ass. He was about to hang up the goddamn phone when somebody answered.

"Hello?" asked a male voice, slightly out of breath. "Hello? I just walked in."

"I've been calling and calling. Who is this?"

"This is Roger. Who is this?"

"Roger?"

"The one and only." He laughed, and Ed identified Roger as gay. This put him at ease somehow.

"I'm looking for my daughter."

"I'm afraid you have the wrong number."

"Is this Gould Gardens?" He couldn't believe he was speaking that ridiculous name in such a serious voice. But it helped, the name. He preferred it to speaking the name of the man whom Jill had not simply screwed but might marry.

"Yes, it is," Roger said, suddenly official, "but Mr. Gould is not available, I'm afraid."

"Okay, Roger. This is Ed Cantowitz. My daughter is Rebecca Cantowitz. My wife—my ex-wife—is Jill. Ringing any bells?"

"Oooh, I'm *so* sorry, Mr. Cantowitz. I'm Mr. Gould's chef, Roger del Parra. And—again, so sorry—but there must have been some kind of communication snafu between y'all, because they aren't here for the holiday. Happy Thanksgiving, by the way."

"What do you mean they aren't there?"

"I mean Mr. Gould and . . . your ex-wife have gone to the Palm Beach house. It's just Christophe and me and the dogs here this weekend."

"Is my daughter with them?"

"Well, I—I didn't think so, but—"

"What's the number in Palm Beach, Roger?"

"I'm afraid I'm not—"

"Roger, give me the goddamn number. Please."

"Mr. Gould has expressly told me—"

"He's told you what? That if Ed Cantowitz asks where his daughter is, if Ed Cantowitz wants to know where his own daughter is spending the Thanksgiving holiday—No, I don't think so, Roger. Give me the number. Please."

"I appreciate what you're saying."

"Thank you."

Roger gave him the number.

"Happy Thanksgiving," Ed managed to say, before hanging up the phone.

He pulled on his clothes before dialing Florida. He sat at the spindly desk in the corner. As he expected, nobody answered. The moonlight remained bright, a lone dog barked in the distance, and as he heard a car door slam and a far-off argument in Chinese, Ed kept dialing. He dialed Rebecca's dorm and the school's office—no answers. He dialed his apartment in New York, and his own voice greeted him brusquely. He thought about calling friends of Jill's, but he didn't have those numbers and promised himself that, next time, he'd travel with more of her contacts. It was difficult to think of a next time, to think beyond this night right here, this unending night, in the strangest place he'd ever been. He might have even dozed off between so many dialings of that Palm Beach number, he wasn't sure, but when someone answered, he was so surprised that he cried out, "Don't hang up, okay? Hello?"

"*Ed?*"

"Jesus Christ, Jill. Jesus Christ."

"Where are you calling from? You sound right next door. Happy Thanksgiving—David," she interrupted herself, "will you please turn that down."

Ed emitted a hostile laugh. "Right, right, Happy Thanksgiving. Please put Rebecca on the phone."

"Rebecca isn't here, Ed. She's spending the holiday with a school friend."

"A school friend? Well, where the hell is she?"

"She's actually in Anguilla," Jill said, lightly incredulous, as if she'd had nothing whatsoever to do with it. "Her friend sounds terrific; her parents seem like interesting people. Of course I spoke with them before I gave Rebecca the okay, and—this is really funny, and obviously I was going to tell you when you were back from Asia—it turns out the girl's father was in your class at Harvard."

Ed felt not one shred of the usual satisfaction upon hearing Jill sound nervous. "What's his name?"

"Hugh Shipley? And her name is Helen? He was very nice, very friendly on the phone. They both were. Said they couldn't wait to meet Rebecca and, of course, to catch up with you."

If hearing Helen's name on Connie Graff's lips the night before he left for Hong Kong had made him feel sucker punched, then hearing these names, hearing this from Jill, made him feel . . . disembodied. Up he floated to the cracked-plaster asbestos-ridden ceiling and saw what there was to see. He waited for his reaction or for his lack of one. There he was: the same frustrated, determined person with the receiver cradled between his shoulder and ear and the phone between his hands. This was the way he liked his telephones best—not a faggy toy of a cordless but a phone to hold, a *machine*. He held on to a phone the way another man might hold on to a football. It helped him to feel grounded, ready.

There he was, looking around the room, with his potential bald spot and his thick hunched shoulders, and—*Hugh and Helen's daughter was Rebecca's friend*. How could such a thing be true?

It was night in China. In coming here, in making each decision that led him to this trip, to this particular sleepless night, had he—without his knowledge—agreed to live on Chinese terms? Maybe his ancestors were also playing ball now, controlling his life the way that Li claimed she believed. *The more-recent dead deal with the smaller things. The longer dead deal with the bigger things.* She had told him this in the same straight-forward manner that she'd relayed any other manner of Chinese bureaucratic bullshit.

Was his mother long dead or was she recently dead? As always, it was tough to say.

"Ed?" he heard Jill ask. "Ed, are you there?"

"What's the number?"

"Ed—she's really having a wonderful time. I spoke to her after they arrived."

"What's the goddamn number."

"It's such a short trip; she's in a beautiful place. She's made a friend. Please don't ruin this for her."

He waited until she gave it to him.

"What's the flight information."

She gave that up, too. Not without a whole lot of sighing.

"We'll talk more about this," said Ed. Then he hung up the phone.

He never went to sleep that night. He sat by the window and watched the sky go through its hours, the fog obscuring most of the mountains until the sun burned through. Rebecca was with Hugh and Helen. Hugh and Helen were hosting his daughter on a trip to Anguilla. He would have welcomed nausea, but there was none.

At precisely seven A.M., he knocked on Li's door. "It's time to go," he said.

She was already dressed, with her lipstick applied, her eyebrows expertly thickened with pencil. "I'm ready," she agreed.

After several miles of driving in the rented car, Ed spoke up. "I need to go to New York."

She merely nodded.

"I'll get you what you need, all the money you've more than earned. I'll get it for you before I go."

"Good," she said. "That's fine, then."

"And I'll be back soon."

"Yes?"

"I only have to leave because, you see—my daughter . . ."

She didn't ask what had happened.

It occurred to him that she wasn't interested in his life. She may have even been relieved to see him go. "I'll be back within a couple of weeks," he said.

"Good," she said. She smiled, but she didn't show her gums.

"You'll reschedule the general."

"Of course."

"How big a problem is that going to be?"

"I will make it a very small one."

He nodded, relieved. It was still early morning, and they stopped for a coffee first, drank it from small paper cups, and, even though it was nearly undrinkable, Ed did not complain. There was so much he hadn't accomplished here, but he was confident he'd be back soon and that Li would be ready. Construction, security permits—the list was never-ending, and he couldn't do it without her. "If it weren't for you," he said, "I would have packed up and gone back to Hong Kong after a few days with my tail between my legs. This town is not for the faint of heart."

"You are not faint of heart."

"No," he said. "But even so."

"You got lucky," she said. "We both did."

"You know I don't believe in luck."

After saying goodbye to Li and tying up loose ends in Hong Kong, Ed accomplished many tasks before seeing Rebecca again. On the plane he had watched not only *Baby Boom* but also *Three Men and a Baby*. He listened as the nervous Australian sitting next to him held forth on the appeal of Diane Keaton. He read the *Financial Times* and the *International Herald Tribune*. He kept himself fed by scarfing down two Kit Kats, an entire cylinder of Pringles, and one fairly decent fettuccine Alfredo—courtesy of TWA—in addition to three or four cans of Diet Coke and several packets of peanuts. He filled out customs forms, went to the bathroom, plucked a particularly unruly eyebrow hair with his fingers; he tried and failed and tried and failed to fall asleep. Ed knew he'd done all of these things, but after his plane was delayed while refueling in Anchorage, after he realized that he might actually miss seeing them at the airport, after his plane touched down on the runway, allowing him just enough time to—theoretically—catch them at baggage claim, after clearing immigration and running and running through gate after gate—he felt as if he'd done nothing but pray.

He still wasn't exactly sure for what he had been praying.

Since calling Gould Gardens and speaking to Roger the chef, he'd had the distinct sense that Rebecca was in danger, but of course it wasn't Rebecca who was in danger. Because here was Rebecca and she was tan (he hadn't known his daughter *could* tan) and looking more relaxed while hurling a bag from the carousel than he'd seen her in a long time. Here was Rebecca, smiling at Helen, who took the bag from her.

Here was Helen, after twenty-five years, and those years had been perfectly kind to her. It was as if Ed had been seeing her regularly after all, because, although she didn't look the same—she looked older, she *was* older—there were no dramatic shifts and she looked as he'd expected. Though she didn't dye her hair, the texture was still shiny like a younger woman's, and the blend of gray and white with blond was surprising, even striking. Lines fanned out from her eyes, and that *V* was indeed etched into her forehead and made her look just like the worried person he'd always known she was. Her posture and figure remained intact; *coltish* still came to mind.

Which is to say, he felt exactly the same.

He'd been praying for Rebecca's well-being, but Rebecca was just fine.

It was he who hadn't slept in a dangerously long while and who probably stank on top of it, he who had the same dual urges to both deck his old friend Hugh and throw his arms around the handsome bastard (who was cradling an oddly bandaged hand and looking more exhausted than he would have imagined after what had been, after all, a trip to the Caribbean). It was he, he, *he,* who was in danger, when—out of breath—

Ed heard himself cry out, "Will someone please tell me what the hell is going on here?"

"Oh my God," said Rebecca.

"Yup," said Ed.

"Daddy, what are you doing here?"

Helen—who, should she and Hugh go on to celebrate their golden anniversary, would always be Helen Ordway to him—started to laugh. Or she started something that began as laughter and descended into suppressed giggling.

"That's ours," Helen said, but reached for the bag too late.

"It'll come around," said Hugh, rather daftly, or so Ed couldn't help but think. His was a face and bearing that would never change, not really, but there was no mistaking the broken capillaries and the shadows under the eyes. There was no mistaking the smell of vodka as Hugh silently embraced Ed in lieu of saying more, at least for now. Ed felt strange embracing Hugh before hugging his own daughter, but as he felt Hugh clap his back with his one good hand, Ed swallowed down on his anger—they had spirited his daughter away!

"Daddy, what are you doing here?"

"Ed?" asked Helen, though he wasn't sure if she was echoing Rebecca's question or trying to start her own.

Ed pulled away from Hugh and looked at Helen.

"Ed," she repeated, "this is Genevieve—Vivi—our daughter."

Vivi looked like the type of girl he'd encountered on ferryboats while traveling through Greece—chronically unwashed, inevitably Scandinavian, up to nothing good. Her hair was done like Bo Derek's in *10*, which told Ed just about all he needed to know about the Shipley parenting style.

"We've actually met," she said, politely shaking his hand.

"We have? I don't think so."

"On the phone," she said, with a smile that reminded him so much of Helen he felt a twinge in his lower back.

"Right, right, good to meet you again," Ed said, trying not to wince.

"Helen," he managed. He kissed her tawny cheek, the bone beneath still sharp. Even after the years and the airplane and the reputed *bad turn*—even after all of this—Helen smelled like flowers and smoke, absolutely the same.

His daughter stood by her duffel (Jill's old mauve LeSportsac, the one she'd taken the first time they'd gone to Caneel Bay) and looked at him brutally, as if she might prefer to relinquish him as a father than be humiliated by what was sure to come out of his mouth at any second. As if galvanized by her fears about his gruff, possessive, chronically uncool, capitalist, paranoid, insensitive, square self, he repeated, "Will someone please tell me what the hell is going on here?"

Helen said something about talking to Jill, about *coincidence*—

Yes, right, added Hugh. *Who would believe?*—

"I should have been told," Ed said. "Your mother should have consulted with me before you jetted off to Anguilla," he said.

Rebecca stared at those bags on the carousel, and Hugh and Helen gave empty apologies—because what did they know about Jill and the divorce and her sketchy relationship with telling the truth—and Ed nodded, nodded, he shook his head, but really he was just watching them, watching Helen, her wrists, her fingers threading through her necklaces. He was watching Hugh—what was with his bandaged hand?—and he caught their daughter nudge his own daughter, then smile a troublesome smile. He watched them as if all his future successes and failures were pinned to these tanned people, all far more beautiful than he, all differently ill at ease. And the baggage went around and around, some repeats, some new additions, some battered, one no more than a broken box held together with string, and as their fellow passengers retrieved these bags and double-checked and dialed pay phones and searched out cabs at the curb, and as people came and went and fluorescent lights flickered overhead, he saw Hugh lean down and say something to his daughter. He saw her shake her head mildly but say nothing back.

"Rebecca," Ed said, picking up the mauve LeSportsac, "let's get moving."

He realized he'd been braced for her refusal to go with him, and when she simply nodded and hugged her friend and smiled at Helen, Ed took a radically different turn. "Hey," he heard himself say affably, "how long are you all in town, anyway?"

"Not long," said Helen. He looked on with amazement as Helen gave his daughter a hug.

Rebecca said goodbyes to Helen and then to Hugh, and Ed saw that Rebecca was sulking and that she probably didn't realize this made her seem oddly cold to them, even rude.

"That's too bad you're leaving so soon," Ed said expansively. "It would have been nice to have dinner."

"The next time," said Hugh. "Absolutely."

"What happened to your hand?" asked Ed.

"Long story," Hugh replied, as if he'd returned from a particularly wild college weekend.

"Thanks again," Rebecca muttered.

"It was a pleasure," Hugh said.

"Absolutely," said Helen. "We'll do it again."

Ed knew he was the cause of Rebecca's rudeness. He could feel her tension; he could sense everyone's discomfort at his presence. He had ruined this, the last part of their perfect trip, their intimate, heartfelt goodbye.

"Well," he said, "bye, then." He gave a stupid salute, his hand landing on Rebecca's back, and together they walked away.

Ed's driver, Manny, was waiting, and after telling Ed and Rebecca about the storm they'd missed, about the traffic on the Belt Parkway, he turned up his classical music and there was nothing but the drive, gray and ugly, from Queens to Manhattan.

"I don't even know where to start," said Ed.

"I don't want to talk about it," said Rebecca, with her head against the window. "Not right now." She turned her attention to the Van Wyck Expressway, to a bland sky between seasons. *You embarrassed me,* he could tell she wanted to say. *You always ruin everything.*

After bidding Manny goodbye and bidding Sal the doorman hello, after the requisite chitchat about weather and mail, Ed was finally alone with his daughter, finally home.

"Now, you listen to me," he said, before even taking off his coat. "Those people—"

His daughter started to laugh.

"Don't you laugh at me."

"Dad," she said, shaking her head, as if to say, *Stop*. "Those people are Vivi's parents, and they are my friends now. They're nice, and they're fun, and they're interesting."

"Is that right?" His face burned.

"Yes."

Ed took off his coat. He draped it over the closest chair. He barely stopped himself from yelling. "What makes them interesting?"

She didn't sigh or roll her eyes. "They care about other things besides money."

"Uh-huh," he said.

She raised one eyebrow. She'd known how to do this since she was a little kid, claimed to have taught herself.

"I heard what you said. They care about other things besides money. Meaning I *only* care about money."

She said, "Just tell me what you want to tell me. I'm tired. You must be, too."

"Maybe," Ed continued, "they *don't care about money* because they grew up with money. Lots of it. Piles of it. You do know that, don't you?"

"What would that matter?"

"Because, sweetheart, not caring about money when you come from it? That's easy as pie. You, for instance, don't care about money. And I love that about you. But don't confuse things."

"No, you don't," she said. "You don't *love* that I don't care about money. Give me a break."

"Yes," he said, "I do. You'd better believe it."

"The Shipleys—who cares if they come from money! That doesn't make any sense! Plenty of people have plenty of money and they just want more of it."

"Of course," he said, "but all I'm saying is—"

"Hugh has devoted his whole life to caring for poor people."

"That's noble. I'm only saying there's more to it. You have to understand, there always is." What exactly was he so burned up about? Hugh—Ed did realize this—had not wronged him. He had never even judged him. So Hugh chose to live as if he was doing penance for his very existence—wasn't that his prerogative?

"They care about helping people," said Rebecca. "That's it. Why can't you admit that? What did they ever do to you, anyway? And also—" She scraped her hair away from her face, a repetitive gesture that seemed like it would hurt. She secured her smoothed hair with one of the many bands that encircled her wrist.

"Forget it."

"Forget what?"

"Forget their politics, forget their values—"

"Their *values*?" Rebecca raised her voice. "You want to talk to me about Hugh and Helen and their *values*? What is that supposed to mean?"

"Nothing," Ed said. He could feel that bitter smile.

"No, what? Tell me. You seem really pissed off about them, and it makes no sense."

I'm really pissed off because Hugh never once paused to consider that Helen might actually have wanted me, that she might have wanted me badly enough to do something about it. And I'm pissed off because Hugh is a man who lives above it all, and nothing down here—down in the real world, the petty world, the world of fear and greed and bottomless desire—nothing seems to catch up to him and—

"I'm really pissed off because you and your mother didn't tell me that you weren't going where I thought you were going, and the reason you didn't tell me was because you knew I'd never let you go away with people like that. Even before you knew they'd been friends of mine—you knew that I'd make sure to talk to them on the phone and ask all my questions and there would have been no way."

"Because you don't trust me."

"Trust has absolutely nothing to do with any of this. I can't get over when I hear parents saying that. *I trust my kid.* Jesus Christ. There are forces that are beyond our control, Rebecca, and it is my job—*my job*—to control how vulnerable you are to these forces. In a couple of years that'll be your job. Nothin' I'll be able to do about it. You can go live in Africa, too, if you'd like. Knock yourself out. But goddamn if I'm going to be the sucker who looks the other way while you get yourself into trouble before then. *I trust my kid.* No, forget it. I'm sorry."

"Dad—"

He was pacing now, holding his hands together. "I bet you and your friend had no curfew, and I bet you were drinking and maybe smoking marijuana on top of it, and I don't even want to *think* about you having gotten in a car with Hugh Shipley on vacation. People don't change. I'm not an idiot, Rebecca."

"Daddy, I never said you were."

"You want to know why I'm pissed off? I'm pissed off because you're not even sixteen years old and you got on a plane and I had no idea about it. And who is *Vivi*, anyway? Why haven't I heard anything about her?"

"Probably because you are so judgmental about my friends that I tend not to say much about them."

"Oh, please lighten up, Rebecca. Will you please?"

"Also probably because you haven't exactly been easy to talk to these days."

Was she right? Fine, she was right. But one day he would explain it all. He'd explain it and she would understand it. She was smart, incredibly smart. He was always proud of her. Even right now, when she was being impossible.

"So—what?" he continued, trying to gain back his momentum.

"Was it cocktails for breakfast on this island getaway? Catching fresh fish on sailboats and all that?"

"Oh, now you have a problem with vacations? With *fish*? What are you talking about?"

"I just know how they are," he muttered.

"They're *married*. Okay? Vivi's parents are married. Which is a lot more than I'm able to say."

"Give me a break, Rebecca. This isn't a goddamn movie. I did not want to get divorced," he yelled. He went ahead and yelled it again. "You know I didn't want to."

"Also? Vivi's parents don't live their life thinking that the worst thing is about to happen at any given moment." She walked over to the window and put her face right up to it. He watched her there, fogging up the glass, for what seemed like a very long time. "I am so sick of thinking that way," she finally said. "And I do, you know." She turned around to face him. "I think just the way you do." Her eyes were brimming with tears and her nose was running; she didn't even bother to wipe it.

He was ready to ground her for keeping this trip from him. He was prepared to keep her in this apartment and out of that goddamn mistake of a school for an extra few days. That would be the right thing to do. Not the easy thing but the *right* thing.

Instead, he took a deep breath, the way his doctor had shown him. He sat down on the couch, took another breath, and stood up once more. He went into the kitchen and poured two glasses of water. He returned with the water and they both drank up.

"Did you have a good time?" he asked.

She wiped away her tears and her snot and took a deep, shuddering breath. "I did," she said.

"Okay," he said.

Rebecca was crying—weeping, really—and he found himself sympathizing with the fact that she was cursed with a father like him. He put his arms around her, and when she didn't shrug him off, he tried not to feel surprised.

"Why are you crying?" he asked. "I'm not even grounding you."

"I had such a good time," she sobbed.

He kissed her head. He remembered how her hair used to smell like sugar and strawberries, and now it smelled like hair. They stood by the window, and the sun shone weakly in the sky. Ed held his daughter and looked out at the park and so many barren trees.

Part Four

1989–2010

Chapter Seventeen

Columbia and Beyond, 1989–2004

Rebecca and Vivi were both shocked by Vivi's acceptance at Columbia. They each cast about for how this could have happened and agreed it must have been Vivi's final project in her creative writing class that had convinced the admissions committee. During Vivi's senior spring, everyone had to present his or her collected works in some kind of portfolio. Most kids had written them out neatly or used a word processor, stapled the pages together, and called it a day; there had been one girl who'd done hers in purple calligraphy and bound the pages with ribbon. But Vivi had found an old Sunfish at someone's garage sale, rigged up the sail, spray-painted the whole boat gold, and scrawled her poetry on the boat with neon paint pens. Everyone loved it; she'd won some kind of award. And, during Rebecca's senior year at boarding school, each time she walked by the "Poetry Boat," which had acquired a semipermanent position on the Arts Center lawn (Vivi having ignored all requests to come collect it), Rebecca considered how the admissions board of Columbia University must really be studded with suckers.

But then, during her first week at Columbia, while searching for her contemporary civilization class, something finally clicked when Rebecca ran across a lecture hall bearing Vivi's grandmother's maiden name.

One month into Rebecca's freshman year, Vivi was "tapped" for St.

A's, the most exclusive social club on campus. Vivi told Rebecca while they were crossing Broadway, and Rebecca had used the noisy traffic as an excuse to shout. *"What are you talking about?"*

"They asked me." Vivi shrugged. "I want to see what it's like."

She'd been chosen by half-British, half-Texan Marion Childs, who had—according to rumor—recently been sleeping with Ethan Hawke. When Rebecca pressed, Vivi described the most exclusive club on campus as if it were a group of civic-minded students, interested not in black tie or blue blood or (at its most interesting) defying the thriving culture of political correctness but rather in earnest matters of community responsibility and the fostering of close friendships.

"It'll be like a social experiment," said Vivi.

"A social experiment in what? Snobbism? Why would you—you, of all people!—why would you want that?"

Vivi looked away and picked up her pace, as if speed could get her through this conversation. "I tried to join the African Student Club and the members laughed at me. Like in unison. I looked ridiculous to them, of course I did. It doesn't matter that I was born in Africa and that I lived there until I was ten. If I didn't know that before, I definitely knew it when I was standing there looking like a freakin' missionary."

"You might not be a missionary, but—"

"What?" Vivi was a little out of breath.

The light turned red and they stood on the median, smack in the middle of Broadway.

"What?" repeated Vivi. Cars whizzed by.

It was still surprising to see Vivi without cornrows. Her long, layered hair blew away from her face with a sudden gust of wind.

"You're starting to sound like an elitist." Rebecca said this loud and clear, though inside she was nervous.

Vivi looked downright flinty; her eyes might have actually narrowed. "These people from St. A's are interested in me, Rebecca. I like them. They're fun. Some of them are smart—like, smarter than you. They're definitely not a bunch of jackasses." Vivi turned her attention to the passing cars, obviously impatient to get away from Rebecca. "You need to let this go."

Rebecca remembered previously thinking: *Why is there a bench on a median smack in the middle of Broadway?* And then it became perfectly clear: It was as if someone had created seating specifically for those who, while in the midst of arguing, couldn't make decisions—whether or not to keep walking, to keep fighting, whether or not to go on.

As Rebecca's sophomore year began, Vivi spent more and more time at St. A's. Rebecca attended one party there, which was perfectly fine. It was a beautiful building; twinkly chandelier. No people in ascots, no burning crosses, and yet she never returned. Though Vivi had never once acknowledged any family fortune or any legacy besides one of social service and borderline alcoholism, now that she'd joined a club known for issuing invitations based on old-money origins, Vivi's non-disclosure about her own increasingly evident old money had started to seem less like a desire to follow in her father's earnest footsteps and a genuine by-product of having grown up in Africa and Haiti and more like straight-up hypocrisy. Rebecca did not want this to be true for so many reasons, not the least of which was, of course, that this would vindicate her father's cynical point of view. Rebecca never returned to St. A's because she felt that, within such a context, she didn't know very much about her closest friend.

So she hung around the Hungarian Pastry Shop with Francisco, the self-described asexual heir to a Puerto Rican shipping empire. She studied and talked with Francisco about politics, philosophy—everything except anything resembling popular culture or living breathing humans. Francisco had also gone to boarding school but had been kicked out due to the fact that he'd (having never seen *Harold and Maude*) faked his own death. He had a unibrow, a contagious laugh, and excellent knife skills. One Saturday night he made osso bucco on his dorm stove for Rebecca and Bob—a wiry, unsmiling, self-described liberation theologian from Troy, Michigan. Bob smoked Pall Malls and drank Jägermeister and did a weekly night shift at a Bronx soup kitchen. He got straight A's, played cards with old men in Riverside Park, and seemed to have read every book ever written, and when, two weeks later—at her suggestion—he relieved Rebecca of her virginity, his crucifix dangled in her line of vision and she didn't even close her eyes.

And to whom did Rebecca place a call, the morning after her deflowering?

"What do you mean a crucifix?" asked Vivi. "It's probably just a little cross, no?" Vivi had befriended several Italians on campus and had already absorbed their expressions and inflections.

"No. It's a crucifix. It's Jesus. On a cross. With blood."

"Blood?"

"Approximation of. It's all silver."

"Bet your dad will love that."

"I doubt my dad will meet him."

"Why not?"

"Because."

"Because he wears a crucifix?"

"No!"

"You'd better be careful," Vivi said. "Don't start lying to yourself."

"What is that supposed to mean?"

"You know."

"I don't know."

"All I'm saying is that it wouldn't be the worst thing to piss your father off again. You can do that more than once in a lifetime."

"Coming from someone whose father thinks everything she does is downright dreamy."

After that, she saw less of Vivi. In the winter they met while it was still dark out, swam laps in the university pool. They were at their best when they weren't talking, when they were—like the toddlers Rebecca read about in her psych class—doing something like parallel play. Outside, with their hair still wet, they drank café con leches and ate sweet rolls; their hair froze in the snow. When they hugged goodbye, Vivi was the last to let go. *I miss you,* she sometimes said, as if they weren't living not only in the same city but also attending the same school.

Rebecca never did introduce Bob to her father. And after they'd broken up after less than a year, for plenty of good reasons—Rebecca made out with several other people; Bob, it turned out, was a pretentious alcoholic—she never once regretted it.

But, somehow, once Vivi graduated and moved to Los Angeles, Rebecca and Vivi's history of tension ceased to matter. They talked on the phone more than they ever saw each other in college. Vivi's development job seemed to mean she was licensed to meet for drinks with attractive guys who'd graduated from film school, full of expectations. Unsurprisingly, Vivi was very good at this. She was soon promoted. When she came to New York for a meeting, she told Rebecca to meet her at the Royalton. Vivi expensed it. Vivi was Hollywood; Rebecca, a do-gooder: That narrative seemed to work. But then Rebecca went to law school, and Vivi met a Buddhist monk at a party in Venice Beach, and by the next week Vivi had quit her job and agreed to work on the monk's documentary about Bhutan.

Vivi wrote Rebecca one long letter from Bhutan, through which Rebecca basically deduced that the film was going nowhere. But the film, as it turned out, was not only completed but it won some kind of German humanitarian award, after which Vivi worked consistently, for a good two years, as a producer of another indisputably substantive film. And then, after she confided she was not cut out for producing (*Not even you could keep all this shit straight,* she'd explained at the Carlyle, before literally falling asleep at the bar), instead of moving on to the next thing, as Rebecca had imagined she would do, Vivi somehow managed to convince enough people that—despite their usually minuscule budgets—she was indispensable as a visual consultant/location scout. She made it happen.

Rebecca not only stopped being so self-righteous (she was a summer associate at Davis Polk, writing briefs on behalf of a . . . *tobacco com-*

pany), she also stopped keeping track of where Vivi was, knowing that she'd blow through New York soon enough and would call her from a hotel bar. They justified the astronomical prices by the fact that they never saw each other.

They were both—when you got down to it—two girls who loved a treat.

Now, ten years after her Columbia graduation, and three years after the obliteration of the World Trade Center, not one mile away from where she was now battling her way through an unexpected, torrential downpour (it was December—where was the snow?), Rebecca Cantowitz was bone-cold, exhausted, and already certain she felt a nascent scratch in the back of her throat. When she passed through the doors of this new downtown hotel—ambient lighting, expensive currant scent—the chill and the rain were immediately distant.

"Rebecca?" asked a tall Asian man at the front desk.

Rebecca nodded, fighting the urge to wipe her nose with the back of her sweater sleeve.

"Your friend is in the drawing room. May I take your coat?"

Checking items always seemed to overcomplicate matters—why involve more people in one's entrance than absolutely necessary? Why couldn't she simply drape a coat—such an elegant gesture—over the back of a chair? But she nodded, and, fighting her more-natural instincts (*eccentricities,* said her mother), Rebecca flashed her best pretty smile and handed over her trench coat before moving forward. Her spike-heeled boots—likely ruined in the rain—clicked across the marble floor.

The drawing room was absurdly cozy, and she scanned the room for Vivi, who'd last been in town about a year ago, doing postproduction consulting for the fifty-something German director, whom she had dubbed *the Sentimental Penis.* Vivi had worked on his film about a village in Malta, where he'd spent a seminal summer as a child. The three of them had gone out late one night and Rebecca had been impressed with Vivi's command; she told him where she wanted to eat, what wine to order, and, when he'd reached over to touch Rebecca's leg, Vivi had stopped him cold.

Out of your league, she'd said.

And there she was now; there was Vivi at a table by the window—rising slowly and hugging her quickly. When she felt those willowy, strong arms around her, Rebecca was afraid she might start crying, something she swore she wouldn't do today. Vivi held on a little longer than the usual embrace, the one Rebecca knew in her bones. "You look so *great,*" Vivi said, after pulling away.

"I sort of believe you," said Rebecca. "Because I'm finally sleeping."

"Oh, thank God."

"Ambien," she said. "I relented."

"You're so stubborn about taking drugs."

"Wait," said Rebecca suddenly. She stared at Vivi openly. "Something's different."

Vivi shrugged, but Rebecca detected a twist of a smile.

"It's something. Your *boobs*?" mouthed Rebecca. "Did you—"

Then Vivi started to laugh for real, in the way that meant something more than the answer.

"What can I get for you?" asked the waiter, foreign and handsome.

Vivi smiled at him, not flirtatiously but somehow attentively. "My very best friend will have a *very* dirty martini." Then, glancing at Rebecca, "Am I right?"

Rebecca nodded. She'd planned on avoiding hard liquor tonight, but now such an idea seemed ridiculous. Here in the profoundly unfamiliar world of joblessness, she not only had to work so much harder to avoid her father's phone calls but she'd taken to going out frequently; there were more overeducated unemployed people than she'd ever imagined. They emailed links: some to potential jobs but mostly to travel bargains and excellent sample sales. They met for drinks well before five.

"And I'll have . . ." Vivi glanced over the wine list. "I'll have a glass of the Bordeaux.

"So I'm worried," she heard Vivi say, after the waiter walked away.

When Rebecca turned her attention to her, Vivi wasn't smiling.

"I've been worried about you," she repeated.

"I know," said Rebecca lightly. "You said so on the phone."

"Listen," Vivi said. Her face shed a layer of pretense that Rebecca hadn't noticed was there. "What's going on?"

"What are you talking about?" She shook her head, as if to shake off the direction this conversation was taking.

"With you. What is going on with you."

"What's going on with me is that I'm looking for a job. Or looking into getting another degree. I've taken up running. What else? I don't know—I've been going on some dates?"

Vivi just stared.

"You read the *Times* article," said Rebecca. "You read all the articles. You said so on my voice mail. So I know you know what's going on."

Vivi sat up straighter, looked out for the drinks, and when they were not in sight, she returned her attention to Rebecca. "You're acting insane," she said.

"I'm acting insane?" asked Rebecca.

"Yes. Listen. You are my best friend," said Vivi, as if—at the moment—this might not be an altogether welcome truth. "Your father made a series of bad decisions, but that doesn't give you the right . . ."

"The right to *what?*"

The waiter returned with his appropriately lascivious waiter grin. They both turned their attention to him so completely that it seemed amazing to Rebecca that he neither blushed nor fumbled the tray. He set down their drinks with care. Not a drop spilled from the chilled martini glass, and Rebecca had to sit on her hands in order not to grab it before it was fully relinquished.

Vivi took a discreet sip of wine. "That's perfect," she told him approvingly, and then, to Rebecca after he took his leave once more, "I must have left you ten messages."

Her skin, Rebecca noticed with a stab of pure envy, looked particularly good. From the first moment Rebecca saw her tonight, Vivi had looked younger, and Rebecca finally realized it was because Vivi had actually gained some weight. Huh. She carried it well. Back before they'd conversed about something other than the all-encompassing lawsuit against him, Rebecca's father had been in the habit of asking her to please gain five pounds. Rebecca wondered: If she'd done so, would she look mysteriously younger, like Vivi, or simply thirty-two years old and five pounds too heavy?

"I know you've been calling," Rebecca said. She took a long sip of her martini. "And I'm sorry. It was rude of me not to return your calls."

"I don't give a shit about your manners."

"I know," said Rebecca, and suddenly she really did know. She knew that Vivi was truly worried and that here she was acting like a pain in the ass. Just as she knew that if she'd understood the seriousness of the lawsuit brought against her father by the justice department on behalf of the IRS—if her father had been remotely straight with her—she might have in fact followed Gabriel's advice and not gone through with quitting her own lucrative position at the firm. She might have followed Gabriel's advice, and maybe she would have finally pushed through her chronic, mostly professional dissatisfaction, and maybe—it was possible!—they would still be together. But knowing all of this did not make it any easier to stop acting like a pain in the ass. In fact, the knowledge that she was acting this way made Rebecca more impatient than ever. *"What's going on?"* she repeated. "My father—who, as you know has always made a big deal about being an honest guy, wronged by my cheating mother and all that—has been nailed for tax fraud. *Fraud.*"

"Well, yes," said Vivi, "but how is he?"

Rebecca shrugged. Once she knew—courtesy of the *New York Times* business section—exactly how much money he'd hidden in offshore accounts for over fifteen years (and on which he'd avoided paying those much-discussed taxes), she'd had a hard time not bringing greed and hypocrisy and irresponsibility into every conversation. The last time she'd seen her father, he was moving into a Midtown rental the size of his former study. This, after so many years of flying back and forth to China in pursuit of . . . what exactly? She'd lost track of his ambitions. First it was BMW, and when that never amounted to anything, he'd invested in some Western-style hotel—but nothing had ever brought him the success that he craved, the success for which he'd gotten risky and stupid and screwed with the IRS. She'd gone with her father to the diner on the ground floor of the new building and ordered sad weak coffee that neither of them drank. He'd continued with his plentiful excuses. He repeated that he hadn't done anything that any schmuck with a business degree and a passport wasn't doing all over the globe. He said, yet again, that he was being unfairly targeted.

But you broke the law, Rebecca said.

And this was how he'd looked at her: as if all those decades of discussing honesty and strong character and being a decent person had added up to nothing. As if, really, *he* was disappointed in *her* because she hadn't been paying attention to what he'd actually been saying all these years. As if they'd been engaged the whole time in a kind of double-speak: Don't do as I *say,* do as I *do.*

You think it was easy, he'd asked, *keeping you in the manner to which you'd been accustomed?*

She barely hesitated before throwing money on the table and walking out that smudged glass door.

Rebecca, he yelled after her, but if he was anything besides angry, he hadn't shown it.

"He must be terrified," said Vivi now.

"I don't think so," said Rebecca. "But, then again, what do I know?" She swallowed slowly, savored the kick of gin. "I wouldn't know."

"What are you talking about? You can't pretend you and your father aren't close. Whether or not he's a shady businessman, he's still your dad. He's still Ed!"

"I haven't talked to him in three months."

Vivi sat back on the banquette, clearly at something of a loss. Rebecca, perhaps unfairly, was pretty sure how Vivi had thought this evening might go: Rebecca dishing about her dad, dishing about the court case; venting and maybe crying and certainly realizing how lucky she was to have Vivi, who was (she really was) particularly good at joint venting.

"I don't want to talk about it," said Rebecca. "I'm too angry."

Vivi nodded.

"And," she continued, "you can't tell me that you'd be so compassionate if you found out that *your* father had done this."

"I don't know," said Vivi.

"That's because you know it could never happen."

"Maybe," Vivi acknowledged.

Rebecca looked down at her ragged fingernails. She tried to picture Hugh in a situation remotely similar to her father's. She could not. Hugh was too transparent for corruption. *You saved my life* is what Hugh had whispered to Rebecca at the airport sixteen years ago, when they'd said the strangest of goodbyes. She'd felt Vivi watching, she'd felt her father watching, and she'd been intensely awkward. Hugh had smiled when he'd seen Rebecca's father at the airport. He had smiled for real when her father approached them, out of breath, his face in a serious scowl. *Will someone please tell me what the hell is going on here?* She would always remember how her father was sweating through his usually crisp Italian white button-down shirt. Knowing what she knew now—that he had returned not an hour before from that first trip to China, the trip that had played no small part in the chain of events that led to his undoing—rendered this already uncomfortable memory that much more so.

"All right," Vivi finally said. "So are you hungry?"

Rebecca nodded. This was what she'd wanted from this evening: to live in the fading sphere of their genuine common ground, and if that was currently limited to a shared love of food and drink, so be it. When they'd fought on that bench in the middle of Broadway, they were on their way to a falafel lunch, and they'd both later admitted that part of their mutual distress was that—on top of their conflict—they were depriving themselves of eating that falafel together. Their one conflict during the whole summer they'd Eurailed was on a Naxos beach, midday: Rebecca wasn't hungry and Vivi was disappointed.

Rebecca signaled for another martini. "Go ahead and order. You know what I like." Then she stood up and made her way to the ladies' room. As soon as Vivi was out of sight, Rebecca felt chastened, remembering the night Gabriel had moved out and how she'd cried and cried into the phone and how Vivi had listened. And then, when Rebecca hadn't been able to stop crying, when Vivi told Rebecca that she'd stay on the line but that Rebecca needed to go stand on her head because it really would make her feel better, Rebecca had yelled, *Fuck that, fuck you, I'm not standing on my fucking head,* and Vivi hadn't argued.

In the single bathroom of this downtown hotel: light so dim she could barely find the toilet paper. In the mirror: a dark-haired animal, a waif applying lip gloss. On exiting: another woman with the familiar (and strangely conspiratorial) post-ladies'-room grin of women all over the globe. She felt the martini. Rebecca floated above the floor this time; she didn't hear the clicking of her heels.

When she returned, she sat right next to Vivi on the banquette. "So tell me something else," she said. "Something good."

Vivi's face cracked into the smile that Rebecca would always think of as *the best*. As if life really worked like a yearbook or a tabloid: *best legs, best voice, best smile.* "I'm pregnant," Vivi said.

"You—"

"Yup."

Rebecca recalled the two different waiting rooms for both of Vivi's abortions: one in college (the father was in her Italian poetry class; a sweet, brief encounter), and one that had put an end to a spectacularly bad affair in her mid-twenties, during which Vivi was frequently and uncharacteristically weepy.

"Are you going to—"

"Nope." Vivi shook her head definitively. "Not this time."

Both times Vivi was sure that she'd done the right thing. And now? Rebecca scanned her friend's face for anxiety. She saw none. Vivi seemed concerned only with her placement of pillows, and as she arranged herself on the window banquette it took several tries to get the velvet ones against her lower back just so. Vivi had always made a production of sitting exactly the way she wanted.

"I'm sure about it," she said now. "Four months," said Vivi, placing her hand on her belly, which Rebecca only now noticed but for some reason had no inclination at all to touch. There it was: the bump; minor but there. And Rebecca realized then that Vivi was happy, really happy; during the past half hour, she'd been actively repressing the extent of her joy. Rebecca was suddenly aware of heat rising to her own cheeks, aware that this heat was a result of feeling too many things at once, including embarrassment, because Vivi was clearly worried how Rebecca would handle this news.

"You're pregnant," Rebecca said weakly. She felt dizzy. "Boy, I should have called you back."

"It's okay," Vivi said.

As Rebecca took in the smile, the posture, the slightly bowed head, it became evident that Vivi had found her pregnant persona. Rebecca couldn't quite put her finger on it, but Liv Ullmann came to mind. A splash of Ingrid Bergman.

"I'm happy for you," Rebecca managed. "I don't know who the father is, so that's a little weird, but I'm really happy for you."

"You do know who he is, actually."

"The Sentimental Penis?"

"Ew. Rebecca. It's Brian," said Vivi. She was nodding.

As Vivi said Brian's name, *whoosh* came the pine needles, the rush of nicotine, and the particular longing that accompanied being sixteen years old. It was a different class of longing—more desperate but also more hopeful—from the kind Rebecca had these days. "No way."

Vivi continued to nod.

Rebecca pictured his shiny brown hair, that freckle-tan skin. She pictured his ease, the way he smiled while sitting on the branch of a tree. "*Brian?* The Dirty Hippie King?"

"The *who?*"

Rebecca shook her head fuzzily. "You had sex with Brian and you're pregnant? You *do* know how to steal my thunder." They were both smiling now, but Rebecca realized she was also shaking.

"It's been crazy," said Vivi. "I was in Baja shooting with these leatherback-sea-turtle people—whole other story—and I bumped into him. On the beach. He had just finished surfing," said Vivi. "That's when I first called you," she said. "I hadn't even seen the *Times* article yet. And, listen—I know you don't want to talk about it and I know your father dug his own hole, but I just want to say that it *did* cross my mind that the reporter was out to get him."

"So does Brian live in Baja?" Rebecca asked.

"San Francisco. He's a journalist, actually."

"What does he write about?" Rebecca inquired as if, at this point in the conversation, Brian's bylines really mattered.

"Food, politics."

"Food politics?"

"Not really. More like separately—food and also politics. *Rebecca,*" said Vivi, suddenly impatient, "I'm so sorry about that article. I'm so sorry about your dad."

"I know," she said.

"And I know this isn't great timing, my news—"

"Don't be ridiculous—*please*. It just makes it worse. It's better right now if you talk."

And—almost obediently—Vivi began to ramble: "I never thought I'd even *want* to be pregnant before I was forty. Let alone before thirty-five. I was sure I'd wait till that last shriveled egg was crying out for mercy. That, or adopt. And, it's funny, but for some reason I always pictured doing it on my own. . . ."

Rebecca half-listened to Vivi, grateful to know that she *could* half-listen, that Vivi fully expected her to. She was not sure what she'd expected this evening, but this was definitely not it. Brian was from Greenwich, Connecticut. His father and Vivi's father learned to sail at the same club on Fishers Island. Vivi had traveled around the world and attached herself to a pretty diverse sampling of men, but at the end of the day it was Brian she would choose, Brian Kells Avery (Rebecca remembered his full name from their boarding school facebook, as well as his puka-shell necklace in the picture, his sweetly mischievous grin). She felt her face flushing from the alcohol in a way that always brought it all back—drinking wine with the Shipleys in Anguilla and everything that followed.

"Do your parents know you're pregnant?" Rebecca asked now, even though she knew. Vivi had always told them everything.

Vivi nodded. "They're excited about the baby, but they're worried that if we don't get married now we might drag our feet too long. Or something. I'm not sure exactly what they're afraid of. But I just—" Vivi took another slow sip of wine. "We'll have a big party after the baby is born. My friend Marion—remember Marion?—she got married when she was six months' pregnant, and she looked around at all the tables like: *What the hell am I doing here?*"

Rebecca gnawed on an olive pit until it was smooth. "Did you just ask me if I remember Marion? As if I might not?"

"It was a turn of phrase," said Vivi.

"Aha. Well, I'm surprised her family went for a big shotgun wedding. As I remember, they were pretty conservative."

"Yeah, *well*, Marion's their only daughter," said Vivi, neither acknowledging Rebecca's slight aggression nor backing down. "I guess the idea of missing the opportunity to host her wedding trumped their politics."

"I guess so," said Rebecca. "Good for them."

And suddenly she remembered a window. Or was it a terrace? Sitting by the window with Marion and Vivi. Rebecca couldn't help remembering what Marion was wearing: a nubby wool miniskirt and Wellington boots. Spring.

Rebecca: I heard you have to submit your parents' tax returns in order to get into St. A's.

Marion: Bullshit.

Rebecca: One of the members Maced an African American student outside the building last year. They said it was an accident. Like, whoops— sorry—we thought you were dangerous.

Marion: Total and complete bullshit. Where do you come up with these fabrications?

Rebecca: They have an undisputed history of anti-Semitism and racism.

Marion: Welcome to America, where things can actually change.

"So how is Marion?" she asked.

Vivi looked at her shrewdly. "You don't care about Marion," she said.

"You're right," said Rebecca, "I don't."

She hadn't smoked a cigarette in sixteen years—not since the night that Hugh lost two fingers—and, not for the first (or five hundredth) time, she really really wanted one.

She settled for finishing her drink. She looked at Vivi, sitting on a banquette: black wrap dress and incomprehensible symbolic tattoos, the familiar way she ran a multi-ringed hand through her neo-hippie, still-blond hair. It struck her that—more than the fuller face and the lovely skin, more than her new no-joke cleavage that she was not afraid to flaunt—Vivi's power lay here: Not once during the whole time that Rebecca had known her had Vivi ever made a negative remark about her own appearance. She could be bloated beyond recognition and she would—Rebecca knew—find a way to telegraph that look as the way a woman *should* look.

"You know what I thought of when I saw Brian again?" asked Vivi. "When we started talking on that beach?"

Rebecca shook her head.

"How you sounded after you met Gabriel," she said. "I never imagined I could feel that level of pure interest."

She remembered that morning perfectly. Kissing Gabriel goodbye outside her apartment building. Taking her cordless phone onto the fire escape and watching the sunrise. Then calling Vivi, who mumbled, *Hello? Hello?* And *Who is this?*

Just kill me now is what she'd said. What a drama queen.

She'd taken a rare day out of town for a friend's birthday. People lay around a swimming pool in the sun-dappled woods of the Catskills. That she'd chosen to surround herself with people, she realized—as she often did, a little too late—was a bad idea, because she wasn't in any kind of social mood. She closed her eyes and tried to relax but instead found herself casting about for how, during law school—somewhere between wanting *to help people* and realizing she didn't have a great legal mind—she'd been sucked into accepting a summer offer from a prestigious corporate New York firm despite never having wanted to work in corporate law, and how it was that she'd been at the same firm for over three years.

But, for a second, none of it mattered—not her tenuous career track, not her antisocial tendencies—when this stranger arrived and waved a general friendly hello. He wasn't particularly fit or spectacular-looking, but when he took off all of his clothes and jumped into the water, she felt it in her toes. It wasn't that he'd stripped completely naked without modesty but that he'd somehow accomplished this without even a whiff of exhibitionism. She'd sat up taller, watching for what he'd do next. When he finally came up for air, he'd caught her staring, and she hadn't looked away.

Have a swim, he'd said. He didn't sound foreign, not exactly, but he didn't sound American, either.

I forgot my suit.

He laughed.

I'm not into public nakedness. She'd shrugged. *For me, that is. Works for you, though.*

Oh, you reckon?

Later that day, when—fully clothed—he'd revealed himself as a corporate litigator, she'd been even more intrigued. He was passionate about his job, and for a while (six months? a year?) she saw her own work differently, because she saw everything differently, because—as Vivi had pointed out—that's just how far gone she was.

"So now you have that *level of interest*?" asked Rebecca. "In Brian?"

Vivi nodded. "I mean, I think so."

"Proceed with caution," Rebecca laughed, and she hated her own laugh, so dark and dry.

"But would you ever trade what you had?" Vivi asked.

"In a heartbeat."

"I'm just talking about the beginning," maintained Vivi.

But Rebecca had nothing more to say. Vivi's insistence on romance—which had once been enthralling, then mildly annoying—only made her seem further away than ever. Rebecca couldn't—or wouldn't—relate.

Vivi had barely touched her wine, but now she basically swilled it. "You know he asked if you were a surgeon or a CEO or something," she said. "He assumed you were doing something important."

"Who did?"

"Brian," said Vivi.

"The father of your child," Rebecca said; again her dark laugh.

"People always expect that you're doing great things." Vivi said this without a hint of pity. She said this as if to say: *Pay attention*. Rebecca wanted to stop her. She wanted to stop Vivi's efforts to shore her up and also the sob that was spiraling upward from her gut with not a single, tolerable, possible resolution.

But Vivi didn't stop. "Because you are that person," she said, deadly serious. "You were in high school, you were in college, and you are now." Vivi leaned forward, so close that Rebecca could smell the sour-sweet warmth of Bordeaux. "You're just in a funk. You've had a shitty shitty year."

"Shitty shitty bang bang." Rebecca mimed a gun to her head.

"Not funny."

"No," Rebecca said, contrite, "you're right."

By the time the food arrived, she was dizzy with hunger. She tore into bread and cannellini beans, the paper-thin prosciutto, the big green olives, and the cheese.

"I can't believe he really left," Vivi said, quietly.

"Well," Rebecca said, "that's because you're an optimist."

"Is that so," she said. "Because you know that when you say that, what I think you actually mean is *dumb*."

"I'm not going to even respond to that. You're an optimist and a romantic. You are."

"Fine, but—"

"From the moment I quit my job, we were doomed. I thought it wouldn't matter to him, but it did. Sometimes things are simple."

"I guess," said Vivi. "But he had been operating under the impression that you both wanted the same things. Right?"

"What are you saying?"

"Nothing. I'm just saying that when you met, and for a good couple of years, he thought you were after the same life. So he probably felt judged when you stepped off—what do you call it?"

"The moving sidewalk," Rebecca said.

"Right," Vivi said. "I love that image."

"Judged?"

"Yes, judged."

"What are you trying to do to me? It's over. Vivi, he left me."

"I know."

"And *I* know you're a great big fan of his, but Gabriel only loved me when he thought my drive was really drive and not sheer anxiety."

"I just can't believe that."

What Rebecca chose not to mention was that, despite how driven Gabriel was (and he *was*, and she'd loved that about him!), he'd always made a point of turning his BlackBerry off when at all possible. What Rebecca also chose not to mention was that his impatience with her had more than a little something to do with the fact that she was constantly checking messages and returning phone calls and that, when she finally went ahead and quit her job and *still* couldn't manage to find a way to stop doing either one of these things, when she was still anxious and resisted his (and her therapist's) suggestions to make time for him even when she had nothing *but* time—this was when their relationship took a truly bad turn.

"Look," Rebecca insisted, "people like Gabriel get it done. And he didn't have the patience for my . . . current ambivalence with, well, pretty much everything. I was—I *am* pretty directionless right now. I'm not entirely sure I blame him. He's basically a good person. Whatever that means."

"Don't you know?"

Rebecca slowly shook her head.

"Well, that makes sense," Vivi acknowledged. "That you would feel confused about that these days. I mean, with your dad—"

"I said I don't know," Rebecca said, hoping to put an end to this thread of conversation.

Vivi, to her credit, went silent. Until: "Sometimes you just remind me so much of my father."

Rebecca's stomach was suddenly far too full. She felt nerves spike her gut and wished she'd stuck to olives. "I remind you of your father?"

"What—I've said that before."

"No, you haven't."

"Yes, I have. Of course I have."

"How do you mean?" asked Rebecca, as if she was only vaguely interested in knowing.

"Well, you know, you're both kind of idealistic and passionate and also kind of difficult." She winced. "You're both difficult to talk to sometimes. Sorry."

She shrugged. "Don't be."

The waiter, with excellent timing, set down another martini. Rebecca took a greedy sip.

"Okay," Vivi said, dispensing with her worried expression. "Okay, listen. I have a brilliant idea."

"Yes?"

"Go see him."

"Go see who?"

"My father."

Rebecca felt her stomach flip straight into her throat. As if she hadn't thought of that already, over so many years, with accompanying fantasy scenarios of how such a visit might go. Thinking of Hugh never changed. No matter what her life looked like. And though she'd seen him at Vivi's college graduation—and several times during that visit, once with her own father present—when Rebecca thought about Hugh Shipley it was always the two of them together in an unfamiliar room.

"Go see your father?" she finally managed.

"I mean go work for him," said Vivi.

"Volunteer?"

"You obviously need a real change. And of course he always needs help. You have an Ivy League law degree and you've just—of your own accord—left one of the most powerful firms in the free world. So you need to figure some shit out. My parents are good at hosting confused people and—"

"I don't want to be that person."

"What person?"

"That person—you know—who travels to Africa because they're *confused*."

"My father did it." Vivi shrugged.

"That was the sixties. We know better now."

"You should call him. You should go."

Rebecca started to feel an uncomfortable pounding in her chest. She imagined sitting down at her butcher-block table and dialing Hugh and Helen's number in Dar es Salaam. *Hello?* She could imagine Hugh's voice—the somehow intimate timbre of it—and, stomach dropping, ears popping, she felt as if she were taking an elevator to the world's highest floor.

"Really?" she asked Vivi.

"That's what I'm saying."

Rebecca sat back. She set her drink down. "You know, your parents did invite me."

"When?"

"A long time ago, but they did. They said it was an open invitation to visit wherever they moved in the world." She neglected to mention that Helen had issued the invitation during Vivi's high school graduation and that Rebecca was pretty sure that, even then, she hadn't meant it.

"Open invitation?" said Vivi now. "Well—so if they said that . . ."

Rebecca smiled at Vivi's enthusiasm, at her unflappable belief in dramatic solutions. Inside, though, she was already mentally creating a checklist: vaccinations, sublet her apartment, find someone decent to cover her volunteer shift at the domestic-violence hotline, decide whether or not to let her father know . . .

"It's funny about your parents. All this time and I've never seen them at home. I can't quite picture them at home anywhere."

Vivi shrugged. "They're liminal creatures."

Rebecca took the last delicious sip of her drink. "Maybe I am, too."

"You?" asked Vivi. "I don't think so. I think you like to be right in the juicy center. Right now you're just not sure exactly which center."

"That's generous," Rebecca said. And she meant it. "That's a very generous read." And right then—as if the news had taken exactly this long to sink in—she put her hand on Vivi's belly.

"You're going to be fine," Vivi said.

Rebecca found that her breath was matched with Vivi's, and for the first time all evening, she actually felt like talking. "My father's going to jail."

"You don't know that yet," Vivi said.

"I do," whispered Rebecca. "I found out yesterday. He was sentenced to a year."

She was grateful for Vivi's silence. How she only put her hand on top of Rebecca's and together they waited for movement, some simple proof of life.

"He's not moving now," said Vivi. "He's a morning kind of guy."

"A boy?"

Vivi nodded.

"You found out?"

She shook her head. "But I know."

Rebecca did not say that she had only a fifty–fifty chance of being correct. And she also didn't take her hand away.

Chapter Eighteen

Africa, April 2005

Hugh made his way slowly through the airport in Dar es Salaam. Past the lipstick-red chairs and the hand-painted signs, past Indian women in saris and African men in dashikis and tracksuits and baggy jeans, through a group of pale spotty teenagers—whom Rebecca pegged as missionaries—Hugh Shipley came forward. His face was as tanned and craggy and stubbornly handsome as ever, and his hair—though thinner in front—still reminded her of all those boarding school boys. He was wearing his uniform—white linen shirt, khaki pants—and looked as if he hadn't changed clothes since the last time she'd seen him, ten years earlier with Vivi, when they'd all had an early dinner not far from campus, somewhere on Broadway.

His two fingers were still missing. The lack of those fingers was such an integral part of him; one could argue it was the most notable aspect of his appearance, and it amazed her not only that the lack was permanent but that she'd been the last person to see Hugh with ten fingers. No one was more entrenched with the story of that particular loss.

Now he kissed Rebecca's cheek, and—when she briefly closed her eyes—she tricked herself into smelling not his ripe and unfamiliar stink but the mussels and French fries they'd all eaten together, the salt he'd sprinkled in his beer. Hugh needed a shower, yes, but there was also something unequivocally pleasing about this familiar greeting; they were friends, old family friends. She felt relieved and also—what? Apprehensive? *Was* she apprehensive? Because here was Hugh and she was still maddeningly attracted to him. All the alcohol and tropical maladies hadn't claimed him, not yet.

"Rebecca," he said.

Hugh exchanged greetings—*Jambo! Mambo! Habari!*—with so many people as they continued through the airport that Rebecca began repeating *Jambo* or *Mambo* or *Habari* along with him. Two men and one woman separately said, *Hello, sister,* as she passed, which made her blush with ridiculous pleasure, even if this greeting was twice followed by offers to sell her bargain DVDs.

As they walked toward the baggage claim, Hugh calmly explained that there wasn't any time for her to so much as say hello to Helen and spend one night with them. "In fact," he said, finally stopping and glancing at his watch, "if you need to use the bathroom, now's the time."

"You mean we're going this minute?" asked Rebecca. She'd been traveling for nearly twenty hours. Her mouth felt like a petri dish and her joints were aching; she could smell herself in this heat, and the scent was *eau de airplane blanket, eau de airplane lasagna.* She had counted on at least a shower and a meal at Hugh and Helen's before heading into one of the world's most remote regions, to a town that wasn't listed on most Tanzanian maps.

Hugh nodded. "Helen is embarrassed that I'm not letting you rest. But the trucks are arriving tomorrow and we have to be there—if not to receive them, then *right* after—or the whole operation will be shot to hell."

"Of course," said Rebecca, not comprehending a thing.

Hugh took Rebecca's bag, said something in Swahili to two men, and told Rebecca to follow him. What else would she do? She'd even explicitly agreed to this—to follow what he said—during the one brief phone conversation they'd had before she booked the ticket. She'd hoped to offer legal services—something specific—but he said she'd caught him at a moment when what he needed most was an extra set of hands and company he could stand. He'd offered her heat (and he wasn't kidding; it must have been well over one hundred degrees) and the opportunity to visit Lake Tanganyika, where she could help distribute mosquito nets.

Sign me up, she'd said.

And though she knew that to some extent she wanted to do this in order to put off her own unpleasant personal decision-making, she also knew that she'd always had a healthy interest in Hugh's career, quite apart from her debatably healthy interest in Hugh himself.

You're sure you want to come? he'd asked, before hanging up.

I'm sure.

I have to tell you, I'm surprised. You have never struck me as that girl who's always dreamed of an African adventure.

Well, I'm not, she'd said. *Of course I'm not.*

There was silence. And in that silence: worn rubber handlebars sloughed off onto her sweaty hands; Hugh leaned solidly onto her back; and there they were on an island road—blazing bright sun and dark-green shade—up into the hills.

But, she'd said, *delivering mosquito nets to impoverished people hardly sounds like safari.*

And she could picture his grin, his vodka sweating next to the phone in a place that she'd never seen. *Okay,* he said.

Okay, you want me to come?

Good ol' Rebecca. You've always tried to be helpful.

Why does that sound insulting?

It isn't. He cleared his throat. *You want to help? You can come.*

I do, she said. *I want to. And I've seen pictures of the lake. I won't lie—beauty doesn't hurt.*

It never does, he said.

On the runway, the light was painfully bright and their five-seater had ominous-looking red flames painted on the wings. Either way, she had vowed to herself not to express anything close to fear over flying. Or reptiles or insects: She'd mentally prepared herself for snakes coiled in corners and spiders crawling out of drains. Still, when Hugh pointed out the window to the shockingly blue expanse of water, she wished she could simply marvel, instead of imagining falling straight out into it—sky, lake, death. She stiffly gave Hugh a thumbs-up and was pleased that at least she got a laugh.

Two hours that felt like less and more all at once and then finally down, down on the ground. Oh, how she loved that moment. She could imagine forgetting the landing strip, the rocky brown earth and fat trees, but never the pitted dirt roads whose shocks she felt in her bowels, or the low huts, tall grasses, and three brown bulls stolidly blocking traffic. She would never forget the cluster of boys who emerged with the traffic and crowded the Land Rover, to whom Hugh gave pens and candy. They were wearing strikingly clean plaid button-down shirts, as if a bonanza of American Eagle overstock had come in just that week. With their oddly grown-up posturing and their wide warm smiles, they could have sold her anything. She'd never forget those boys. Or the one girl among all those boys, a yellow polyester cheongsam hanging down to her bony ankles.

Just before dusk, against a pink and purple backdrop of a sky straight out of the early days of Technicolor, they arrived at a series of conical huts built along the lakeshore. There was a main bar area in a larger hut with swept-clean floors, flowers in vases, and billowy white curtains. There were tea candles, tables set for dinner.

"Are you serious?" asked Rebecca, punch-drunk; her giddiness went beyond jet lag.

"What."

"This is a bit more Isak Dinesen than I pictured."

"It won't all be like this," Hugh said, somewhere between sheepish and proud. "See you in twenty minutes?" he asked, without exactly asking. "I prefer to sleep in a tent," he said, wandering off. She had to roll her eyes—*of course you do.*

A young African man with round wire eyeglasses carried her bag and showed her to her room. He was tall and slender, and she could just as easily picture him walking a runway in Paris or nursing an espresso in a Brooklyn café, busy on a laptop.

"Now," he said, pointing toward where a mosquito net was tied up but ready to envelop whomever lay down on the immaculate-looking white sheets. "Let me show you this," he said. "This is the bed."

"Thank you," she said.

"This is your first time to Tanganyika?"

"It's my first time to Africa."

"Ah." He nodded. He couldn't have been older than twenty-five, but he took his time, embodying the rhythms of a much older person. "And how do you like our country?"

"It's gorgeous," she said, "of course."

"Traffic very bad in Dar, very bad in Moshi. Very bad. This is better. This is very nice, very tranquil."

She nodded. "It is."

"Now, this," he continued. "This is the bath." The small room looked out over a vegetable garden. She recognized Swiss chard sprouting from soil-filled tires. "Now, this—let me show you—this is the soap for the body. This," he said, "is a cup."

"Thank you," she managed, so grateful for it all that she wasn't even tempted to giggle at his tender and absurd attention to detail. "Thank you so much," she said.

After she'd showered (warmish water! decent pressure!), she changed into gauzy pants and a worn T-shirt, both of which were innocuous enough to give off the impression that she hadn't given a thought to what she'd packed for this trip. This particular T-shirt and pants said: *I am of the belief that there are far more important things to think about than clothes.* They said this while still being mysteriously flattering to her figure. These garments were time-tested and had been peeled off her in East Hampton, Key West, and Fire Island over the last several summers.

Do I really think this way? she asked herself, half self-loathing, half amused.

Yes, seemed to be the answer, *yes, it seems that you do.*

She managed to resist lip gloss; she made her way to the bar.

There were candles and salads and wine and the stars. There were no other guests. The serious young man who'd showed Rebecca her room was also the waiter and bartender. The Dutch owners came out for a chat and then they disappeared. And then here was Hugh. Hugh Shipley, looking a shade more dapper after bathing or maybe even just dousing his hair with water. Here was Hugh, who made Robert Redford look like a total wuss. It was ridiculous, but she felt no urge to laugh.

They were looking out at a landscape so pure and at a sky so clear that to remark upon the beauty would be to taint it. She was sure—positive—that he thought this way, too.

Nobody was talking.

"How did you end up coming here?" she finally blurted.

He squinted, as if trying to recall. "I had an adventurer friend."

"As one does."

He grinned. "Oh, yes? And who's your adventurer friend?"

"Vivi," she said. "Of course."

"Right," he said warmly. "Of course."

"So your friend?"

"His boat got stuck in a typhoon and he was stranded on the lake for days. This was before—you know—this place existed." He gestured to the bar, and when he realized it had looked as if he was signaling for more wine, he didn't bother to correct the young man's assumption. "When he finally made it back to Dar, he said that while he was stuck, he realized that there were all these people living on the lake so completely cut off from the world, how there was no health care, absolutely none. There were a couple of clinics that were theoretically supposed to refer people to the national hospitals, but those clinics didn't even have water or electricity—never mind that any access to the interior is severely limited because of the terrible roads. At any rate, he'd known most of this before, but it had taken his getting stuck to understand what it really meant. So he got stuck and then came to me."

"Does that happen a lot? People coming to you and asking for help?"

"What—" He smiled. "You mean like you?"

"Ha. Well, yes, I guess. But I was talking about your field, your experience running clinics. The need is so great. And you've been here for such a long time."

"That's certainly relative." He watched as the young man poured more wine. "Thank you, Omar."

She smiled at the young man—Omar—who nodded and left. If Omar and the Dutch owners considered them at all, what did they think? Father and daughter? Doubtful.

"But," she persisted, "people must come and go with all kinds of plans."

"Oh yes. Lots of plans," Hugh said tightly. "We all have lots of plans."

"True," she said, waiting for him to explain his sarcasm. "And?"

Hugh visibly grimaced. She tried and failed not to take his expression personally. She waited for him to speak.

He didn't.

"Are you all right?" she finally asked.

"Don't pay attention to me right now," he said. "It's not productive."

"I didn't know we were being productive right this minute. I thought we were finishing dinner."

"Vivi thinks I'm a depressive. Did you know that?"

She didn't. But she wasn't surprised to hear it. She neither nodded nor shook her head. She didn't, she suddenly realized, want to talk about Vivi.

Hugh motioned toward the bar, and this time there was no mistaking his intent. Omar brought Hugh a different bottle, without a label, and two small glasses. "What was I saying?"

"Depression?"

"No, not that."

"Then . . ." She hesitated; did she really want to have a conversation about Hugh's mental health? "Then why did you mention it?" Evidently she did.

"I'm not depressed," he said. And he smiled. "I'm not depressed right now."

"What does Helen think?" she asked, both without planning to do so and instantly regretting it. "She's always seemed—I don't know—intuitive." *What was she doing?* "I've always had the feeling she could somehow—this sounds strange—that if I were in trouble or something"—*Stop talking,* she told herself, to absolutely no avail—"or if I needed someone, she's always seemed understanding. Not that I know her all that well, in a way. Not that I really have any idea, actually." She finished her wine and waited for Hugh to put an end to this embarrassing ramble.

He did no such thing.

"She just seems like a really good person. And she's so beautiful," she said. "I mean, obviously."

He nodded.

"Your friend," said Rebecca. She wanted to leave the table and dive into the water. She wanted to go to her nice clean bed and read the copy of *Vogue* that she'd bought at JFK and already read cover to cover. "You were talking about your friend. How he was stuck."

"Right," said Hugh. He poured her the liquor from the mysterious bottle, and though she thought she might very well pass out if she had more than a sip, she didn't stop him. "Let's just say this fellow knew me well."

She took a sip and nearly retched from the poisonous chalk-acid taste. "Don't laugh," she sputtered at his bemused expression. "I'm not much of a drinker," she lied. "Besides, anyone's a lightweight compared to you."

"True," he said. "Bottoms up."

She took another sip. It tasted marginally better this time, like the way she imagined moonshine would taste. And with only two sips, she felt her body simultaneously spring to life and revolt, much like how she felt when she dreamed about sex but woke with an intense need to pee. "Who coined the phrase *moonshine?*" she heard herself ask.

"No idea. How about white lightning?" He shrugged. "Or kill me quick."

"Sorry?"

"Kill me quick. *Kumi Kumi.* That's what they call it in Kenya."

"Oh," she said, "I like that. Cuts right to the chase." She sipped some more. "So how," she asked, "how did he—the adventurer friend—how did he know you well?"

"Oh, I guess he knew I'm always up for going farther and farther away."

"Farther away from . . ."

He took a slow swallow. "There's always another level of isolation." He wasn't smiling.

"Isolation."

"Another spot." His eyes were solid, not glittery, not dull. "Another place."

"In the world? Or in your mind?"

Hugh shook his head. "I'm not talking about my goddamn psyche."

"I wasn't—"

"Four million people live directly on the lake. Eleven million live farther inland. And this is one of the only towns even accessible to the interior at all. If anyone needs to get out of here for real medical care—if anyone has the wherewithal to do so—there's one ship."

"A ship?"

"She was built in Germany and used here to control the lake during the First World War, before being scuttled by the Germans. Years later, the British Royal Navy salvaged her. And *now* . . . she's a ferry," he said, shaking his head with a certain incredulity that made her suspect his mind had ventured further than this history lesson.

"Does she have a name?" Rebecca asked.

"Who?" he asked, looking oddly defensive.

"The ship," she said. "The one you were just telling me about."

"I'm sorry," he acknowledged. "I'm distracted."

Here was the same man who'd looked at her madly while he was in pain and who, during a brief private moment in an Anguillan doctor's clinic, told her that she was an angel. She felt the alcohol rush through her now with so much sensation she thought she might get up from her chair and just sit in his lap. Just fold around him. As if, in doing so, she might flood him with the same feeling. To rid herself of it. Get it out. Get it done.

Instead, she took another sip. "You're distracted by . . ."

"Listen," he said. His wild brows were furrowed. His elbows were on the table.

"Hugh?"

"Helen left me."

"What?" She thought, for one crazed moment, that he must be lying, that he would mine her sympathies at any cost. And then she thought, *No, she's actually left him.* She could see it in his eyes. But how was that even possible? It was possible. And he was telling her this why? Why? Because he wanted her to know that he was free.

Shut it down, she thought. *Get ahold of yourself and—Forget about your father, but for Vivi. For Vivi, just shut it down.*

"I—it's been coming."

"What do you mean, *it's been coming?* Vivi didn't even say anything."

"That's because—" He shook his head. "That's because Vivi doesn't know."

"You've got to be kidding me." She was reeling—both with shock and a sheepish streak of utter, selfish delight.

He shook his head. "We're going to tell her. We'll find the right time. I'm afraid I just had to tell you. I'm . . . I'm not doing all that well."

"Oh," she said. "Oh. Well, that makes sense. That you wouldn't be, I mean."

"I'm sorry," he said. "I shouldn't have said anything."

"No," she said, relaxing somewhat. She had the first stirrings of sadness for Vivi, for whom—maybe now especially—this news would be devastating. She might have known more than she ever let on about her parents' discontentment, but there was no way she'd be prepared for this. "No, I'm glad you did."

She was suddenly desperate to find out if he was telling her this news—at least in part—as a way to ignite what had been lying dormant between them for all these years. She wanted to search his face for clues, but she was too cowardly for that. And so, for lack of a better alternative, she looked up at the stars. She imagined all the humans throughout time in socially uncomfortable situations who'd done the same thing with those same constellations. She could imagine the stars whispering: some disdainful, some amused. *Mortals,* they'd say, pointedly throwing off a bit more light.

"Let's not talk about it further," he was saying.

"Okay," she agreed.

"And, look," he said, brightening, "this is a valuable trip you've taken." She couldn't help but notice that his upbeat turn was entirely unconvincing. "I'm glad you've come," he continued. "When I was young, it was considered shocking that I went off to Africa in the first place, forget about not coming back. But I was a dilettante—I can say that now—and I didn't start with any real ambition. And it's not like my absence was any sacrifice for the American workforce, that's for certain. Not like your father—he always knew what he was doing, and he always knew how to get what he wanted."

"Yes, well, we both know how that turned out. I would imagine that even you saw the *Times* article."

In the absence of Hugh's response, there was only the slightest breeze.

She continued: "He's in jail, you know. Jail. For corruption—years of it. You do know he's in jail, right?"

Hugh looked out at the water and drank. She noticed that his eyes closed slightly as he did so.

"Rebecca?" He leaned forward at last. "Do me a favor and don't knock your dad."

"Okay," she said, taken by surprise.

"And don't count him out. Not yet."

"Fine," she said. Her face was burning; her head was spinning. How could Hugh Shipley be the one to suggest that she was being too harsh?

"Rebecca?"

"I said fine. I hear you."

Omar arrived once again, set down two small plates. "Ginger cake," he announced.

"Delightful." Hugh smiled.

"Thank you," said Rebecca.

They each took a bite.

"This is delicious, isn't it?" asked Hugh.

"Completely," said Rebecca.

She looked up at the thatched roof, out at the still black water. For that moment it was hard not to feel as if she and Hugh were simply away on vacation together a couple of years from now. She let herself imagine that, after the Shipleys' quick and painless divorce, Helen was elsewhere, ecstatic with a second husband. She let herself envision that Vivi, who had it all now—baby, career, Brian—stood behind all of her years of insistence on romance and gracefully accepted the fact that her best friend and her father were in love. In this fantasy, Rebecca realized, her father had to be dead. He was dead and she was guilty and grieving. That was why, she realized—as if any part of this fantasy had any foothold in reality—she and Hugh were on a lakeside vacation: He was helping her through her grief.

A pale pig was rooting around in the sand. A brown dog came up beside the pig. Rebecca pointed to the animals, and Hugh raised his glass in their direction.

She said, "There's a pig on the beach."

"And a dog," said Hugh, finally lightening up.

The water gently lapped on the shore. Candle flames slanted one way and then the other. "I can't believe I'm here."

She was no longer fifteen. She was, in fact, a woman in her thirties. She wasn't going to do anything about the feeling, so she might as well go ahead and admit, if only to herself, that in the absence of nuance—

fantasy, infatuation, girlhood crush born of an accidental intimacy—this is what she'd have to call her feelings for Hugh: love. And not just in her fantasy. She might be a grown woman, she may have come to understand Hugh and the world at large a bit better than she did sixteen years ago, but here she was and it felt basically the same as it had when she was with him in the kitchen in Aunt Kitty's Anguillan villa. She allowed herself to hear her father's words and to acknowledge that he might just be right about this one: *People don't change.*

"Right," he said, suddenly pushing back his chair. "So, I doubt you'll need to set an alarm, but you might want to." He stood up in three neat stages. If he was drunk, there was no way to tell. "We need to leave by six-thirty."

He didn't touch her shoulder or even look in her direction before heading for his tent, stumbling under the cover of darkness. And this absence of touch felt *more* thrilling somehow, as if he couldn't possibly touch her at this hour in this place without an obvious absence of propriety. The breeze was so light and the air so warm, but she was not distracted by the beauty of it all or even by the strangeness of where she was sitting. She wasn't distracted, not exactly. But it was as if everything—not only malaria and the absence of basic health care for nearly fifteen million people (how was that even possible?) but also her own minuscule embers of personal failure—everything seemed as far from here as civilization, which seemed even farther than the sky.

She couldn't have said what exactly happened between sleep and the morning's pitted road, but she knew that her head was pounding and a bug bite throbbed behind her knee. She knew she'd overslept and she knew that Hugh was aggravated (*What happened, Rebecca, with the alarm?*). He was aggravated but he was quiet, so when they pulled up to the missionary's hut and Hugh—suddenly furious—said, "Where the hell are they?" before banging his fist on the steering wheel, it was like hearing a car backfire: She had to catch her breath. Before this trip Re-

becca had certainly seen Hugh angry, but—excepting the long-ago moment when he'd insisted that she drive him to the doctor (and that was
scared, she reasoned)—she'd never seen him truly mad with anyone
besides himself.

"Goddamn it!" he said, getting out of the car and stretching his legs.
"Where in God's name are the trucks?"

"Hugh, please," said a stout pale woman who was standing in the
dirt drive and sipping from an aluminum mug. "I know you and I both
agree that *He* has nothing to do with this."

"Veronica," he yelled. He slammed shut the Land Rover's door.
"Where are the trucks?"

"Good morning," she said sternly. Irish.

"They promised," said Hugh. "They swore to me that the trucks
would be here with the nets. Trucks. Nets. Jesus, it is just not that complicated."

Veronica shook her head. She was probably somewhere around
Hugh's age and had a blond pageboy that was basically a bowl cut, but
the hair itself was gorgeous; she probably grew it and cut it yearly, sold
the hair, and gave the money away. Hugh had told Rebecca that Veronica was a missionary and that she'd been living on the lake for a good
thirty years. She had the eerie calm of someone who knows that she is,
in fact, indispensable.

"Yes, well . . ." Veronica squinted at Hugh with something like sympathy. She was obviously waiting for him to remember that he was too
old and too experienced to expect more than this.

"The problem with this country is that people stop expecting anything to work." Hugh stood with his feet firmly planted in the dirt of her
drive. "I'm not getting on that train. Okay?"

"Okay," said Veronica. "And who's this, then?" she asked, nodding
toward Rebecca, who took it as her cue to get out of the car.

"Rebecca here has come all the way from New York City. She's
young and able and I am not paying her a dime. And, believe me, she's
not going to hang around forever."

"I'm not that young," said Rebecca.

"Pleased to meet you," said Veronica. "Are you a doctor, then?"

"No," said Rebecca. "Lawyer."

"Well, then." She looked at Hugh oddly. "I see."

Rebecca watched as Hugh made phone calls, trying to track down the missing trucks. He yelled into his cellphone, and, when that connection failed because his battery died, he yelled into Veronica's. Veronica's house was small—a hut, really—but it had a generous back porch, where Rebecca watched a beetle nearly the size of Hugh's cellphone dig around in the dirt. A cat slunk beneath a drooping palm. The violet sky was cloudless, save one massive gathering at the edge of this morning's horizon, shot through with milk-white sun. And as she watched Hugh yell and curse at the local trucking outfit, she noticed that his agitation did nothing to detract from his appeal; she was only mildly ashamed that witnessing someone's so normally charming manner undergo such a complete transformation could produce this kind of thrill.

He lost it, she imagined telling her father in earlier, happier days. *He really did.*

Then again. She did not want to think about her father.

She'd received eight letters since he'd started his prison sentence two months earlier. *For the first time in my life,* he'd written, *I've gone ahead and grown a beard. Let me tell you, I look like a terrorist, but I figure, if not now, when?* His lawyer had secured him a spot upstate in Otisville—a prison that was evidently not nearly as cushy as the one where Martha Stewart had recently served, but it had been built (with a kosher meal option, with an in-house rabbi) as an answer to the evidently significant number of Orthodox Jewish criminals in the tristate area, who'd tried to make the case that serving time forced them to give up their religious lifestyle and thus violated their First Amendment rights. Talk about chutzpah, her father's lawyer had said when he suggested Otisville. Her father had agreed that a jail populated by Jews sounded safer, even if it irked him to think this, even if it was, in fact, a medium-security prison filled with a diverse assortment of criminals, including the coke dealer played by Johnny Depp in the movie *Blow.*

After a lifetime of being uninterested in cards, he'd borrowed a book from the lending library, taught himself poker, and joined a biweekly card game with a loan shark, a counterfeiter, a bank robber, and a "very bright" drug dealer from Nyack. He'd soon celebrate Passover in the only federal penitentiary that hosted a seder. She imagined him mumbling the kiddush, singing *Dayenu,* drinking grape juice instead of wine.

She'd written him back but not often, and she'd let him know about her last dentist appointment, when she was forced to keep her mouth open while Dr. Glasser speculated about her father's case. *What the hell was he thinking?* asked Glasser. *Okay, you can spit now.* She told him about the pharmacy on Madison, where she stopped for her favorite lip gloss and bumped into Mrs. Switt from their old apartment building, and although Rebecca had tried to avoid her, Mrs. Switt had greeted her not only as if someone had died but as if maybe Rebecca were the murderer.

He hadn't allowed her to visit, and she had been relieved.

In fact, she'd debated even telling him about her plans to come to Africa, not wanting to hear his inevitably strong opinions, but that inner debate didn't last long, because the guilt was simply too fierce. And because she was her father's daughter and was raised to imagine the worst—her own death by small-plane crash, for instance—she couldn't do that to him without at least the knowledge that she had gone in the first place. She'd expected him to immediately discourage this trip, and he had. In fact, five of the eight letters had consisted of diatribes against her plans.

She booked the ticket anyway and sent him a letter saying so. Neither of which had been remotely easy for her to do. In a shocking turn of events, she received a letter back, which said: *Okay, then. See Goldfarb for the shots and the antimalarial prescription.* Followed by exhaustive advice—pages—about the pitfalls of exchanging money.

"I sent the deposit," Hugh now said into the phone. "There was an explicit expectation that those nets were going to be here before me. Is that what happened?"

"Hugh," said Veronica.

Hugh waved her away. "I am asking you, is that what happened?"

"Rebecca," said Veronica. "He needs to get off the telephone."

"I'm sure he will, but—"

"Hugh," Veronica insisted loudly, and when he continued to ignore her, she turned to Rebecca and said, *"Come."*

Rebecca felt like a poorly trained dog as she followed Veronica around the house to the drive, where an African woman in bright pink cloth was sitting on the ground. She was holding a baby and weeping. "Shush now," Veronica soothingly told the woman. "Shush now, darling. You're here."

Rebecca came closer and saw that the baby's head was swollen so that he looked like a caricature of an alien baby, his forehead enormous and broad.

"This woman has walked eight days to find me," Veronica told her. "Now go get your friend Hugh."

So Rebecca—reeling—ran to get him, and when he waved her away, she found herself literally yanking the phone from his hand, shocked at her own gall. Shocked at how such proximity to Hugh was completely exhilarating. "You'll call back," she said, her heart speeding.

"How dare you?" he asked. His face was red, his voice hoarse. But though she'd surprised him, he did not look thrown off balance.

"Just come," said Rebecca, with a good approximation of calm, but she was sweating and shaken from not only the look that had passed across his face when she'd grabbed the phone but the strength in his resistance.

Still, he followed her around to the drive. And when Hugh saw the woman and baby, his face lost every stitch of aggravation; he knelt down on the ground and greeted the mother. She was wearing yellow beaded earrings, she looked tired but elegant, and Rebecca tried to conceive of how she'd managed to put in those earrings at some point before endeavoring to walk eight days. How she had managed to tie the sling, to put the baby inside. Hugh took the baby in his arms, stroked the baby's cheek. He spoke to the mother in Swahili, and the mother nodded and nodded. She didn't cry.

Hugh nodded as well. "There's a procedure," he said. "They need to get to Dar."

He spoke to the mother again, and Rebecca assumed this is what he told her, but her expression still didn't change. He said something else to the mother before returning her baby.

"Can you go?" Hugh asked Veronica. "Can you go with her to Dar?"

It was an enormous request and an expensive one (even if Hugh was presumably paying), and Veronica's face reflected this. But Rebecca realized that this was Hugh's alter ego, the side of him that came alive only when in crisis, the part of him that could easily ask for whatever it was he wanted.

"I don't know," Veronica said, "I—"

"I'd take them myself," he said. "But right now more nets are coming, Veronica. One truck's worth, anyway. It's on the road. If you take them to Dar, I promise I'll join you as soon as I hear from you that the surgery is a go."

"What can I do?" asked Rebecca. "Can I do something?"

"You? You're going to help carry the nets. And you're going to take pictures."

"Take pictures?"

"You still take pictures, don't you?"

"Well, yes, but—"

"How do you think I raise money for all of this? The pictures are important, trust me."

"If it's so important, why didn't you mention it before now?"

"I'll go to Dar," said Veronica.

"Good," said Hugh. He took the mother's hand and—looking as if he had all the time in the world—began to explain.

———

The nets came the next morning. They came before sunrise and, within a day, Hugh had made contact with a team that he'd obviously assembled long before Rebecca arrived. She was beginning to understand the way he worked, if not *why* he worked this way, and would bet he had at least two other photographers lined up besides her. She wondered why he'd neglected to mention the scope of this operation. Six people came by boat—volunteers from Tanzania, the U.K., and the United States. Donning orange life jackets, they arrived as the sun was rising. They disembarked; introductions were made. The nets were packaged in large plastic bundles, and Rebecca joined in hauling them from the truck containers into the low wooden boats manned by local men.

Hugh informed her that not only would she be taking pictures but she'd also need to demonstrate how to *use* the nets. He showed her how to do it, and though she explained how she'd spent a lifetime shying away from public speaking, she also realized that it was ludicrous to say no to this request, to any of it. They delivered the mosquito nets from morning until evening, and she found herself wondering if Hugh had known that without a camera she would have missed so many details. She zoomed in on children's faces, on old men and women standing by, and snapped away on her digital Sony.

Each time, with every village, as their boats grew closer to the beach, the men called into their bullhorns and the shoreline swarmed with people. As she took in the crowds assembled in their brightly colored clothing, it was impossible not to smile—even though she felt that smile spring quickly into embarrassment, because, my God, how little they were actually handing over. But the people gathered. The children sang. Teenagers—one girl in a black head scarf and white sunglasses, one boy with a serious expression that reminded her, curiously, of her father—mugged and boasted; they gathered and they cheered. There were speeches in Swahili, which she didn't understand, and a Zambian doctor translated into a bullhorn as Rebecca demonstrated how to use the nets. In the face of kids dancing and singing over mosquito nets, one's ego really did look like a little gleaming turd.

———

After they'd delivered nets to eleven villages, after Rebecca had discovered and then grown used to the idea that she *liked* standing up in front of the crowds, the boat docked back at the lodge. Her ears were ringing and her body ached and her cheeks were sunburned, sore from smiling. The light was violet and silver.

"The magic hour," sighed Carol, the RN from Johns Hopkins, who was around the same age as Hugh. A speck of diamond glinted from the side of her aquiline nose.

"The mosquito hour," quipped Hugh, sitting down to the dinner prepared by Omar and the Dutch couple. "All these years I've been here—most of my life, really—and the goddamn little bugger's still winning."

A round of agreement. Then everyone sat down: the two bearded American doctors (infectious diseases and tropical medicine— she'd missed their names), Carol the RN, Jerry the policy wonk, Omar, the Dutch owners, Rebecca, Hugh, and the two Zambians—Dr. Makasa and Dr. Alwani. Even though they'd all done their parts and had accomplished a great deal in one day, there were at least ten more villages that had been left out of this mission, due to the other trucks gone missing. And the reason those trucks didn't arrive was the same reason that it took the mother of that poor alien-head baby eight full days to get to Veronica and Hugh: the pitted, flooded, much-lamented roads. The government, an NGO, USAID, the UN—*somebody* had to fix the goddamn roads.

But after one beer (never had beer tasted so good), when Rebecca asked Infectious Diseases if the incidence of HIV would go up if those roads ever improved and there was more and more trucking access, the answer she received was an unqualified *yes*.

Tropical Medicine held forth on malaria: rates of incidence and what these rates meant. But it was an argument about Mother Teresa that really became heated. Carol the RN had worked with her in the late sixties and had nothing but praise, while Jerry the policy wonk maintained that anyone who'd take money from the Duvalier family and in turn praise their rule was, at the very least, no saint. "*Abortion is the greatest destroyer of world peace?* She said that, you know. She did say that."

"So she was a Catholic!" cried Carol. "As are—face it—most of the people doing most of the good in Africa these days."

There was a great deal of drinking.

As the evening wore on, Rebecca found herself considering Hugh again at a distance. Hugh wasn't a doctor. He most certainly wasn't a Catholic. He wasn't a nurse or an anthropologist or an agricultural consultant. He hadn't won any major prizes. If he'd improved the lot of any Tanzanians or Haitians—and he had, she'd done her research: His clinic in Dar had reduced malarial incidence rates by 68 percent the previous year; the clinic he'd set up in Haiti was thriving, staffed by Haitians and serving several rural villages—what set him apart from other well-meaning Westerners working in the Third World was this: He drew people in and he put them together and he seemed to know when to step back. He had assembled all of these impressive professionals who were interested in working with him; he'd raised the funds (though she guessed that much of his own, still-vague Shipley capital went into every project) and he'd worked with the necessary suppliers, making sure those supplies reached the people most desperate for them.

She watched him rolling a cigarette, looking even more attractive than usual, and she decided it was because he seemed shy. She considered his self-deprecating nature, and what she realized then was that he'd likely been—much like her—afraid to fail.

It struck her now that Hugh wasn't really her father's opposite, as she'd always thought of him. He was more like his complement. And though her father, too, had a distinct fear of failure, he didn't ignore it—not at all; it positively drove him until he and the failure were in burning competition. It had driven him—she still couldn't believe it—straight into prison.

Rebecca wondered if Hugh and her father had ever talked about these things when they were young—when they were friends. She could picture it with such eerie clarity: her father saying to Hugh, *You're lucky.*

She could almost hear the pitch of his younger voice, a voice she'd never know. And she imagined Hugh looking physically pained to have that kind of attention. He had probably wasted time—years?—resenting the gift of his tremendous appeal, even as he'd learned how to use it.

After nightfall, everyone went swimming. The water was warm, and these were loosely linked people in a foreign place. It was foreign even to the Zambian doctors, who both admitted they'd required persuading to come this far into the bush. People acted like friends in the water; people acted like children. The moonlight illuminated funny tan lines and nasty sunburns; an informal competition began for the worst one. Dr. Makasa taught a couple of local boys karate moves, and they practiced the moves on the shoreline.

Hugh swam out into the distance, beginning laps back and forth, which for anyone else would have seemed strange at that hour, but with Hugh she was not surprised. It was only when everyone else had retired that he even looked up. When he did, Rebecca waved.

He swam a plodding crawl, and when he came out of the water she looked away, aware of being too interested in his body. His skin was older, of course, but he had the kind of height that held everything in place. He wrapped himself in a towel and looked down at her sitting in the sand.

"Thank you," she said.

"You're welcome."

She appreciated that he didn't ask what she was thanking him for. She also appreciated that he hadn't asked her any questions about her life.

"I would sit next to you, but let's spare us both the embarrassment of my needing your help to get up."

"Oh, come on."

"You think I'm joking. I have a long, evidently *very Western* spine. And also sciatica. Old goat's got sciatica."

Rebecca stood up. "Vivi has sciatica," she said.

He gave a fleeting smile. "My daughter's very pregnant," he said. "I'm afraid that's different."

"Sciatica for a good cause?"

"Indeed." He shook out his hair like a dog. "And she's young. *Hers* will vanish once she's no longer carrying around an extra thirty pounds."

They walked to a bench. The air was still warm. Hugh sprayed them both liberally with a repellent called Doom; the smell was nasty but also enlivening. "Are you happy about the baby?" she asked, after a bout of coughing.

"I am." He nodded, clasping his hands together. Despite missing the better part of two fingers, he still had the best hands she'd ever seen. They were big and expressive; she imagined how her fingers would feel laced through each of his. "Brian's a good kid."

"Although Brian's not really a kid."

She waited for him to meet her gaze. When she had it, when she had his blue eyes with their bleached lashes and big dark pupils, when his eyes settled on hers, she said, "None of us are kids anymore."

She wasn't sure what she wanted. Nothing could ever happen. Because if it did, she'd never be able to look at Vivi again. She knew this. But she was heady and exhausted from the events of the day, and exhaustion made her reckless. She began working her fingers through her damp hair, wincing with nervousness each time she untangled a knot.

"I'm just pleased to hear *she's* happy," Hugh went on. "You know, I wasn't sure Vivi wanted children, but of course she does. Most people do, you know. I know I did."

Rebecca felt her face unfold into a weary grin. "Even though most of the world's problems are due to overpopulation?"

Hugh nodded. "I absolutely did. Do you?"

She was flushed, not only with a sudden and unexpected longing—longing for children with a different, younger, unmarried, impossible Hugh—but also with embarrassment at this longing, which was no less than absurd. And she was angry with Hugh for bringing her own desire for children into the context of Vivi and Brian, for pointing out what they had in contrast with what she did not. She *hadn't* been seeing Vivi's pregnancy through that kind of selfish lens. But in this elemental setting, in the grip of undeniable, untenable desire—she was seeing it that way. There she was, thinking of herself as some kind of empty vessel. Or, to be accurate, she wasn't thinking. She was wanting. And at the moment she wanted everything.

"Why didn't you tell me that this—today—would be such a big operation?" she said abruptly. "You made it sound like the two of us would be doling out some nets, nothing more than a weekly routine."

"Like a paper route?"

"Something like that, yes." She shook her head. "Those doctors are from top universities. These are volunteers with all kinds of credentials. Did you not want me to feel intimidated?"

He considered it, shook his head. "I don't think that was it. Your CV is plenty impressive. You have your own intimidating qualities."

"Oh." She grimaced. "Right. And why, again, didn't you tell me more about today's project?"

"I don't know, it's the way I do things. Maybe I was afraid of something going wrong. In fact—yes, okay? I was afraid of something going wrong. It happens. As you have seen already, it happens quite a lot; it's . . . built in. So, as much as I'm focused, I try not to dwell on any one plan."

"Or on any one element of a plan."

"Right."

"Or any one person."

"Fine."

"Maybe that's why you seem so aloof."

He didn't seem surprised. "Maybe."

The sky was tauntingly oppositional—ink black but also pale with the moon and clusters of stars—brighter and darker than any sky she'd ever seen. She smelled something mineral-dark, cold. She suddenly realized that she was incapable of seeing Hugh as separate from every other part of her life. She could not consider him without also considering her father or Vivi—and also her work (both what she had and hadn't accomplished). He'd even roamed the perimeter of her consciousness during various romantic entanglements—Gabriel included—offering himself up as comparison. Because how could she have felt what she had felt on that day, that night, if he hadn't felt it, too? But she had been fifteen, his daughter's best friend. What did that mean about him, about Helen, if he had?

Maybe it meant nothing. Nothing, after all, had happened.

But, no. She always came back to *no*. The friction between them stemmed from a mutual transgression. Or the mutual desire to have transgressed.

And now they were across the world in a wholly new place, but—and she wasn't sure what this meant—every new place reminded her of an old place. The moon, after all, was still the moon.

"I don't mean to be aloof," he said.

"That's like: Don't hate me because I'm beautiful."

"I don't hate you," he said.

"Oh, come on."

He wasn't looking at her. He wasn't holding a drink, a cigarette, or a set of keys; he wasn't looking for them, either. But he still wasn't looking at her.

And then he was. His eyes were partially obscured by damp hair, but there was no mistaking his expression.

The fine hairs on her arm stood up, and there was her body slipping into paraffin wax—warm, bewildered, stuck. She put her hand on his shoulder. His skin was still damp with the finest of lake-water silt. She felt heat and muscle, cool water and bone. He didn't flinch, but he also didn't move.

"Rebecca," he said. He shook his head.

"I know," she said. Because she did. She knew how painful it was to have this much sheer sensation and to know it was wholly wrong. *Even if Helen has left him?* A small voice asked. *Even still.*

He shook his head again.

"Tell me," she whispered, "what."

He sat up straighter. She took her hand away.

"Let's just—let's leave it," he said.

No was all she could think. *No, let's not.* She returned her hand to his skin, closer to his neck, more confidently this time.

But he grabbed her hands between both of his own. Those hands were finally touching hers, but it didn't feel the way it had just a moment ago, when the air was charged.

He was, she realized, trying to stop her. Shocked—even mortified—her mouth went utterly dry.

She cleared her throat, parched. "I think I need to hear you say it." Her voice was low, unfamiliar. She watched as a part of her bolted up and ran straight underwater. "I think you need to explain." She kept looking for clues, searching his face, but his only expression was something like . . . *patience.* And so she looked away, locked eyes with the sand.

"Rebecca," he said gently, still holding her hand. "You're Ed's kid."

She shook her head. She took her hand away. "What does that even mean?" When her voice broke, he put his arm around her and she stopped fighting. "My father—" she started. Then she leaned into his chest: bare and wet and not for her. "You're not even in touch with my father," she said, laughing through the beginning of her tears. "You haven't been friends for years."

She could feel him shrug as he held on to her. "Doesn't matter."

Rebecca wasn't exactly sure if she was crying because Hugh had rejected her or because she was experiencing embarrassment on an unprecedented level or because, at this distance, she could finally consider how her father was sleeping in a cell each night. She could finally think about the prison's inmate's handbook, which she'd read online, and how it contained a section nearly two pages long entitled: *How to Prevent Sexually Abusive Behavior.* Her father was in prison; he was in danger.

"I'm sorry," she whispered. "I'm so sorry."

She tried to get up, but he didn't let her go.

She thought of the missing mosquito nets, the missing trucks, her father and his cellmates—all missing from their desperate, exciting, pathetic, wretched, amazing lives. That baby's swollen head and narrowed eyes no bigger than his mother's yellow beads.

Here was Hugh with his arm around her. They had no timeless, mutually transgressive understanding. He was her best friend's father. Once upon a time—a time that evidently meant something to Hugh—he had been her father's friend. This had been no one's fantasy but hers, and here she was: a white woman in Africa, part of a *misunderstanding*.

And so what? *So what*.

This time, when she tried to pull away, he let her.

"Thank you." Her voice caught again, but as she stood, she looked out at the lake; she pulled herself together. "This has been a great opportunity."

As she walked away, she had a sudden flash of herself at sixteen, sitting at school assembly in a pair of black tights. She was scratching at the last of her poison ivy, snagging her nails over her thighs and calves. *What are you doing?* whispered Vivi. Why did she remember this? But she did. *Careful*, Vivi said. *You're going to make a hole.*

She stayed another month. A routine unfolded: At the clinic, she learned how to prepare medicines—crushing the tablets and mixing the liquids. The work was menial, and it suited her. She assisted Tropical Medicine—Dr. Al Horowitz—who taught her how to take vitals. One morning a young man wandered in with an infected cut on his foot. An old woman stumbled in, crying that her uterus was falling out. She saw how Hugh spent most of his day on the phone: with the clinic in Dar; the local net company, which still hadn't delivered the rest of the nets; the pharmaceutical representatives.

She and Hugh barely spoke during the day. When she wanted to find out about logistics—meal times, meeting times, what to bring where—she asked Omar or another volunteer. If she passed Hugh at the clinic, she kept her head down. She kept a pocket journal with her at all times for the purpose of emergency scribbling. She developed an unprecedented ability to focus on plant life and found she was often squinting at imaginary faraway birds.

But at night, while she drank the same three beers amidst doctors, workers, and missionaries, she and Hugh would inevitably end up in discussion, first among the others but eventually alone. Their conversations became increasingly personal. They talked about Helen, how he had cheated on her for years and how she'd finally had enough. How—as far as he knew—Vivi had no idea, not unless Helen had told her. Rebecca felt an odd lack of surprise at this news and felt even more unburdened from what she'd begun to think of as her crush. Also, she was flooded with memories that took on sudden meaning: How Hugh had obviously been in Anguilla before they all went on that trip. How that woman in the hammock nursing a newborn was beautiful. How Helen had seemed sad around that baby. Rebecca knew she was seeing everything through a particular, retrofitted lens (could he have really fathered that child?), but it *had* felt odd how he'd so clearly been to the island before and yet neither Helen nor Vivi seemed to acknowledge it.

She asked if he was sorry, and he told her how *sorry* was irrelevant when it came to such matters, especially after so much time.

"Even so," said Rebecca. "Are you?"

"Of course I am," said Hugh. "Jesus."

"I don't mean to press you on it," she said quickly.

"Sure you do," said Hugh. "And I deserve it."

But he excused himself soon after that. And the following evening, he had his dinner—and presumably his after-dinner drinks—elsewhere.

One night, on the shore, she sat with Hugh atop an overturned boat. Behind them, on the terrace, a birthday dinner continued: clinking bottles and laughter; Carol the RN was sixty.

"So what happened with you and my father?" Rebecca finally asked him.

"What do you mean?"

"I mean why did you lose touch?"

Hugh didn't answer immediately; he took a drag of his cigarette. "Your father cut me off."

"He—what? No, he didn't."

Hugh shook his head, as if this fact surprised him, too. "Over some pointless conversation about the goddamn nation of Israel." He added, "No offense."

She found she was unable to look at him, out of something like embarrassment on everyone's behalf. "But, *really?* I mean, I know he can be . . . forceful on the subject, but he never mentioned anything like that. He only said you drifted apart."

"There was no drifting. Have you ever known your father to *drift?* In any way whatsoever?"

When she turned to look at him, he was staring out at the water.

"Hugh?"

"Look," he said, and pointed. And while at first she was irritated with his shifting focus, she saw that, in the distance, there was an unmistakable glow.

He slowly stood up as a ship came into view. "There she is," he said. "The only passenger and cargo ferry for the entire lake. She's it, and she's extraordinary, so make sure you get a good look." He called out to the tableful of people behind them, "The *Liemba,* ladies and gentlemen!" He gazed across the water, as if this ship were, in fact, his new romance. "Just watch," he whispered. Before he sat back down, he held up his hand, as if marking the location of the boat. For a moment he looked almost infirm, and then it dawned on Rebecca that Hugh was exceptionally drunk.

The table quieted; someone blew out the candles so they could get a better look, and within moments the dark lake erupted with small kerosene flames, lanterns shining from small wooden skiffs laden with sacks. *Rice,* Carol explained. *Sugar. Pineapples. Cassava.* Rebecca could see the glinting silver of what Hugh identified as piles of dried fish. He explained with peculiar reverence how the goods were transferred from the bobbing wooden boats up onto the *Liemba*'s deck. Most goods were going to the Congo, he explained, which was larger than the U.K., France, Spain, Italy, and Germany combined.

If Rebecca strained, she could hear passengers crying out to one another in the universal language of impatience. She could imagine the crowds, determined to find their place on the ship for the night. She took out her camera and aimed it toward the ship, so regal and glittery from where she was sitting, though she could only imagine the foul-smelling chaos of so many people and their belongings.

Weeks later, after the swollen-headed baby (whose name, she'd learn, was Abasi) had made it through a successful surgery, after he'd returned to his family with bright eyes and a tiny scar, and after Rebecca was back in her own apartment, which looked out on a row of brownstones and one ancient cigar shop, she would log hours staring at her laptop screen in the midst of an unavoidable job search. One day when she was particularly discouraged, she distracted herself by downloading this particular series of photographs: the *Liemba,* all blurry glows and traces of sparkle on a background of solid black. And there was another picture. She realized that she must have aimed slightly to the right, because, just for one mistake of a shot, there was no *Liemba,* no blur of light—only the edge of Hugh in flash-blighted profile, with the tail end of his cigarette dangling from his lips, as if he'd forgotten about it.

Soon after, she got a phone call in the middle of the night—*Hello?* she asked, breathless, assuming it was Vivi, gone into labor. But it was Hugh—so odd to hear from Hugh—and he didn't even say hello. *You won't fucking believe this* is how he started, and he explained how Abasi—sometime after the follow-up visit—ran a high fever. He relayed how the baby was admitted to the hospital, the same national hospital where he'd had the successful surgery, and how, there in the hospital, the nurses determined—*without a blood test,* he shouted, *without administering antibiotics*—that there was nothing to be done.

The mother would have been there, too, of course. The mother would have been there in that hospital in Dar es Salaam. Rebecca had learned her name but would always think of her just this way: *the mother.* She would think of her when Vivi's healthy baby was born. And years after that, when her own children made their way into this world: *the mother.*

They talked for hours that night, Hugh and Rebecca, their disembodied voices rising and falling. About an hour into the conversation it came to her again: She was talking on the phone with Hugh. Even stranger: Whatever spell she'd been under for lo those many years—it had evidently lifted. And so she kept talking to him: She lay on her bed, wandered to the kitchen; she cradled the phone between her ear and shoulder and felt such tremendous relief because, my God, what a mess she'd almost made.

Toward the end of their conversation, some three hours later, toward dawn, Rebecca lay down on her bed and closed her eyes. She was abruptly back on that single-prop plane, flying over Lake Tanganyika. The propeller whirred loudly, sweat was drying on her skin, and before she remembered to be terrified, she found herself looking out the window and thinking: *what a view.*

"A few what?" asked Hugh. "Did you just say *a few?*"

"I must have been dreaming," said Rebecca, disoriented. "I must have fallen asleep."

"You should be asleep," he said.

"No, no, I'm awake," she reassured him. Her heart was suddenly racing. "I'm awake now."

Chapter Nineteen

An Invitation, 2010

Vivi and Brian are getting hitched.
(Only family)
Won't you come celebrate the very next day?
Sunday, September Twenty-Sixth, 2010
Eleven o'clock in the morning.
Veuve Clicquot and brunch.
Grandmother Ordway's house on Fishers Island.
Circle YES PLEASE or NO THANK YOU
and send this paper back to us!
XOXO
Vivi, Brian, Lukas, Sabine, and Gisella

The invitation looked as though someone had scrawled the information with a Sharpie, while in a rush, on a paper bag. It came with an accompanying "Travel Information Kit" and a picture of Vivi and Brian and their three blond children, who had presumably kept the couple so damn busy that they'd never found the time—up until the *very second* when someone had scrawled this pathetic invitation—to consider getting married.

Despite his early suspicions that she was a bad influence on Rebecca, and despite the exceptionally strange fact of who her parents were, Ed was fond of Vivi and always had been, ever since the moment she'd shaken his hand at JFK, looking like the spawn of Bo Derek, after Rebecca (still a shocking fact) had snuck off to Anguilla with the Shipleys. But this was ridiculous. If Guy Ordway had lived to see this invitation, trusts might have been revoked.

And what kind of schmuck did they take him for? Evidently one who would travel all the way to an island off the coast of Connecticut for a day trip, for a glass of bubbly and some bacon.

Though he did wonder which one of them had come up with the idea of inviting him. Was he simply Rebecca's father now? Rebecca's father, who had been morally and financially gutted? Or was he Hugh's old friend? And, most relevant, what was he now—if anything—to Helen?

This shoddy and affected invitation, which had been waiting for him when he'd returned home that muggy evening, was the ostensible reason for his daily phone call to his daughter. He sat at his desk, in his crappy Hell's Kitchen (*Midtown West*) rental, looking over the view of buildings upon buildings, the nothing-special view of bright lights and traffic to which he'd never grown accustomed, and he complained. He ranted about how nothing was taken seriously anymore. How nobody had any respect for life's rituals, life's ceremonies. Forget about how people were swearing on television and joking about every last thing—not that he didn't have a sense of goddamn humor, but did *every last thing need to be a joke?*

He was fine with the fact that his daughter was only half-listening. Because Ed's actual thoughts were about the mother of the bride-to-be, who had (according to Rebecca) been *spending time in Europe.*

Rebecca now explained over the phone, "I haven't seen it yet, because, obviously, *I'm still at work,* but, Daddy, I'm betting the invitation looks that way because the paper is recycled." She was using *the voice,* which advertised that were she not at work, in the presence of other earnest, hardworking professionals, she would surely be saying something like, *Enough*. Like, *What do you care? The voice* let him know she felt she ought to be congratulated for not acting as impatient as she felt.

"Recycled," he scoffed. "I do know about recycling, Rebecca. And I support it—though you know the only ones really profiting from the recycling industry are the goddamn Mafia—"

"Please let's not start about that right now, if you don't mind."

"I'm not saying anything about recycling. What I'm saying is that this invitation has an intentional look. Grubby. And if they're so concerned about the environment," he asked his daughter, "why didn't they just send out an email? You should see this thing. It's a sad excuse for a wedding invitation."

"That's surprising," Rebecca said, obviously unconvinced.

"What do you mean?"

"I mean it's surprising because Vivi has great style. It's kind of her thing."

"Style over substance?"

"I'm not saying that," she said evenly. "Daddy, I really have to go. I'm going to be here all night to begin with."

"All I'm saying is that it's embarrassing, and I doubt I'm the only one who feels this way."

"I doubt you are."

"That's all I'm saying."

"And I hear you. But I have to go."

"Fine," he said, pissed. And then, more pleasantly: "Go get 'em."

"How are you?" she asked, suddenly sounding a little guilty. "You're okay, right? I mean, aside from being horrified by Vivi's brunch invitation?"

"I'm okay," he said, "I am. Things are looking up."

"Do I want to know the details?" she asked, though she kept her tone light enough. She had a habit of insinuating that she still considered him a crook, and this had ceased to bother him, because he believed she made these insinuations only to make herself feel better. He could tell that her continued belief in him annoyed her, made her feel too soft and too tenderhearted for the kind of person she had become: the dogged, Ivy League—educated kind of person who toils away in a windowless community justice center on behalf of the accused who don't have the dough to be white-collar criminals.

"We'll ride up together," he announced. "We'll ride up to this thing."

"Oh, so you *do* want to go?"

"Sure," he said, knowing full well she never doubted he would. "Why not?"

"Oh," said Rebecca. "Well, that's great." She wasn't doing much to hide the fact that she would have been happier if he'd declined.

"But?"

"I'm going up a day earlier. I'm actually going to be at the ceremony."

"I thought it was only family."

"It is," said Rebecca.

"What—are you a Shipley now? Are you an Ordway or an Avery?"

"It's—you know—family and me. Those are my godchildren."

"Of course," he said, feeling oddly jazzed. He glanced out the window, where the cars were shooting down Ninth Avenue now that rush hour was over. "Hey," he said, "that divorce finally go through?"

"It did," she said. "Vivi's still in shock."

"Is that right?" And, to calm his sped-up heart, he sank into the couch. He grabbed a kilm pillow he'd bought on a whim while on a second date in SoHo over ten years ago. He'd had to sell most of his belongings. How was it that he'd held on to this pillow? Lying flat on his back, he gazed up at the cheapo drywall ceiling, at the inert ceiling fan with the lamp in the middle, which never failed to light up when he wanted air or to start whirring when he wanted only light.

Where, he wondered, did Helen lie down at the end of yet another day?

"You read about Hugh, right?" asked Rebecca.

"Read what?"

"The award," she said, obviously annoyed that he somehow hadn't already known this. "Use those prison skills and Google him. It's prestigious."

"Good for him," he said quietly. He still bristled each and every time she mentioned prison. "Hugh won something big?" he asked, surprised at the pleasure he felt in hearing this.

After he'd hung up the phone and watched the sky go as dark as it could while drowning in a sea of lights, Ed considered how Rebecca knew nothing about his current state of affairs. Besides that it was simpler not to tell her anything, she had more than made clear her disinterest in the rise and fall of his fortunes. It wasn't as if she was some kind of Marxist, but she genuinely seemed to be content with what—at least to him— wasn't much. Although she might have been accepting her mother's money from time to time, it seemed just as likely that she wasn't. She rarely traveled; she worked hard. She happily lived in one of those neighborhoods in Brooklyn that boasted some *New York Times* press clippings about well-lit bars and charming bistros but still basically looked like crap.

She didn't even know that he'd bumped into his old friend Hy in the lobby of the St. Regis, where—post-prison—he'd sometimes spring for a cup of coffee just to make an appearance, to see who was meeting whom for breakfast. Even though years had passed since his release, it was the first time he'd seen Hy since his life had fallen to pieces, and, while saying goodbye, Hy had gripped him in an ungainly hug. Hy had not said, *I'm sorry, Ed*, or *I'm sorry I screwed you*, as Ed had so often envisioned he would.

Instead, Hy had said one word: *Brazil*.

Brazil, Hy had repeated as he'd pumped Ed's hand. Hy knew exactly how unlucky Ed had been. He also knew how smart Ed was and that he would figure out the rest from there.

And because Hy had become (it was Ed's worst source of vexation) literally one of the most successful investors on Wall Street, and because if guilt was not the single most motivating factor Ed didn't know what was, and because the market had utterly crashed and he actually *hadn't* lost his shirt (the scraps that were left of it), and because he'd always had the good sense to never—even when he could have easily have gotten a seat at that table—invest with BadForTheJews Madoff because he had just never believed the guy, Ed said goodbye to Hy, went straight to his aesthetically offensive studio apartment, and for a solid week he filled his every waking moment with research. He barely slept; he stopped bothering with his weights and his walk and, instead, indulged his love for Chinese takeout. For the first time since prison, he even stopped shaving and then, on the following rainy Monday, he showered and shaved and called a housekeeping service. Up until then he'd been cleaning the place himself—he'd become a pro on the inside—not wanting to spend the money. While two women named Teresa and Marisol cleaned, he walked around the Central Park Reservoir, and when he returned—soaking wet—the apartment smelled like ammonia; he tipped and said *muchas gracias.* Then he began to sell much of his then-measly portfolio and buy Brazilian stocks.

And now—he still couldn't quite believe it—after watching those stocks rise, he had sold many of them and, after having almost no liquid assets for more than five years, he had liquidity. He had some actual capital. No one would know this by the way he lived: If he was good at anything now, it was saving money. It had become a game: *How little can I spend?* He saw nobody but Rebecca. He walked everywhere. After an awkward moment in a café near her office when she had offered to pay, they usually met in City Hall Park and not during mealtimes. Sometimes she brought her little Tupperware containers anyway and—when he offered to take her to a late lunch, an early dinner—insisted that she preferred her own food: her greens, her grains.

He knew his daughter thought he had changed. She thought that he'd realized he could live with far less, and he *had,* but truthfully he still hated living this way. He had plans to export cars to Brazil. The plan was in its initial stages, but though the concept was not without risks (not only the historical precedent of Brazil's growth preceding dramatic collapse but also—obviously—his own previous failure importing BMWs to China), he thought the risks were worth taking in exchange for the possibility of his golden years (ha!) spent with good tables and overpriced wine and what he remembered as the sense of having traction in this city. He never complained but absolutely dreamed of buying back his old apartment, craved the day when he'd never again have to lay eyes on the pathetic exile of these crappy digs with the gypsum board and exposed 1970s radiators and tacky black linoleum countertops and could return to the walnut-paneled hush, the Carrara imported marble, the trees.

On his colossal loss of income, Rebecca often said: *I think this could be a good thing.*

But Rebecca didn't have children yet. And didn't even the most ascetic sorts of people change their tune about money and personal comforts when children came along? (*I'm not remotely ascetic!* she'd yelled at him once. *Where do you come up with these insane ideas? Have you taken a good look at my shoes? Loeffler Randall, Daddy! I'm not proud, but, believe it or not, I have a clue what it's like to live beyond my means.*) Even though she'd remained stubbornly unattached for years now, Ed allowed himself to picture his daughter coming to her reclaimed childhood home with her own children one day.

He wasn't sure when he'd transferred wanting more children into wanting grandchildren, but he knew he'd made the leap—he wasn't delusional about his age, not to mention his current precarious situation— somewhere along the way. He tried not to nudge Rebecca about any of it—the going on dates, the *getting out there,* the unconceived babies—but he was also acutely aware of the fact that his only daughter was closer to forty than thirty. How was this possible? Even though he was no less than stern with her if she ever waxed nostalgic about Gabriel (if he said anything on the subject, it was how she needed to snap out of it and get over him), Ed was certain that he and his daughter shared an unspoken understanding that letting Gabriel get away had not been her finest moment.

The truth was, *he* was crushed when they'd split. Ed had really liked—even loved—Gabriel, who was raised in Belfast until he was twelve and was fiercely ambitious, who was of the opinion that since there was no way in hell he was going to remain a Catholic, he'd be happy to raise any future kids Jewish, if that's what Rebecca really wanted. Gabriel didn't approve of religion, but he loved the law and liked the tradition of the Talmud. He liked how Ed's rabbi had told him that should he choose to convert to Judaism (he did not intend to) and still not find a way to believe in God, then he would find himself in good company, because theirs was a religion based on the act of doubting. Ed loved that Gabriel was happy to say such things aloud and that he had a genuinely photographic memory and so could easily discuss articles Ed felt the need to foist upon him about Israel or the stock market, even though Gabriel wasn't all that interested in either topic.

It had, in fact, taken every last reserve of Ed's self-control not to call Gabriel when he moved out of the apartment he'd shared with Rebecca for several years (another source of bitter fighting with Rebecca: *Why hadn't they gotten married* before *they'd moved in together?*). It had taken all Ed had not to tell Gabriel he'd never find a better woman than his daughter, who was brilliant and gorgeous and loyal and who needed—Ed agreed!—to get her head on straight and figure out what she wanted out of life. But Ed was being sued by the justice department at the time and thus had *not* gotten involved. And after quitting her highly coveted, well-compensated position at a top-tier Manhattan law firm because she'd been (she claimed) *anxious every minute of every day, and for what, and for whom?*, Rebecca sulked around for a while before going off to Africa to work with—or rather *for*—Hugh Shipley.

Had he worried? He had worried. But his daughter had returned seeming, if anything, nicer. Also, she had a renewed—if gravely altered—sense of purpose. She'd immediately started to apply for fellowships and internships, dead set on working with the most underserved populations in the city. Ed hadn't allowed her to visit him in prison—seeing her there would have been worse than not seeing her for a year—but during a rare phone call, when Ed had brought up how she could likely do more good taking on pro bono work at one of the bigger firms and had braced himself for a furious response, she'd only responded—with remarkable composure—that she was certain now, absolutely certain, about the work she wanted to pursue.

So Ed had *not* gotten involved about Gabriel, he had *not gotten involved*, and shortly after the breakup Gabriel had taken up with someone else and—though never marrying (what was it with this generation?)—immediately had a baby. Which Ed knew only because, during another precious phone call, Rebecca had cried, and when he asked what had happened, she told him, but only after he agreed not to ever mention Gabriel again. He'd stuck to this and never did mention Gabriel, or not unless Rebecca did so first. It wasn't like he didn't know a thing or two about holding on to someone long after they'd—to put it politely—let you go.

Over the telephone, an expression he loathed: *I'm going to let you go now.* Not: *I have to go.* Not: *Holy shit—look at the time!* No:

I'm going to let you go.

Once, in an attempt to make his daughter feel better, he'd almost told her everything about Helen—how he'd never wanted anyone or anything as *clearly* ever again, how he'd felt the loss of Helen like a physical blow that was truly not unlike being punched in the gut during one of the few times he'd entered a real boxing ring, before becoming a Harvard man. Ed had almost told Rebecca about the night at the Y, how Helen had just *been there*, sitting in the dank, hot hallway, but thankfully he'd come to his senses about this kind of storytelling once he realized that his particular experience could impart neither wisdom nor comfort.

On the morning of the wedding brunch, Ed rented a car. He drove out from the darkness of the underground garage and into a dawn where the air was exactly crisp enough to announce the presence of fall. He made his way through the Bronx, onto I-95, and—indulging in a habit that began while visiting Rebecca at boarding school—he stopped at Dunkin' Donuts for a half-dozen chocolate Munchkins and sweet dark tea, which he'd work through on the highway.

You look sharp, he imagined Helen saying.

Is that right? Ed would laugh—disingenuously, as he'd taken unusual care with his appearance this morning, doing serious battle with the nose-hair clipper and even (he would never admit this) blow-drying his hair.

He knew he should be wondering what she looked like, but he wasn't. He was convinced he already knew: that she'd never cut her hair shorter than her chin, that she would always have the same essential shape with the same worried expression, which would always be softened by her coloring and by some ineffable youthfulness. Even if she went gray (which he doubted she'd allow, no matter how far into the bush they'd lived), he imagined the gray hair would be the soft kind. She had always been a study in softness despite a pronounced angularity, and he couldn't imagine that these essentials didn't remain.

Driving usually calmed him down like nothing else could, and yet, on imagining Helen and after the last of the chocolate Munchkins, he was hit with a jolt of not just sugar but also of serious nerves; in fact, he became almost foggy with the notion of seeing her. He gripped the wheel tighter, only to think about seeing Hugh. They were going to judge him. They both were. He'd spent a goddamn year in prison.

When he'd met Hugh and Helen, he was a rough kid who wanted to be a gentleman. And he'd done it; he'd become that gentleman, only to reverse all his accomplishments by landing himself in the can, by pissing all that polish away. Or at least he was certain that was how they'd see him. Who could look at him without imagining a prison cell? He shouldn't even be showing his face today. He should not be running the risk of embarrassing Rebecca with the potential whisperings about him. But he also knew he couldn't stay away. He switched on sports radio; the Red Sox had beaten the Yankees last night. He could count on baseball. Not to lift his anxiety—or at least not exactly—but to provide the sound—that constant hum—of every fall, spring, and summer of his life. Baseball on the radio; he was grateful for this, the ultimate white noise.

Nostalgia was besides the point. Yes, the ferryboat looked basically the same as it did in the early summer of 1963, and, yes, his heart fucking swelled when he stood on the deck, not even taking the time to look around and see if there was anyone he might have recognized on this ferry, on their way to this party, too.

NOSTALGIA—WHAT IS IT GOOD FOR? He remembered this headline and the article: how, according to several studies, people who considered themselves very nostalgic also had corresponding high levels of self-regard and sociability. So, okay, fine, he thought. Fine. Okay. And maybe that's why he'd decided to come today? Nostalgia as a naturally occurring antidepressant? Because Ed had to concede that, among the many things he was right then, depressed was definitely not one of them. Nervous? Check. Ashamed? You bet. Agitated? Horny? Absofucking-lutely.

He'd read a big fat book on meditation when his personal fortune was first in the toilet, and even though he had never meditated, he found the explanations of the brain terrifically, even entertainingly, comforting. *There goes my amygdala,* he forced himself to think now, as the smell of potato chips and expensive perfume and saltwater came over him in brutal, ungentle waves. *There go my almond-shaped clusters of nuclei, deep within those medial temporal lobes. There you go again—you limbic system, you—throwing yourself into it, rearranging my memories.*

He'd half-expected Kitty Ordway James (or whatever her name was now) to be waiting for him in the parking lot in a yellow Mercedes, but there was neither Kitty, nor Rebecca, nor anyone he recognized. After sitting in the car for a good ten minutes and flipping the mirror down, up, then down again, in order to stare at his fairly jowly—though September-tan and astoundingly not bald—sixty-nine-year-old self, he turned the key in the ignition and began to follow Vivi's directions.

The rolling hills were not as green as in his June memories (some of the trees had even started to lose their early fall leaves), but the hills still made him feel twenty-two years old, and, oh, how he wanted to speed, to clear these hills like someone he'd never been, not even at twenty-two—especially not then—because his experience of youth went against the accepted truism. He had never felt invincible. Not even close. He'd felt completely out of control: a ball of nerves coiled tightly, rolling down the steepest hill. It was unfathomable how he'd spent a weekend here in this lush and heady setting and had still managed to conceal—even to himself!—the extent of his feelings for Helen.

Because, in retrospect, he'd been totally focused on her.

He remembered that her sister had been a knockout and that she'd overtly flirted with him one night at dinner. And while he certainly remembered feeling excited by the attention, what he recalled most vividly was Helen's expression as it was happening. He remembered Helen's face—that finely etched study in agitation—and this notion: *She's jealous.* And though he'd dismissed this budding thought before it could properly flower, Helen's agitation had been so much more exciting to him than the many glimpses of her sister's stupendous cleavage.

He had been focused on Helen—her gestures and her hips and her family and every one of her nuanced reactions to each and every moment.

Or at least that was his memory. It wasn't easy now, after so many years, to remember how he'd loved Hugh, too.

Ed had seen a shrink for a while after his divorce, and though this shrink had been irritatingly vague—never answering when Ed asked what he thought about Jill's behavior, never answering any remotely personal questions, such as if the shrink himself was Jewish—he had come right out and asked if Ed harbored any sexual feelings for Hugh. After all the pussyfooting around this shrink had done about his *anger,* this insane question had arrived as a strange sort of relief. Because he could feel properly indignant. Because he could say with great certainty: *No.* Because he'd never wanted to go to bed with Hugh Shipley. If only all desires could be reduced to a simple roll in the hay.

But it wasn't as if desire of a different kind hadn't played a part. Desire always did. And he'd desired the proximity to Hugh: the always slightly faraway gaze, the reassuring physical presence—reassuring not only because Hugh was squarely from the then-mysterious world of privilege but because, man, was he ever tall and handsome. To this day, Ed was certain that all those years ago they had each taken a deep and, yes, partially explicable solace from each other. But while Hugh—a Shipley from Boston—conferred upon Ed—a Cantowitz from Dorchester—a certain kind of confidence, and while Ed had presumably been something of a curiosity for Hugh, a budding anthropologist (plus the fact that he'd credited Ed for getting him out of bed for nearly a month), these were only the most obvious aspects of their friendship. For as far back as they could remember, they'd both felt like outsiders. That they'd shared this feeling—that they shared anything—was surprising to both of them. Surprising and tremendously comforting.

Chapter Twenty

The Wedding, 2010

If there was an ideal time to see your recently single ex-boyfriend, the night before you leave for your best friend's wedding was probably not it.

Especially if your father was going to be at the wedding celebration.

And especially if the *bride's* father had—until several years prior—been the (secret) object of your ongoing obsession.

Also not an ideal time to see the recently single ex-boyfriend? After 9:30 on a Thursday night.

Even if—as determined by the flurry of brief and logistical messages left for each other during the course of that Monday—this was the only time that either of you could meet until the end of the following week? Even if, after a year of no dating and then several years of what one might conservatively call *a healthy dating streak,* you were fairly certain that this recently single ex-boyfriend was, in fact, still the only man to whom you could imagine coming home?

Especially if.

Let's repeat, she told herself. *Not ideal. Really not.*

And then she picked up the phone to call him back, to set the time and place.

———

By Friday morning she was on the train to New London, alternating between dozing and running her hand over her raw, stubble-scratched cheeks. She looked out the smudged train window and reassured herself that, no, neither of them had had more than that single glass of wine and that they hadn't done anything more than talk over a wobbly table and make out on a street corner. There had been nothing promised, nothing at all. And yet she felt stubbornly certain that this was not just some kind of scratching a familiar itch. That she'd meant it when she told him she had some real regrets. That *he'd* meant it when he said, if hesitantly, *So do I.* And if she was unclear, exactly, to what extent he had meant this, it didn't really matter when he'd followed it up with a flinty look and *It's so good to see you.* They'd walked and walked. Neither of them mentioned their breakup or his subsequent failed relationship. The only conversational evidence of the past six years was the frequent mention of his son, Declan, of whom he had joint custody. He walked her over the Brooklyn Bridge, all the way to her apartment. *Have fun at the wedding,* he said. Then he put his arms around her and—sort of awkwardly, sort of beautifully—lifted her off the pavement.

But she came back to the facts that they hadn't made any concrete plans for the following week and that, just because they had drunk some wine and shared some kisses, this did not preclude him from doing this with many other women all over New York City and beyond. These were facts. She made herself mouth these facts, repeat them as if she were once again studying for the bar. More facts: He was attractive and successful. He could bed and date and marry any number of not only gorgeous women in their twenties but also intelligent and successful and kind and gorgeous women in their twenties. Why would he return to her? Did they not make each other miserable? Was she not—if nothing else—smart enough to understand the chances?

But she was unable to refrain from sudden bouts of smiling and was too stubbornly happy about the previous night to be properly distressed about what she knew was the likely outcome.

She also made herself a promise:

She would not call Gabriel until she calmed way down.

Then she made herself another:

The Shipleys will not throw me.

She'd resolved whatever she'd needed to resolve with Hugh several years before. This was Vivi's wedding and she would be there. She was on her goddamn horse and she wasn't getting thrown.

By Friday afternoon she was on the ferry from New London to Fishers Island with Vivi and Brian and the children, juggling bags and snacks and running after Gisella—their youngest—who was at an age when all she wanted to do was nurse greedily or flee from everything and everyone familiar. Rebecca had not babysat as a teenager—even now she had a surprisingly small number of friends who had kids—but she'd spent a great deal of time with Vivi's, and it was Gisella's age—between one and two, when time was still doled out in months—with which she identified most completely. Gisella was so exhausting, but Rebecca understood her. She understood her interest in seeing exactly how far she could push any vaguely authoritative figure before they told her *no*. Which was funny—she reflected now, as the sea air made her sneeze— because every description of her own childhood revolved around how mature and self-possessed she was. She couldn't help but think that either this was utter nonsense and her parents had been kidding themselves or maybe she *should* have been more out of control way back when.

She picked up Gisella and brought her back to her parents. "We're sitting down," she told her. Miraculously, though not without a bit of drooling laughter, Gisella complied.

"So let me get this straight," Vivi said to Rebecca, picking up the thread of a conversation that had started about an hour before. "You and Gabriel. Last night. You didn't do it?"

Rebecca glanced at four-year-old Sabine, who was ostensibly napping in her mother's lap, and five-year-old Lukas, who was focused on the possibility of whales.

"It's fine," Vivi assured her. "Just don't use any specific words. You'd be amazed at how much you can say without saying anything at all."

"In general?" asked Brian, with his dead-serious expression that Rebecca could now instantly recognize as the face that meant he was being anything but. "Or . . ."

"Ha-ha," said Vivi, with a bit of edge. "You're hilarious."

"We didn't do it," Rebecca told them.

"Not even a little?" Vivi insisted.

Brian said, "Honey, what are you asking? How could they do it *a little?*"

"*We* kind of did," she protested. "That first time we met up again."

"Okay," he admitted. "This is true." He looked a little wistful as he took a swig of Mountain Dew, which he claimed he drank only when he was on a boat.

Rebecca sat back on the wooden bench, closed her eyes to the gentle sun. Vivi and little Sabine—who'd perked up—began their habitual fiddling with Rebecca's rings, which were all stacked on her left pointer finger. The seven rings had originally belonged to her mother's grandmother, who'd evidently loved clothes and jewelry. When her mother had—with uncharacteristic tears—given her the rings at her college graduation, they'd been too large to fit on any other finger. Rebecca had intended to have them all sized and wear one at any given time, but Vivi had convinced her otherwise. Now she couldn't imagine her own hands without them.

"Puppy," Vivi said to Sabine. "You're looking a little green around the gills. Bri, give her some of that odious drink."

"What does *odious* mean?" asked Sabine.

"It means terrible," Vivi answered. "But, you know, sometimes terrible *odious* corn-syrupy soda makes us feel better when we're a little seasick."

"Are you seasick?" asked Rebecca—her eyes wide open—recalling one hell of a car trip with Sabine the previous summer.

Sabine nodded somberly at Rebecca, then happily chugged Mountain Dew before attempting to climb into her lap. Rebecca—not without slight hesitation—passed Gisella to Vivi, who waved to Lukas, who didn't even see her; he was sitting next to his father, still focused on the sea.

"Do you think there is something we're all wired with," mused Vivi, "the three of us—or maybe the four of us, if we can count Gabriel, *which you know I am dying to do*—that tells us we must recycle people, that, after the age of, say, twenty-five, there is literally nobody new?"

"I don't love the idea of recycling people," said Rebecca. "Not crazy about how that sounds."

"Me, neither," agreed Brian.

"But I don't mean it in a bad way."

"Of course you don't." Rebecca gestured at the two of them as if she were presenting *a brand-new car!* She took them in, this couple whose marriage was more familiar in many ways than that of her own parents. She had seen Vivi and Brian dewy-eyed with each other and also fighting bitterly—especially after Lukas was born—and she knew far too much about their sex life, due to Vivi's relentless—and often unflattering—disclosures. She knew them so well and yet sometimes she still had no idea what made them happy or unhappy with each other. Sometimes she'd think Vivi was angry with Brian, and then Vivi would blurt out how much she loved him. Sometimes Brian seemed to dote on Vivi and she'd complain—as soon as he left the room and with total conviction—that he was doing it only to make her feel bad. But Rebecca couldn't imagine them not together. To this day she still wasn't sure why they'd waited so long to get married.

"I just think," Rebecca attempted, "that it's so unusual to connect with somebody. Or rather—I think it's unusual to want to spend more than a limited time with somebody. And because it is so . . . so . . . cosmically unusual—"

"Rebecca, you just used the word *cosmic!*"

She realized she was playing to Vivi the way she'd always done—the way they both had always done—as if they were performing for each other in their own private piece of theater. "And because *it is so cosmi-*

cally unusual, you have to follow through sometimes more than once in order to get it right."

My God, did she want to check her phone. The desire had plagued her for every moment of this pleasant ferry ride, but she had sworn to herself—and out loud to Vivi and Brian—that she wouldn't. She'd made a vow to wait until she was in "her room" at the Ordway house, where the sheets were the softest and the floorboards creaked, and the white-painted oval-framed mirror was the best place she had ever found for applying makeup in natural light. She could almost taste the privacy and the delicious buzz of checking her phone after a significant spell.

They were getting close to sailing into the harbor now, and she felt the full extent of her exhaustion—recalling, once again, the previous and seemingly impossible night. "Oh, and listen," Rebecca told them, "I might be in danger of getting *verrry* sentimental during tomorrow's long-awaited ceremony."

"*You?*" mocked Vivi. Or, that is, Rebecca thought she was mocking. She wasn't entirely sure.

Rebecca had always thought it was funny how even the least yogic types of brides always seemed to want to get in some quality poses on their wedding day, but here, on the Ordway lawn, though the grass poked up around their mats and there were several persistent flies, Rebecca was grateful that this was what Vivi had wanted to do. Staying away from her phone was not easy. The urge to check for any messages from Gabriel was disturbingly strong and felt no less than a physical dependency. And so here they were. No distractions. Hugh had been dispatched to pick up a few items for the party being held the following day; Mrs. Ordway's "girl" had helped the great lady retire to her room, Brian had taken the kids to *his* grandparents' house (they, too, had a home on the island), and Helen—who had apparently been quietly practicing yoga since the late 1970s—led Vivi and Rebecca.

Aside from their horselike breaths, there was total silence, which was virtually unprecedented for Vivi and Rebecca while in each other's company. There was the breeze, the buzzy insects, infrequent motorboats, and the somewhat incessant ringing of the telephone from inside the house. The house phone only served as a reminder of her own fuchsia-encased cell, lying on the oak nightstand, switched on to vibrate so that even if it was in fact ringing at right that very moment she'd never be able to hear it. Besides, she reminded herself, Gabriel wasn't going to call her. He knew where she was, that she was busy with Vivi's wedding, and he'd mentioned he wasn't much of a texter. He was probably with his son, consumed with playing soccer or buying a bagel or any number of weekendy, parenty activities that prevented him from making contact. But if he was thinking of her, if he was unable to stop himself, wouldn't he just go ahead and send a little text? He'd always been at least slightly compulsive. Had he really changed that much?

When Helen suggested they close their eyes, Rebecca tried, but all she saw was Gabriel, and not in a peaceful, visualize-your-future kind of way but just—there he was—caught in the egregious act of not attempting to make contact, which was maddeningly easy to do these days. The whole wireless 3G network seemed to be a conspiracy to prove *exactly how little* anyone actually cared to be in touch.

How would Helen handle Gabriel? Helen would be cool. Were it not for her concern for the environment, she'd probably toss her cellphone into the water and go get an upgrade on Monday. Rebecca marveled at how Helen had managed to retain not only her sanity and composure but also her sense of humor while living for so many years in such close proximity to poverty and suffering. Not to mention how she'd seemingly dodged any outwardly stressful effects of the long marriage to Hugh. Maybe, Rebecca considered, while stretching toward the sky, Helen was becoming lighter and lighter as she aged. Maybe she had started out under a dark portion of the mythic Ordway cloud (Vivi loved her grandmother, but, though Rebecca couldn't quite put her finger on it, there was something frightening about Virginia Ordway) and was moving steadily out from beneath its shadow.

"All right," said Helen, "let's find our way to corpse pose."

"Can't you call it savasana?" asked Vivi. "I like it a whole lot better in Sanskrit."

"Sweetheart," said Helen simply. "We're all going to die."

"But not today," said Rebecca uneasily.

"Not today," Helen said, but she was already lying down, arms out to her sides.

Before any semblance of relaxation could take place, "For Christ's sake," came a booming voice—unmistakably Hugh's. Rebecca opened her eyes to see him walking down the lawn, cigarette in hand. "I've been calling and calling," he cried. "On the *telephone*," he added, as if resorting to telephone usage was somehow more than he could take.

Vivi bolted upright. "What is it?"

"Well, nothing," he said. "I was just worried when nobody answered, so I came back."

"*You were worried?*" asked Helen, more dumbfounded than angry, but anger was certainly in the mix. "*You?*" she repeated. "Did you pick up the drink order?"

He shook his head. "I'll go back," he muttered. "But, Vivi," he said, "I did get the lobsters."

"That's great." She beamed. "Really great. Thanks, Papa."

"I'm going," he said, trudging up the hill once again.

"You don't have to give him such a hard time," Vivi whispered.

Helen lifted her head. "You do realize he just interrupted this one half hour of yoga, which the three of us have been planning for a good six months, to tell us he managed to do an errand," said Helen. And then she started to laugh—still in corpse pose, on the ground.

At five o'clock they all gathered on the porch. Grandmother Ordway's hair had been teased and set and—as if she'd actually planned it—was the exact color of the pale-lavender mums that had been cut for the vase in the entryway. The Ordway kitchen staff presented trays of champagne, and everyone happily accepted. Brian's parents and sisters and grandfather—a pleasant, well-mannered bunch—talked about the club and people Rebecca didn't know, and as the kids climbed all over Vivi, who looked exquisite and happy, with a yellow silk flower in her hair, the sun hovered above the Long Island Sound. Hugh was perched (a bit precariously, Rebecca couldn't help notice) on the porch railing, as if he wanted to be closest, above all, to the sunset.

"No rain," said Vivi. "And it's the magic hour."

"The mosquito hour," echoed both Hugh and Rebecca in tandem—a vaguely amusing and awkward moment that, in years prior, would have felt no less than electric. Now, as Rebecca looked at Hugh, who grinned and nodded back at her, she felt only vague warmth.

Brian's Buddhism professor from Wesleyan asked everyone to make a circle around Vivi and Brian, and everyone set down their glasses.

"This is a beginning," said the professor. "It might seem like the middle, because here you are, already a family, but this is a beginning and you need to know that. Do you?" he asked, and Rebecca could tell that Vivi, who was slightly pursing her lips, was about to cry.

"I do," Vivi managed.

"I do," said Brian, with conviction.

And, at that moment (truthfully, throughout much of what followed: the vows and Hugh's e. e. cummings reading; Brian's sister's lovely yet strangely depressing Celtic love song), Rebecca cried. She cried openly (trying to stop the force of her tears only made her sound stifled and disturbed), because whenever she saw Vivi tear up, she was somehow incapable of not doing so herself. She cried throughout the ceremony because she loved Vivi and Brian as a couple and she was moved by this act of commitment. She also (mostly) cried because of how badly she wanted to run upstairs and check her phone and how the strength of her desire to do so was actually terrifying. Because after many years of not feeling this way, she felt, acutely, how her sense of well-being seemed absolutely tied to—and, yes, dependent on—another. The same other. And because she regretted how during the last year of their relationship she'd rebuffed Gabriel's mostly thoughtful suggestions and begun to blame him for everything, and finally because—not long afterward—

she'd behaved so carelessly with Hugh. She'd come dangerously close to removing herself from Vivi's life, making certain she'd miss being on this porch for the Buddhist-Lite, Universal Church of Life–sanctioned ceremony that Vivi surely would not have been able to have on this property (and Rebecca took an odd pleasure in knowing this) if Grandfather Ordway had been alive.

Hugh was crying, too. Rebecca looked at him briefly—seeing him like that felt too intimate—and right then she was assaulted with how changed he looked, how *old:* puffy eyes and age spots and a shocking slackness to his carriage. There was simply no connecting with the truly painful desire she'd felt for him for more than half her life. And there was also this: the nearly unbearable gratitude for how he'd prevented her erasure from this moment.

Later that night, after lobsters and white wine, Helen called everyone outside. A sheet was hanging down from the second-floor windows, and she began projecting a video. As the images started to roll—little Brian, little Genevieve—Rebecca couldn't help but remember sitting in Vivi's dorm room and looking at her photographs. She'd never known anyone her age who talked about her parents like that—not only with unmitigated affection but with such dramatic flair.

She'd always been a talented storyteller.

As the images flashed, Rebecca noticed that Hugh was standing beside her. "Look," he said, pointing up at the screen. There was Vivi—many years before Rebecca had met her—standing, like an acrobat, atop her father's shoulders.

"Beautiful," said Rebecca.

"And melancholy," he said. "Most good images are."

Less than a decade ago, she would have agreed with him, but right now she was simply annoyed that he couldn't look at these home movies and pictures and just watch. Just watch and maybe get tearful all over again. Like everybody else.

"Are you okay?" he nearly whispered.

"Am I—Yes." She nodded, obviously spooked by his intimate tone. "I'm definitely okay." And then, a bit contrite: "How about you?"

He shrugged. "Jury's out."

"Oh," she replied, softening. "I'm sorry."

They watched the rest of the presentation in appropriate silence. When it was over, and the migration inside toward dessert began, they both hung back. They watched the house and its golden light from the distance of the lawn.

"You want to know something?" he asked. "I'm pissed at your father." He gave his twisted-up smile, slowly shaking his head. "I'm still angry at him."

"But, Hugh . . ." She hesitated, because she of course understood how irrelevant this line of reasoning was. "It's been so long."

"Don't I know it," he said. He was staring up at the blank white sheet, as if waiting for another image to appear.

A door slam woke her up the next morning, and for a moment Rebecca's stomach pitched. This was the same irrational moment she'd had for years now, in which she imagined that Vivi knew that Rebecca had—*oh yes, she had*—made a pass at her father. This type of dread popped up infrequently, so distanced was she from the original impulse, but each and every time it did, she felt an urge to throw up. As she fled to the bathroom, she suddenly realized that she'd slept late—light was blasting the floorboards—and by the time she splashed her face with cold water, the need to vomit (if not the fear) was thankfully gone. She rushed to pull herself together and marveled at how she'd managed to sleep late with so many people in the house. She was even a little hurt that no children had come to wake her. *Surprise!* Lukas and Sabine had been known to cry out in unison, well before seven A.M.

In the kitchen: the same wicker basket on the counter that she'd come to expect; the same slightly stale donuts and muffins.

"Oh, good, you're up," said Vivi, who was holding a pink-frosted donut.

"What time is it? You should have woken me."

"Listen to this: My father screwed up. I knew I should have just had my assistant place the order, but he wanted to be useful and now there's not enough. My mother is quietly fuming."

"Not enough . . ."

Vivi started to laugh, and Rebecca was alarmed to see that her best friend, who had a career, three children, threw impromptu parties, and who—as a rule—did not sweat the small stuff, seemed atypically unhinged. "I asked him to order booze." Vivi gestured for emphasis, and Rebecca was surprised the donut didn't fly right out of her hand. "Wouldn't you have thought I could trust him with that one?"

"I would have." Rebecca nodded, poured the dregs of the coffee. "So, what can I do? Do you want me to call my dad? He can go buy booze somewhere. He'll have plenty of room in the car."

"It's a Sunday! Liquor stores are closed!"

"No, they're not. Not in New York. That law changed."

"It did? Excellent! How did I miss that? Anyway . . ." She finally took a bite of the donut. "My dad's on the way to the country club. His plan is to beg them to sell some of theirs. Although—"

"See? Okay, then."

"He's not exactly beloved there."

"It's going to be fine."

Vivi took another bite of donut. "This is disgusting," she said.

"Hand it over," said Rebecca, who took a bite. Though she agreed, the sugar made her feel more settled.

"This was supposed to be a simple daytime brunch thingy," Vivi moaned. "So casual, so—*whatever*. My stupid invitation was supposed to make this perfectly clear."

"I liked the invitation."

"Thank you. This day is not supposed to be a big deal."

"I know."

"I'm going to kill my father if there is nothing to drink at my simple, casual thingy."

"Listen," Rebecca said, "why don't you go take a bath?"

"I can't *take a bath*!"

"Why not?"

"I can't take a bath."

"Where are the kiddos?"

"Watching something—who knows what—with Brian. They're all lying on our bed, eyes glued to the TV screen. Total clueless relaxation."

"Cute."

"Sure," she said, starting to laugh. "Okay."

"You finally got married," said Rebecca.

Vivi nodded, her laughter trailing off. "I'm going to go take a bath."

By the time everyone was dressed and the mimosas were flowing, Hugh was on the lawn and at his best: one or two drinks in and doing impressions for several of Vivi and Brian's friends about his recent trip to the club. "Let's just say they did not make it easy for me," he said, swilling the remainder of his mimosa. "I said to the fellow, *I would like to purchase some alcohol; this isn't exactly water from a stone.* He looked appalled."

"How'd you convince them?" asked Marion Childs, the one friend of Vivi's whom Rebecca truly (still) could not stand.

"Quite a bit of tap-dancing," he said. He started counting people.

"What are you doing?" Brian's cousin asked.

"Almost everyone here is married," Hugh said. "And I'm not."

"*Quelle horreur,*" said the dreaded Marion, clearly flirting. She was wearing the kind of dress that looked simple and almost tentlike but likely cost at least six hundred dollars. Her husband was a few yards away, speaking urgent Spanish into a cellphone. "Many of his clients are in Mexico City," she explained. Rebecca couldn't tell what Marion felt about this—pride? resentment? embarrassment?—though it was clear that she felt something.

Brian's best friend, Joe, and his band set up. "Is this too loud?" the singer inquired into a microphone, but no one answered. "Is this too loud?" she repeated again, and this time everyone said yes.

"Be my date?" Hugh asked Rebecca, as they both watched more and more people arrive. "Just let me—you know—stay beside you. I'm not very popular with some of the guests," he said. "As you might imagine."

"And why would that be?" Rebecca asked. Hugh suddenly seemed . . . distasteful. The thought of him tap-dancing for alcohol at the club he so detested, the thought of how he'd screwed God only knew how many women during his marriage to Helen—the sun was too bright to contemplate all the reasons she felt as she did.

"Fine," he said lightly. "Don't be my date. I don't deserve you any-way."

"Glad you got that straight," she said with a smile. And then she thought: *What the hell are we talking about?* She turned away from Hugh and Marion and the growing cluster of guests and was annoyed to feel that her face was flushed.

"Let me know when your dad shows up," Hugh called out, but Rebecca only raised her hand in some vague acknowledgment that she would—*sure thing!*—let him know and also that she was walking away.

Her heels dug into the grass, and she tried not to trip as she walked by the croquet set, where Brian was cautioning a Lukas-led pack of kids not to go down to the water. She walked past them, past the slope of lilac bushes that obscured the generator where Vivi had—the summer after her graduation from high school—hid their jointly bought envelope of psychedelic mushrooms. Rebecca climbed the dilapidated stairs to the side entrance. In the corner of the railing, a spider was in the final stages of an elaborate web. And as she heard the sound of her father's arrival—the too-loud voice proclaiming his own name—she had an urge to poke a finger through it.

Later, while Rebecca watched Hugh play the piano from the mossy shade of the side porch, she saw her father, too, right behind Hugh at the front of the crowd, gripping a lyric sheet with both hands. He kept his eyes trained on that piece of paper as if he was really *trying*. It was this kind of quotidian effort from him that never failed to interest her; he truly believed there was a right way to do every last thing. Though she'd never seen Hugh play, she was unsurprised to learn that—though he avoided eye contact with his crowd and added unnecessary flourishes to every number—he was a natural piano man. She could imagine him living a parallel life in a small town somewhere—Ireland? Maine?— boozily gathering tips at the end of the night, going home with widows.

By the time she came in from the porch, the crowd had dwindled and her father was nowhere in sight.

"My wife left me for Obama," declared Vivi's cousin J.K., who was talking too loudly and drinking from a can of Budweiser.

"You just love saying that," said Hugh.

"She loses her job, so I suggest she does a little campaigning and, what do you know? She has a knack, she loves it, so she hits the campaign trail. Do I object?"

"You do not," said Hugh, in a way that made it clear that Hugh and J.K. were friends, that Hugh had, in fact, known much of this family tree, with all its gnarled and complicated branches, for most of his life.

"Goddamn Barry Obama," said J.K., knocking back the rest of his beer. "At least the bastard won."

"Rebecca, do you see this man here?" Hugh put his arm around J.K. "You have never seen a cuter kid than J.K. as a youngster."

"Bet you can't believe that," said J.K., and because J.K. was a good thirty pounds overweight and sunburned and losing his hair, and because Rebecca knew that he'd been in and out of rehab for as long as she'd known Vivi, the moment was uncomfortable.

"Do you know what?" asked Hugh. "You two have something in common," he said.

"What's that?" asked Rebecca.

"You both came to see me in Dar," he said. "You both needed a change of scene."

Rebecca froze. She didn't want him to talk about that trip, and certainly not like this.

"Those were some times," said J.K., a bit creepily. "Those were some goddamn different times."

"Yeah, well, I'm going to leave you two to take a stroll down memory lane," Rebecca said, backing away, wondering where everyone was. "Gonna leave you to it."

When she retreated to the side porch again and saw that most of the party had migrated down to the dock, she wanted to go upstairs to her room and lay her head down. Maybe she'd take a peek at her cellphone. She was about to give in and do just that, when Hugh came outside and they nearly collided. She backed up—shot back, actually—and he said, "I'm sorry."

She shrugged. "For what, exactly?"

He didn't answer. Instead, he tried to hug her.

She didn't really want him to, but she also didn't want to make more of something by refusing a simple hug. Did she have to be so rigid? She saw he realized he'd made her uneasy with his reference to her visit, that he'd been careless with her most secret and awful memory. And so she let him.

He was familiar—his tallness, his potent earthy tobacco scent, his calloused hands missing two fingers at her back—and not at all unpleasant. But then she realized that he wasn't letting go, and . . . "Hugh," she said, gently at first, but when he still didn't release her, she felt her heart start racing. Where were they? Could anyone see them? Probably not—they were hidden from the lawn, to one side of the door—but she broke out in a sweat, had a sense of being trapped, and did not know what else she felt besides the fact of him pressing into her, and she could not breathe and she wrested herself free, crying out *"Hugh,"* in a hushed angry way that, if anything, created the very scene that she would have done anything—really and truly anything—to avoid.

"Excuse me," uttered Helen, who was of course of course of course standing on the threshold, holding the screen door away from her body.

And, in that awful moment, Rebecca thought her mind might shut down from the noodle-y piano riffs that would not stop their loop.

"Hugh, what are you doing?" Helen demanded. She stepped out onto the side porch, letting the screen door slam behind her. Though Rebecca knew that—after a terrible struggle—Helen had quit smoking years ago, she immediately smelled cigarette smoke and was flooded with sympathy. Something must have set Helen off today, something bad enough to break her will.

"I—" Hugh looked off balance, Rebecca noticed, as if he might literally fall down. "I was giving Rebecca a hug," Hugh said. Even to Rebecca's ears he sounded guilty, as if this was a familiar scenario and he was simply saying his lines.

"You were giving Rebecca a hug."

"Helen, he hugged me," Rebecca confirmed. She tried her best to toss this off, to laugh even.

"Why?" Helen asked bluntly, although it obviously didn't matter why. Her face looked as if she'd cast off a previously imperceptible mask of inhibition. *"Why?"*

Rebecca stared at the screen door, watched it blur and unblur and blur again.

"I'm sorry," Helen stumbled, "but did you need a hug, Rebecca? From the looks of it, you were struggling to break free."

Without any warning, Vivi opened the screen door and stepped onto the porch. She immediately asked, "What's wrong?"

"Really," said Rebecca quickly, ignoring Vivi for the moment, "I think he saw that I was upset about something—I've had a strange week—and, look, he's had a lot to drink and it's an emotional day—an emotional *weekend*—and—"

"Rebecca," said Helen, who was biting her lower lip and clasping her hands together. "Did he hit on you?"

"Mom!" Vivi cried.

"Christ, Helen," hissed Hugh.

Helen's eyes were steely—many stages past shock. "Just . . . *did he?*"

"No," answered Rebecca, as clearly as she possibly could. "Absolutely not."

"Why would you ask her that?" cried Vivi, astonished, who looked too beautiful in her silky dress of all her favorite underwater colors to be stressed and seized by this embarrassing situation. She came to her father's side. *"Mom,"* she whispered with hushed force, before eventually breaking into yelling. "I know you're divorced, I know you have your own opinions, but what is wrong with you? *What are you even saying?* Papa isn't like that. He hasn't—"

"Yes, he is. Shit," blurted Helen. *"Shit."* She avoided looking at any of them. "I really don't want to have this conversation now."

"Then leave," said Vivi cruelly. "Stop yourself now and get out of here."

"I just—I have to—" For a moment Helen looked back nervously at the living room—miraculously free of guests—and, when she faced them again, Rebecca thought she might fall apart. Instead, she seemed to revive. "I know this is your day, sweetheart. And I wish more than anything that this was not happening, but I came outside to look for you. I came to say goodbye, and what I saw—"

"You're angry with him," said Vivi. "Look, *I* know he's an alcoholic. No one's ever come out and said that, so there you go. It's said." She turned to Hugh with exaggerated formality. "Papa, you're an alcoholic and not easy to live with. And, Mom, I know it was worse for you. He *wasn't* easy, but—"

"Rebecca," said Helen sharply. "Look at me."

But Rebecca was looking at Hugh; though still standing, his head was in his hands.

"Was my ex-husband hitting on you just now?"

Rebecca swallowed the shame. At this moment she imagined it would remain a part of her always, something like her very own inoperable growth—permanent if not cancerous—to carry around forever. This was, without a doubt, all her fault. "No," she answered. "No, of course not."

Rebecca could feel Helen assessing her. She understood that Helen wasn't sure whether or not she was telling the truth. Maybe Helen even suspected she had done something to provoke Hugh's attentions or—worse—that something had actually happened between them, but Rebecca could also see that Helen was going to hedge her bets; she was going to use this as an opportunity.

"Vivi, your father . . ." Helen started.

Vivi wouldn't acknowledge she was speaking.

"Just—Vivi, please—"

She remained impassive, her gaze far away.

But when Hugh simply walked away, down the stairs of the side porch and—predictably—toward the bar, Vivi didn't follow him.

"Think about it," Helen said gently, after they all watched him go. "For one second. How can you not already know?"

"How can I not *already*—what kind of bullshit is that?"

Helen repeatedly ran her hands through her hair but didn't have an answer.

"Answer me," cried Vivi. *"What are you even talking about?"*

"Your father was never faithful," Helen blurted. "Ever."

"What?"

"Your father—"

"Well, were *you?*"

Helen looked briefly insulted but quickly recovered. "Once we were married, yes. I certainly was."

"What do you mean, *once we were married?*"

"What I mean is that, once your father and I were married, I was faithful to him."

"But there was someone else?" Vivi asked.

Rebecca could swear she saw the slightest smile pass across Helen's face, but it was gone in an instant. "Yes," she said. "But I chose your father. For all kinds of reasons, that's the choice I made."

"Look, do you mean he had an affair? Or affairs?" asked Vivi, obviously grasping. "Because—I mean—over the course of a long marriage, a lot of people do."

"That's true," Helen said, obviously trying to control her mounting frustration with Vivi's insistence on incomprehension. "But this wasn't—" Helen stopped abruptly, as if to remind herself to keep it simple. "This was something of a different order."

"Okay," Vivi relented. "Okay, fine. But why are you telling me this now? I mean right *now?* At my *wedding celebration?*"

"I shouldn't have," said Helen, her voice cracking. "I'm so sorry." She went to take Vivi's hands, and Rebecca was surprised to see that Vivi did not, in fact, yank them away.

"Wait—earlier—did you say you were *leaving*?"

Helen nodded. "I decided to head back a bit early." She sounded defeated, but when she put her arms around Vivi, it was clear she wasn't. Her grip was strong.

"I'm so sorry," Helen whispered over and over; she continued to hold Vivi tightly.

Rebecca left them like this, before heading out on a search of her own.

Chapter Twenty-one

Fishers, 2010

Mrs. Ordway was ancient, gnarled and positioned in a wicker chair on the wide porch, looking out to sea. Ed took her frail hand in his, but of course she didn't remember him. She'd grown nicer. He loved when that happened. Since his own father was always so mean, it had been shocking—disturbing, even—when, near the end, the home-care attendant noted that his father was *such a sweet and gentle man.* And Ed did not think she was simply angling for an excellent tip, because— amazingly—he'd witnessed it. In the last few months of a life consumed by fighting, Murray Cantowitz had finally gone docile, as if dying alone in that same miserable tenement in a neighborhood that was finally finishing up a decade-long crack epidemic was all that he'd ever really wanted.

You won, Ed told him, minutes before the very end.

You better believe it is what he thought he heard, but he couldn't be certain; his father's speech had been slurred for a long time by then.

"I remember your garden," said Ed now.

"What's that, dear?" said Mrs. Ordway.

"I was here many years ago, and I remember your beautiful garden."

"Oh yes," she said, "beautiful." She smiled. "And what a bitch to maintain."

"But you enjoyed it," he insisted.

"Well, of course I did," she said, and he realized she hadn't entirely changed. "Who are you, did you say?"

"My name is Ed." He smiled, too. "Ed Cantowitz."

He looked out across the lawn and saw Hugh; he was heading for the bar. While preparing for this day, Ed hadn't allowed himself to dwell on how he'd ignored several letters and messages from Hugh over the years, even two during the very last five. After Rebecca had left Tanzania, Hugh sent him a brief note in prison just to let him know what a fine person she was. Ed had told Rebecca about the note (she'd seemed oddly flat in her response), but he hadn't replied to it. Then Hugh sent another note comprised of two sloppily written lines:

> *Dear Ed,*
> *What, exactly, did I ever do to you?*
> *Helen's left me.*
> *—H.*

He'd written back that time, but it was something equivocating and empty. As he saw Hugh now—in person, at a distance—he sustained what were today's first—though surely not the last—stirrings of serious shame. And it occurred to him that maybe, in fact, he owed Hugh more than he could ever offer, more than he could possibly explain.

"Daddy!" he heard, and there was Rebecca, flushed and urgent in the way she was about greetings.

Hugh suddenly looked up in Ed's direction but turned away before Ed could offer so much as a wave. But—Ed tried to reassure himself—he also wasn't sure whether or not Hugh had even seen him.

"You made it," Rebecca said, and planted a kiss on his cheek.

"This is my daughter," Ed told the old woman, who nodded.

"Hello, Mrs. Ordway," said Rebecca. "Do you have everything you need?"

"Every last thing," she said. She clasped her hands together as if a game were about to begin.

Rebecca led Ed down to the lawn, where croquet was set up but no one was playing. Under a tall oak tree, two dapper fellows were playing a banjo and an upright bass; a woman was singing along.

I'll see you in my dreams. And I'll hold you in my dreams—

They seemed like ghosts from another party, one from before even Ed was born. The woman's lipstick was bright red, and she was pretty and plump in the way women so seldom were anymore. She was wearing a lacy white sundress and what looked like high-heeled orthopedic shoes.

Someone took you out of my arms. Still I feel the thrill of your charms—

"How was the ceremony?" Ed asked.

"Lovely," said Rebecca, and Ed could tell she meant it. "There was a lot of crying."

"Hugh cry?" Ed asked, looking out to where a sailboat glided across the water.

"Big-time."

They walked toward the bar, which was set up in the reedy place where the grass became the shoreline, and there was Hugh, accepting a drink from the bartender.

"Hugh," said Rebecca. "My dad's here."

Hugh turned around and said, "Well, hello there." He took a step back and shook his head. "Christ almighty, hello." Then he stuck out his hand, which Ed ignored, opting for a hug instead. He clapped Hugh on the back several times.

"Hugh," said Ed, "congratulations." The setting here was so pastoral, and the scent of sea air and lavender was so particularly *clean,* that Hugh Shipley's own scent was just that much more of a contrast. There was the alcohol, of course, but also tobacco, which was so rare to catch a whiff of these days in civilized company that it immediately reminded him of prison, and he felt briefly revolted. But something besides alcohol or tobacco was even stronger, and Ed couldn't place it. When he drew back and got a good look at his old friend—his friend from another life—Ed had his first surprise.

Hugh did not look great. He didn't even look good. His eyes were the same—a little bloodshot, though still they had the same leonine gaze—and he wasn't pot-bellied or bald, but somehow he looked different. Was it bloat? Maybe he was sick and on some kind of god-awful medication? Or maybe, Ed thought—as Hugh looked bemused, mumbling about Vivi and Brian's expensive taste in spirits, while indicating his drink, which he then spilled on his tan lapel—maybe Hugh had become a drunk. And not the functioning kind that proliferated on this island and in the halls of Shipley family homes dotted along the East Coast, or even his own father's kind of boozing, which had seemed aggressive and grief-stricken, but rather the kind that qualified for the title when Ed and Hugh were children in the 1950s: *a drunk*—someone who pretended not to be and for whom the common practice of ignoring and pretending didn't work anymore.

Ed's second surprise was when he realized just how fervently he didn't want this to be the case. He didn't want to feel sorry for Hugh Shipley. This was something for which he was completely unprepared.

And so he started to talk. And once he started, he found he couldn't stop. "I read about the prize, Hugh. Congratulations. Really. Congratulations on that."

"Thanks," Hugh said.

"I mean it." Ed clapped him on the shoulder. "Very goddamn impressive. I read all about it."

"Did you?"

"All the articles. I got to see what you've been up to. I mean, I knew you'd been up to a hell of a lot—I always knew you'd been productive—but it's another thing to read all about it. See it in print. Do you know what I mean? Even though these days you can read pretty much anything in print. Do you remember when print really meant something? All the bullshit publications on the Internet these days make it that much harder to see the genuine articles—so to speak—but not with your work. That was easy to find. I'm telling you . . ."

Rebecca drifted away; the 1920s band stopped playing; Ed had yet to see Vivi and her husband; he'd yet to see Helen; but still he continued to stand on the lawn with Hugh.

"Seen any good films lately?" Ed asked, pleased with himself on account of how he'd remembered the perfect way to start Hugh talking and save them both from Ed's inability to stop. Ed prepared himself for a long diatribe about an obscure tribal practice in a country rarely traveled to—if such places even existed anymore. But:

"I haven't seen a real film in years" is all Hugh offered.

"No?" Ed felt unreasonably disappointed. He waited for Hugh to clarify.

But Hugh only shook his head. "When I do, it's on an airplane and I find myself looking forward to the ones about spies and the future, that sort of thing."

"But what about those—y'know . . ." He was at a loss, both to describe the films properly and on seeing Hugh's blank expression. "What about those films you loved? Anthropological? Ethnographical?"

"Ethnographic. I always disliked those terms."

"I do recall they all seemed to be either over three hours or under five minutes."

Hugh shrugged. But he finally grinned.

"The one about the violent tribe?" Ed probed. "You loved that film. You loved all of them."

"Like watching paint dry," said Hugh.

"But what about your mentor? Charlie? That was his name, right?"

"You got it, Ed. You got it." Ed was suddenly aware of a distinct angry sarcasm. "That mind's still a steel trap."

"What happened to Charlie?" Ed asked, attempting to sound unperturbed.

"What happened to Charlie," Hugh said. "Sounds like a play, doesn't it?"

"You're thinking of the play *Charley's Aunt*," Ed corrected him. "Or the musical *Where's Charley?* Two Oxford lads and their cross-dressing hijinks."

"Right again." Hugh raised his glass in acknowledgment.

"Rebecca was in the musical——eighth grade. 'Once in Love with Amy.' Don't you know that song?"

"I'm afraid not," said Hugh.

"Everybody knows that song."

"Everybody except me," said Hugh.

Ed wasn't sure why he was so convinced of this, or why it even mattered, but he was certain that Hugh knew that sweet, romantic song and simply wouldn't admit it. "So tell me," he pressed on, "what *did* happen to him?"

"Charlie Case made a terrible picture in Hollywood about 'cave people.' He's taught at Harvard for several decades—beloved by his students, ignored by the rest of the world."

"Well, I'm sorry to hear that he's ignored by the masses, but being a beloved Harvard professor hardly sounds like a tragedy. You know who should have been a professor?"

"Who?"

"Me," said Ed. "That's what I should have done. A professorial life."

"Ha," said Hugh.

"No, really," said Ed, but he was aware he was actually only trying to get another smile out of Hugh.

"Charlie and I fell out long before the Hollywood picture."

Hugh's tone was so bitter and even mournful at the idea of falling out with a friend that Ed had to look away. Because though it was true that time and geography—as he'd always claimed—certainly served to distance even the most diligent and closest of friends, Ed had always known that it had been he who'd cut Hugh off, and he'd cut him off without warning. He also knew that Hugh had done nothing to deserve this contempt, aside from the fact that he'd gone ahead and married Helen. Which should not have come as any kind of surprise. And though Ed could not abide the marriage—at least not up close—how the hell was Hugh supposed to have been expected to understand this?

The breeze kept steady, the boats continued sailing, and Ed felt—why?—that he had to keep this conversation going. It was as if he was trying to get through whatever this kind of talk could be called (was there any other word besides *bullshit?*) and get to the other side, another shore. It felt somehow necessary to get there, as if *there* were a particular place—like *the club,* where they'd been met with towels and cheers and hoppy cold beer after swimming through a mess of seaweed. As if *there* were not simply a shared authenticity, which they'd both abandoned long ago.

"You know," said Hugh, clapping Ed on the shoulder, "I'm going to tell you something, Ed. I have thought, you know, over the years, that maybe, if I cared so much about *contributing* to the world—and I did, you know—that's what I've wanted to do—even when I loved those boring, useless films, because you're right, I did love them—I have wanted to *contribute something*—"

"I know you did," Ed reassured him. "I know. And who says those films are useless? You know I've always been a goddamn Philistine. You were probably right to love them."

"I've thought—I admit it—maybe I should have done what Ed did. Maybe I should have gone and made some *real dough*—"

"Okay," said Ed, forcing a laugh, not wanting to continue with this particular theme.

"You remember that's what you said to me that first night at Cronin's? I couldn't get over it." Hugh smiled. "No one I knew ever talked about money."

"Now, listen here," said Ed, not only keen on redirecting the conversation but suddenly downright pissed. "You and I both know that you don't mean a word of this nonsense. If you're trying to stick in the knife further, why not just come out and say it?"

"What are you talking about?"

"Prison," hissed Ed. "My stint in prison." He looked around, anxious to have mentioned it. *"Jesus."*

"I only meant—"

"You've just won a goddamn seriously impressive award for a fucking lifetime of selfless service. And whatever mood you're in—excuse me, but you need to pull it together, because as far as I can tell this is a goddamn happy occasion." He was not up to this kind of bitter talk right here, right now, although he did realize this was childish. Because—aside from the most banal chitchat, of which he was nearly incapable—what other kind of talk did he think might transpire today, nearly fifty years since their first conversation, their lives still improbably entwined?

"But you know I could have done that," Hugh persisted. "I could have made some real dough, like you. Doesn't mean I would have made the same choices."

"Right," said Ed. But he was *still* unable to walk away.

"I could have," said Hugh, "especially with times what they were when we graduated, before the world woke up—I probably could have inserted myself into any number of firms, even despite my awfully meager academic achievements. *You* know—what with all those *family connections*, which I now shamelessly tap for contributions to my clinics."

"It's not as easy as you think," said Ed.

"I should have made some real money," said Hugh, clearly not even making a pretense of listening to what Ed might have to say. "I should have made money and I should have given it away," said Hugh. "*Bam. Contribution.* That's what I should have done."

Ed had settled into nodding, into a pattern of nodding and shifting weight and drinking his glass of champagne. "Maybe," said Ed tightly. "But I don't think you mean that."

"No?" asked Hugh, and his tone sounded conspiratorial now, as if they'd gone into hiding together, far away from this celebration that either was or was not responsible for sending Hugh into anything but a celebratory state. "No?" he repeated. "You don't think I mean what I say? Why? Because you know me so well?"

"Of course not."

"Because we both know you don't know me at all."

"True," Ed said. He let himself look at Hugh directly. "Or," he let his eyes apologize, "I might."

Hugh breathed the saddest kind of sigh. Then, as if refusing to be sucked under by this display of sentiment, he kicked at the ground; he shook his head. "We both know, *actually,* that as soon as you met Helen's father and had every connection you could ever need, you were done with me, done with both of us."

Ed swallowed hard, stupidly stunned. "That couldn't be further from the truth."

Hugh shrugged, as if there was so much more that he wanted to say but he was choosing not to.

Ed knew he should have taken this insult as his cue to excuse himself, if not to simply walk away, but he didn't do either. There was a part of him that felt oddly more relaxed now, having heard what Hugh really thought of him all this time and hearing it with little to no provocation.

They stood not together exactly but side by side, looking out to sea like a pair of whaling widows. And when the water no longer held the attention of either of them, they still didn't part ways. Instead, they turned and shifted their focus up the lawn, where people seemed to be enjoying themselves tremendously. Men in their prime held babies on their shoulders. Women held their long hair off their damp necks. An Indian woman was playing croquet in an emerald-green sari. Vivi and Brian's friends belonged in one of those politically correct fashion ads for a fantasy version of a picnic on a country estate or an otherworldly kind of tailgating—where several ethnicities were represented and pretty much everyone looked interesting if not overtly attractive. But this wasn't an ad; this was their life, and Ed could not get over it. The physical landscape of this island had not changed one bit as far as he could tell, but time had left its mark here, at least at this one house. Because at this generation's Ordway house party, Ed was not a remotely exotic visitor. In fact, in the eyes of some of today's guests, he might have even belonged on the side porch, where the older folks—decidedly less colorful—were seated at rented chairs and tables, eating deviled eggs in ample shade.

When Ed saw the woman with the pixie-short hair, he recognized her instantly, even though she was across the lawn with her back turned. He saw her pale narrow shoulders and her long neck and felt his heart not in free fall but rather exploding into his knees and throat. She was wearing a blue sundress. Her figure—at least from this vantage—looked the same. He realized that some might have said the dress was better suited to a younger person, and yet he also saw that on Helen this dress was perfect. When she turned around, her face was just as he'd imagined: bright eyes, high cheekbones, no discernible help from science and thus—older. And still . . . pretty. Oh my God, was she pretty. As he watched her cross the lawn and give the Indian woman a warm embrace, as she behaved perfectly normally and the party continued as if there were not an asteroid breaking up inside a man pushing seventy standing near the bar, Ed tried not to look so obviously focused. He had come here to see her and here she was—older, with short silver-blond hair— and though he tried to remain at least a little bit tough, steeled against her more than probable lack of interest, he felt weak—even inexperienced —at the sight of her. He forced himself not to ask Hugh about her, not to start the inquiries.

"I still can't believe it," said Hugh.

"Can't believe . . ."

"That she really left me."

Ed wanted to ask if Hugh had deserved it, but he refrained. He knew how idiotic such a question was. He, of all people, knew.

She'd gone and cut her hair. If anyone had told him she'd cut her hair, he would have mourned the corn-silk loss of it, but he mourned nothing, not even the passage of time, when he saw her now standing on that lawn. When she spotted Ed standing with Hugh, her expression didn't change. If she was startled, if she was happy or disconcerted, her face did not reveal it. He wanted to go to her immediately, but he didn't. He couldn't. He waited with Hugh, if not patiently then quietly, until she made her way to the bar.

"Gentlemen," she said; her smile was contained. He was on high alert, watching for hints of what remained between Hugh and her. They seemed neutral enough with each other, but he wanted surety. They were divorced, he reminded himself, which oddly didn't help. If he could get definitive proof that there was nothing left between them, he'd feel—what? Free to proceed and be rejected?

"Congratulations, Helen," said Ed. And he offered a kiss—his lips landing on the air next to her slightly flushed cheek. All these years he'd assumed that she understood exactly why he'd bowed out of their life, but as he stood facing Helen now, he suddenly wondered if she didn't share Hugh's clearly mixed if not completely harsh opinion of him. It took all he had not to ask for her judgment right there and then. "I still haven't seen your daughter."

"Oh, she's around," Helen said. "Probably with one of her children somewhere—putting out fires, you know."

"Cute kids," said Ed. "Do you see them much?" he asked both of them.

"Yes—I'm afraid I can't get enough," said Helen.

He noticed that Hugh was keeping his gaze on the water, as if watching for signs of a squall.

"And," she continued, seemingly unruffled by Hugh's disengagement, "you must be so proud of Rebecca."

"Very proud," said Ed. And even though he *was*, he realized he sounded oddly reserved about expressing it. As a rule, he generally disliked people who were too modest about their children. Jill, for instance, was accomplished in this regard. Plenty of people who'd been seated to her right and left at dinner parties in Manhattan, Palm Beach, Southampton, Milan, hadn't a clue she even had offspring. So why did Ed now have the unfamiliar impulse to deflect any praise about his kid?

He hated to think it was because Hugh was keeping disconcertingly quiet on the subject. He hated to think that, after all, Hugh Shipley still basically intimidated him. Or, worse, that Hugh's silence was due to the fact that Hugh and Rebecca had discussed him during her trip to Tanzania—that they'd torn Ed apart, examining his many flaws.

"Hugh had the chance to see what Rebecca is capable of. She still says that trip changed her life."

Hugh only nodded.

"She worked hard, I guess?"

"Sure," said Hugh. "Sure she did."

Ed felt like asking: *Really? Who can't find at least one nice thing to say about Rebecca Cantowitz?*

But he also knew this had nothing to do with his daughter or her trip. Hugh *actually thought* that Ed had been some kind of social-climbing, ambitious mercenary. The way Hugh had said it, Ed could tell he meant it. *Was* it possible that Helen agreed?

"Excuse me," Ed said, "I just realized I have an appetite."

"You just realized this?" asked Hugh, and Ed still couldn't tell if he was trying to be chummy or cruel.

"I think I'm going to help myself to some of the brunch that invitation promised."

"That invitation . . ." said Helen, with the lightest touch of an eye roll, making it perfectly clear that she had not been a fan, either.

He turned away, taking with him the slightest dose of immature pleasure both in their shared reaction to the invitation and that, for the first time since he'd known them, Hugh and Helen were not a couple. There was a line snaking down the hill from the buffet table, and he took his place in it, watching from afar as his old friends parted quickly, though neither of them joined him. He waited, listening to snippets of people greeting one another, reporting on their summers as if it were the first day of school. He made himself a plate and, in lieu of sitting, hovered at the side of the buffet table, not wanting to get stuck talking to anyone. He considered the house from a distance. It was not smaller than he remembered. It was still sprawling, still as magisterial as it was faded. While looking for Rebecca, he somehow failed to notice the oncoming woman until she was literally in his face.

"Ed!" she cried, before positively enveloping him. She held on a tad longer than was socially acceptable on the East Coast, and when she drew away, she still held on to his hands. "Ed Cantowitz. Well, look at you! You know, I have to say, I didn't know you'd age so well."

He greeted her warily, failing to see what was—seconds later—so obvious. Her bosoms had bosoms; her freckles had freckles; the hair was spiky and layered but still red, dyed even redder.

But after some initial banter about how insulted she was that he hadn't recognized her, they defaulted quickly to politics, and shortly after laughing surprisingly hard at her dead-on imitation of Sarah Palin, Ed found it almost difficult to conjure what Kitty had looked like as a young woman. It was hard to be wistful in the face of such a commanding presence.

Here she was in a dramatic white silk blazer, with her throaty voice and complicated necklace and rhinestone-encrusted reading glasses suspended on a chain. Here she was, referencing a dizzying number of friends (two of whom were ex-husbands) and insisting he ought to come visit her in Santa Fe.

"I have a ranch," said Kitty. "Do you ride?"

"Me? No," said Ed. "I fall off horses."

"Oh who cares," said Kitty. "To tell you the truth? I don't ride, either." She gave a wayward smile. "Oh, Ed, I'm glad to see you're okay. I know a fellow in securities, and they put him away for *twenty*." She made a tragic face and he must have looked confused, because she said, "I do *read*, you know."

"Right," he said. *Jesus*, he thought, but he was also frankly touched by her decisive sympathy. "I'm a-okay," he said.

"You're out!"

"That's right," he said. "I'm out."

Before dessert, Brian called everyone into the living room. He was a handsome fellow with a beard that made him look, if anything, younger. Ed idly wondered if Hugh had managed to sail through the seventies and eighties without a beard or the inexplicably popular bushy mustache. "Well," Brian deadpanned, "Vivi finally said yes."

"I'm a procrastinator," she cried, a little loopy. "A late bloomer!"

"Hardly," said Brian. "And," he raised his glass to her, "I love you," he said, to approving murmurs and *hear hears*. "Thank you for coming,

everyone. Thank you to Grandmother Ordway, especially, for her patience with our brood and for hosting this wonderful occasion."

As he continued the brief toast, his children hung around his legs and
he gathered them closer. *He's classy,* Ed thought, disappointed with himself for the teensiest bit of jealousy on Rebecca's behalf. He'd been expecting a more pretentious tone.

Then Vivi stood on a chair and read out loud from a crinkly piece of
paper.

"Among you," she began, "is a talented chef who taught me how to
dance, a person who can make me laugh no matter how shitty—sorry,
Grandmother!—my mood, a poet who taught me to stop using all my
unnecessary adverbs, and," she looked up, "at least two people who are,
very literally, changing the world."

She continued with these descriptions, never naming names. She
progressed to discussing her upbringing; her parents, who'd taught her
everything; her struggles with her career; her inability to separate from
both her parents and her children. The (purposefully overstated) theme
of the toast became: *What Poor Brian Has to Endure.* The room was
overheated—from the Oriental rug came a whiff of old canned soup—
and though a part of Ed recognized that Vivi was being more than a little
self-indulgent, he also could not take his eyes off her. He found himself
wanting her to get back to the mystery descriptions and even wondered
if some of them—*you're an example of fierceness; you're New York to
me*—could have possibly been about him. This was the attraction of
self-indulgent people: They gave you permission to be self-
indulgent, too. No wonder Rebecca had been drawn to Vivi, especially
at fifteen. He remembered his daughter in eighth or ninth grade, throwing a fit because he'd insisted she go to sleep; she hadn't wanted to be
unprepared for school the next day. *I have a responsibility to my classmates,* she'd insisted. *I'm accountable, Daddy.* He'd been so proud of her
diligence that he hadn't noticed—had he?—that in addition to being
serious-minded and conscientious, she'd also been a very stressed-out
kid.

And there she was—*his daughter*—no longer a kid but so much the same, intently listening to a tall old man in a wheelchair. Ed sidled up beside her. "Excuse me," he said, with a smiling glance at the man. "Nice toast, huh?"

She looked down at the old man. "Daddy, this is Mr.—I'm sorry, sir, I only know what Vivi calls you."

"You can call me that, too. So can he. Who're you?"

"He's my dad," she said, and Ed placed his hands on his daughter's shoulders.

"Ed Cantowitz," he said, reaching out his hand, which the man ignored.

"Well, you can both call me Uncle Larry. Why the hell not? Old geezer like me."

"Uncle Larry," Ed said, "no kidding." This old geezer had blown a goddamn bullhorn in his ear. He almost wanted to remind him—but something held him back: Pity? Empathy? Yes, he realized, it was empathy, or something closer to empathy than was exactly comfortable.

"We know each other?" Uncle Larry squinted; the skin around his eyes sagged and pouched so that his eyes looked barely open.

"Nope," Ed said, while giving Rebecca's shoulders a squeeze, as if to say, *Time to go.* The old man looked benign now, but there was no point in sticking around to find out; he wasn't in the mood to be insulted in front of his daughter. And then, as a kind of farewell: "I've only heard the stories."

"Hope you'll ignore them," he shouted out as they headed toward the piano, as if this was his favorite line.

Kitty was handing out song sheets. Having written some original lyrics for the occasion, she'd titled the song "Hello, Marriage," (to the tune of "Hello, Dolly"), and everybody sang—softly at first, despite uncomfortable laughter, and then, as the satiric edge fell away, everyone sang out louder. These were the voices of people who'd been drinking during one of the first days of fall, who largely didn't belt out karaoke or attend religious gatherings (or if they did: High Holidays, a caroling service), and so singing was a rare enough occurrence that they'd forgotten how good it felt. To sing! Ed accepted a glass of bourbon. Everyone sang in the Ordway living room as Hugh Shipley banged it out on the baby grand.

"Hello, Marriage" turned into "Some Enchanted Evening," which turned into "My One and Only." Ed didn't see Rebecca or Vivi or anyone under sixty. Also, he didn't see Helen. He told himself he needed some air, and when he hit the lawn, he realized just how true this was. He planted his feet in the grass, took one of Dr. Goldfarb's deep breaths, and walked on toward the tennis courts, where there was neither the pop of balls on the Har-Tru nor the grunts of self-laceration with which he was now so familiar, after decades of playing. On the court there were no players, only several children taking turns jumping over the middle of the sagging, fraying net.

Past the courts was where he was headed; he wanted to see what had become of the garden. Though he realized, as he drew closer, that he was actually filled with dread at the thought of seeing all that bounty gone to seed, and he was relieved to see a sunflower blossom poking through the various trees and shrubs that created such privacy within. Of course the garden wasn't entirely abandoned—he was foolish to think so; surely such a property as this employed at least one gardener.

He remembered being alone in Mrs. Ordway's garden in the middle of the night. He remembered the heady scent and the humidity and the lingering shame and confusion he'd felt at having upset Helen, who'd been in a touchy mood. He had teased her about wanting babies. Now he understood the reasons for her outsized reaction. But the thought of how she'd snapped at him so bitterly, it filled him—even now—with fear. He was afraid he would inadvertently replicate that feeling, that he would somehow ruin whatever time was allotted to him today.

"Hello, stranger," Helen said now. She was wrapped in a pale shawl; she was smoking a cigarette. Hydrangeas drooped off the overgrown bushes, the blooms barely holding on. She regarded the cigarette as if it were a foe. "I quit," she said. "For almost fifteen years."

"Put that thing out, then," he said. "Just go ahead and put it out."

While maintaining eye contact, she took another drag and then she crushed the sucker into the bottom of her beaded sandal. Her toenails, he noticed, were opalescent, like the inside of a shell.

"You did it," he marveled.

"You look amazed."

"Well," said Ed, "I guess I am." He took the crushed cigarette from her long cupped fingers and put it in his jacket pocket. He'd throw it out later. He tried not to think of later. He opted not to think beyond this: Helen; her fingers.

"So here we are," she said.

The garden had nothing of the wildness that he remembered, and yet it was still a garden. Aside from the patch of sunflowers and hydrangea bushes, there were several climbing vines merging with wisteria trees, Japanese maples. Ed felt himself working to contain a smile and wondered why he was doing that; what did he care if she knew he was happy to see her? What did he care if she knew that he was, in fact, ecstatic to find her here, specifically away from the others, away from the distraction of both of their daughters and her grandchildren, her mother, sister, Hugh.

"What?" asked Helen gently. "What are you smiling about?"

"Well, I was thinking that here you are," he said, "hiding."

"I'm not hiding."

"Sure you are. You're like a princess in some dark fairy tale: hiding in the garden, trying to break a curse."

"With a stolen cigarette?"

He shrugged. "You tell me."

"Maybe I'm a young princess trapped in the body of an old hag."

"Hardly." And it did come as something of a relief to feel in every cell of his body that he was telling the truth.

"Then what's the curse?" she asked. For a moment she stepped into a patch of sunlight, and her eyes looked almost golden. "And what's the princess after, if not to be young again? Isn't that what all those princesses want?"

"I thought they wanted to find their way home."

"I'm never at home," she said. She didn't seem particularly bothered by this. "You?"

"Sure," he said, not mentioning that he hadn't lived there in years. "So," he said, "Vivi's married."

"Yes."

"Are you happy?" he asked her, ostensibly about the wedding, though it came out with far more portent than he'd intended. He didn't want to open the door to speak about their actual lives.

She picked up a hydrangea blossom that had dropped to the ground and rubbed its petals between her fingers. She smelled her fingertips and, with a familiar burst of giggling, rubbed at the flower some more. "At the moment?" she asked.

"Sure," he nodded. *Please.* "Let's stick with the moment."

"Then, yes," she said. "I guess I am."

"Okay, then," he said. He wanted to take hold of her hand, her neck, and her tufted hair. "I thought—" He stopped himself.

"You thought what?"

"I thought you'd stay with me." He hadn't planned on saying it, hadn't even dreamed of it, but once he did, he knew it had been inevitable. His own breath echoed in his ears the way it had on so many turbulent flights he'd taken; then as now, he prayed for his own survival. "You have any idea how badly I wanted you to?"

Helen didn't say anything. But she also didn't look away. He took a few steps closer.

When the girl came running into the garden, Ed felt ungenerous toward the little interloper. But then Ed saw Helen's skin flush from her chest, up her neck, and up to the tips of her vaguely elfin ears, and his ungenerous feelings melted into gratitude, because he could tell that Helen was embarrassed, and what did she have to be embarrassed about? What, indeed.

"Nana, there's cake," said the little girl. "And we made the cake? And so I think you should eat a lot of it, because I know you love cake so much?"

"I do, darling," she said, scooping her up onto her hip, with surprising —even shocking—ease. "Bina, this is Ed. Auntie Rebecca's daddy. Ed, this is Bina—*Sabine*. But Nana doesn't call her that—too grown up for now, in my humble opinion."

"Nana doesn't like candy so much," Sabine said, by way of a greeting. "She doesn't like gum or lollipops."

"No?" asked Ed. They began to walk back to the house.

"But cake?" said the girl, with her eyes comically wide. "Cake or cookies? Forget about it! She LOVES cake."

"Forget about it?" Helen was laughing now, and it was so different from any of her familiar giggling spurts. It was a laugh that made him realize not only that there was little current information he *did* know about her but that he was really curious; he wanted to know. He wanted to know.

He wanted to know.

As they approached the house, Sabine spotted Brian, crying out, "Daddy, I found Nana. *Now* can we have the cake?"

Helen sighed. "She doesn't take me for granted or anything."

The sun went behind a patch of clouds, and Ed was struck by the fact that this day would turn to evening, and sooner than he'd realized. "That's a beautiful thing, you know."

"What is?"

"To have a grandmother to take for granted."

She looked at him for seconds longer than she strictly needed to. "I want you to have something," she said, as they entered the house through the kitchen. "Do you mind waiting here? I'll just be a second."

"What is it?" he asked, and then, "Never mind. Of course."

While he waited for her—what was she getting?—Ed sat on a bar stool and ate grapes from a fruit bowl, although he was anything but hungry. Helen hadn't mentioned his questionable business practices or the *Times* article or prison, and he wondered if and when she would. It then occurred to him that she might see him as nothing more than some kind of colorful character, a notion that made him queasy.

"Can I get you something?" asked the caterer, a woman who looked like any number of teenage boys from his youth, complete with brilliantined hair.

"No thanks," he said, before starting with his mantra of self-comfort: interrogation. Did she work in the city? Where did she buy her meat? Her produce? Did she go to college? Cooking school? Why not? Pastimes? Tennis? Gym? Concerts? He found that the details of other people's lives worked to soothe his nerves. He wasn't interested in people, per se, but rather in the mundane details of living; everybody— *everybody*—had to pass the time.

Just then Vivi came into the kitchen, looking upset. "Hi, kiddo," he offered.

"Hi," said Vivi flatly. She put her fingertips to her eyes. "Ed," she asked, "what are you doing here?" And though he knew she meant here in this kitchen, it did sound as though she meant here—at this party, today.

Though always ready with a comeback, Ed had absolutely nothing to say. The caterer busied herself with vast sheets of plastic wrap; the dishwasher washed dishes; from the living room came the sound of laughter.

What are you doing here? It was a fair question.

If he could have, he would have said this to Vivi with the utmost sincerity: *I am here for your mother.*

But even that wouldn't have been the whole truth. Because he was here for Hugh, too.

He was here to have Hugh condemn him not only for cutting him off but for *why* he'd cut him off. What happened with Helen: He did want to be condemned for it. Ed realized that for this to happen he would have had to show up at this wedding party and not only confess to having slept with the mother of the bride almost fifty years ago but he would have had to reveal the (perhaps deranged) extent of his torch-carrying.

What are you doing here?

He was here for Hugh to look him in the eye and—just as his own daughter had—condemn the illegal manner in which Ed had made *real dough* for fifteen years. He was looking for Hugh to seem disappointed in him. To say: *I just thought you were better than that.* But all Hugh had seemed was wounded. He'd also seemed bitter.

Ed watched Vivi drink a glass of water standing over the sink, obviously not caring that Ed had neither answered her question nor left the kitchen.

He wasn't going to buy back his old apartment. He wasn't going to start working on any risky new car enterprise in Brazil. He was going to take his fresh, still fairly meager capital and invest it conservatively, and he was going to set about ingratiating himself onto a board or two. He knew this in a way that was so suddenly, deflatingly obvious that he even thought of telling Vivi that *this* was what he was doing here: figuring out how to live.

"I'll see ya, kiddo," he said to Vivi. "Congratulations."

Vivi gave him a dour wave.

The screen door banged too loudly behind him; autumn had crept into the air. A group of children finally played croquet, and a crowd of adults—mostly women, many shivering—gathered around to watch.

It occurred to him that, even though she'd sounded genuine in her intention of giving him something, Helen might have, in fact, ditched him yet again. It was time to leave this party.

And there was Hugh, down by the bar, even though the bartender had packed up and was hauling crates away. Before he took the time to consider it, Ed found himself walking down the lawn.

Ed's heart was racing no less bombastically than when he'd faced Helen in the garden. He stood beside Hugh, who was watching the water, unwilling or unable to acknowledge his presence. They would be dead relatively soon. They lived on different continents. Ed cleared his throat. He kept clearing it and clearing it, and in that moment he knew there was no denying how much he sounded like his father. His hands were shaking; the salt air was bracing but not enough to stop this pitiful clarity. He knew what he had to say. "We were friends," Ed found himself saying. "We were." Quiet, gravelly—he barely recognized his own voice. "I can't leave here with you thinking that I used you. That I cared about the connections more than—" He couldn't bring himself to finish.

Hugh gripped his shoulder then; he put his arm around Ed and held him tightly—a hold that belied his poor posture and bloodshot eyes. This was still a strong man, and his grip fell somewhere between aggression and affection.

Ed waited for Hugh to say something.

But he didn't.

He just gripped Ed and looked out at the water; Ed didn't rush to fill the silence then. Even if he'd had the urge, the hitch in his throat would have prevented it.

A boat floated across the horizon. The sun disappeared behind a skein of clouds. "We were friends," Ed repeated.

Hugh's grip lessened, and then he gave Ed's back a pat. An unquestionably reassuring gesture. As if to say—*I know.*

But when Ed allowed himself to reconcile the fact that Helen might, in fact, be searching for him, when he finally turned toward the house and asked, "You coming?" Hugh shook his head.

"I'm going to stay out here a little longer," he said.

"Okay," said Ed, nodding.

"Okay," said Hugh.

A minute must have passed before Ed walked away.

Helen wasn't anywhere to be found. The porch, the house—it was all eerily quiet. "There you are," he heard Rebecca say, as if she'd been looking for hours. She shivered. "It's so much colder."

"You want a ride?" he asked, handing over his jacket.

She shook her head but put the jacket on, pulled it close. "Thanks," she said. "You're leaving?"

He nodded. "Where've you been? I saw your friend the bride in the kitchen."

By the way Rebecca nodded, Ed could tell that she knew the cause of Vivi's distress.

"Weddings can be rough," he offered lightly.

"Right." She looked out in the distance. Ed saw water, sky, reeds, Hugh. He wondered what she saw.

"A group of us are supposed to stay an extra night," said Rebecca miserably. "I took off from work and everything."

"So you'll stay. What—are you two in some kind of fight?"

She shook her head. "No," she said. "No, of course not."

"Well, I'm sure she'll snap out of her mood."

"I don't know about that."

His daughter seemed suddenly younger, as if she were a teenager and what she really wanted was for him to force her to leave. He realized just how long it had been since she'd looked at him that way: as if he had any kind of power.

"You'll stay," Ed said again. "You'll enjoy yourself." They walked around the house toward the driveway. Ed gave the valet his ticket.

"I want to tell you something," Rebecca said. She still looked younger and scared—maybe tipsy, too—but there was also something else.

"What is it?" he asked. "You okay? You don't *have* to stay an extra night, you know. Only stay if you want to. You might be done here. Whatever the problem is, I'm sure it can—"

"I went out with Gabriel," she blurted.

Hallelujah. Baruch HaShem. Images of his own little grandkids running through—if not this very majestic lawn—the miracle of Central Park. Ed forced himself to merely nod.

"Aren't you going to say anything?" Rebecca demanded.

"Is he—"

"He's available," she cut him off; boy, was she tense. "He's available and he called."

"How many times have you seen him?"

"Just once."

"You gonna see him again?"

She nodded. "I really hope so."

"Okay," Ed said. "Okay, good."

"Okay, good?"

He nodded.

"I thought you'd be upset," she said, and her voice was trembling. "You've always told me to move on!"

While he did feel kind of badly that she'd anticipated such a response, he couldn't help but also take pride in the evidently great job he'd done at hiding the fact that their breakup had been so personally devastating. "Well—" he started.

"He has a five-year-old son!" Rebecca cried.

"So?"

"*So?*"

"Do you think you'll like the kid?"

She was nodding emphatically, bordering on maniacally. "Absolutely."

"Will he have more kids?"

"I don't know. Probably."

"Well, then?" he said, inwardly beaming. *"Okay, good."*

His daughter took a shuddering breath. "We'll see," said Rebecca, and now he couldn't tell if she was shaking because of the change in the weather or if, in fact, she might just cry. "I mean—we'll see," she repeated. "Who knows?"

He gave her a good strong hug. "Nobody."

Ed stood with his car keys in his hand, not sure what he was still doing there, lingering in the gravel driveway minutes after Rebecca had handed over his jacket. What was there left to say to anyone? He hadn't said goodbye; he'd send letters instead, especially—he decided—to Hugh. He'd send Vivi and Brian the same glass bowl from Bergdorf's that he gave every pair of newlyweds, plus an extravagant gift for each child. He might live like a pauper these days but, thanks to credit cards—the new debt-ridden American way—he'd never scrimp on these presents. He hadn't figured out what he would do about Helen, but once he was finally behind the wheel, he found himself looking into the rearview, as if she might simply appear—the way she had in his hallway nearly fifty years ago at the Y and over an hour ago in the garden. So when he saw her walk out of the house onto the porch, it seemed, once again, no less than magical. He didn't consider that maybe—just maybe—she might have simply made a decision to follow him.

She'd changed out of the sundress, and in the khaki pants, blue sweater, and colorful scarf, she didn't look quite as youthful. She was wearing tennis sneakers and had dragged a carry-on with wheels down the porch steps, but due to the grass and the gravel, she was definitely having some trouble on the driveway.

He got out of the car. "Let me help you with that."

She nodded thanks, as he brought her bag as far as his own car. She didn't motion for the valet, so neither did he.

"Where are you going?" he asked, surprised that she was going anywhere.

"Manhattan," she said. "Oh." She reached into her pocket. "This is what I wanted you to have." She handed over an envelope. "It's just a picture," she said.

And for some reason he was certain that it was the same picture he'd also held on to, the one in front of the round house, captured by Hugh's Leica in the hands of an old man who'd been out walking an old dog, both of whom—by now—had to have been dead for decades.

He hadn't actually seen the whole photograph in years. Soon after he'd read about the Shipley marriage, and in an act he'd immediately regretted, Ed had cut Helen out of the picture, so that the photo that lay in his desk drawer—in Midtown, right this very moment—was of only Ed and Hugh.

"Should I open it now?" Ed asked.

"If you want," she said.

He didn't.

"Can you give me a lift?" she asked. The fading sunlight shone on her face and he could see her lines, her damage.

He barked a kind of incredulous laugh, which came out strangely.

"What was that?" Helen asked.

Ed popped the trunk. He picked up her bag and hurled it—lower back be damned—into the spotless trunk.

"*What?*" demanded Helen. "Why are you laughing at me?"

"*Can I give you a lift?*" His voice was too loud, and he was breathing heavily from the exertion of lifting that deceptively small bag. He opened the passenger door for her and closed it once she was safely inside. He looked up, for a moment, at the darkening sky.

Ed sat down in the driver's seat, turned the key in the ignition. "Can I give you a lift?" he repeated, softly now, or—at least—softer. They both fastened their seat belts. "Please, sweetheart," Ed said. "As if you don't already know."

Epilogue

Clinking glasses and muffled conversation, gravel from the driveway crunching underfoot, the blending scents of perfume and grill smoke and fertilizer—it all floated up through the floor and the windows of Rebecca's room at the Ordway house. She took in the stillness after so much turmoil and wondered how much Vivi would want to know about what had happened on the porch. Would she end up blaming Rebecca? It was not inconceivable. She looked around: the dying light; the embroidered bedspread; her favorite oval mirror. She didn't know if she'd be back.

And maybe it was because what happened with all three Shipleys that day did, in fact, eclipse most of her other memories of Vivi's wedding, but what Rebecca would always remember, with exquisite detail, from that strange and joyful and terrible weekend was the sensation of packing her clothes. She folded silk and cotton and balled one pair of running socks and stuck her high-heeled sandals in the side pocket of her bag. She cleaned her long hairs and smears of toothpaste from the sink, wanting to remove every trace of herself. She sat down on the edge of the bed and hyperventilated. And then she walked from the bed to the window to get some air, feeling uncertain of everything. Of what could possibly come next.

Rebecca might have been able to guess how gracefully Vivi would, in fact, forgive both of her parents their foibles, but she never could have guessed how and in what context Vivi and she would talk about not only this day but also this moment. How in kitchens and bars and while walking down city streets and once in the woods and twice by the ocean, Vivi and she would talk about it. Until it was inseparable from every other fact of their shared history. Until it was together that they remembered Rebecca's walk from the bed to the window as if it were in slow motion—the chill of the hardwood floor on Rebecca's bare feet, the curtain straight ahead, slightly undulating.

Did you really see it happen? Vivi Shipley asked Rebecca Cantowitz, so many years in the future that it—the whole day—scarcely seemed possible, if only because of everybody's youth: even—or especially—their parents'.

From the window, Rebecca always answered. *At first my father was just sitting in his car.*

This exchange—first confused, then overwhelmed, and later gleeful—had become merely a wistful one. Their personal stories were so intertwined by then that the details of how they'd gotten there—though entertaining for younger generations—just didn't seem to matter anymore.

Acknowledgments

Huge thanks first and foremost to my uncle Marshall Cogan, whose brilliance and patience were essential to this project. Also to the amazing Robert Gardner and all of Robert Gardner's work—specifically the wonderful films *Dead Birds* and *The Nuer,* and the inspiring book *The Impulse to Preserve.* Tildy Lewis Davidson was tremendously generous not only with her time and memories, but also with her insights.

I'm indebted to Florence Phillips, Maureen Cogan, Walker Buckner, Jonathan Eisenthal, Gregory A. Finnegan, Sarah and Robert LeVine, Shefa Siegal, Daria Levin, John Lewis, Sarah Gay Damman, Dr. Stephen Gluckman, Jesse Drucker, Robby Stein, Rob Gifford, Sara Mark, Alyse Liebovich, and Dr. Amy Lehman and the Lake Tanganyika Floating Health Clinic website (www.floatingclinic.org).

To my stellar crew of writer/readers who provided inventive suggestions, excellent edits, and fierce support along the way: Ellen Umansky, Sarah Saffian, and especially Lizzie Simon and Jennifer Cody Epstein, who hung in until the final chapter. It's impossible to imagine where this novel would be without all of your voices.

To Jen Albano, Ondine Cohane, Tanya Larkin, and my husband, Derek Buckner, all of whom read the first draft and in their own inimitable ways, knew how to make it better.

Thanks to my talented editor, Susanna Porter; her assistant, Priyanka Krishnan; the excellent Dana Isaacson, Kathleen Lord, Lisa Barnes, Rachel Kind, and *everyone* at Ballantine; thanks also to Gretchen Crary. And to my treasured agent, Elizabeth Sheinkman, your early support of this project made all the difference. Also to Dorian Karchmar, whose arrival feels, indeed, *beshert*.

The Real Deal: My Life in Business and Philanthropy by Sandy Weill and Judah S. Kraushaar, *The Partnership: The Making of Goldman Sachs* by Charles D. Ellis, and especially *The Year They Sold Wall Street* by Tim Carrington were all helpful books. Also: *Boston Boy* by Nat Hentoff, *The Death of an American Jewish Community: A Tragedy of Good Intentions* by Hillel Levine and Lawrence Harmon, and the exquisite *Shadow of the Sun* by Ryszard Kapuscinski.

I'm grateful to my parents, Judy and Stuart Hershon, for—well—everything.

And finally to Derek, Wyatt, and Noah Buckner, who make my daily life so compelling that it's a wonder I ever managed to write this book.

ABOUT THE AUTHOR

JOANNA HERSHON is the author of four novels: *Swimming, The Outside of August, The German Bride,* and *A Dual Inheritance.* Her writing has appeared in *The New York Times, One Story, The Virginia Quarterly Review,* and the literary anthologies *Brooklyn Was Mine* and *Freud's Blind Spot* (among other places), and was shortlisted for the 2007 *O. Henry Prize Stories.* She has taught in the creative writing program at Columbia University and lives in Brooklyn with her husband, painter Derek Buckner, and their twin sons.

ABOUT THE TYPE

This book is set in Fournier, a typeface named for Pierre Simon Fournier, the youngest son of a French printing family. He started out engraving woodblocks and large capitals, then moved on to fonts of type. In 1736 he began his own foundry and made several important contributions in the field of type design; he is said to have cut 147 alphabets of his own creation. Fournier is probably best remembered as the designer of St. Augustine Ordinaire, a face that served as the model for Monotype's Fournier, which was released in 1925.